BLESSED CHILD

TED DEKKER
AND
BILL BRIGHT

WestBow
PRESS

A Division of Thomas Nelson Publishers
Since 1798

visit us at www.westbowpress.com

BLESSED CHILD

© 2001 Ted Dekker and Bill Bright.

Scripture quotations used in this book are from *The Holy Bible,* New International Version (NIV). Copyright © 1973, 1978, 1984, International Bible Society. Used by permission of Zondervan Bible Publishers.

Library of Congress Cataloging-in-Publication Data

Dekker, Ted, 1962–
    Blessed Child / by Ted Dekker and Bill Bright.
       p. cm.
    ISBN 0-8499-4312-4
    I. Bright, Bill. II. Title.
    PS3554.E43 B58 2001
    813'.6—dc21

2001026271
CIP

Printed in the United States of America
05 06 07 08 RRD 19 18 17

A NOTE FROM THE AUTHORS

GOD OFTEN BRINGS HIS CHILDREN TOGETHER in the most unusual ways to accomplish His unique purposes. The way in which we were drawn together leaves us humbled. The seeds of this novel were planted in each of our hearts independently at least a full year before our paths crossed.

From the beginning, our intent extended beyond telling a good story. Good stories, although hard enough to come by these days, don't necessarily trumpet the truth. More than weaving a worthy tale, we wanted to write about the mysteries which lay beyond the skin of this world—to bring into focus that truth which is precious to us who believe in Christ's power and captivating to those who, as of yet, do not.

With this purpose firmly under our belts, we set out to honor the Holy Spirit with an unapologetic rendering of His power, to draw a grand portrait of our God across the canvas of our world, an offering for His pleasure, rather than one for the pleasure of man.

Doing so requires a vivid story of God's power in our world. It requires a clear message, and it requires a canvas on which to paint our portrait. It was in this context that our collaboration was born.

The story and the writing are primarily Ted's; the heart of the message and the canvas, if you will, are primarily Bill's. A thirty-eight-year-old novelist and an eighty-year-old church father; a hand and an arm, members of one body, each gifted for the edification of the other, brought together for His purpose.

We sincerely pray that your short walk through Caleb's world will encourage you to consider the kingdom of heaven in new and maybe even challenging ways. We pray it will spur you on to earnestly seek Him, and above all we pray this journey will fill you with hope. The hope for the true treasures of this life—may you seek and find them quickly. The hope of the glory which awaits us in the life to come. May it come soon.

We would both like to thank the many friends who encouraged us to write from our hearts rather than from good political senses; their names would be too many to mention here. But there is one man whose insight, brilliance, and diligence cannot be overlooked. Thank you, Helmut Teichert, for your unwavering work and inspiration on this project. You have the heart of a champion.

TED DEKKER
BILL BRIGHT

1

DISCOVERY

The greatest difference between present-day Christianity,
and that of which we read in these letters (of the New Testament),
is that to us it is primarily a performance;
to them it was real experience.
We are apt to reduce the Christian religion to a code or,
at best, a rule of heart and life.
Perhaps if we believed what they believed,
we could achieve what they achieved.

J. B. PHILLIPS
in the introduction to his New Testament translation

PROLOGUE

"WE HAVE TO KILL THE PRIEST," Roberts said.

Charles Crandal sat still in the subterranean room's dim light, legs crossed and relaxed. His dark eyes peered from a shiny bald head, past Roberts to the glass cases filled with his precious artifacts. He said nothing, which could mean anything. But looking into those cold eyes, Roberts felt a very gentle unnerving, which considering his own steely disposition, said volumes. He just didn't know which volumes yet. Ambiguity was a prerogative that followed great power, he thought, and power was the air Crandal breathed.

Roberts pressed his point. "He's talking, sir. If Tempest gets out it'll be the end."

Crandal shifted his eyes but he still did not speak.

"You kill the priest and this all goes away," Roberts said.

"This paranoia is asinine," Crandal said. "It's none of anybody's business. I did what needed done."

"Of course. But you're wrong: they'll make it *everybody's* business. And when the public wakes up one morning and learns that you ordered the killing of several thousand civilians—"

"It wasn't an order."

"It might as well have been. And either way I guarantee they'll crucify you. We have a simple solution here, sir. We head this off at the source and it's the end of it."

Crandal unfolded his legs, pushed his large frame from the stuffed chair, and walked to the desk. A green lawyer's lamp cast an amber hue over its mahogany finish. All but one of the study's walls were paneled in the same wood, a rich backdrop for his collection of Rembrandts. The other wall was encased in glass and lined with outrageously rare artifacts Crandal had personally collected from the most remote regions of the world. Another dozen pieces sat in their own cases about the office. The few who had seen this room sometimes referred to it as his museum.

He had furnished his private enclave in majestic fashion, which seemed appropriate considering the kind of decisions that had been conceived here, three floors under the D.C. earth in seclusion from even the agency he had directed for eight years. The National Security Administration's roots ran deep, but the ex-director knew its holes and he lived in one now.

Two years ago he'd left the agency and set his sights on this loftier goal, but he'd never relinquished his power. Not really. He hadn't even lost his command post—he still ran his world from this room.

Crandal reached for a copy of *Time* magazine, featuring his smiling face on its cover with the inscription "The Power Broker" beneath it. "Killing is never the end of it, Roberts. You should know that by now. You end one problem and create another."

"Then tell me a better way."

"Did I say there was a better way? I'm simply telling you that killing someone doesn't always silence them. Especially not a priest in a country that worships their priests."

"It's a risk we can't afford not to take. Sooner or later someone who matters will listen to the old man."

Crandal tossed the magazine back onto the desk. "Then we go all the way. We go after the entire monastery. If we set out to silence, then we silence them all. Including the village around it."

Roberts felt a tug at his lips. Here was the old Crandal talking, putting aside politics for the moment and dealing decisively with the problem at hand.

"What are you thinking?" he asked.

"It worked before, why not again?"

"Another invasion?"

Crandal nodded. "Tempest." He stretched his neck and rubbed his throat with a thick hand. "Did we go this far south last time?" he asked.

Roberts arched his right brow. "You're thinking we should search again?"

"Why not. It's in that region somewhere—I'd stake my life on it."

"But would you stake your presidency on it? The last thing we need is another leak."

Crandal chuckled. "Leak? We plug our leaks, remember? And if you're really worried about leaks, Ethiopia is the least of your concerns."

He had a point there.

Crandal sighed. "Stage the invasion, kill every living soul within ten miles of the Debra Damarro, and then flatten it. But have them at least take a look. Okay, Roberts? Humor me."

1

Three Months Later
Minus 3 Days

JASON BROUGHT THE OPEN-TOPPED PEACE CORPS JEEP to a stop and
turned off its ignition. The engine coughed once and died. He hauled himself up by the roll bar and studied the browned valley ahead. The Ethiopian
Orthodox monastery known to locals as Debra Damarro loomed against the
rolling hills, a square fortress hewn from solid rock. Why the ancients had
built here, in such a remote corner of Tigre in northern Ethiopia, so far from
the beaten track of worshipers, was beyond him, but then so was the tenor of
Orthodoxy in general. And Christianity, for that matter.

Acacia trees swayed in the courtyard, serene in the afternoon heat. Jason
kept his eyes fixed on the iron gate where Daal insisted he would be met and
speedily serviced. The Eritrean invasion was only three days old, but already
the Eritrean Peoples Liberation Front (EPLF) had brought the border dispute as far south as Axum to the west; it was a wonder they had not overtaken these hills yet. But then Ethiopia wasn't taking the sudden invasion
along its northern border lying down. They were obviously keeping the
enemy forces occupied elsewhere, where more than a single remote monastery
was at stake.

It was not the first time Eritrea had made this absurd claim to the land
beyond its drawn borders. Absurd because even the pagans knew that Orthodox
Ethiopians would defend their northern holy sites to the death. The queen of
Sheba had first brought Solomon's wisdom and, according to many, his child,
here to her castle near Axum, fifty miles to the southwest. The Jewish religion
had swept through the hills, and several hundred years later, the Ark of the
Covenant had followed—also to Axum, the priests insisted. A growing con-
tingent of scholars at least agreed with the Ethiopian Orthodox community
that the Ark's last known resting place was indeed somewhere in northern
Ethiopia.

Christianity had first come to Africa here, along this northern border.

And now for the second time in ten years, Eritrea was openly disputing that border. It was like trying to argue that Florida really belonged to Cuba.

Absurd.

Most of the relief workers in the surrounding towns had already fled south to the country's capital, Addis Ababa, with the first evacuation order.

Most. But not Jason Marker. Daal, his Irob interpreter, had begged him for this one favor. To deliver this one orphan stranded at this remote monastery to safety. And why would he risk his life to save a single child in a land where a hundred thousand would die in the next famine? Why would he head north, closer to the EPLF forces, instead of blazing a trail south as demanded by the Corps?

Perhaps because he *was* in the Corps: the kind of man who at least on occasion threw caution to the wind for a sense of greater purpose. Or maybe to appease the guilt he felt at having decided to leave Ethiopia for good.

But most likely because he wasn't really risking his life at all. The Eritreans would probably not harm an American. Daal had sworn nothing less before running off to see to his own family. So Jason would engage in this one last humanitarian mission and close this chapter in his life. And just as well—working in Ethiopia had been like trying to extract water from a bag of flour.

Jason wiped the rolling sweat from his forehead, rubbed his hand on his khakis, and dropped back into the seat. The monastery seemed quiet enough. He reached for the key, and the faint rumble of an engine drifted through the air.

His hand froze. It wasn't the Jeep's engine, of course. He hadn't turned the key. Jason scanned the horizon quickly. The road ran past the monastery and climbed the hills to the right, disappearing into valleys and reappearing on the distant hills beyond like a tan snake.

He saw the trucks then, tiny dots slinking into a valley several miles off. A small grunt escaped his throat, and for a terrible moment he couldn't think. He snatched up his binoculars and peered at the trucks. EPLF! It was an EPLF column, headed toward the monastery, no more than ten minutes off. Which meant what?

That Daal had been wrong?

Jason's doctorate was in agriculture, not military maneuvers, but he hardly needed an education to tell him that this was not good. His heart was doing the job splendidly.

He spun around in a panic and grabbed for the old bolt action .30-06 he used for the occasional hunt. His sweaty palm slapped at the worn wood stock and managed to claw it off the back seat before sending it clattering to the floorboards behind.

What was he thinking? Take on the Eritrean army with a thirty-ought-six?

Jason fired the Jeep's engine, shoved the stick forward, and dropped the clutch. The old World War II vehicle jerked forward. He tore for the gate, blinking against the simple thought that he was headed the wrong way. He should be *leaving.*

It wasn't terribly clear why he did continue for that closed iron gate. At any moment his arms would yank the steering wheel and whip the Jeep through a one-eighty. But they did not.

A figure in robes suddenly ran for the gate and threw it open. Jason roared through and braked the Jeep into a skidding stop, three meters from the monastery's foundation. Wide, sweeping steps cut from sandstone rose to an arching entry. Heavy wooden doors gaped open to a dark interior. Behind him the gatekeeper was yelling in Amharic.

Jason slid from the seat and bounded up the steps two at a time. He ran through an internal circuit and into the cavernous sanctuary. He slid to a stop on the polished stone floor. To say that the room was empty would have misstated the matter. Although Jason was indeed alone in the huge domed sanctum, an imposing silence filled the space, heavy enough to resonate through his skull with a distant ring. His blood pounded through his ears.

High above him a yellow face covering half the dome peered down unblinking, engaging his eyes.

"Sire!"

Jason spun.

The voice echoed across the sanctuary. "Sire, you are not permitted in this room. It is for priests—"

"Where's Father Matthew? Do you have a Father Matthew here? I have to see him!"

The white-draped priest stared at Jason as if he'd just swallowed a small boulder. He held an ancient text in his arms, a huge book browned by time.

Jason lowered his voice. "Please, man. Forgive me, but I have to see Father Matthew immediately. Do you know that there are soldiers—"

"It's quite all right, Phillip."

Jason turned to the new voice. An old priest wearing the same traditional white garb as the other priest shuffled with small steps from a doorway on his left.

"Come, come, come." He motioned for Jason to follow.

"Father Matthew?"

"Yes, of course. And you are the good man Daal promised, yes? Then come, come."

The priest pulled at a wiry white beard that hung a good foot off his chin. He smiled and his large oblong eyes flashed knowingly, as if the whole thing were a play and he held a secret part that he was now executing perfectly. Jason glanced at the first priest, who had bowed his head to Father Matthew.

"We don't have all day, young man. You have come for the boy, yes?"

Jason faced Father Matthew. "Yes." He headed for the old man, who nodded and shuffled hurriedly from the room.

They walked into a passageway cut from the same sandstone as the monastery's exterior. The whole structure was literally one large rock, carved and chipped away over many years, not so unusual in northern Ethiopia. Jason hurried after the priest, who moved very quickly considering his small steps. They descended a flight of steps by the light of a torch's flickering flame and then followed a tunnel farther into the earth. He'd never been so deep in a monastery. Stories of the secret underground caverns were common, but Jason had never suspected they were much more than small enclaves. Certainly not serviced by the well-worn passageways he was seeing now.

"Welcome to the mystery of our faith," the old man said with a hint of sarcasm.

"Amazing."

"And it makes us priests feel rather special, crawling through the earth like moles while the flock wanders above."

This was no ordinary priest. A tad eccentric from his years below the surface perhaps.

"The mortals above are carrying guns now," Jason said. "You do realize that, Father. The EPLF is less than five minutes up the road."

"Precisely. Which is why we are hurrying. You think I walk with such haste every waking hour?"

"You knew they'd be coming? That's not what Daal told me. He said this would be a simple in-and-out trip to collect the orphan and take him to safety. Somehow it isn't feeling quite so simple."

"Ah, Daal. He was always a bit smooth with the tongue. Rather like a lot of priests I know. It's a case of humanity, I suspect; insisting on some brand of the truth altogether unclear, but made clearer with insistence." He shuffled on and held up a finger, half turning. "What you cannot establish with wit you can always further with a little volume, don't you think?"

Ordinarily Jason would have chuckled at the old man's own wit, but the image of those trucks plowing over the hills outside tempered his humor. The priest was muttering now, and his echoes sounded like a chuckle through the tunnel. They hurried deeper into the earth.

"Maybe you could just bring the child out to the Jeep," Jason said. He was having a hard time communicating his urgency to the old senile goat. "Maybe I should go back and—"

"Do you believe in God?"

They broke into a torch-lit room furnished with a single wooden table and two chairs. The priest turned to face him. His long eyes sagged in the surreal orange light.

"Do I . . . yes, of course—"

"Or do you just say that you believe in God to appease me? I see doubt in your eyes, young man."

Jason blinked, stunned. Father Matthew was clearly out of touch. Outside a war was looming and he wasted time philosophizing about God in the bowels of some lost monastery. The old man spoke hurriedly now.

"Do you believe that Jesus Christ was a madman?"

"What?"

"Do you believe that when he announced that his disciples would do greater things than he had, he was delusional?"

"What does this have to do with anything? We have to get out, man!"

"I thought not," the priest said. "You do not believe. And yes, we are short on time. But our lives are in God's hands."

"That's fine, but if you wouldn't mind I would like to get out of here before the bullets start flying. I'm not sure your God is quite so attentive to my interests."

"Yes, I can see that you're unsure."

"And why did you call me here in the first place, if you're so confident that God will save you?"

"You are here, aren't you? I will assume that he sent you. So then he *is* saving us. Or at least the child. Unless we are too late, of course."

Jason shoved the logic from his mind and tried to control his frustration. "Then please help your God along and get me the kid."

The priest studied Jason's face. "I want your word. You will die before allowing Caleb to come to harm."

Jason balked at the man's audacity.

"Swear it."

It was an insane moment and he spoke quickly, to appease the man. "Of course, I promise you. Now get him please."

"We found him at the gate when he was a baby, you know. Abandoned here by a retreating Eritrean commander who had just killed his mother during the last war. She was a European nurse. The soldier left a scrawled note with the boy seeking absolution for his sins."

Father Matthew stared unblinking, as if the revelation should explain some things. But the tale sounded rather par for the course in this mad place.

"The boy is no ordinary child. I think you will see that soon enough. Did you know that he has never seen beyond the gate? You will only be the fourth man he has ever laid eyes on in his ten years of life. He has never seen a woman."

"He's been in this monastery his whole life?"

"I raised him as a son. Where I go he goes. Or in this case where I stay, he has stayed. Except now. Now God has sent you to deliver the boy and I am bound by a vow to remain here."

He reached inside his tunic and withdrew an envelope. He handed the brown packet out to Jason, who looked unsure. "These are his papers, granting him refugee status outside of Ethiopia."

"Outside? I was under the impression that I was taking him to Addis Ababa."

"As long as he is in this country, his life is in danger. You must deliver him to safety beyond our borders."

Jason was about to tell the old man that he was losing true north when a door suddenly burst open to their right. A boy ran into the room, grinning from ear to ear.

"Dadda!" He spoke in Amharic, but he didn't look Ethiopian. His skin was a creamy tan and his dark hair hung in loose curls to his shoulders—he was clearly of mixed race. A simple cotton tunic similar to the priest's covered his small frame.

The boy ran up and threw his arms around the priest's waist, burying his face in the man's tunic. Father Matthew palmed the envelope, smiled, and dropped to his knees to hug the child. "Hello, Caleb." He kissed him on his forehead and looked into the boy's eyes—eyes as brilliant blue-green as Jason had ever seen.

"Caleb, your time has come, my son." He smoothed the boy's hair lovingly.

Caleb faced Jason with those large, round eyes. The priest had prepared the boy already, and Jason wondered what the boy knew.

A tremor shook the ground and Jason instinctively glanced up. It was a shell! A shell had detonated outside!

Father Matthew's hand grabbed Jason's and pressed the envelope into his palm. The old man's eyes were misted by the flame's light. "Promise me, my friend, I beg you! Take him beyond our borders."

"I will. I will. Get us out of here!"

The priest's eyes lingered for a brief moment, searching for truth. He whirled for the boy, who stared at the ceiling as another rumble shook the room. He snatched Caleb's hand. "Follow me! Run!"

The small shuffle steps Father Matthew had employed to lead Jason down gave way to long strides, and Jason raced to keep Father and son in sight. The priest was an enigma but certainly no idiot. His voice called back as they ran.

"They are firing on the village behind the monastery. We still have time. I have asked the others to distract them if necessary."

"Distract?"

"We have a moat behind for water. It will be burning with oil."

The child ran silently, on the heels of his father. They burst into the same sanctuary Jason had been scolded for entering earlier. Now another figure stood at its center, spinning around to face them as they rushed in.

She wore a navy blue tunic not unlike you might see on any street corner throughout Ethiopia, but the woman was clearly not Ethiopian. A hood shrouded a deeply tanned face. She seemed to arrest even the old priest's attention for a moment.

"Oh yes, I'd nearly forgotten about you, dear," Father Matthew said. He turned to Jason. "This is the nurse Leiah. She came to us a few hours ago from a French Canadian Red Cross camp in Eritrea that was overrun."

"A woman," Jason said, not because the discovery was notable, but because everyone knew women were strictly prohibited past the gates of any Ethiopian Orthodox monastery. Yet here was most definitely a woman. A Frenchwoman.

The woman glanced at the door leading to the courtyard and then back to Jason. She approached him quickly. "Take me with you!" she said in perfect English. She turned to Father Matthew. "Father, tell him he must take me with him!"

Her blue eyes begged. She grabbed his shirt and tugged gently toward the door. "Hurry! We have to leave."

A loud detonation shook the sanctuary and Jason ducked with the sound.

"Take her," the priest said. He knelt and took Caleb in his arms again. He drew the boy close and whispered in his ear. When he pulled back, tears snaked from his eyes, wetting each cheek. "Remember what I have taught you, my son. Remember it well. Listen to your heart; the eyes will deceive. Remember." He spoke in Amharic.

"Let's go! Hurry," Jason urged them. For all the talk of delivering these to safety, they wouldn't make it past the front gate if they didn't leave now. Assuming the gate was not already overtaken.

"Dadda . . ." the boy said.

"Go with God, Caleb. His love is better than life."

"Dadda . . ."

Jason grabbed the boy's arm and tugged him toward the arching entry. Leiah, the woman, was already at the door craning for a view on either side. She spun to them.

"Hurry, hurry!"

"Jason," the priest said. "What's soft and round and says more than it should?"

Jason spun back. "Wha—?"

"The hem of a tunic." Father Matthew smiled. "An old Ethiopian riddle about modesty that will make sense to you one day. Remember it."

∽

They ran from the monastery together, Leiah in the lead, with Jason and the boy following behind. The midday sun blinded Jason for an instant. He released the boy's hand and took the steps more by feel than by sight.

Behind him Father Matthew's voice urged a faltering boy. "Go! Run. Run to the truck and climb in. It will be all right. Remember my riddle, Jason."

There was no sign of soldiers on this side of the monastery, but the detonations of what Jason assumed to be mortar fire shook the ground behind them. Black smoke boiled into the sky. Father Matthew's burning moat. Oil.

Jason spun to see the boy picking his way down the broad steps on his tiptoes. His round eyes glanced around, petrified. Jason bounded up the steps, grabbed the boy around the waist, and ran for the Jeep.

"Give him to me!" the nurse demanded, her arms outstretched from the back seat. He shoved the boy toward her. She gathered Caleb and set him on the seat beside her. The boy immediately covered his eyes with his hands and buried his head in her lap.

"Get us out of here! Hurry, man!" Leiah said.

"I am. I am! Hold on!"

The engine roared to life with the first turn of the ignition. Jason rammed the shift stick forward and floored the accelerator. The Jeep spun in a circle, raising dust on all sides. He angled the vehicle for the gate and grabbed another gear.

Behind them an explosion shook the courtyard. They were lobbing the explosives to the front! Ahead the gate was closed. The gatekeeper ran out, pointing frantically to Jason's rear. He glanced back and saw the first truck emerging from a cloud of smoke beside the monastery—a Land Rover painted in desert camouflage.

Jason didn't let up on the gas pedal. He had the engine wound out in third gear, screaming for the closed gate.

"Open it! Open the gate!" he screamed, motioning furiously with his hand.

The gatekeeper flew for the latch, like a ghost in his flowing white robes. He shoved the gates open and ran for the monastery, uttering sharp cries barely heard above the thumping explosions behind them.

The Jeep struck one of the gates with a clang and shot out onto the driveway. Jason shoved the gearbox into high gear, veered off the road in his haste, corrected with a jerk of the wheel, and centered the vehicle on the road leading from the valley.

"Stay on the road! Watch the potholes!"

Her warning came too late and their right wheel pounded through a hole the size of a Volkswagen. Jason cleared the seat a good foot before crashing back down. He glanced back to see Leiah's white face. The boy was still buried in her lap, oblivious to the world.

"Watch for the holes!" Leiah yelled.

"I am!"

Behind them a huge explosion ripped through the air, like a thunderclap rumbling across the sky. Jason's heart slammed against the walls of his chest, loud in his ears, spurred by a mixture of terror and euphoria. Machine guns stuttered in long bursts. This was no abstract attack on a village. They were destroying the monastery wholesale, an unspoken taboo, even during an invasion. The monasteries had survived a thousand years precisely because of the reverence they commanded. Slaughter of women and children was far more common in this land than the destruction of a shrine.

They had nearly reached the crest of the first hill when Jason looked back again. What he saw ran through his chest like a spike on the end of a sledgehammer. He caught his breath. The monastery was without ambiguity history, crumbled and smoking, a remnant of its former structure. No soul could possibly have lived through such a pounding. And if one or two did manage to find the sunlight alive, a ring of trucks with mounted machine guns awaited to make certain they did not savor it too long.

Jason saw the destruction in a glance. But he forgot it almost immediately in favor of another sight that nearly drove him from the road. It was the sight of a lone truck barreling down the road behind them.

Leiah must have seen the look on his face, because she spun to face the valley. Machine-gun fire cut through the air, a small popping sound, like popcorn in a microwave.

"Move it! They're catching us!" she screamed.

Something snapped in Jason's mind. The euphoria of their escape was smothered by horror. They were being pursued.

"Faster! Drive faster!"

"Shut up! I'm driving as fast as I can! Just shut up and let me drive!"

They crested the hill and roared into the next valley. For a few seconds, maybe ten, they were alone with the growling of their own engine. And then the larger Land Rover broke over the hill and screamed after them.

Jason felt panic wash over his spine. They were going to die. He knew that with dread certainty. His life would end this day.

2

THE JEEP MANAGED TO MAINTAIN its half-mile lead only with its engine screaming bloody murder. With the white dust billowing behind them, keeping sight of the Land Rover was nearly impossible. But every time they crested a hill, they could clearly see the vehicle's relentless pursuit.

"You can't make this bucket of bolts move any faster?" Leiah demanded.

"It's not exactly a Porsche, is it?"

Jason could nearly feel her glare on the back of his head. She was a hard one; it took a strong woman to survive in this land. But right now it wasn't the land that threatened their lives; it was an armed truck barreling down on them. He was beginning to regret bringing her. At least she was keeping the kid quiet. Caleb still cowered beside her, his head buried on her knees, silent.

"Do you think they've gained?" he asked.

"All I see is dust. How do you expect me to know if they've gained?"

"I asked if you *thought* they had gained."

She looked back for a moment, then announced her verdict. "They've gained."

"Are you sure?" Jason asked with alarm.

"You asked for my thoughts. I think they've gained."

"Well, that's not good. How do you know?"

"They're closer."

They came to the crest of a hill and Jason looked back quickly. The cloud of dust from the Land Rover was still a fair ways off, but it certainly wasn't falling farther behind.

He spun back to face the road and corrected the Jeep's straying course.

"Keep your eyes on the road. We don't need *you* killing us," Leiah said.

He ignored her for the moment.

For another half-hour they kept their distance, and Jason began to recover from the raw panic of their flight. They had a good hour haul to Adwa, the first town in this parched mountainscape. If they made Adwa, they would have a chance.

They were in canyon lands at five thousand feet. With any luck the cool mountain air would extend the engine's performance. Heaven knew the Jeep wasn't made for this. On all sides rugged mountains rose and fell to deep ravines browned by a dry year. Sandstone cliffs ran jagged lines across the horizon on either side. It was like driving through parts of North Dakota on steroids, Jason had often thought. Seventy miles to the east, the salt-encrusted Denakil Desert fell to the earth's lowest point, nearly 500 feet below sea level. Seventy miles to the west, Mount Ras Dashen rose to over 15,000 feet. It was a land of extremes.

And now the landscape seemed to have rubbed off on the guerrillas behind them.

The boy uttered a small cry of surprise, and Jason twisted to see that he'd finally lifted his head and was gaping at the steep escarpment to their left.

Leiah spoke a few reassuring words in rough Amharic. *"Ishee, ishee."*

Caleb turned his attention to the Jeep itself, staring in stunned silence at the vehicle that whisked him away from his only reality. The boy likely hadn't seen a vehicle, much less taken a ride in one.

Back there at the monastery Caleb's only father had just been killed; Jason was sure of it.

"Make sure he doesn't fall out," Jason said.

"You just keep your eyes on the road. Let me worry about the boy."

He turned and met her gaze. Her eyes flashed a blue brighter than the clear sky, and Jason held back a retort. Like the priest and the child, she, too, was an enigma.

The Jeep suddenly coughed once. A chill ran down Jason's spine. He pressed the accelerator, but it was already flat on the floorboards. The gas meter bounced in the green at the halfway mark.

"We're pushing it too hard," Leiah said.

Jason didn't answer. If they were, they had a problem: they were still a good twenty miles out of any civilization. Maybe it had been an isolated . . .

The engine coughed again, and Jason felt a chill run through his bones. He stomped on the accelerator. The road had leveled off, offering no descents to ease the strain on the motor.

"This ain't good," Jason said.

"No, it's not."

"We have to get off the main road. They're going to catch us if we slow."

"Yes, they are."

"There's a road that heads east a couple miles—"

"The trail to Biset? Are you crazy? There's no way you can take a vehicle through those canyons."

"You have a better idea?" he snarled. "You obviously seem to know your way around, so why don't you lay it on me? At least we have a chance of fooling them."

"Yes, of course. And we could drive off a cliff as well. That would throw a surprise their way. At least on the road we have a chance of staying on all fours. Maybe the engine's just adjusting."

As if to respond, the Jeep lurched once before regaining its full speed.

"That feel like an adjustment to you? I may not be as well informed about the arts of survival as you, but I have learned a thing or two about Jeeps in my two years here. That was more like a death rattle than a midcourse tune-up."

"And in the three years I've lived in this country, I've learned a few things as well. One is that this trail to Biset you suggest we take was made for camels, not Jeeps. It's impassable."

She had a point.

The car suddenly jerked three times in succession. He snatched a quick look to the rear and saw that Leiah had turned as well. The Land Rover had gained. The boy stared at him round-eyed.

That was it. Jason gripped the wheel tight. The turn off was not much more than a break in the rock to their right, around the next bend.

"Hold on. Just hold on tight."

"You'll kill us," Leiah said.

"Hold the boy."

He was counting on the dust to obscure their exit; the more he churned up the better. They were doing forty miles per hour by the speedometer when the sandstone to their right gaped. Jason jerked the wheel without easing off the accelerator. The Jeep bounced over a shallow ditch and snorted into what looked like a sandy river bottom.

Rocks the size of coconuts populated the wash. A thin trail snaked through the center. Leiah's camel trail. Jason swung the wheel from side to side in an attempt to dodge the rocks, but there were too many. The front left wheel slammed into a large rock, sending the Jeep rearing up at an odd angle. Jason's knees smashed into the steering wheel and he winced. He caught a brief glimpse of Leiah, suspended behind him. They crashed to the ground and shot forward. How Leiah managed to stay in the Jeep was beyond Jason. Then again, if anyone could, it would be someone with her determination. And she did it holding the boy.

"Hold on!"

The engine was faltering badly now. They lurched over the sand, avoiding the rocks and peeling around an embankment that rose to their left. Here the path was still wide enough to allow the Jeep's passage, but Jason knew that Leiah was right: the path narrowed to a goat trail within two miles.

But he had no intention of going two miles. Or even one mile. If he could get the Jeep into one of the canyons gaping to their right and shut it down out of sight, they might escape detection.

He angled the vehicle for the second canyon and glanced back. No sign of the Land Rover yet. "Keep down."

"You're going to kill us."

"Just keep your pretty head down!"

They entered the canyon without being seen—that much Jason was sure of—and the relief that washed over his neck felt sweeter than any he could remember. He nursed the sputtering vehicle along the canyon floor. Sheer cliffs rose on either side thirty yards each way. And then directly ahead as well. It was a box canyon—not his first choice, but with any luck he had already saved their skins.

He drove the Jeep into the canyon's long shadows and pulled behind several round boulders at the end. He turned off the ignition and let the engine die.

Jason pulled himself up by the roll bar and peered back toward the opening, three hundred yards off. Nothing. A low wind moaned through the canyon, but it was the pounding of his own heart that filled his ears. He held his breath and strained for the rumble of an engine.

Still nothing.

Jason blew out a lungful of air and looked down at the pair in the rear seat. His right hand rested on the roll bar, shaking badly.

"You hear anything?"

The nurse looked at him without responding. It was the first time he saw her without an impending threat looming over them. Her complexion was dark, but clearly European. Her nose was sharp and her eyes very blue. But he saw something else now, on her neck, at the fray of her navy tunic. Her skin at the base of her throat was badly scarred. Burn scars that disappeared beneath her wrap.

He shifted his eyes to meet hers. She knew that he had seen. Her eyes said so, and she held her posture in near defiance.

"Do you hear anything?" he asked.

She held his eyes for a moment longer and then pulled herself up into a clear line with the canyon's opening. She held onto the bar beside him, and he saw that her arms, though covered with the flowing tunic, were also scarred.

"No," she said.

Caleb climbed slowly out of the back seat and dropped to the sand. He stood on trembling legs and looked at the Jeep in awe. The sight made Jason think of a lost puppy. In all of the commotion, Jason had nearly forgotten about the boy. And yet it was because of him that they found themselves in this predicament. Because of one ten-year-old boy who had been abandoned at the monastery as a baby and raised in total isolation from the rest of the world. And because the priest who had adopted him had gone to great lengths to see that he lived.

It occurred to Jason that the boy's shaking knees were the result of the wild ride aboard this metal monster beside him—not the threat of armed soldiers' pursuit. He probably wouldn't know the threat of a gun if one were to go off in his hands.

They remained still like that for long seconds. Jason listened intently, holding his breath periodically. A lammergeyer cawed high above, and Jason lifted his eyes to the canyon lip. The huge vulturelike bird of prey circled lazily against the dimming sky. A cackle sounded across the canyon. A troop of several dozen gelada baboons peered curiously down on this invasion into their world.

But these were sights and sounds as common as the grass in northern Ethiopia.

"That's what I call a close call," Jason said, hopping over the door to the ground. Leiah did not follow. She had her head tilted, still listening determinedly. Jason stilled.

He heard it then: a faint rumble on the wind. The boy turned to face the canyon's mouth—he'd heard it as well.

Jason's heart spiked.

Leiah suddenly crouched. "They've doubled back!" she whispered near panic. "They're coming!"

The Land Rover's engine now rumbled clearly. In horror Jason watched the truck crawl into the canyon's mouth and then turn directly for them. It rocked its way steadily over the wash, closing the three-hundred-yard gap.

He pulled his head down out of sight and flattened his back to the rock they'd pulled behind. The Land Rover had obviously doubled back and followed the tracks after noting their vanishing act.

They were sitting ducks!

Leiah grabbed the boy and pulled him down to the sand. He uttered a startled cry and Leiah quieted him with her hand. She spun to Jason with wide eyes.

High above, the baboons were starting to cackle loudly, as if they sensed an impending showdown. Jason could hardly think, much less act. They were a nurse, a child, and a man, cornered in a box canyon, facing trained killers who had just come from butchering a gathering of innocent priests. Heavily armed soldiers against . . .

One gun.

The rifle!

Jason scrambled for the Jeep and dove for the rifle on the floorboards. Thank the stars it hadn't flown out. He snatched it out and then fumbled with the glove box. A box of .30-06 shells tumbled out.

Working frantically, he pulled the bolt action back and rammed shells into the ten-round clip. He dropped a round in the sand and left it, thinking he would use it last if need be. The nurse and the boy were staring at his performance, wide-eyed.

"You think you'll accomplish something with one gun?" Leiah whispered.

"Keep down," he ordered. He flattened himself on the sand and crawled to the edge of the rock. The truck rolled forward, no more than a hundred meters off now. If he could get a round into its fuel tank, they might have a chance.

Jason pressed his cheek against the butt of the .30-06 and lined it up with the Land Rover. But his breathing wagged the sights in crazy circles, and he pulled away to take a deep breath.

The vehicle suddenly veered to the left and pulled behind a group of large boulders, seventy-five meters from them. They had been seen!

Jason blinked at the sting of sweat in the corners of his eyes. He lay immobilized. The Land Rover's cab poked out from the boulders, and he watched three men dressed in green military garb drop to the ground and duck behind the rocks. Within seconds the madness began: a staccato burst of machine-gun fire erupted from their position, thundering between the canyon walls. Slugs smacked the rock; ricochets pinged by.

For the second time that day Jason came face-to-face with the simple knowledge that he was going to die. The realization chilled his flesh like a bucket of ice water poured over his head. He had a gun in his hands, but including the round he'd dropped in the sand behind him, he had fewer bullets than were contained in the single burst that had ripped over their heads just now.

Jason pointed the gun in their general direction and pulled the trigger. It bucked and boomed loudly.

The machine guns fell silent. The baboons on the cliff above screeched in protest. Jason grabbed the rifle's bolt and chambered another round. *Surprise, surprise! You're not the only one with firepower!*

As if in response, the air filled with a cacophony of weapons fire and none of it from Jason. The shells came like a stream of lead, thumping and whining on all sides.

Panicked, Jason fired the .30-06 as fast as he could work the bolt action, hardly thinking the maneuver through. It was only when a small remaining thread of reason whispered that he must be down to only one or two rounds that he stopped.

He was hardly aware of Leiah and the boy beside him. He glanced their way and saw to his surprise that the boy had crawled over to a gap in the boulders for a clear view of the Land Rover. Neither he nor Leiah appeared to be hit. And as far as he knew, he wasn't either, but his mind wasn't working so quickly just now.

The machine-gun fire cut off abruptly, and he edged his head around the rock for a look. So now he had one, maybe two, rounds left in the rifle, and one in the sand behind him. Three shots. Facing three men armed with machine guns. Three killers trained to . . .

A figure suddenly broke from the rocks and ran crouched toward another pile of boulders across the canyon. Two thoughts blasted through Jason's mind with surprising clarity. The first was that from the soldier's new position, they would be wide open. This was not good. The second thought was that he had not chambered a round.

Jason flew into action, snatching the bolt back and chambering a round. He held his breath and aimed the wavering sights with as much care as he could extract from his taut muscles. He pulled the trigger.

If the slug came remotely close, the man did not show it. He ran on, only a few strides away from the boulders now.

Jason chambered and fired again in one desperate motion.

The soldier grunted and dove to the ground three yards from the rocks. Only it wasn't a dive; it was more of a flop. Jason moved the rifle for a clear view.

The man lay unmoving, facedown in the sand. The canyon lay still in the tall shadows. No one moved. All eyes seemed to have been arrested by this one impossible development. Even the baboons had fallen silent.

Jason's breath blasted into the white sand two inches from his mouth; sweat trickled down his cheeks. He had shot the man. The lammergeyer cawed high above, but down here a surreal silence had settled.

A soft whimpering sound floated through the air. Not from the figure lying facedown forty meters out, but from Jason's left. He turned his head.

What followed seemed to proceed in slow motion, in a distant place beyond Jason's control. Caleb was standing. And then he was walking forward.

Leiah reached out for him, and Jason saw her mouth open, even heard her cry of protest, but even that sounded muted. Maybe it was the deafening of the rounds he'd fired; or the deadening realization that he was down to one round, buried in the sand behind him; or maybe the certainty of their death. But whatever the reason, Jason's senses were shutting down.

The boy was suddenly running across the open sand, straight for the fallen man.

Jason dropped the rifle and shoved himself to his knees, waiting for the reports of weapons fire. But none came. Perhaps because the two remaining soldiers were as stunned as he over the development.

Caleb ran silently, with his tan tunic fluttering in the breeze. His wavy hair flew behind him. Leiah left the rock and jumped out into the open, as if she intended to follow. The soldiers could have shot her as well as the boy, but they held their fire.

Caleb reached the fallen man and dropped to his knees with his back to

Jason. He whimpered again and then bent over the man in silence. The circling lammergeyer stopped its cawing. The valley stilled completely.

"What's he doing?" Jason heard himself whisper. "What's he doing?"

Leiah didn't respond. She took a single step forward and then stopped.

For what seemed like long minutes, but could have only been ten or fifteen seconds, they remained fixed, watching the boy knelt over the man, like
a priest administering last rites.

A thought skipped through Jason's mind: the thought that the .30-06's
chamber was empty. The thought that he should be thinking things through
instead of staring out dumbly.

The boy stood, turned his back on the fallen man, and began to walk
calmly back to them. Still the soldiers did not fire on him—perhaps because
he was a child. A hot gust blew across the sand, whipping the boy's tunic
about his ankles.

Leiah called out in a weak, desperate voice. *"Fetan, fetan!"* Hurry, hurry!

But the boy did not hurry.

A cough suddenly echoed through the canyon. Another. Behind the boy,
the fallen man moved on the sand.

Jason's heart bolted in his chest. He instinctively jerked the bolt on the
rifle, but there were no rounds to chamber. Behind him! The last round was
behind him.

Beyond Caleb's shimmering figure the fallen soldier sat up and Jason froze.

Leiah ran out a few steps and stretched her hand to the boy. "Caleb!
Caleb, fetan!"

The man suddenly scrambled to his feet in a defensive posture, like a
wrestler facing his opponent. In this case the boy, now thirty feet from him
and walking steadily but unhurriedly away. The soldier felt his chest as if rubbing a bruise and then spun around in search of his rifle. He snatched it up
and stared after the boy. He patted his chest one last time and then ran for
the Land Rover, yelling words in a foreign tongue.

Still expressionless, Caleb turned back when the man began his yelling. The
nurse rushed out, lifted the boy around his chest, and rushed back to the cover.

Jason watched in stunned disbelief as the soldiers piled into the Land
Rover. The truck snorted to life and spewed dust through a sweeping turn.
Within seconds it disappeared from the canyon in a hasty retreat.

Jason became aware that his jaw lay open, and he closed it. Grit ground between his teeth and he attempted to spit it out, but his mouth had dried. He staggered to his feet. Caleb was looking after the Land Rover. Leiah had her hand on the boy's head. Tears marked trails down her dusty face.

They remained unmoving for what seemed a long time, staring down the canyon. Whatever had just happened, Jason's mind was not understanding it so clearly. They were alive, and that was good. That was incredible.

"Let's go," he finally said.

"Are they gone?" Leiah asked.

"For now. But they'll be back." He turned to the Jeep. "I guarantee you they'll be back."

3

H E OBVIOUSLY WASN'T HIT," Jason said.

Leiah sat in the front passenger seat and glanced back at Caleb's frail, bouncing figure staring off at the sharp, angular landscape. The boy hadn't offered any explanation, at least none that she or Jason could understand. He'd rattled off a string of words in Ge'ez, the language preferred by most Ethiopian Orthodox priests, but they meant nothing to her. She wasn't even sure if the boy spoke English, although it wouldn't surprise her. If the priests had taught him Amharic and Ge'ez, they'd likely exposed him to English as well.

She looked back at the American. "What? The bullet just frightened the soldier and he fainted?"

"No. But it obviously didn't cause any damage. Dead men don't run back to their trucks and drive off."

"And neither do soldiers who have the enemy pinned down."

He looked at her with a raised eyebrow—a *don't-be-smart* look. "You always mock men who save your neck?" His eyes were nearly as blue as her own. He could be of Scandinavian descent with the blond hair.

"Save my neck? You mean like you did with that peashooter of yours? Forgive me, I'd nearly forgotten."

"You're alive, aren't you? Last time I looked, the monastery was pretty much leveled. You may not be thrilled with this ride, but like it or not, it's saved your neck."

He's right, Leiah. This man saved your life. "You're right. It hasn't been an easy day."

Jason stared ahead without responding. They would head straight for Addis Ababa, he'd said, an eight-hour journey on these roads. From there they would see.

She watched the muscles on his arm flex as he gripped the wheel. It took a strong man to live in this country, and he'd done it for two years, he'd said.

He wore blue jeans and a well-worn khaki shirt rolled at the sleeves, both layered with dust—typical American.

"Maybe the soldier was wearing a vest of some kind," she said. "Or you hit his belt or something. Enough to knock him out without hurting him."

Jason nodded. "Makes sense." He shook his head. "What doesn't make sense is why they haven't picked up the chase again. But they're coming. There's no way they chased us this far if they had any intention of letting us go. Something's not adding up."

"And why do you suppose they took off in the first place?"

"They fled because they were terrified by my carefully placed shots, that's why," he said, grinning. "Either way they did. For now anyway."

She smiled, slightly amused. "So you're with the Peace Corps? They've already been withdrawn from Eritrea."

"And from northern Ethiopia. Trust me, I'm not out sightseeing. I did this as a favor to an old friend who I'll probably never see again."

"How long have you been with the Corps?"

"Almost two years on this assignment. Before that, two years in the Congo. Not much better than this."

"So you don't approve?"

He looked at her past her furrowed eyebrows. "I wouldn't have given four years of my life to this place if I didn't care for the people. I don't see *you* running back to Eritrea."

"My camp was wiped out. I saw hundreds of unarmed civilians killed in less than an hour. I'm not running from the people."

"And neither am I."

Neither spoke for a few minutes. She had never been good with men. At least not North American men. It was part of her reason for leaving Canada seven years earlier. A head doctor—*Dr. Flannagan,* his gold door sign read—had once given her some psychobabble about insecurities brought on by her burns, but she rejected the reasoning wholesale. She could hardly be more secure.

And what if Dr. Flannagan was right?

So what if he was right? Everyone on the planet struggled with at least a smidgen of insecurity.

She shook her head at the thought. "I'm sorry. Like I said, it's been a bad day. So what are you running from?" That sounded bad, so she quickly explained. "They say that everybody in Africa is running from something."

Jason stared ahead without turning, his jaw line firm. It struck her looking at him that his complexion was as pure as she had seen. Darkened by the sun and silted with dust, but unbroken.

"I have a degree in agriculture," he finally said. "I've spent the last two years with the Irob people on the border, propagating an unusual method of soil conservation they developed."

"Really? How so?"

He looked at her carefully, as if to judge whether she had genuine interest. "They build sandstone walls along the escarpments leading down to the Red Sea to collect soil that washes from the highlands."

"The Alitena gardens. I've heard of them," she said.

He looked surprised. "You have? And what brings you?"

"Me? I'm just a nurse." She didn't let him pursue the question. "So then, here we are, the Peace Corps and the Red Cross. Regardless of how we got here, we're now on the same mission. We might as well make the best of it."

"And what mission would that be?"

"The boy, of course."

"*Your* mission?"

"Ours. Why not?"

She shifted her gaze to a small cluster of stone huts on the outskirts of Biset. A young man leaned on his cane next to a smoldering field of *tef* grain. The man watched them pass with a blank stare.

Leiah looked over her shoulder. Caleb had his head twisted back, watching the scene. He must have sensed her, because he turned around. His large aqua eyes locked onto her, questioning and thoroughly innocent. He stared into her eyes without blinking. What kind of boy was this who had never seen beyond the monastery until today? And what did he make of these two people arguing before him? For that matter, could he even understand their words?

She suddenly wanted to reach out and take the boy into her arms.

Leiah cleared her throat and spoke slowly in her broken Amharic. "Are you all right, Caleb?"

He hesitated and then nodded. *"Hara,"* he said softly. Yes. He looked away then, without changing his expression.

Leiah felt a sudden lump rise to her throat. The boy was like her in many ways. They were both alone. So much alone.

"Let me take the boy to Kenya," she said.

Jason didn't answer.

"There's a refugee camp on the border. I was thinking of possibly going there. Or I could take him to the coast. Either way he would be safe with me." She would've thought Jason would jump at the suggestion. Instead he avoided her look and stared ahead.

"Father Matthew wanted him out of the country, didn't he? I'll take him for you," she offered. "In a way his evacuation provided for mine. It's the least I can do."

"We'll see," he said.

They drove south on a paved road now, quiet in their own thoughts.

∞

Caleb's mind spun with the new world. When he climbed into the truck and buried his head in the woman's garment, he'd told himself that it was all another vision—a dream in the night. It had to be, because even though Dadda had told him that the world was going to change, nothing in real life could be like this.

But when he'd opened his eyes, the world had not changed. He was still in the truck (he knew it was a truck because he'd seen a picture of one in the book Father Timons had shown him once), and he was still moving very fast on the hard path. What was this, a part of the kingdom of heaven? Or maybe hell—he was being shown hell. But it wasn't a vision, was it?

The mountains seemed much bigger than he would have guessed. Dadda had told him that the hills around the monastery went very far and reached very high, but looking at them now for the first time he thought they were touching the sky. If he could climb up one of those, he might be able to see God.

He looked at the man and woman in the front. They called each other Jason and Leiah, and it was obvious that Jason and Leiah were both angry people. They didn't know how to speak kindly. It was no wonder Dadda had suggested he not leave the monastery until it was time. And if he was leaving the monastery as Dadda had told him he would one day, he didn't know how he could manage with such odd men and women. Even the ones in the other truck had been angry. The world was full of grumpy, angry people who wanted to hurt each other.

But Jason did not mean to hurt him—he knew that. Miss Leiah loved him. So did Jason, he thought, although he wasn't very good with showing his love. He should spend a few years with Dadda.

Caleb heard the sound of a bird, and he turned to a gaping valley beside the road. Below them, but high above a tiny river, glided a big bird. Maybe as big as he. The sight sent a chill down his spine. What a lovely creature! They had pigeons and doves and some other small birds at the monastery, but nothing so big.

When he returned he would have to tell Dadda about this bird.

If I could be a bird,
If I could be a bird,
I would fly to heaven and land in my Father's hair.
He smiled.

∞

Jason drove south with a feeling of disconcertion gnawing at his mind, as if a tick were working discreetly away up there. He had a surplus of excuses, of course: it was not every day you saw a monastery obliterated seconds after stepping from its sanctuary. And how many of this planet's inhabitants would ever have a stream of bullets part their hair while they lay sweating on the ground? It was no wonder his head was throbbing.

Then again he was alive, which was in itself a wonder.

It's the boy, Jason.

He grunted and was rewarded with a quick look from Leiah. The nurse with the stunning face and the scarred body and a mouth big enough to swallow Africa. It was her offer to take the boy that dug at him, he thought. Which made no sense. He could be rid of both of them with the nod of his head, for crying out loud. And this was not good?

Not really.

No? And why not, dear Jason? Father Matthew would approve.

It suddenly occurred to him that he hadn't examined the papers Father Matthew had given him. He pulled the envelope from his breast pocket, steadied the wheel with his left knee, and tore it open. Inside were two sheets of paper. He managed to unfold them without running off the road. An immigration form and a letter.

He scanned the pages quickly, surprised by their content.

"What is it?" Leiah asked. It was her first question in over an hour.

"Nothing."

But it was something. The form was a consular general recommendation for Temporary Protective Status under section 44 of the Immigration and Naturalization Law, completed and signed by the priest and an embassy official. If Jason wasn't mistaken, an Immigration and Naturalization Service officer had been persuaded that the boy might have claim to U.S. citizenship as a birthright. His mother may have been an American nurse.

The commander who had deposited the boy at the monastery's gates had killed an American nurse. Or so the theory went, but the evidence was inconclusive. Still, enough cause for investigation.

Furthermore, as long as Caleb remained on the African continent, his life was at risk. Father Matthew had signed custody of the boy over to World Relief's resettlement program. All it required was the signature of an authorized agent of custody in the event of the priest's death.

Father Matthew wanted the boy in the United States.

Of course that was insane. There was no way Jason could take the boy back to the States with him. He shoved the papers back into his pocket.

"They're for the boy?" Leiah asked.

"Yes."

"And?"

"And we'll need to pull over for gas in Woldia. Maybe, just maybe, we've made it far enough south to avoid any more run-ins with the EPLF. I don't want to hold you up. If you want, you could take a bus to wherever you're going."

"Take a bus from Woldia? To where?"

"You mentioned Kenya."

She hesitated. "With the boy?"

"I'm still thinking about the boy. Either way you could go."

"Why do I get the feeling you wouldn't mind my going?"

"I didn't say that. You're headed for Kenya; I'm not."

"I really think the boy should stay with me. I'm with the Red Cross, for goodness' sake. He's now a refugee; let me take him."

He didn't respond.

She turned away from him and stared at the passing hills. They fell into an awkward silence.

Jason considered apologizing. She hardly deserved the cold shoulder he was dishing out. Thing of it was, he didn't even know *why* he was so bothered by her. She'd done nothing to hurt him or the boy. She was strong willed; that much she couldn't hide if she wanted to. But then he was usually attracted to strong women.

It's the boy, Jason.

They rolled on to the hum of the road. Jason looked back once and met the boy's eyes. They stared large and innocent. His dark, wavy hair fluttered in the wind. He sat with his hands limp in his lap, and it occurred to Jason that he was in shock.

Jason smiled. *"Tadius."* Hello, friend.

"Tadius," the boy returned, smiling sheepishly.

It was the first smile since leaving the monastery, Jason thought. His heart suddenly felt heavy staring into those innocent round eyes. He faced the road and swallowed. Maybe it *was* the boy.

∞

Beside him Leiah had nodded off with her head against the roll bar. Her hair lay against her cheek in delicate black strands. Her complexion was smooth over her nose and her lips, down past her chin to the base of her neck, where the burn scars began. Looking at it now, Jason blinked at the sight. Judging by the scarred tissue at her wrists, he surmised that her whole upper torso had been baked in a fire. The fire had either missed her face, or reconstructive surgery had given her a new one.

Either way, the result was a stunning display of contrasts. Watching her at any distance in her tunic, you would see only a beautiful woman with a silky tanned face and the eyes of the sky. But under her garments lay a mangled mess of skin.

Jason removed his eyes and studied the asphalt rolling to meet them. He had been too hard on her. Whatever had brought her to this rugged land was no less than his own reason for coming. What are you running from? she had asked. *And what are you running from, Leiah?*

She was right about one thing: they were now both running with the boy . . . this enigma behind them, who had never before today seen an automobile, much less fled for his life in one. Who did not hesitate to run into the field of fire to see a wounded man up close. The boy was either badly disturbed or so totally innocent he simply could not understand even the most obvious threat. He would be lost in a UNHCR refugee camp.

They rolled into the outskirts of Woldia with the sun nudging the western slope of the Great Rift Valley. The dusty concrete streets were a maze of activity, filled with more than the usual fare of drawn carts and old automobiles spewing plumes of gray smoke. News of the attacks farther north had obviously quickened the pace even this far south.

"We're here?" Leiah looked around, dazed by sleep.

"Welcome to the lovely metroplex of Woldia."

She chuckled. Jason braked for a crossing horse-drawn cart loaded with bulging gunnysacks. Wheat. The driver shot them a stern glare and pulled in front of the Jeep without concern for his own safety.

They pulled into a dilapidated BP gas station five minutes later. An attendant ran out, eager to service them. Even as far south as Woldia, jean-clad Europeans were immediately branded as tourists loaded with cash. Jason asked for a full tank of fuel and an oil check and climbed out. Leiah was already out, extending a hand for the boy, who sat gazing about from his rear-seat perch.

"Come on, Caleb," Leiah urged. "Stretch your legs."

The boy had settled his stare across the road where a street merchant dressed in a bright red tunic sat surrounded by his caged birds. Jason saw the boy's interest and motioned to Leiah. "You go ahead and visit the rest room. I'll take the boy across the street to see the birds."

Leiah hesitated before dropping her arm and heading for the small tin shack labeled "Rest Rome" in broad black letters on a cockeyed wooden sign.

"Come on, kid. You want to see the birds?"

The boy glanced at him and returned his eyes to the cages. He suddenly stood and hopped to the ground. Without waiting for Jason, he struck out across the street.

"Hold on!" Jason took after the boy into the busy street. A small pale yellow Fiat honked its horn and slid to a stop three feet from the boy.

The driver's face puffed red with angry objections, but the Fiat's window was up, and Caleb only looked curiously at the man's shaking jowls. He walked past the car, fixated once again on the birds.

Jason lifted his hand in a hasty apology to the driver and hurried after the boy. The incident had gathered some attention from pedestrians strolling along the cracked sidewalk. "Caleb . . . Caleb wait."

But Caleb did not wait. In fact he was suddenly running. His eyes were

now wide in a look of sheer horror, and he ran right up to the merchant's collection of thirty or so cages.

They were the typical tubular cages which frequented markets throughout Ethiopia, holding a variety of birds, in this case mostly white-collared
pigeons. The merchant had his back turned to Caleb, but at least a dozen
onlookers had now stopped and focused on the boy. He was of mixed race,
an unusual sight to be sure. But it was his expression, Jason thought; his face
held such a blend of innocence and anguish that it would have stopped a
dumb mule had one been in front of the boy.

At the last possible moment, Jason knew what the boy intended to do,
and he broke into a run. He spoke sternly but quietly, not eager to draw attention, although with the running he was beyond that. "Caleb, stop! Don't
touch the birds . . ."

It was too late. The boy reached the first cage, flipped the gate open, and
pulled a rather strange-looking bird free. A look of delight splashed across
Caleb's face as the bird flapped noisily to the sky. He giggled.

The merchant spun around at the sound, but before either he or Jason
could reach him, Caleb had repeated the process with another cage, setting
free another bird of the same species. He was turning to a third cage when
Jason reached him and grabbed the arm extended for the cage.

Had Jason not been there, the merchant would have probably slapped the
boy's head from his shoulders. As it was he screamed a string of obscenities
and flung his hands to the sky. A crowd was gathering, delighted at the show.

Jason pulled Caleb back. "I'm sorry. I don't know why he did that."

The merchant immediately switched to English. "You must pay! You
must pay!" He looked at the sky, lifted his arms as if beseeching the sky for
mercy, and swore in Amharic. "These are very rare birds, you know. Very rare!
Abyssinian catbird! You will pay for these now!"

Jason was reaching for his wallet already. "Yes, of course. I'm sorry. I don't
know what got into him. Please, how much?"

Around them the crowd was cackling and pointing to the skyline, where
the two birds had perched themselves on a three-story building.

"Very rare, you know. These are very rare, very expensive birds." The
merchant now had his eyes on Jason's wallet.

"Of course, and I'm very sorry. Please how much do you want?"

Caleb stepped away from Jason and stood looking up at the merchant.

He spoke in a dialect of Amharic usually reserved for Orthodox religious cer-
emonies. "What will you do with these birds?"

The sound of the language from the boy's mouth cut through the crowd
like a sword. A hush swallowed their laughter. The merchant looked from the
boy to Jason and then back again.

"Please, tell me what you will do with these birds," the boy repeated.

"I will sell them."

"And why would you sell them?"

"They are a delicacy. What do you care, you thieving young scoundrel?"

"He's hardly a thieving scoundrel," Jason said. They were speaking in
separate languages now: the merchant and the boy in Amharic and Jason in
English. "He's an innocent boy who obviously loves birds. Not everyone is set
on killing every piece of meat they can find."

The merchant's face grew red. "And what do you know, you *farenji*?
Perhaps you need to be taught a lesson."

"I meant no insult. Just tell me what you charge for the birds."

"In the cages, two pounds each. But they are not in their cages. They are
on the roofs. Now you must pay five pounds each."

A rumble of agreement went through the crowd, as if this ploy were a particularly clever move on the merchant's part.

"And that's highway robbery, my friend," Jason said.

A note sounded very softly, like a tuning fork, quiet but pure, echoing at
the back of Jason's mind. Someone was singing. Jason extracted some small
bills from his wallet, and the crowd hushed.

The note sounded like the perfect C, held unwavering, and it occurred
to Jason that it wasn't his wallet but this singing that had hushed the crowd.
He looked down to see Caleb's chin lifted lightly and his eyes closed. The
boy's mouth was parted in a pure, crystalline note that carried on the air,
effectively silencing the crowd. Even the merchant had frozen and now
stared at the boy.

From the corner of his eye, Jason saw Leiah step from the rest room and
pull up at the sight. He turned to her and their eyes met. It must be strange,
he thought, to look across the street and see him and the boy surrounded by
a crowd while the boy sang this odd note of perfection. The entire street
seemed to have turned its attention to the boy now. A donkey drawing a cart

twenty yards up the street stopped and turned its head to the scene. Even the drivers in the cars that drove by were craning their necks for a view of the commotion by the bird merchant's cages.

Still the note hung in the air, undisturbed and soft. The crowd now stared at the boy as if he were performing an astounding feat right before their very eyes. But it was just a note sung from the thin lips of a ten-year-old boy.

And then it was more. Because then the two Abyssinian birds who had flown to freedom took flight again. Only this time they flew to the boy. On wings that seemed to flap too slowly for their flight, they fluttered through the air, over the street and over the crowd, which lifted its eyes as one and watched. The birds hovered just above the boy for a moment and then settled onto his shoulders.

Caleb opened his eyes and smiled. He took the birds from his shoulders and set them back in their cages. Now the crowd found its voice: murmurs of incredulity.

Caleb looked up at him, and Jason knew precisely what the boy was thinking. He wanted the birds. Jason pulled out four pounds and paid the reduced price to the merchant. "Your price for the birds?"

The man nodded.

"Jason!" The piercing scream came from the gas station, and Jason spun to see Leiah frantically pointing up the street. He followed her arm. A truck blared its horn as it picked its way through the crowded traffic.

Jason saw the markings clearly then. It was an EPLF Land Rover identical to the one that had cornered them in the canyon!

Panic crowded his throat and he spun back to the boy. Caleb had one bird out and he threw it in the air. He laughed and went for the second bird, oblivious to the danger behind them.

"We have to go, Caleb! Leave it!" He grabbed the boy's arm.

But Caleb pulled away, snatched the second bird from its cage, and threw it into the air.

Jason lifted the boy from his feet and spun to the street. Someone from the crowd had spotted the EPLF vehicle and was shouting frantically. The street broke into pandemonium. From the truck's direction a machine gun began to pop, and the Land Rover broke through the traffic.

Jason saw all of this in the time it took for three draws of breath, and by then it was too late. He'd left the Jeep across the street, and the Land Rover was closing the gap with a full-throated roar.

∾

"Jason!" He snapped his head back to the street before him. Leiah was shouting at him from the driver's seat of his Jeep. She had swung the Jeep around! "Hurry!"

He reached the Jeep in three strides, hefted the boy into the back seat, and piled in beside him. The Jeep lurched forward before he had seated himself, and he nearly toppled off the back.

Machine-gun fire ripped through the air, and Jason shoved the boy's head down. Caleb cried out in surprise.

"Stay down! Move it, Leiah! Floor it!"

"It *is* floored."

They careened around a corner, beyond the sight of the EPLF truck. Jason had driven the Jeep cautiously over the last hundred miles, and it had just received a change of oil, both factors that may have contributed to its healthy pace now.

"Same truck?" Leiah yelled back.

"I don't know. Keep it floored!"

"It's going as fast as it'll go, believe me!"

The EPLF truck came into view, nothing more than a small speck now, just emerging from the town. The sound of weapons fire popped adjacent to the truck: the Land Rover was taking fire. It made a sharp turn onto a side street and disappeared from their view.

Jason released the boy's head and climbed over the passenger seat. "Just keep her pegged."

"We okay?"

"Maybe."

Leiah stared ahead, her knuckles white on the steering wheel. Jason glanced back at Caleb, who sat staring at a rust bucket on the side of the road that looked as if it might once have been a Model T. His hood had flown off, freeing his shoulder-length hair to fly wild in the wind. It struck Jason that had his own son lived, he would be Caleb's age. He might not have looked so different.

"What happened?" Leiah asked.

Jason turned to face the road. "I'm not sure. Animals seem to like him. So does the EPLF."

"Or hate him. Isn't this a bit far south for them?"

"A bit far? Honey, we're halfway to Addis Ababa. There's no way they should be this far south."

"And what does that mean?"

Red hues drew the first lines of a sunset in the western sky. There was more happening here than Jason could even begin to piece together. What was it about this boy? Even beyond his unique innocence, there was a sweetness that had worked its way into Jason's heart.

"It means that I'm taking him," he said.

"To Addis Ababa?"

"To the United States. To California. It's where the priest wanted him."

"You . . . how can—"

"The papers are already drawn up. Father Matthew was no idiot."

Her jaw stiffened and she looked ahead. The Jeep's tires whined incessantly, speeding them down the deserted road.

"I thought you were going to allow me to take him."

"You assumed. And you assumed wrong."

"Then I'm going with you," Leiah said.

He faced her, surprised. "Don't be ridiculous. I thought you were going to Kenya."

"I said I was *thinking* of going to Kenya. But really I have no reason to go to Kenya or to any other place. The boy needs a careful hand. No offense, but it's not something I'm sure you have."

"Thanks. And you're Canadian, not American. What do you think you can possibly do in the States that I can't?"

"I can be with him. The last time I checked, the Red Cross was an international organization. I'll go with you to California and then return to Canada. I may be more help than you might think, Mr. American." She paused and looked to the horizon. "Besides, it's been a long time since I've been home; maybe it'll be for the best."

She said it with a finality that silenced him for the moment. In reality, as a Red Cross evacuee she had as much right to take a flight to Los Angeles as to Nairobi. She was also a nurse who had obviously taken to the boy. He had no reason to suggest she do anything against her wishes, regardless of how wacky they seemed. It was a wacky world.

"Fine," he said.

She nodded. "Good."

4

Minus 2 days

CHARLES CRANDAL STOOD TALL AND COMMANDING, a confident smile curving his lips just so, basking in the winds of political favor, his arms thrust over his head in a victory sign. Four thousand of San Diego's citizens had discarded any notion of spending a day at the beach in favor of hearing this man shake the rafters with his call to power. They stood on the park's green grass with fists lifted to the sky, young and old, male and female, mimicking the victory sign. Paying homage to Charles Crandal, who had persuaded them that he should be the next president of the United States.

Blane Roberts watched him from the side of the podium, intrigued by the man's ability to bring out their affections. Crandal's shiny bald skull flexed with his smile. He wasn't particularly handsome, but even there, looking at the women crying out to him, you would think him a rock legend. John Lennon resurrected. In these moments even Roberts wanted to believe the stump speech. There was a sort of redemption in unity alone, he thought, regardless of its focus. It could be Hitler up here with a flat palm saluting the fine residents of Southern California and they would hardly know the difference.

They were chanting, *"Power to the people. Power to the people,"* which was a slogan Roberts had come up with *(yuk, yuk)*, and it might just as well have been, *"We'll follow you to hell. We'll follow you to hell,"* for all they knew. Either way it didn't matter; people like Crandal were destined to rule. This campaigning stuff was America's road to power, but in reality, when you really got behind all the flags and the dancing girls, true leaders made their own roads. And in the case of Charles Crandal, Roberts was as much the road builder as the man San Diego was going batso over at the moment.

Crandal turned, made one last gesture to the people—an open-armed *we-are-family* gesture—and walked toward Roberts, who smiled and nodded supportively.

They walked off the platform together and headed directly for the black limousine waiting on the park's driveway. Their bodyguards, Bone and

Carson, followed at ten paces as demanded by Crandal. "You had even me going there," Roberts said with a chuckle.

"Keep smiling, Roberts. I know it doesn't come natural, but humor me."

"I'm smiling; I'm smiling. I heard from our people in Eritrea."

Crandal turned to meet a reporter who had slipped past the line and ran to catch them. A security man was striding to intercept, but Crandal waved him off with a casual hand. It was Donna Blair, political correspondent for NBC, her trademark blue eyes smiling even now at twenty feet. The blond anchor-turned-correspondent did not possess the muscles required to frown, Roberts thought. The wind had disheveled her short hair, but the look only complemented her.

"No interviews, Donna. I thought I made that clear." Crandal said it with a grin, but his voice carried a slight bite.

"Who said anything about an interview?" She pulled up and smiled pointedly, a gesture that made most men blink. "How does it feel to be ten points up on your opponent eight weeks before the election?"

"Sounds like a question to me." Crandal paused, studying her. "Ten points, huh? Which poll?"

"Ours. And it's a word of congratulations, not a question. How about a sit-down in Los Angeles next week?"

"When?"

"Monday?"

"No, when was the poll taken?"

"Came out this morning, taken last night. How about Monday?"

"Come to the press conference Wednesday. I promise you I'll give you the leadoff." He turned and strode for the limousine and then looked back. "And if you think ten points is something, stick around, honey. We're going to re-define blowout. You can quote me on that."

Roberts's gaze lingered. Even the media in all of their supposed unbiased neutrality couldn't resist Crandal's charm. He stepped after the man quickly.

"And the report on Tempest?" Crandal asked.

They were alone now, with only the chauffeur in possible earshot. Roberts spoke quietly. "Like clockwork. The news has it as another African border skirmish, but the guerrillas penetrated all the way to Debra Damarro."

"They find anything?"

"No."

He paused. "The monastery?"

"Leveled."

"No survivors?"

"No."

"Good. Tell them not to get carried away over there."

"There'll be the typical posturing for another month, but they've already started pulling back."

"Good." Crandal turned one last time and lifted his arms in his patented victory sign. "It's amazing what you can get away with when you have the power, isn't it?" The band was playing and the chants were still full on, but a fresh cheer rose above the din and Crandal smiled wide. He was getting to like the feel, and truth be told, Roberts wasn't hating it either.

"Yes, sir."

Crandal suddenly thundered his war cry, startling Roberts beside him. "Power to the people."

Yes indeed. *Power to the people.*

5

Day 0

THEY BROUGHT THE BOY INTO THE UNITED STATES on Saturday, flying American Airlines from London. The International Office of Migration arranged the short-notice tickets through regular evacuation agreements with the Peace Corps and the INS.

Late September in Southern California felt warm, considering the season. They rented a Yellow cab for the trip to Pasadena, where Jason would keep the boy until his processing Monday morning.

Caleb had hardly spoken since their departure from Ethiopia, and when he did, it was usually in Ge'ez, in an off-the-cuff reaction. He spoke a few times in Amharic in response to questions put to him in Jason's or Leiah's broken Amharic.

Approaching Addis Ababa near midnight Thursday, he had awoken from a long sleep and entered his first modern city. He had shaken his head repeatedly as if doing so would wake him from a dream. They had driven directly to Bole International Airport and caught a flight to London on Ethiopian Airlines at six Friday morning, but the few short hours in the large city, albeit Third World, were enough to send Caleb into a tailspin.

Watching the boy's unblinking stare as they wound their way through cluttered highways, Jason found it hard to imagine what it must be like, seeing for the first time such strange wonders. It gave the term *culture shock* new meaning. Leiah and he had agreed to let the boy discover the new world on his own, offering explanation only when he asked.

By the time they boarded the DC-9 that would take them to London, Caleb's stare had become glazed. His mind had retreated into some familiar place where things made sense. He slept most of the first leg. The London airport was his first exposure to mass modernization, and he took it in with a dumb stare. Even when Jason asked him what he thought of this new world, he said only, *"Dehan,"* nice, in a small, meek voice and looked around as if bored by it all.

The flight over the Atlantic and the United States on the Airbus was surprisingly quiet, and Caleb had slept through most of it. They exited the 210 freeway at 10:00 P.M. and pulled into Jason's driveway on Hollister ten minutes later. Fifty-four hours had expired since Father Matthew had rushed them out of his monastery.

Caleb was asleep and Jason carried him in without waking him. The house had sat empty for four years now, except for several short visits, and it smelled musty. But the linens were clean—he always left with freshly made beds in the event of his return. He walked down the hall and tucked the boy into the same bed his son had occupied seven years earlier.

When he returned to the living room, he found Leiah waiting by their duffle bags. During their layover in London she'd used most of her money to purchase Western clothes for her and the boy. When she'd approached Jason after changing in the airport, he'd hardly recognized her out of the tunic. The blue jeans she wore now fit her thin frame well. The turtleneck was maybe a bit warm for Los Angeles, but he understood why she would choose it. Either way she looked quite striking.

"Want a drink? I've got warm soda pop in the kitchen."

Leiah smiled thinly. "I'll pass." She opened the top of her duffle, pulled out Caleb's dirty tunic, and zipped the bag back up. She held up the tunic. "His possessions." She tossed it to him. "That's all he has. You might want to give it a good wash. We should get him some more clothes as soon as possible."

"Maybe I should burn it. Either way, it's a bit late for laundry, don't you think?"

"No, don't burn it. It's all he has from Ethiopia now. Wash it."

Jason stepped down the hall, tossed the tunic into the laundry room, and walked to the kitchen. He flipped the refrigerator on and dug out a lukewarm Coke.

"You can sleep in the guesthouse out back until you leave Tuesday. It's not much, but it'll beat an Ethiopian shanty any day."

"I still think he should go with me," Leiah said. "The poor child's in shock. An orphanage will have no clue how to deal with someone in his shoes."

Jason straddled a dining chair. "Like I said, his case has already been assured by World Relief's Garden Grove office. We're restricted by the immigration laws, and in this case they've allowed him into the country with the understanding that he'll be in the custody of World Relief's assignment. Don't worry; they're good people. We're not talking Oliver Twist here."

"He's no ordinary refugee, and you know that. For starters, he's an orphan—"

"Which is why he's been assigned to an orphanage. One run by an Orthodox church, for that matter. John Gardner, the *director* of the World Relief office, assured me that he couldn't think of a better place for an orphan from an Ethiopian Orthodox monastery than in an orphanage run by a Greek Orthodox church. Orthodoxy has its similarities. It'll be good for the boy."

"He's no ordinary orphan either. You see him, Jason. He's beyond himself. No orphanage could be prepared to handle a case like his. Can't we talk to the INS about transferring him into my personal care until we understand his needs better?"

"Send him to Canada? With someone who hasn't lived there for over five years? I don't think so. Besides, one of the reasons he's been granted Temporary Protective Status is because of the fact that he may have citizenship rights."

"And while they're deciding his rights, he may very well lose himself. Have you considered that? You see him now and you see a cute little ten-year-old who makes you want to cry. But put him under the wrong care and he could snap. He's never seen the outside of a monastery until a couple days ago, for goodness' sake!"

"I know, Leiah!" Jason surprised himself with his tone. "I know. I like him too. But this isn't Ethiopia. We have laws. You can't just take the boy to Canada and adopt him."

"I didn't suggest adopting him. We spend our lives helping people." She stood and paced his beige carpet. "We sew up their wounds and try to keep them from starving; it's what we've given our lives to. So now we have a single boy who is desperate for help. How do we help him?"

"We help him by saving his life! We deliver him to the blessed United States of America in one piece. We give him the opportunity to live a life few can even dream about where he came from. What are you talking about? Don't turn him into your little pet, Leiah. You may feel all messed up limping back home, but that doesn't give you the right to use him as your sweet little bundle of validation."

"How dare you say that!" She let the question ring through the room.

"How dare you say that? You have no idea about me. You think that's all he is to me? Some teddy bear to keep me from crying at night? Who could make a comment like that?"

His ears were ringing and he suddenly felt hot. "Who? Someone who hasn't consigned themselves to hiding from the world."

"And that would be me, right?" She spoke bitterly. "You see me as the poor burned nurse who has fled the world in shame? You, on the other hand, are the world's savior, rushing about tending to the less fortunate. Is that it?"

"I didn't say that."

They sat quietly for a few moments. Jason shook his head, angry at their harsh words. She was a stubborn woman; that much had been obvious from the start. But in the three days he'd spent in Leiah's company, he had seen beyond the shell she wore and he knew a good heart when he saw one. Hers was better than good. It was an odd chemistry between them that allowed them to squabble like this, as though they had known each other all their lives and held no compunction in dumping their thoughts on one another.

"Maybe, just maybe the boy deserves better than either of us," he said, and he knew it made no sense. "Either way, our hands are tied."

She didn't respond, but neither did she break her glare.

"Look, the kid's going to the orphanage, and that's it. I'm an agriculturalist, for heaven's sake, not a nanny. I can't believe we're even having this conversation."

"Excuse me."

They both spun to the small voice at the same time. Caleb stood in the hall, staring at them with wide eyes. He was out of bed and he'd just spoken in English.

"Excuse me. Could you not speak so loudly, please?" he said.

With that the boy simply turned around, walked back down the hall, and disappeared into his room.

Jason stared after Caleb, stunned by his use of such clear English. He'd understood everything, then. Not just here, but in the Jeep and on the plane.

He turned to Leiah, who had fixed her jaw. She looked at him sternly, as if to say, *You see? And you want to throw him to the wolves?*

"It's late; we're both tired," Jason said. "We should get some sleep." He shook his head. "I'm sorry; I don't know why I said those things. I had no right."

Her expression softened a little but not much. "Like you said, we're both tired." It was all she offered.

Jason stood and retrieved a key from the wall. "I'll show you to your room."

He led her out back to the detached garage he'd converted into a small guesthouse for his mother-in-law's extended stay after Stephen's birth. The main house was too small to share with in-laws for three months, he'd decided. That was before taking a pickax to the cement slab in the converted garage to make room for the bathroom's plumbing. Suffice it to say that the project had sharpened his use of profanity. After Ailsa's untimely departure from his life following little Stephen's death, he'd considered tearing the structure to the ground to rid his world of the lingering mother-in-law talcum-powder smell.

He pushed the door open and flipped on the light. "Like I said, it's not much, but it beats—"

"It's fine. Thank you." She stepped past him and tossed her bag on the bed.

He wanted to tell her to lighten up and show a little appreciation, but it occurred to him that he wasn't exactly dealing from a position of strength here. Instead he offered a meek, "See you in the morning," and closed the door without volunteering any further assistance. He wasn't sure if he'd left toilet paper in the bathroom; he would soon find out. Knowing her, she'd cross her legs till morning to make a point.

It was midnight when Jason climbed under the cool sheets he'd placed on the bed two years earlier. He turned off the familiar brass bedside lamp and smiled. It was good to be home, actually. He was getting used to sleeping alone and for the first time he could remember, he hadn't come home to a house full of memories. He had new challenges, of course—Caleb, Leiah— but he wasn't slumping through the house fuming at Ailsa, and that was something.

Yes, it was good to be home.

6

Day 1

JASON FELT A TUG AT HIS ARM, and he rolled over with a grunt.
"Excuse me, please."

The voice drifted through his mind with a distant familiarity. A voice calling from his dream.

"Excuse me, please."

Jason opened one eye and saw the small boy standing. The boy? He jerked up and looked around the room. His home in Pasadena . . . with the boy, Caleb, standing beside his bed, at nine in the morning according to the analog clock on the wall. He sat up and rubbed the sleep from his eyes.

Caleb stood with his arms at his sides, dressed in the gray cotton slacks and white dress shirt Leiah had bought him in London. The brown sandals fit him well, although they didn't really complement the outfit. He had chosen them over the black shoes Leiah had shown him. His hair lay in tangles to his shoulders.

"Good morning, Caleb. You're up bright and early."

"Sir?"

Yes, he did speak English, didn't he? At least basic English. "Just a saying we use in America. Did you sleep well?"

"Sir, we must go to the church." His choice of words certainly didn't sound childish, but then again he hadn't grown up with children, had he? In Ethiopia it would be proper English.

"Church? Yes, of course. You'll have lots of time to go to church."

"We will go now, then?"

"Now? No, heavens no." Jason chuckled and plopped back on the pillow. "It's nine o'clock in the morning, middle of the night Ethiopian time."

The boy's round aqua eyes blinked. He looked out the window and then back. "I would like very much to go to the church."

Jason sat up. "Yes, I'm sure you would, but we can't. I don't even know which churches are open or when the services start. It's been years since I've stepped foot inside a church, my boy." He threw the covers aside to stand. "Now, what do you say we go get us some breakfast? Ever hear of McDonald's?"

Caleb seemed not to have heard. He took a step back and blinked several times. "I would like very much to find the church."

Poor child was feeling lost. The church was the only home he knew. "We will, Caleb. We will. We'll take you to the Orthodox church on Monday."

Caleb suddenly seemed frantic. His eyes shifted to the window, welled with tears, and then returned to Jason. He brought his hands to his chin in a praying gesture and begged. "We must go to the church! Please, sir." The boy's little body trembled and Jason felt the first pang of alarm. What if the boy did snap as Leiah suggested? He'd certainly never seen a ten-year-old looking like Caleb did now. "I beg you, good sir. I beg you—"

"Okay, Caleb." He held out his hand for the boy to settle down. "Okay, we'll take you to a church. Maybe we can find one open tonight."

The boy stilled for a moment and then he began to pace frantically, four feet one way and four feet back. His eyes were searching the floor desperately.

Jason stood, frightened by the behavior now. "Okay, Caleb, settle down. Please settle down. We'll get Leiah and go to the church, okay?"

The boy stopped midstride and spun to him, his eyes round with relief. He rushed forward, grabbed Jason's right hand, and began to kiss it. "I thank you; I thank you," he said.

Jason felt his chest constrict at the sight. *Dear Caleb, I'm so sorry.* He placed a hand on the boy's head and pulled him close. He wanted to say something, but his throat was aching and he couldn't speak.

The boy wrapped his arms around Jason's waist and held tight. Then he broke away and pulled Jason by the hand. "We will go now?"

"Well, I do have to get dressed, boy. I can't very well fetch our dear nurse in my underwear, can I?"

He dressed quickly and led Caleb to the guesthouse. Leiah responded on their third attempt to raise her. She stood in her blue tunic, her dark hair messy and her eyes squinting.

"The boy insists we go to church," Jason said, smiling.

"Now?"

"Yes, trust me. Now. He doesn't seem interested in accepting no for an answer."

"Goodness, I haven't been to a church in a dozen years." She hesitated.

"Well, give me a minute to throw myself together here." She shut the door without waiting for a response.

"There you go, Caleb. Church it is."

It occurred to Jason then that the Greek Orthodox church which ran the orphanage would probably be having their Sunday Mass soon. Church services usually started at ten or eleven, didn't they? He had attended the Greater Life Community Church on the east side of Pasadena for three months leading up to his son's death seven years ago. It would take an army of angels to drag him back into that sanctuary again.

Fifteen minutes later Jason piloted his white Ford Bronco down the Hollywood freeway toward the valley. According to the yellow pages, liturgy began at ten-thirty Sundays at Holy Ascension Greek Orthodox Church in Burbank—the church responsible for Caleb's future. Their large color-splashed ad included a small picture of Father Nikolous, dressed in white-and-gold robes with a towering white headpiece that reminded Jason of pictures of the pope.

Leiah had managed to wash and dry her new clothes before turning in, and she wore them now, white turtleneck and all. Jason thought about offering her some of his clothes, but quickly decided that he could hardly do it without embarrassing her. He wasn't sure that jeans were standard fare in Orthodox services, but hers were clean and they fit well.

Caleb sat in the rear, face pressed against the window, gawking at the mix of metal and concrete flying by. It was the first time he'd seen a Western city by daylight, Jason thought. Speeds within the monastery hadn't exceeded walking or the occasional run. It was a slow life with enough time to hear your own breathing and consider its source. Watching a mouse scamper across the room would qualify as a highlight. Now the boy was confronted with eight lanes of lumbering trucks and flashing cars, roaring at breakneck speeds. It would be akin to stepping into a Jetsons cartoon and watching futuristic cars hover by.

Leiah sat in the front passenger seat, looking back at the boy with furrowed brow. "You ever bring a Third-World refugee to the States?" Jason asked.

"No. You?"

"No. At least we've established that Caleb speaks English, haven't we, Caleb?" Jason asked, glancing in the rearview mirror.

The boy looked at the back of his head but did not respond.

Jason tapped the mirror. "Caleb?"

He looked up, saw Jason's image, and smiled.

"Father Matthew taught you English?"

Caleb didn't answer. Why, Jason didn't understand, but the boy just looked out the window, presumably distracted by a huge tractor-trailer that rolled by on their left. The boy muttered something in Ge'ez and fell silent.

"He'll be in shock for days," Leiah said quietly.

"I don't understand. He spoke so clearly this morning. I mean it wasn't just broken English, but proper English, like last night."

"So he speaks proper English. That doesn't mean he speaks more than a few dozen words. Either way he's like a fish out of water."

Jason glanced at the boy's image in the mirror. He was growing rather used to the idea of having him along. Nostalgic, even. Maybe Caleb was bringing something out in him: a sense of purpose that he'd buried with Stephen.

∞

At first sight the large Orthodox church looked like something that belonged in an encyclopedia under the subject of religion rather than on the streets of Burbank, California. The circular drive swept by a crystal-clear pond complete with splashing fountain and large orange carp before running under a causeway in front of the entrance. The lawns were manicured and the palm trees carefully placed to give symmetry to the landscaping. Towering brickwork supported huge bright blue dormers on either side of the entrance. But it was the copper dome arching over the otherwise square structure that gave it the religious feel. These boys knew how to put their money where their hearts were.

Jason parked the Bronco in a visitor's slot and climbed out. They were late, judging by the hundreds of cars sitting quietly in the lot. He walked around to help Caleb out, but the boy had already found his way to the asphalt and was crossing to the large dome.

"Caleb, hold up." Jason glanced at Leiah and they hurried after the boy. "Well, he recognizes something."

"Of course he does. The dome. I feel underdressed."

"You'll be fine. We'll slip in the back and sneak out early."

"You ever been in an Orthodox church like this?"

"No."

"Me neither. I really feel underdressed."

The foyer was lined with Greek pillars rising twenty feet to support a ceiling painted in gold leaf. Leiah rested her hand on the boy's shoulder. They passed a large writing desk that reminded Jason of a concierge's station, and the man who peered past his bifocals at their entry seemed to fit the part. A business manager perhaps. Someone had to keep the coffers full.

The door leading into the sanctuary was at least ten feet tall and made of solid oak. Jason pulled a brass handle three times the size of his hand and ushered Leiah and the boy through it. He followed them and let the door close softly behind him.

Nothing could have quite prepared him for the atmosphere that met him. The dome spanned over them in brilliant gold, divided in a dozen sections, each section framing huge paintings of robed men with eyes too large for their faces. Presumably Christ and his disciples. The rectangular walls were covered in a burgundy velvet cloth. Three huge crystal chandeliers, glittering with a hundred bright lights, hung over the sanctuary. The sight was enough to stop all three of them for a moment.

A rich scent filled Jason's nostrils—an incense Jason didn't recognize or possibly the smell of the candles blazing on the platform. Every detail was in perfect order; not a soul moved from their place. The congregation was seated in long pews on either side of the plush aisle at their feet. They sat like puppets, fixated on the ceremony conducted by Father Nikolous, who Jason immediately recognized from his picture. Had a stray sheep in the flock turned to take note of the slight disturbance, they would've seen three sadly underdressed strangers who looked as if they'd just entered the wrong facility by mistake.

Fortunately, it wasn't the kind of atmosphere that invited the sheep to turn and stare. *Un*fortunately, the Father didn't need to turn to see them. His eyes held Jason's for a long moment before dropping back to the large book in his hands.

Jason tugged on Leiah's arm and sidestepped into the last pew. She followed quickly, slipping in beside him.

But the boy stood staring ahead, transfixed by the sight.

Leiah reached out and gently laid her hand on his shoulder. "Caleb," she whispered softly.

Caleb was not listening. He stepped forward and Leiah's hand fell off his shoulder. It was a small, slow step, but it was away from them, up the aisle.

Caleb had taken three more steps forward before Jason realized that the boy actually intended on walking to the front. His heart skipped a beat, and he let his instincts take over for one terrible moment.

"Caleb!"

His harsh whisper might as well have been a yell. A dozen parishioners near the back turned and dipped their heads to offer stern stares.

But Caleb walked on, slow and frail, with his arms hanging by his sides. Leiah had buttoned his white shirt up to the last button and combed his hair so that it parted in the middle and fell neatly to his shoulders. He stared directly ahead and moved as if lost in a world beyond the one captured under this gold dome.

On the platform Father Nikolous came to the end of a stanza. One of the priests next to him began to sing in a high warbly voice and the congregation joined him like a well-practiced choir. A bowl of smoking incense hung from a chain in the priest's right hand and swung like a pendulum at his knees, keeping surreal time with his chant.

Caleb walked on, and Jason stood, as if doing so might stop the boy. What was he going to do now? Leiah rose slowly beside him. Jason made a move to exit the pew, but Leiah held out her hand.

"Leave him," she whispered.

Of the five hundred faithful gathered that day, roughly twenty-five had lost their focus on the liturgy and now watched the strange boy slowly gliding up the aisle. He was halfway to the front, a stray child whose head hardly reached the top of the pews, when the congregation seemed to sense wholesale that something unusual was happening in the aisle. A hush settled over the crowd, beginning at the back and spreading up the thirty or so rows, until only the most devout, seated up front, boldly continued their liturgy.

And then it was only the priest beside Father Nikolous, in a voice that echoed loudly through the auditorium. He caught himself, pried his eyes from the book in his hands, and stopped on the word *and* . . .

Father Nikolous frowned and stared at the boy, but he did not speak. The service at Holy Ascension Greek Orthodox Church in Burbank, California, had come to a dead stop.

All eyes were fixed on this one small child who walked up the aisle, seemingly unaware of his boldness, his large eyes fixated on the podium.

Jason moved quietly down the pew to the outer aisle and eased closer to the front, where Leiah joined him. From his vantage point he could see the boy clearly. He scanned the platform and once again met Father Nikolous's disapproving glare. He shifted his eyes and saw then what the boy was staring at. Behind the priest stood a tall wooden cross, with the naked form of Christ hanging in death. Caleb was fixated on the one icon that could easily have been transported here from his monastery at Debra Damarro for its similarity.

The poor child was grasping for a root to his motherland and he had found it here, in this cross with the dead Christ. "He's staring at the crucifix," Jason whispered.

Leiah nodded. She'd seen it too.

"Should I get him?"

"No, leave him," she said.

Caleb stopped at the platform steps and stared up at the cross. Ahead and to his right the priest's swinging incense bowl barely moved now. Absolute silence had gripped the church.

The boy's face suddenly wrinkled with sorrow. A wet tear slipped from his eye and left its trail down his cheek. He closed his eyes, lifted his chin, and opened his mouth in a long, sustained, quiet cry.

Jason felt as though his chest had been caught in a vise. Caleb's hands slowly lifted and he cried quietly before the cross while the congregation looked on in stunned silence. Jason thought Father Nikolous might interrupt the scene, but he, too, was immobilized.

The boy fell quiet and seemed to become aware of the surroundings. It might have been the first time since entering that he'd removed his eyes from the cross. He looked at the Father and smiled softly. Nikolous did not return the smile.

"Mama, what's happening?" a young voice from across the room asked aloud.

"Shhhhh!"

Jason saw a mother bend over her child on the far front pew. He looked to be about Caleb's age, all dressed up in shorts with suspenders and a bow tie. His hair was slicked back above glazed white eyes.

The boy was blind.

It was why he'd asked the question. *Mama, what's happening?* What kind of disease would turn a boy's eyes white at the age of ten?

Caleb had turned his head to the boy. The congregation still hadn't found themselves in the moment, and now it appeared that Caleb hadn't either. He was walking toward the mother and her boy.

A slight murmur ran through the crowd. Caleb approached the boy and stopped within arm's reach. The mother had a dumb look on her face, a mixture of anxiety and wonder. Her mouth opened when Caleb reached for the blind boy's hand, but she said nothing. Caleb leaned forward and whispered in the child's ear, then stood and took a step back.

The child looked in his mother's direction for a moment, and then stood. The mother watched her son, frozen in the moment. Caleb smiled and gently pulled the boy along, toward the center aisle. They walked like two brothers sharing some innocent secret, oblivious to the crowd—the one child because his eyes were blinded by a white tissue, and Caleb because his might as well have been.

Caleb held the other's hand and guided him back to the spot before the platform. Together they turned toward the front with Caleb's guiding hand. They stood in silence, facing the cross.

Some of the parishioners shifted uncomfortably in their seats. For an awkward moment nothing moved.

A gasp suddenly filled the room. Jason thought it might be the boy's mother, finally come to herself. But it wasn't. It was the blind boy. And now he was crying. He was standing with his hand in Caleb's, with his back to the audience, and his shoulders were shaking with sobs.

Cries of protest erupted from the sanctuary. Half a dozen men stood, and for a few seconds what could only be described as bedlam in such a stately place broke out.

"Quiet! Be quiet!" Father Nikolous had his hand raised to the crowd, but his eyes were fixed on the boy, who was now raising his hands with his fingers spread wide, as though grasping at the air. The congregation fell quiet.

The boy suddenly began to bob up and down, still sobbing. The bounce became a short vertical hop and the cry grew to a wail. Chills broke down Jason's spine. Beside the boy Caleb only smiled.

Then Jason understood the boy's words. "I can see!" he was screaming. "I can see; I can see; I can see the cross!"

The boy whirled around and faced the crowd. His eyes flashed with delight and not a spot of white covered them.

Leiah's gasp beside him was lost in a hundred others. She instinctively grabbed Jason's arm. The priest stared dumbfounded. The boy's mother stumbled across the auditorium, mouth wide open.

The boy spun to Caleb and threw his arms around him, nearly knocking him over in the process. He was blubbering unintelligibly now. The congregation dissolved into pandemonium. Some shouted for order and respect; others cried out their confusion; no less than twenty stormed the front to get a closeup look at the boy, whom they called Samuel.

"Sit down! Sit down, everybody!" Father Nikolous thundered.

It took him ten minutes to return his flock to a semblance of order. The blind boy, Samuel, who could now clearly see, had calmed down, but he couldn't stop looking around. His eyes flittered over the sanctuary's bright colors and then over his hands and then they would settle on Caleb for a few seconds before returning to the drapes or some other brightly colored object.

Caleb sat on the front pew beside Jason and Leiah, head bowed, staring at his hands. The commotion in the church had pushed him into a withdrawal of some kind. The incense had stopped its smoldering, and the Father stood before them all with a frown plastered on his face.

It felt like a moment of gravity, one in which the Father should make a grand announcement. What that announcement would be, Jason had no clue, because he had no earthly idea what had just happened. Some would undoubtedly call it a miracle for lack of better understanding. Or perhaps some psychic phenomenon, triggered by Caleb. But in any case, the occasion of a blind boy finding his sight in the blink of an eye needed a few words of commemoration.

But Father Nikolous said nothing of the kind. He simply stood there in his white robes, looked from Samuel to Caleb, and closed the service with a "Let us pray."

It was the end of the liturgy for the Holy Ascension Greek Orthodox Church that day.

∞

"So you came to our church because the boy has been assigned to the orphanage?" Father Nikolous asked, looking up from the INS forms Jason had given him.

Jason sat next to Leiah, watching Caleb, who looked lost in the overstuffed chair they'd set him in. It had taken them ten minutes to dodge a host of questions, escape the auditorium, and find their way to the Father's office at his request. The boy would not make eye contact. He was clearly shaken by the attention.

Jason nodded. "He wanted to go to church."

"And you say his life is at risk?"

"Father Matthew seemed to think so. Not now, of course, but we were chased several hundred miles in Ethiopia. His Temporary Protective Status was granted on the grounds that he might have citizenship rights."

"Yes, that much I can read." He turned to the boy and frowned.

Father Nikolous did not strike Jason as the kind of man who would rise in the middle of the night to fetch a bottle of milk for a crying child. But he had the proper staff in place to run the orphanage. He was tall and wore a black mustache, which generally followed the frown on his lips. His brown eyes were cupped by large dark bags, and his nose was perhaps the largest Jason had seen—definitely not the perfect picture of Mother Teresa.

"We have taken several Orthodox refugees in from Ethiopia, although never an orphan. Orphan refugees to the United States are rare, you know."

"He's not an ordinary boy," Leiah said.

"Of course not. He's of mixed race and raised in an Ethiopian monastery."

"It's more than that. You saw it yourself."

Father Nikolous dipped his head and looked at her carefully. "And what did I see, my dear?"

She didn't answer.

"You tell us, Father," Jason said. "What did we just see out there?"

Nikolous faced the boy. Caleb had picked up a magazine from the end table by his chair—a *National Geographic* with the caption "The Wonders Down Under"—and was engrossed in its contents.

"You say he speaks English?"

"Yes. At least some."

Nikolous waited a moment, as if he expected the boy to offer an explanation on his own. "Well, what about it, young man? What happened out there?"

Jason knew the boy had heard, because his eyes strayed from the page for a brief second. But he refused to acknowledge the priest.

"Leave him alone," Leiah said, standing suddenly. She walked over to stand beside him. "Can't you see that he's in shock? I don't see how pushing him on things he himself probably doesn't understand can help him."

She was right, Jason thought. The loving mother.

"We'll give him the care he needs," Nikolous said. He picked up a pen and pulled the INS form closer.

"What are you going to do with him?" Leiah asked.

"We're going to take him into the orphanage, my dear. Isn't that why you brought him?"

"No. We brought him because he insisted on attending a service. But we had no intention of just signing him over to you." She glanced at Jason for support.

"Well, well, miss. I do have a form in front of me that states otherwise. The boy has been granted Temporary Protective Status and his care assigned to World Relief by his former guardian, this Father Matthew. You see, his signature is right here." He looked down at the paper. "Right beside this statement stamped by the immigration officer at LAX, which orders the boy into the care of the Sunnyside Orphanage, as assured by World Relief." He looked up and grinned condescendingly. "The Sunnyside Orphanage. That would be me."

"Yes, but you just can't *take* him!"

Nikolous kept the snotty smile on his face and turned slowly to Jason. He might be right on technical grounds, but he was pushing the wrong buttons. Leiah looked at Jason, her eyes begging him to say something that would contradict the Father.

"A little less sarcasm wouldn't hurt," he said to Nikolous.

"He's been in the country for less than twenty-four hours, for goodness' sake," Leiah said. "You can't just take him away from us!"

"Ah, you have grown fond of him." The priest's lips fell flat. "Well, he's not an object we grow fond of and toss around as if he were a ball. He's a refugee and an orphan, and he belongs in a facility that cares for refugees and orphans. The sooner the better. You think dragging him around Los Angeles for another day will do him any favors?"

"Maybe not, but surely we don't *have* to turn him over now. He could spend the day with us," Leiah said.

The flat grin returned to the Father's face. "You know, you are quite right." He lowered his head, abruptly signed the form on his desk, slapped the pen down, and looked up. "And now you are quite wrong. You will kindly leave the boy in my charge."

"Jason?"

Fingers of heat already spread over Jason's head. The Father had no right to take such an offensive tone. He ignored Leiah and addressed Nikolous.

"You're pushing it, pal. If anyone's treating him like a ball, it's you, snatching him away with the stroke of your pen. Where's your decency?"

"Forgive me, perhaps I did speak with a touch of cynicism. But I do know orphans, and there is good reason why this boy was assigned to us."

"Okay," Leiah said. "Then let me ask you: please can we keep Caleb until the morning? We won't haul him all around Los Angeles; we won't even take him out of the house. We just want to say good-bye to him. He saved our lives and yes, we have grown fond of him. Surely a little love won't hurt him."

"He saved your lives?" the Father asked with a raised brow. "I was under the impression that you saved *his* life."

Leiah glanced at Jason, who cut in. "Yes. We did save his life. Either way, I think Leiah's request is reasonable. It's the least you can do."

Father Nikolous sighed and straightened the paperwork on his desk. "Yes, perhaps you're right. But I'm going to deny the request."

They both blinked at him. Leiah stared at Jason, dumbstruck.

"Now if you wouldn't mind, I have plenty to do. I thank you for bringing him safely into the country; God will reward you. We will see to the boy from here."

"Just like that?" Leiah asked.

The priest only looked at her with a raised brow.

"But—"

"Leiah, please," Jason interrupted. "He's right. He may not be going about it in the most respectful way, but he does have this right."

"And what of the boy's rights?"

"That's enough!" Father Nikolous snapped. "Now you're confusing him, and I can promise you that will do him no good. Please leave us. Now!"

Jason stood. "Come on, Leiah." He had an inkling to take the priest by his mustache and shake some sense into him, but he shoved the notion aside. Instead he walked over to the boy and laid a hand on his shoulder.

"You take care, Caleb, you hear?" The boy lowered the magazine and looked at him with those round aqua eyes. A sadness lingered deep in them, Jason thought. *What are we doing?*

He knelt and pulled the boy's head to his shoulder. "You'll be okay," he whispered. "I promised your father I wouldn't allow any harm to come to you. I won't let you down. I promise."

When he pulled back, there were tears in the boy's eyes.

Jason stood and Leiah immediately stooped to the boy. She held the boy tight, swallowing visibly. "I love you, Caleb," she said in his ear. She wiped her cheeks quickly as she stood.

Leiah faced Father Nikolous with fire in her eyes. "Now you listen to me, Mr. Religion. If you hurt one hair on his body, you'd better pray to your God to strike me dead, because I will become your worst nightmare, you understand?"

Nikolous looked at her and frowned.

Jason finally took her arm. "Come on, Leiah."

He led her to the door and turned for one last look at Caleb. The boy was staring at them, lost and innocent. But there were tears running down his face. *Goodness, what have we done?* Jason swallowed the lump in his throat and faced Nikolous.

"For a Father, you're quite a jerk, you know that? Someone needs to teach you some manners."

He pulled the door closed and walked Leiah from the office.

7

THE NEW PEOPLE PUT HIM IN THE BIG HOUSE behind the church. Caleb didn't know why Miss Leiah and Jason had to leave, but he was sure that they did. He also knew that Father Nikolous was very different from Dadda.

And Dadda was gone. That's what Jason had told Leiah yesterday, and he knew it was true.

Caleb sat on his haunches in the room and rocked back and forth, trying to decide what to do with the feelings that ran through his chest when he thought about Dadda. He knew that he was with God; he did know that. But he didn't know why that made him sad.

His father's brown face floated through his mind. "Remember, Caleb, words are weak instruments of love. They can do many things, but they do not carry the truth like your hands do. People need to be shown, not told."

"Then why don't we go show them, Dadda?"

"But you will. You will. And I am showing you, am I not?"

Caleb swallowed and stood. The woman that the other children called Auntie Martha had left him in this large room a long time ago, and it was now dark outside. Maybe they would bring the other children in to see him soon. He'd seen five in the yard as they were walking here, and they had seen him too. It had made his heart run very fast.

Let the little children come to me. Jesus had said that, and Caleb had always wondered what it would be like to jump on his lap with other children. A song he learned from Dadda ran through his mind.

You must be a child;
You must always be a child
If you want to see,
If you want to walk in the kingdom.

Caleb walked to the window and looked out to the dark yard. Lights blazed in a window across the grass. A figure walked past it and Caleb's pulse jumped. It was one of the boys! He walked out of view.

Hello, child. My name is Caleb. Maybe it was Samuel, from the church. The one who had seen the cross with him.

Caleb rolled away from the window and stood with his back to the wall, swallowing. The cross in the church was the first he'd seen since leaving the monastery, and it had nearly stopped his heart. They had killed God on that cross. Not that one, but one like it. The worlds had collided on those beams, Dadda used to say, and standing there this morning, it had felt like his worlds were colliding.

He'd seen some things then.

And then he'd helped the boy Samuel see some things too.

The door suddenly opened and Caleb started. It was Martha. "Hello, boy. Did you miss me?"

She had a plate of food, which she put on the table. "Eat up. We can't have you goin' hungry."

Caleb shifted on his feet, shy of her.

"Well, come on, boy. You may be special to everybody else, but not to me. To me you're just another boy, and the sooner you learn that the sooner you and I will get along."

What did she mean by that? Her voice made him feel funny, and although he knew that she wanted him to go over to the food, he was having a hard time moving his feet.

She suddenly slammed the table with her hand, and he jumped a foot off the ground. "Eat!"

Caleb walked forward on wobbly legs. She was dark; he could see it as much as feel it. Not in her long black hair or her dirty brown eyes, but in her heart.

"And I don't want you whining, you hear? Nikolous may insist I give you special treatment, but that doesn't mean *better* treatment! You'll receive no favors. If you're going to grow up and become a man, you'll need no special favors."

He sat at the table and bowed his head. The food looked like a heap of earthworms, but it smelled like cheese. Cheesy worms. He didn't want to eat.

She humphed and walked for the door. Her hips were large, and the brown dress she wore looked as though it might split. The black shoes on her feet appeared too small, so that the straps pressed deep into her ankles. They clacked loudly on the wooden floor.

At the door, she turned around and looked at him crossly. "I'll be back in one hour to turn the lights out. Your room is down the hall on the left." She motioned to the dark opening that led to the rest of the quarters. "That food had better be gone when I get back. If I ever catch you outside of this building, I will whip you. And don't pretend that you don't understand; Nikolous told me that you speak English."

She stepped out and shut the door.

Somewhere a cricket sang in the night. He didn't know what she meant by *whip,* but it did not sound like a good thing. Surely it couldn't mean she actually intended to strike him.

Caleb stared at his food and wondered at the feelings that hurt his chest. He began to bob his head. He bobbed his head, and he began to sing in a high, quiet voice. It was a song in Ge'ez, a chant that he and Dadda often sang, thanking God for his love.

A warmth settled over his shoulders, and he remembered that cross in the church. The cross.

"What does it mean to die, Dadda?"

"It means to find life fully. To be with God."

"And when will we die?"

"As soon as we are done showing his love here, my son."

Caleb nodded and smiled. He picked up his fork and stuck it in the food. He was a child and Dadda was dead. Both were good, he thought. Both allowed access to the kingdom.

8

Day 2

THE PHONE CALL FROM THE GREEK ORTHODOX CHURCH came at eleven on Monday morning. There was a problem with the boy. "He won't do anything," Father Nikolous said.

Jason and Leiah had left the church the previous day and driven back to Jason's house in silence. Working among oppressed peoples as they both had, they'd learned to shut down emotionally in order to survive. Not a distasteful response, simply a human one. It felt oddly like that to Jason driving home from the Greek Orthodox church. As if they had just been to a funeral—a rather strong emotion, considering they had only known Caleb four days now.

He'd taken her to a Super Eight motel Sunday afternoon, and after a brief, rather awkward discussion about their future plans, they wished each other well and parted ways. Leiah would catch a flight to Montreal Tuesday and take a short sabbatical before deciding whether or not to return to Africa. She probably would, she said. There was no place for her in North America. As for Jason, he really had no clue what he would do now. Probably return to some famine-stricken land to help the people struggle through impossible odds.

"What do you mean he won't do anything?" Jason asked into the receiver.

"He won't do anything. I went to see him this morning, and he told me flatly that he'll do absolutely nothing unless he first sees you and the woman. It's ridiculous."

"Me and the woman? You mean Leiah?"

"Yes, of course!" Nikolous snapped.

"And what won't he do?"

"I've told you! Nothing! Everything! He refuses to eat or dress or talk. He sits by the window and pretends to be dumb."

Heat washed down Jason's back. "And you're doing what to him?"

"Nothing. Martha has done nothing but try to encourage him to eat."

"I'll be there in an hour. Don't touch him."

The phone went dead in his ear and Jason hung up. He wasn't sure how well Nikolous knew immigration law, but the Greek might have just opened the door for removal of custody.

He called Leiah's hotel, hoping she was in her room. If he knew her, she was probably propped up on the bed, reacquainting herself with the Western world by flipping through television channels rather than taking to the streets.

Leiah answered on the first ring and immediately agreed to go with him. The flight didn't leave until 4:00 P.M., and she'd been thinking of taking a cab to check on Caleb anyway.

Leiah walked out to meet him in front of the hotel thirty minutes later, and Jason saw that she'd gone shopping. She wore faded jeans and a green cotton blouse with long sleeves. A red bandana hung around her neck. Walking across the driveway in tan leather hiking boots and flowing black hair, she could pass as a pinup model for John Deere tractors, he thought. *Our lady of Africa has found her new home.* Now there was an image: a model with third-degree burns from her neck to her ankles.

She slid into the Bronco. "So . . ." She smiled.

He nodded. "You good?"

"Better now."

Jason pulled into traffic and headed to Burbank. "I thought you might be concerned with this news of Caleb."

"It's hardly news. Did you expect any different? There was bound to be a problem with that charlatan."

"It might end up being more than just a visit."

"Meaning what?"

"Meaning that if Nikolous and his staff have legitimate difficulties with Caleb, then we stand a good chance of finding him another home."

"A home for how long?"

"It'll take several months for the courts to determine his citizenship rights. They'll have to demonstrate that his mother was an American. Just because Father Matthew claimed that some guilt-ridden commander confessed to killing the boy's supposed American mother doesn't mean she actually *was* an American. She could've been Canadian, for that matter. Or European. Point is, it'll take time. In the meantime the court will grant guardianship to a legal party. That's the first step, sometime in the next few days. For most refugees, guardianship is given to a relative within the United States, but with an orphan like Caleb, World Relief appointed Sunnyside Orphanage. The judge would normally rubber-stamp the appointment and turn full custody over to Sunnyside."

"Unless there are problems with the case."

"Unless we can convince the judge at the guardianship hearing that Nikolous and his outfit are unfit to care for this particular boy."

Leiah placed her hand on his forearm. "Then we do whatever we can in our power to make that happen, Jason. I'm telling you, they will destroy him."

He glanced at her hand. He could just see her skin, wrinkled at her wrist. He nodded. "I think you're right. And where would he stay?"

"With me."

"In Canada? They'll never go for that."

"No, here. I don't know. I'll find someplace. I am with the Red Cross; I'm sure something can be worked out."

"Maybe. We'll see. First we have to stop the Greek."

≈

They arrived at the Greek Orthodox church and pulled into the same visitor's spot they'd parked in a day earlier. The large lot was vacant except for a half-dozen cars near the building's west wing. A tall, skinny man with a very short nose that made Jason think of a stuck-up butler led them through the offices to a back door. They entered a grassy courtyard surrounded by three identical long gray buildings. Dormitories. The layout looked like what you might find on a college campus. Or a prison camp. A pale yellow swing set sat idly on the lawn. The setting was as drab as wet concrete.

Lighten up, Jason. This is a fine facility. The tall man led them down covered walkways to the far-right building. They left the courtyard and rounded the structure. The outer walls facing the main street were constructed of cedar and lined with flower boxes full of blue carnations. A high fence encircled the perimeter of the property fifty feet off, between the dormitories and the street—to keep the unwanted out, no doubt.

Nikolous had told them yesterday that they housed five to ten children at any given time. There wasn't any sign of them here; perhaps they were at lunch now.

Butler-man opened a door and showed them into the building and then left. The room they entered looked like a large waiting room, with gray sofas on the side closest to the door and a Formica-topped dining table on the far side. Black-and-white-checkered tile covered the floor, and the white ceilings stood a good twelve feet above their heads. Long warehouse fluorescents hung from white chains, lifeless now.

Nikolous stood by a window near the dining table. He glanced at them, walked over to the entrance of a hallway that ran farther into the building, and pushed a small red button on an intercom. "Bring him, Martha."

The Greek could have passed for a trader on Wall Street in the black suit he wore—a far cry from the robes of yesterday. He approached them with his hands behind his back.

"Good morning," Jason said.

"We should make this quick," the Greek said. "I have a meeting at one o'clock and I haven't had lunch." His hair was slicked back with grease, a stark look that seemed to exaggerate the dark bags under his eyes.

"I'm not sure what you expect us to do, Nikolous, but I can promise you it won't be quick."

The man grinned. "Father Nikolous, if you please. And I expect you to help this child understand that you are no longer his guardian. He seems to have latched on to the notion that you are responsible for him. And when I say quick, I am referring to this meeting only."

"Do you mind if we come in and sit?"

"Of course." The Greek walked to the gray couches and sat in a folding chair adjacent to them. He smelled of linseed oil. Jason glanced at Leiah and saw that she was watching the hall. He took her elbow and they joined Nikolous.

"Where is he?" Leiah asked.

"With Martha. His caretaker. They will be out momentarily." One look at Nikolous and any judge with his head screwed on tightly would want testimony on his worthiness. Jason would give testimony, all right, but it wouldn't be to worthiness.

"Now, I want to be perfectly clear," Nikolous said. "If you have any misguided notions of making new arrangements for this boy, you should dismiss them. We have full custody of the child." He frowned confidently. "I'm not interested in your taking him off my hands. What I am interested in is your help with Caleb's transition. The first days in such a new environment can be difficult, as I'm sure you well know. He seems to have taken a liking to you."

"And not you? Why not?"

The frown deepened. "No need to be smart. These things take time. In the meantime you can help him. He will live here, under our care, but it might be useful for him to receive visits from you until he grows accustomed to his new home."

"Well, to be honest with you, Father, I'm no longer sure this should be his new home."

"And I'm really not interested in what you're sure about, Mr. Marker. I'm more concerned with the child. And I need your help with the child."

A heavyset woman with long black hair, wearing a dress that was two sizes too small, suddenly marched from the hallway. Caleb stepped out from her shadow and stopped. He still wore the same gray slacks and white shirt they'd dressed him in yesterday. His face lit up at the sight of Leiah and Jason, and he walked quickly for Leiah. He slid onto the couch next to her, and she put an arm around his shoulders.

"Hello, Caleb."

"Selam," he said with a smile.

"And that's another thing," Nikolous said. "He simply must stop talking in this nonsensical language of his. You did say he knows English—"

"Ge'ez," Leiah snapped. "His language is Ge'ez. And why do you insist on making comments like that in front of him? He understands you."

"If he understands, then tell him to speak when spoken to."

"He's in shock. You can't expect him to answer every question you throw his way."

Nikolous motioned to the woman. "Please sit, Martha."

She sat without expression.

"This is the boy's caretaker, Martha." She dipped her head. "Now he's been positively insubordinate to Martha. And perhaps you are right. Perhaps his insubordination is the result of shock. Which is precisely why we need your help in easing him past this initial phase of transition. We have decided that daily visits immediately following the lunch hour would be good for the child."

Martha sat like a frog on her chair, bunched up and unmoving. This whole sham was absurd. It felt like something out of a Charles Dickens novel. The judge would take one look at this woman and refuse guardianship.

The boy was absently examining his fingers now. Jason looked at Nikolous sitting stiffly in his chair. "I think I've had enough of this craziness. There's no way we're leaving this boy in your charge. He's clearly not suited to you. You're too impatient and too heartless to be this boy's guardian. I'm going to recommend the judge deny guardianship."

"On what grounds, my friend?" Nikolous asked.

Jason had expected a bolt of lightning from the priest. The revelation should have at least caused a spark. Certainly more than this simple even-toned question. And it was a good question at that. He had no tangible evidence that they were not suitable. It would have to be the judge's good sense at seeing them at the hearing.

"He doesn't like you," Jason said. "And frankly I don't think you like him."

The priest leaned back and grinned through a chuckle. "Dear man, you are far too sentimental. We are raising good citizens, not winning lifelong friends. This child needs good rearing, not hugs and kisses. Isn't that right, Martha?"

The woman shot the boy a stern stare. "He is positively insubordinate and undisciplined."

"And I suppose you think it's your job to bring him into submission, is that it?" Leiah demanded.

"Please watch your tone," the Father cautioned. "You are liable to upset the boy. Hardly what we need."

Jason stood to his feet, flush with heat. "That's it! We're taking him!"

"Taking him? You can't just take him. He's in my custody. Sit down."

"He may be in your custody now, chump. But until a judge gives you guardianship, you don't have squat."

The priest chuckled and his lips bunched smugly. Martha's mouth had settled into her first smile. "I'm afraid you don't understand, young man. I've already seen the judge and been granted guardianship. Whether you like it or not, he's under my care for at least some months, and there's nothing short of kidnapping that you can do about it. You really are here to help me, not fight me. Do you understand this?"

Jason's mind spun. They'd already had the hearing? Leiah's eyes had grown round. The boy was still engrossed in his fingers. "This morning . . . ?"

"Yes, of course. Now please sit down."

Jason sat on the edge of the couch. The man was right; there was nothing he could do if guardianship had already been granted. Yesterday he could have intercepted the process, but not now. Not without a prolonged legal battle. Leiah had lowered her head, but she could not hide the flexing of her jaw. She understood clearly enough that it was Jason's reluctance to take the boy that had brought them here.

"Now, you can either help me or not. That much you can choose," Nikolous said. He stood and straightened his tie. "I really must be going. If you are willing to help Caleb by visiting him each day at the one-o'clock hour for a week, it would be appreciated. If not, we will find other ways to encourage his cooperation."

"Listen to you!" Leiah cried. "You talk like he's some kind of machine you're trying to get working. He's a boy, for crying out loud!"

Father Nikolous's lips fell flat. "A yes or no will be adequate."

If Leiah were able to translate her thoughts into action, they'd be giving the morgue a call, Jason thought.

"Yes," he said.

Leiah spun to him, glaring.

"He's right, Leiah. I'll make a few calls, but it's probably all we can do."

A silence settled over them, and Father Nikolous sighed with satisfaction. "Don't worry. Martha is wonderful with children. And we hope you will be able to persuade the boy to be a little more congenial."

He nodded at Martha, who stood and walked over to the boy. She took his arm and pulled him up.

Leiah held his hand. "Hold on! We just got here. We can't spend more time with him?"

"No, I'm afraid not. Not today." Nikolous motioned to the hallway, and Martha took the boy, who followed like an obedient puppy. Leiah stared after them, dumbstruck. The caretaker and Caleb had taken ten steps when Nikolous stopped them.

"Wait, Martha. Let's make sure they understand me." He watched Jason without moving his head. "I have arranged to have the boy tested at UCLA's parapsychology research laboratory tomorrow morning, but I fear the boy won't cooperate. There'll be no visit tomorrow. You may see him at the university at ten o'clock. That is if the boy agrees to cooperate."

"Tested for what?" Jason demanded.

Still the priest did not remove his stare. "Tested for psychic response, of course."

So that was it, then. The Greek was basically blackmailing them into persuading Caleb to go along with his agenda. *If you want to see the boy again, persuade him to allow me to pry into his mind. If you don't, my mean witch here will teach your precious boy some discipline.*

"UCLA? They do that kind of thing?" Jason glanced at Leiah, who was drilling Nikolous with her stare.

"I was informed this morning that they are at the top of the field. They are quite eager to test the boy."

"I suppose we don't have a choice."

"No, I want you to ask the boy if that will be okay."

"Now?"

"Now."

It was feeling like some distant cousin to prostitution, but Jason saw no alternative. He faced the boy. Caleb was already looking at him. He smiled. "Caleb, do you understand?" He switched to broken Amharic to spite Nikolous. "Do you understand?"

Caleb answered quickly in the same language. "Yes."

"And you . . . agree?"

"Yes."

"What did he say?" Nikolous asked.

"He said yes."

The Father smiled. "Good. Take him, Martha."

She pulled Caleb's arm and they walked into the hallway.

Jason spoke again, still in Amharic. "We will not leave you, my child."

Caleb stopped and turned around. For a long moment he just looked at Jason. Then he spoke. In English. "I believe you."

They left the complex in silence. The boy had used English to frustrate the Father, Jason thought with some satisfaction. And that meant he had some spirit. That was good; he would need spirit to survive the Greek. Somehow the fact seemed patently obvious now.

And it had been he who'd placed Caleb in the Greek's care. Against Leiah's advice.

The fact sat in his gut like a bitter pill.

9

Day 3

IT WAS EITHER THE COKE OR SHEER COINCIDENCE that changed Donna Blair's life forever that day. She chalked it up to coincidence, because everybody knew that when you really thought about it, most everything could be blamed on coincidence. A long string of events and decisions that deposited people to the moment.

If you wanted to get real psycho about it, you could go way back to her decision to switch her major at UCLA from psychology to journalism in '85. Ten years later she became the youngest anchor NBC had ever thrown before a live camera in its prime-time slot.

Or you could go back to her decision to leave the anchor job and hit the road as a correspondent. If she were still sitting at the newsdesk, she'd never have been assigned to cover Charles Crandal. And if she hadn't been assigned to cover the presidential candidate, she wouldn't have found herself on the UCLA campuses midweek, despite her favorable memories of the place. As it was, she'd come to cover a lecture by his choice for vice president, Moses Simon, who had been forced to cancel his appearance when his plane was grounded in Las Vegas due to brake problems.

But simply being at UCLA wouldn't have done it; she had to be in the psych department, which simply wouldn't have been a reality if the Coke machine upstairs had been working. So maybe it was the Coke after all.

Knowing the building from her old days, Donna clapped down the concrete staircase to see if, perchance, the Coke machine outside of Psych 101 was still in the same cubbyhole they'd stuffed it into fifteen years earlier.

It was.

And so was the granddaddy of all coincidences in this train of chance—none other than the student she had fallen head over heels for in her sophomore year: Jason Marker. Well, he wasn't *in* the cubbyhole. But he was there, facing the machine, a green 7-Up bottle tipped to his lips.

She froze and gawked for a second. He turned, the bottle still in his mouth, and his bright blue eyes transported her back in time.

"Jason?"

He lowered the bottle and looked dumbly for a moment. "Donna?"

"It's you. Holy Moses, it really is you!"

He grinned wide. "Donna Blair. What in tarnation are you doing here?"

Hearing his voice brought back a hundred memories, and suddenly she was very glad for this string of coincidences. "I'm here for NBC, covering a non-speech." She walked toward him and kissed him gently on the cheek. "How are you? Haven't heard a peep out of you in years."

"Long story." They looked into each other's eyes and smiled. "A non-speech, huh?"

"Long story," she said. "So what brings you back to the playground of our youth?"

She caught his blush, but he covered quickly. He tilted his head. "Very long story."

"Well, as it turns out, I just happen to have the time for a very long story."

He glanced down the hall, uneasy, it seemed. For all she knew he had a wife and three children waiting around the corner. "Then again, maybe it's not the best time. I just have—"

"No, it's okay," he said, turning. "If you don't mind unusual situations, that is." He shifted on his feet and took another sip from the bottle. "So are we a Mrs.?"

"Actually, no. We're a correspondent. The two are mutually exclusive."

He chuckled. "News, huh? Always knew you'd put that pretty face to work one day."

In the early days she'd insisted that her rise through the ranks had absolutely nothing to do with her face, but truth be told, nobody got excited about hearing a hag run through the news, no matter how eloquently she dispensed it. It was only in the last year that Donna Blair had grown comfortable with the fact that beauty, although only skin deep, brought a favorable dimension to the news hour. And beauty was a quality she'd been blessed with.

"So really, what brings you here, Jason?"

"Well . . . a boy."

"A boy? A boy brings you to the psych department?"

"The Parapsychology Research Lab. They're running tests on him as we speak."

"You're kidding. What on earth does agriculture have to do with parapsychology?"

"Like I said, it's a long story."

"I've got all morning, kiddo," she said, taking his arm. "Show me what you've got. I was a psych major once, remember?" It was the correspondent coming out of her, she thought. Once a hound dog, always a hound dog. She flipped out her phone and punched her cameraman's number. "Hi, Bill. Go ahead without me. I'll catch you back at the studio in a while—something's come up." He grunted his approval and she pocketed her phone.

∞

The feel of her hand in the crook of his arm had Jason's mind spinning through their six-month whirlwind romance. Breaking off had been a joint decision, but he'd always known that it had been she who had cooled first. Now he couldn't help but wonder if she heated as quickly as she cooled.

She'd released his arm when they entered the small viewing room that overlooked the main lab. Nikolous stood with one hand on his chin and the other supporting his elbow, peering into the adjoining room through a large one-way window. He eyed them like a hawk. From the opposite side of the window Leiah turned, arms crossed. A dozen empty folding chairs sat facing the glass. The lights had been dimmed to ensure privacy.

"This is ridiculous, Jason," Leiah said, casting Donna a quick glance. "He's been in there for over two hours, and she's done nothing but push him further into his shell."

Jason explained to Donna. "Dr. Patricia Caldwell's running some basic tests on the boy." He motioned to the glass and then addressed Leiah and Nikolous. "I'm sorry; this is Donna Blair. She wanted to have a look."

"I wasn't aware we were running a zoo," Leiah said.

Jason chuckled nervously. "She's an old friend from school, Leiah. A correspondent for NBC."

"And this is news?"

Donna smiled. "Leiah. Pretty name. By your speech I would guess you're French Canadian. Am I right?"

Leiah ignored her.

"Let's just say accents interest me," Donna said. "With a face like yours and the French voice, you really should consider finding work in front of a camera. Don't worry; I won't hurt a soul." Donna walked up to the glass and nodded at Nikolous, who dipped his head in return.

"So what's the boy's name?" she asked.

Jason stepped up between Leiah and Donna and gazed at the table below. Dr. Caldwell sat stiffly on one side of an oak table studying her subject. She wore a bundle of blond hair in a bun, held together by a long wooden pin. Thick round glasses perched on the bridge of her sharp nose, effectively nullifying the soft smile that had fixed itself on her face. Behind her, a freestanding chalkboard stood like a teepee, wiped clean of all but a few white smudges. Two huge yellow beanbag chairs were stuffed into each corner. Between them sat a large box of alphabet blocks and other geometric objects. A long counter with a dozen drawers ran along the wall, where an oscilloscope of some kind displayed a horizontal amber line.

"His name's Caleb," Jason said. The boy sat slumped in a folding chair, fiddling with a pencil. To say he looked bored would be an understatement. Leiah might not have completely grasped the meaning of tact, but she did understand Caleb better than any of them, Jason thought. "Nothing yet?"

Nikolous humphed.

"I'll take that as a no."

"He's gone from answering with one or two words to not answering at all. This can't be helpful," Leiah said.

"What kind of tests has she been giving him?" Donna asked.

"You know anything about psychokinesis?" Jason asked.

"Mind over matter."

"Something like that. Evidently UCLA made a bit of a name for itself in the seventies—some parapsychology research with a healer they studied."

"Dr. Thelma Ross," Donna said.

Jason looked at her with a raised brow.

"I was a psych major, remember? She studied a man named Jack Gray, a supposed healer."

"And?"

"And it depends on how you interpret the research, but they claimed he was capable of assisting in a person's recovery over a period of time. I don't remember too many professors taking the case seriously, but it was a flash point for the parapsych people in the department. So you think the boy's exhibited pyschokinetic powers of some kind?" she asked with a twinkle in her eye.

Jason returned his gaze to Caleb, who sat innocently in the folding chair across from the harsh-looking doctor. It all seemed a bit silly just now. Bringing a boy into UCLA to have him tested for magical powers. *Yes, Donna. We have landed some evidence that green men do indeed live on Mars, and we are here to break the news to the world.* Leiah was right; this whole thing was nonsense.

"We're just having some tests run on him. I'm sure it's nothing."

"So they've asked him to bend steel rods and see through walls and guess the president's third cousin's birth date, is that it?"

Jason smiled, suddenly embarrassed for even coming. "Pretty much."

"I see. Interesting."

Leiah reached to the wall and flipped a black switch. A small square speaker in the corner hissed to life. "If you don't help me, I can't help you, Caleb," Dr. Caldwell's voice crackled gently.

There was no sign the boy heard her. He simply sat in his chair, swinging his legs and staring at the pencil in his hands.

Dr. Caldwell reached into a drawer, pulled out two large cards, and stood them on edge so that only she could see their markings. "Let's try something simple again. Have you ever played a guessing game? Hmm? I'd like to play one now, if you wouldn't mind. Is that okay?"

This time the boy hesitated but nodded slowly.

"Good. That's good. Now I have two cards here and I want you to tell me if they have colors on them or numbers on them. Can you do that?"

He stared at them for a moment and then looked over to the mirror behind which Jason and the others watched.

"You're sure he can't see us?" Donna asked quietly.

"That's what the good doctor told us," Jason said.

Dr. Caldwell spoke again. "Please, Caleb. Try to concentrate. There are some people who think you may be able to do special things, but how are we ever going to know unless you cooperate. Hmmm?"

He looked up at her. "I'm a simple boy."

"Well, maybe you are. But we'll never know unless you play our little games, will we?"

"Do you know why I am put in this house at the church?"

The doctor stared at the boy and then set her cards facedown, clearly frustrated. "I'm not here to talk about your housing arrangements, Caleb. I'm here to try to help you."

Jason could almost hear Leiah grind her teeth. She glared at Nikolous, who ignored her entirely. She faced the window again. "How can she talk to him like that? Is that the way you talk to a lost child?"

"She's a doctor," Jason said. "She's got to know what she's doing."

"She's a spook. Clearly not a child psychologist."

"If you wouldn't mind," the Greek spoke up. "I am listening."

Leiah swatted the switch off and turned to the clergyman. "Haven't you heard enough? You've watched her administer written tests, which he clearly shows no interest in taking; you've heard a hundred questions, which have produced absolutely nothing but the child's clear need of love; you've even watched while the good doctor has suggested Caleb move a marble along the table by looking at it! And somehow you hold the illusion that this is instrumental? What in heaven's name are you thinking?"

"Nonsense!" Nikolous boomed. "A boy comes into my care and exhibits the power to give sight; you think I have no obligation to have him properly examined?"

"Then you've examined him already and he seems normal enough. You have an obligation to see to his well-being, not explore his mind."

"She's right, Nikolous," Jason said. "The boy's had enough."

"We will allow professionals to decide what is enough. You are here on my request; do not forget that."

"We're here for the *boy's* sake, remember. Including you."

Donna cleared her throat. "I hate to interrupt, but it may not matter." She nodded to the room and they looked as one. Dr. Caldwell was talking toward the window. Leiah hit the audio switch.

" . . . so if you wouldn't mind coming in now, I think we can wrap this up."

Evidently the good doctor had given up.

"She mean all of us?" Jason asked.

Leiah turned toward the door without responding. The Greek quickly followed. Jason looked at Donna, who had her arms crossed and was smiling, as if enjoying this show. "You go ahead, Jason. I'll wait here, if it's okay with you."

He nodded. "Don't go anywhere. I'll be right back."

"I'll be here."

When they entered the testing room, Dr. Caldwell smiled a tad condescendingly and asked them to sit at the table. He and Leiah seated themselves adjacent to the doctor and across from Nikolous. Caleb watched them with round eyes, but he seemed unruffled.

"I'm sorry this has taken so long, but you must understand that I can only follow the subject's pace." Caldwell looked from Jason to Father Nikolous. Her coke-bottle glasses flashed with the reflection of the room's overhead lights. Surely with today's technology she could have found a better presentation for her eyesight correction, Jason thought. Contacts would have suited her sharp features better.

She continued. "Unfortunately, I can see no evidence for psychological anomalies of any kind. He is traumatized perhaps, but otherwise he shows no signs of characteristic behavior."

"No one suggested that he had any anomalies," Leiah said.

The doctor faced her. "Father Nikolous told me that a boy regained his sight after his interaction with Caleb. I don't know about you, but in my book that's rather unusual. Assuming of course that Caleb had anything to do with the event. And assuming that the other child actually did regain his sight. Most cases of this nature are simply misinterpreted events."

"No, no," Nikolous objected. "Samuel did receive his sight, and it was only after the boy's interaction with him. *I* am not blind, Doctor."

"Of course not. But you must understand that I've spent two hours administering a string of tests specifically designed to betray even the slightest paranormal occurrence and I've found nothing."

"And these tests of yours are accurate?"

Dr. Caldwell stiffened slightly. "I assure you, Father, we're not talking about the dark ages here. I've run tests for micro PK without any indicative results. The macro PK tests were even less responsive. You see that machine behind me?"

He glanced at the monitor with its single flat line.

"That's a REG machine. A Random Event Generator. It creates a pattern of random electrical events. Through concentration a subject with psychokinesis can repeatedly vary that pattern. It's no longer a question of whether the human mind *can* change physical events; it's a matter of how. In fact, portable REGs like the one behind me have been placed in blind studies—the Academy Awards and the Super Bowl for example—and the patterns in the electrical events have changed to reflect the audiences' reactions to the shows. In other words, a roomful of people have unwittingly influenced the pattern of a machine by their thoughts alone. We are talking science here, Father, not faith."

The diatribe left them silent. It sounded impossible that a person could change anything by thinking about it.

"And Caleb?" Nikolous asked.

"It turns out that psychokinesis is more common among children than adults, and environments of high stress often trigger the events. That was what interested me about him when you explained the situation. But I'm telling you that I found nothing. Not even a blip."

"We're dealing with a healing here, not a blip on a machine," Nikolous pushed. And what did the Father want in all of this? Why was he so determined to demonstrate the boy's abilities anyway? Jason had considered the matter earlier, but hearing the Greek now, he felt a nudge of concern.

"Healing is generally accepted as a form of psychokinesis," Caldwell said. "In fact Dr. Thelma Ross made the case pretty strongly here at UCLA over twenty years ago. But either way, healing or not, the boy here shows none of the signs."

Caleb had been studying the machine behind the doctor with mild curiosity. Now he crossed his legs and stared at the wall to his right, still slumped in his seat. His right leg swung over the other in short, absent arcs. Jason had the notion that his mind was still trying to understand what had become of him since his rude departure from the quiet monastery. Their conversation was probably the furthest thing from his mind.

"So your final analysis?" the Greek asked.

Patricia Caldwell sighed. "My final analysis is that you may have a disturbed child on your hands." She looked at Caleb. "Maybe one who is retarded . . ."

Jason felt Leiah stiffen beside him. Caleb's legs stopped their swinging, but he didn't remove his eyes from the wall. An uncomfortable silence descended over them.

"But otherwise he is normal."

Jason wanted to leave then—take the boy and leave the campus for good. But Dr. Caldwell was not in the frame of mind to hold her thoughts captive.

She put on a plastic grin. "As I see it, your Caleb here is no more a psychic than Jesus Christ was God's son. But then we all make mistakes, don't we?"

Something in the room changed with those words. A pin could have dropped, and Donna would have heard it like a bell in her perch above them. There were two people in the room who presumably thought much of Jesus Christ: Father Nikolous and Caleb. But it felt like the good doctor had just cast a gauntlet before the pope himself.

The boy looked slowly at first toward Leiah, then Jason, and then at Dr. Caldwell, who held her smug smile. He stared at her as if she'd just suggested that they all jump into a meat grinder or something. The scene stuck like that—with the boy drilling Caldwell with his round stare and the others sitting in an awkward silence.

The smile was still stuck on Caldwell's face when the coke-bottle glass in front of her left eye suddenly cracked.

A single line from top to bottom that sounded like a small whip cracking in the heavy silence. *Crack!*

The good doctor caught her breath and her smiling lips twitched, but she did not budge. A second crack grew from the first at a forty-five-degree angle, slowly, etching white along the thick glass.

It all happened so very deliberately, freezing them all with incredulity. The crawling cracks spread to the other glass, the right lens, horizontal this time.

And then the left coke-bottle lens exploded outward as if Patricia Caldwell's eye had become a cannon. *Pop!* The right eyeglass followed a split second later. One, two. *Pop! Pop!* Small pieces of glass scattered over the table, rattling like beads.

The doctor shrieked and threw her hands to her face. As one, Jason, Leiah, and Nikolous bolted to their feet, spilling all three chairs. Caleb did not flinch.

"I'm blind! I'm blind!" Caldwell shrieked.

It occurred to Jason that he wasn't breathing. His heart thumped in his chest. The doctor's trembling hands covered her eyes so he couldn't see what had happened, but he half expected to see blood seep between her fingers. Maybe he had imagined the shattering glass thing. Then again, the table lay covered in shards of the stuff, and it hadn't come from thin air.

"Somebody help me!" The doctor was hyperventilating.

The door behind Caleb burst open and Donna stood in the frame, white-faced. "What happened?"

Precisely. Jason found his voice. "Dr. Caldwell . . ." He couldn't formulate the correct question. Somehow *Did your eyes just pop out?* didn't feel quite right. He turned to Caleb, who wore a faint grin. "Caleb? What happened?"

"Oh, my heavens!" Caldwell exclaimed. Only this time it was surprise, not panic. Jason spun back to her.

She stood with her hands a foot from her face, staring through circular wire frames, her eyes as round as full moons. "Oh, my heavens!"

Donna stood by Jason's side now, and she gripped his elbow. "What? What's wrong?"

"Oh my!" Caldwell stared at her hands and then turned them over. "I . . . I can see!"

"What do you mean you can see?" Donna asked.

Caldwell reached up, plucked the empty glass frames from her face, and gawked at them. "I mean I can see! I can see clearly. Without my glasses."

Five heads turned to Caleb as one. The boy lowered his eyes sheepishly.

∞

It took a good ten minutes for the small entourage surrounding Caleb to achieve a semblance of civility. But then it's not every day you see eyeglasses popping and eyes seeing at the whim of a child either.

Caleb had retained a shy disposition, seemingly unhearing of the dozens of questions heaped upon him once they found their voices. Leiah rescued the boy by demanding they all shut up and give the child a break. He'd had enough for one day. And how would they like it if aliens captured them and prodded them for hours with nonsensical questions? She had taken him by the hand and led him willingly from the room to get a soft drink.

That left Jason, Donna, Nikolous, and Dr. Caldwell in the room.

Caldwell had remained relatively quiet. She kept picking up her wire frames and looking at the empty holes where the glass had been a few minutes earlier. But now she asserted herself in the wake of Leiah's leaving.

"He has to be studied. You do realize that, don't you?"

The Greek looked at her without responding, and she turned to Jason for support. "Of course you must understand that the boy has to be analyzed. You can't just let a subject like him go without careful study."

"I thought you said he was normal."

"Don't be ridiculous! This level of psychic ability may come along once every thousand years, if the human race is so fortunate. We must isolate him and understand how his mind works."

"The boy's under my care," Father Nikolous said.

"Of course he is. But surely you'll turn him over to the university, or at least the medical center, for thorough analysis!"

The Greek didn't respond. And Jason wasn't sure if that was good or bad.

"Don't be a fool! Do you know what knowledge of this sort would do for the human race? If we could learn how to tap into and reproduce psycho-kinesis of this magnitude, the world as we know it would be changed. And the knowledge is locked up in that little boy's mind. He has to be studied; anything less would be asinine!"

"I think you're forgetting the boy," Jason said. "He's not exactly a poster child for the average well-adjusted American kid. He's only been in-country for a few days."

"And that's exactly why we must bring him into isolation. His exposure must be controlled."

"Meaning what?"

"Meaning in all probability his extraordinary power comes *because* of his isolation. You take a child with psychic abilities at birth and you allow nothing to dilute those powers, but instead you foster a strong belief in those powers, and you end up with an uncompromised subject with extraordinary access to his psyche."

"A noble savage."

"Exactly. A noble savage, so to speak. You put him out in the general population and he'll lose himself in a sea of mediocrity. Psychically speaking. There's no telling how much damage he's already sustained in the last few days alone."

Jason sat back and let the pieces fall into his mind. It seemed logical enough. The soldier he'd shot in the desert: Caleb must have healed him, he realized. And he brought the bird back. The boy had shown the extraordinary powers from the first. Maybe it was why Father Matthew had insisted he be saved. He knew, of course. That didn't explain his fear for the boy's life. Unless by life he meant his mind. Or his understanding of spiritual life. But it seemed more than that. Father Matthew had been worried for Caleb's life.

The Father's riddle came to Jason's mind. *Remember Jason. What's soft and round and says more than it should? The hem of a tunic.* A riddle about humility. He didn't want the boy to lose his humility? Or perhaps his innocence.

And what if the boy's powers were more spiritual than psychic? The notion made Jason cringe. His own experience with his son flew in the face of the possibility. He dismissed it.

"It's still not as simple as you might think," he said. "For starters, Caleb's not a subject you can prod with your mind readers. He's a frightened child who deserves to discover life the way any child should."

"And that's not possible. Like you say, he's not just *any* child," Caldwell returned.

Nikolous cleared his throat. "Is it possible that his power comes from faith rather than from his mind?"

"Forgive me, Father, but is there really any difference? Faith? Pick your faith. Christianity, Hinduism, Islam, Scientology. Pick your healer. Faith is no more than belief fixed on a higher power, a God, because of our own insecurities with the mind. Call it faith if you like, but trust me, the boy's power comes from his own mind—his psyche—not some external being who has chosen him to show off to the world. Which is all the more reason to protect that mind of his. It is a phenomenon."

Father Nikolous nodded in agreement, and Jason was hardly surprised. The explanation certainly lined up with his own experience in the muddy waters of faith.

"Then when can you turn him over to us?" Caldwell asked. "I'll need to make some arrangements, of course. But I think it would be best for the boy to remain in strict isolation until we can unravel this."

Again the Greek nodded, and Jason was about to protest when Nikolous spoke. "Unfortunately, Caleb will not be leaving the orphanage. I'm sorry, but Jason is right. He's not simply a subject for your tests."

"What? You can't be serious!"

"Oh, I'm afraid that I am." The humanitarian in the man hardly fit Jason's perception of him, but it was a welcome change. "Caleb stays with me."

"Excuse me." Donna's voice carried a slight waver. She sat in the chair Caleb had occupied and she looked up to face them. "Excuse me, but wasn't your last test of the boy one in which you asked him if the cards had numbers or colors on them?"

Caldwell glanced at the cards now facedown before her. "Yes. And?"

"And they were numbers, weren't they?"

"Yes. Why?"

"And the number was five, wasn't it?"

Dr. Caldwell looked at Donna for a moment and then lifted one of the cards. A few shards of glass rattled to the tabletop. She turned the card over. On its face was a large number five. "How did you know?"

"The boy knew," Donna said. She pointed to the table in front of her. Jason leaned over and saw the lead markings clearly. Caleb had used his pencil to edge four vertical lines crossed diagonally with another. A five. "This boy does more than move things with his mind."

Patricia Caldwell stood and walked back to the REG machine. The amber line across its screen still ran flat. She took a deep breath. "Father Nikolous, I'm begging you." She turned around. "Please let us study him."

"No. The boy stays with me."

"Then bring him into prominence," Donna said.

Jason looked at her with a raised brow. Prominence? And what good would that do the boy?

"Let the world know that you've found proof positive of radical psychic phenomenon. At the very least it will create unprecedented funding for the field of study. Dr. Caldwell is right about one thing: this could change the way humanity views itself. Who knows what else is locked up in our minds?"

"You actually expect Caleb to sit down with Larry King and have a chat?" Jason asked.

"Of course not. Use me. I may not be Larry King, but I pull a good audience."

So she wanted to give her career a boost on the boy's back.

"And before you accuse me of exploitation, you must realize that Dr. Caldwell's instincts are right. You can't just hole the boy up."

"You've seen him. He's not exactly the most talkative boy in the world." Jason shook his head. "And it sounds an awful lot like exploitation to me."

Donna's eyes brightened, undaunted. "How does he react in public settings? You've had him for what, four . . . five days? Have you even put the boy in direct contact with others?"

"As little as possible. We're here for his sake, not others."

"Of course! But you saw what I saw, right? When was the last time you saw glasses shattering like that, Jason? Never. What if he loses that ability? If you don't want him picked apart by doctors in white coats, then at least let him begin to interact with the world he'll soon become a part of anyway. If you don't want him isolated, then put him in controlled social settings and study him from a distance."

"And this has nothing to do with your being a journalist, right?" Jason said with less than a full deck of sincerity.

"Okay, so I am a journalist. Like I said, use me."

"And how will this do me any good?" Nikolous asked. His eyes twitched. "How will this help the boy?"

He'd said the second quickly, to cover the first, and Jason's earlier perceptions of the man raged to the surface. The Father was not as concerned for Caleb as he let on; that much Jason felt like he felt the running of his own pulse.

Donna hesitated, perhaps aware of the same thing. "I don't know. What happens when the world discovers a little church in Timbuktu with a bleeding crucifix? They're drawn like flies."

"Come on, Donna," Jason said.

"This is the most ridiculous thing I've heard of!" Dr. Caldwell snapped.

Donna ignored her. "I'm just being realistic. Look, you can hide the boy and bring him out slowly if you want, but if Dr. Caldwell's right, his abilities may be lost to the world. Twenty years from now the five of us will be telling our grandchildren what we once saw, the popping-glass-trick once done by a ten-year-old child. It'll just be another story that'll make us sound either stupid or senile, depending on when we get around to opening our mouths. But put this boy on the record and you've changed history. And what harm to Caleb if the setting is controlled?"

"And what guarantees do you have for controlling the environment?" Jason motioned to the glass scattered on the far end of the table. "Doesn't strike me as something you or I have any control over."

"So you run and hide? Because you're not sure if he'll do something that will upset your world?"

"I didn't say that."

She smiled at him and suddenly she looked like the Donna he'd held tenderly fifteen years earlier. Her deep blue eyes sparkled brightly, and he felt a tug in his gut. Memories. What was she doing here anyway? She'd dropped out of the sky because of a Coke. Not that he was complaining. She would be in her early thirties like he was; age did her well.

"I know you didn't, Jason." She said his name, *Jason*, and that tug in his gut rose into his heart.

"What do you have in mind?" Nikolous asked.

Dr. Caldwell sat back in her chair and crossed her arms. "You really think this is constructive? At the very least you should have him accompanied by a professional."

"I don't know," Donna responded to Nikolous. "Something inconspicuous." She bit her lower lip lightly and glanced at the Greek. "There's a press conference with Charles Crandal at Frazier Park tomorrow at noon," she said, using her hands to point in some arbitrary direction. "I'll be all set up. Why don't you bring him down to the park half an hour early and let me shoot him in a natural setting? Who knows what might happen? He's already shown that he isn't keen on stuffed-up environments like this; maybe he'll loosen up in a more organic setting."

"Charles Crandal?" Jason asked.

"What, you've been living in the desert all your life? Charles Crandal, presidential nominee?"

It came back to Jason. He'd read of the man, of course. But in the highlands of Ethiopia one tended to lose sight of such nonsense.

"The news conference isn't significant except that our equipment's in place," Donna said. "What do you say?"

"You're saying you'd interview the boy there?" Nikolous asked.

She shrugged. "No, not necessarily. Just bring him and see what happens. Think of it as a small test. A compromise between what Dr. Caldwell wants and what you might want."

She was a player, Jason thought. No wonder she'd reached her level in such a short time. And truth be told, he wasn't even sure she was trying to exploit the boy. Her reasoning had a ring of sincerity to it.

"This isn't what I'd call scientific," Caldwell said. "But I suppose it's better than not studying him at all. What time tomorrow?"

Nikolous stood abruptly, before Donna could answer. "Your presence won't be required, Dr. Caldwell. If I decide this is best, you may view the tape. Now we must go. I thank you for your time."

He walked toward the door, and after exchanging glances, Jason and Donna followed, leaving Dr. Caldwell seated in stunned disbelief.

They found Leiah and the boy in the outer lobby.

Donna handed cards out to both Father Nikolous and Jason. "Call me," she said. She put her hand on Jason's upper arm and squeezed gently. "It was good to see you, Jason. Maybe we'll have some time to catch up later. I have to run." And then she was off.

Jason caught Leiah's firm stare and shrugged it off. If any explanation was required, he would offer it later. Now another concern filled his mind. It was for Caleb. This scheme of Donna's may or may not be in the boy's interest, but either way he would find a way to stay by the boy's side. He had given his word to protect Caleb and he intended to do just that.

Leiah had already missed one flight to Canada for the boy's sake, but he suspected she would miss more. She held his hand as if she were his mother. Caleb would listen to them, he thought.

He bent to one knee and smiled into the boy's eyes. "Caleb, I want you to listen to me. Listen to me very carefully."

"What are you doing?" Nikolous objected. Jason ignored the Father.

"I want you to make me a promise. Can you do that?" Jason went on.

The boy nodded once.

"Stand back from him," the Greek said. "What do you think you're doing?"

Leiah thrust a warning hand out with enough authority to make him hesitate.

Jason continued. "I want you to promise that no matter what happens, you won't leave your new home without me or Leiah in your presence. And if they force you, you'll pretend to be stupid. Can you do that?"

"Yes," he said immediately, as if the idea were not new.

"Good." He leaned forward and hugged the boy gently. Caleb released Leiah's hand, reached his arms around Jason's neck, and pulled him tight. For a moment he would not let go. When he did step back, his face was expressionless. Caleb was playing the part of the strong boy, Jason thought. He turned from them to swallow.

They left the campus with a string of objections and vile threats from the Greek.

II

LIFE AND DEATH

As a result, people brought the sick into the streets
and laid them on beds and mats so that at least
Peter's shadow might fall on some of them
as he passed by.
Crowds gathered also from the towns around Jerusalem,
bringing their sick and those tormented by evil spirits,
and all of them were healed.

ACTS 5:15–16

10

CALEB STOOD AT ATTENTION IN THE LARGE ROOM they called his new home, facing Martha, who wore a deep frown. They had given him brown shorts that came to his knees and a soft white shirt with a collar. The black shoes hurt his feet and she insisted he wear the socks up to his knees, but in some ways he felt at home in the strange clothes. They were what the other children he'd seen running outside the window wore.

"So what are we going to do with you, hmmm?"

The woman seemed upset, and he didn't understand her. In the three days he'd been here, she had left him alone to stare out the window and wander around the large eating room. Each night she'd marched him down the hall to the small bedroom where she told him he must sleep. Each night he had left the dark room for this one with its tall ceiling and soft couches. She'd found him twice early in the morning and scolded him.

Now it looked like she meant to scold him again.

"Father Nikolous tells me that you're not to watch the other children anymore. Do you understand me, boy? He doesn't want you to look out in the play yard at the others any longer. He says it will mess with your head. But if I leave you alone, I know that you'll look anyway, won't you? I know that because every time I come in here you're staring out that window. And that just won't do."

She sighed and glanced at the large window. "And I'm not about to cover up that window. It would look ridiculous in this large room, wouldn't it?" She kept asking these questions without really waiting for an answer.

"Which means we'll just have to keep you in your room when you're alone." She studied him for a moment, as if expecting him to say something, but he wasn't sure what she meant.

"Let's go."

Caleb stared at her, still not sure what she wanted him to do. Go where?

Her face twisted into a snarl. "Don't just stand there like you don't understand me, boy! Move it!"

He felt a twang of fear at her anger, but he could not move. How could he move unless she told him where to move to? He suddenly wanted Jason or Leiah to be here. And he'd promised Jason that he wouldn't go anywhere without him.

The woman took a large stride toward him, snatched up his right wrist, and yanked him behind her. Pain shot up his arm and he yelped.

"You'll do what you're told, you understand? I don't care if Nikolous does think you're God's gift to man; you don't fool me. When I say go, you go!"

She dragged him down the hall and he stumbled to catch up. They marched right into the small room on the left, and she flung him toward the bed. Caleb caught himself on the mattress and sat with a bounce. She gave him one last glare and slammed the door shut. Darkness filled the room. A click sounded in the latch and then her footsteps clacked away.

He waited for a few moments and then ran for the door. The knob wouldn't turn. He spun around, suddenly frightened. The dim shape of the bed with its white sheets lined the darkness. To his right a big glassy box sat in the corner. He had no idea what it might be.

A scene from the monastery flashed through his mind.

"Dadda, Dadda, it's dark! I'm afraid!"

"Dark? Nonsense, child. It's as bright as day in here."

"It is?"

"It is. Open your eyes."

"My eyes? They aren't open?"

"Not if you can't see the kingdom. Not if you can't see the light. Open your eyes."

"Ouch!"

"What?"

"I touched my eye. It *is* open, Dadda."

He chuckled. "Open your other eyes, Son. The eyes of your heart. You will see that it is very light in here. It's always light in the kingdom of God."

He was a small child and it was the first time he'd seen the light. The kingdom, as Dadda liked to call it. It occurred to him that this was no different than that.

Caleb crossed to the bed and climbed up. He sat against the wall, pulled his knees to his chin, closed his eyes, and began to hum. No, this was not different at all. The kingdom was not just bottled up in a monastery somewhere.

It smothered the world. That's what his father used to say. "It smothers the earth, Caleb."

A thin film of light lapped at his mind and he smiled. He began to sing in Ge'ez. Words. Kingdom words. Then he walked in and his world went white.

11

JASON AND LEIAH CRUISED DOWN THE FREEWAY in somber silence at eleven the following morning. The Greek's black Mercedes led them ten meters ahead, speeding Caleb to the park as Donna had suggested. It felt like a funeral procession. Jason's request that the boy do nothing without them present had paid off; at least for that they could be thankful.

They had arrived at the Orthodox church an hour earlier, eager to see the boy, only to discover that the Father had expanded his restrictions. Not only was their visitation limited to the one-o'clock hour each day, they could only see him in the main room, and only away from the windows. The boy was to remain isolated from any contact with the outside world, and that included watching the other children in the play yard.

Leiah had expressed her outrage in true form. It was child abuse!

But Nikolous had merely chuckled. "He's been confined to the walls of a monastery for ten years, and now you decide it's better for him to wander the streets of Los Angeles? We're simply keeping him in an environment more familiar to him. I don't think Dr. Caldwell would disagree."

The circumstances allowed them only twenty minutes with the boy and that with Martha standing guard like an overstuffed black crow. The boy walked from the dark hallway dressed like a proper parochial schoolboy. Leiah knelt to hug him and then the boy walked to Jason and lifted his arms for an embrace. A huge grin split his face when he pulled away. But he still hardly spoke. A simple yes with wide eyes, or a no. *Are you happy, Caleb?* Yes. *Do you need anything?* No. Leiah kept eyeing the hallway with a furrowed brow. *Are the quarters okay?* Yes.

Nikolous had taken his decision to isolate Caleb to the extreme. He could drive in no car other than the Mercedes, which had been appropriately prepared. Martha had marched the boy to the waiting car, hustled him into the back seat, and attempted to shut the door before Jason could stop her. But he'd grabbed the door and moved her aside with a stern stare. Inside, the windows had been blackened, and a burgundy velvet sheet closed off the front seat so that the rear was completely sealed off from any outside view. Caleb sat with his hands between his knees, lost on the large seat.

"We'll be right behind you in my car," Jason promised him. Then Martha had rattled something off in Greek and angrily slammed the door, very nearly on his fingers. She was wicked, that one, and he shuddered to think that she had any influence on the boy at all.

They turned off the freeway and entered heavy surface traffic. "I still can't believe we're running off to some park because some snotty reporter decided it would be the best thing for him," Leiah said with a frown.

"Nikolous agreed to it, not me," Jason returned.

"I didn't hear your objections. And I can certainly think of more courageous ways to reignite an old flame than at the expense of a young boy."

"Please. This isn't about reigniting old flames."

"Of course not."

They came to a stoplight and pulled up to the Mercedes' bumper. Jason held his tongue and wished for a change in subject. He got one.

"Do you think he's happy?" Leiah asked.

"I'm not sure he knows how not to be happy," Jason said.

She bit the fingernail on her index finger and stared ahead. "This isn't right, Jason. We have to get him back. We can't just sit by and let them destroy him."

"And how do you propose we get him back? By gunpoint?"

"Of course not. But there must be legal remedies. Surely there are laws for the protection of children in this country."

"He's a refugee. You heard Nikolous; he'll simply say he's keeping Caleb's customs."

"You can't talk to John Gardner at World Relief and explain?"

"I already have. But there's no evidence of abuse, is there? Honestly, Nikolous has everything on his side. We don't even have cause to file a petition for a new hearing."

"So we do what?"

"So we stay with him and jump all over Nikolous at the first sign of impropriety."

"He deserves more, you know."

She was right. He deserved a loving mother, and Jason wondered if Leiah had decided to contend for the spot. And what would Jason's own life be like if his ex, Ailsa, had possessed Leiah's loyalty? What if his Stephen had had a mother like Leiah?

Of course that was ridiculous. He hardly even knew Leiah.

Jason glanced at her. She'd left her motel and taken an apartment on a weekly rent, not far from his house. She would stay for the boy until satisfied that he was in good hands. Like the Peace Corps, the Red Cross would pay her a small monthly salary to cover her expenses for up to a three-month break between assignments.

Her scars were well concealed under a white blouse today. At a glance you wouldn't know that she even had the scars, but look closely at the edges and the disfigurement took shape. And if you were to look past a button, you would find what?

She looked at him and they held stares for a brief moment. The light turned and Jason pulled after the Mercedes.

The next question came from him without his full blessing, but there it was. "So what happened to your neck?" Actually it wasn't her neck. It was her body, but he couldn't very well ask what happened to her body. Still it wasn't her neck, was it? "I mean what—"

"I know what you mean. You mean why is my body covered in burn scars? Don't worry; it won't bite."

"Actually, it's hardly noticeable." His face heated with a blush. "You're really quite beautiful."

Goodness, what was he saying?

"You don't have to patronize me."

"I'm not patronizing you. You seem to be concerned about your skin; I'm simply telling you that you're a beautiful woman, with or without the scars. You really should learn to take a compliment."

That quieted her. It was true, of course. One look in the mirror and she must know that most women would kill to have a face as striking as hers. Then again, one look in the mirror with her blouse off might have them blanching. It was an image Jason had difficulty framing.

"I'm sorry." She was staring ahead now. "Everybody has some beauty, you know. Their hands, their hair, their legs. For me it's my face. But the rest of my body is a wrinkled mess of pitted flesh. Either way it's me, take it or leave it."

Jason had no clue how to respond.

She sighed. "I was in a car accident in Ottawa when I was twenty years old. I was on the national track team, headed for the Olympics in Korea—two and four hundred meter. I think I might have medaled too. The car caught fire and I couldn't get out. Fortunately the window was down enough to get my head out or I would've died from the smoke. When they dragged me from the car, my skin was gone. It took twenty-two separate surgeries to get me to where I am now."

She turned to stare out her window. "I tried to return to normal life and gave up after coming to the conclusion that North America is not well suited for people covered from head to toe in disfiguring scars. I volunteered for the Red Cross, found Africa, and vowed never to return to Canada."

A shiver passed through Jason's bones, thinking of the flames licking at her skin. He swallowed. "And now you've returned."

"Yes."

"Not many would do what you're doing."

"Not many have seen what I've seen in the Third World."

Jason nodded. True enough. She wasn't confined to a wheelchair. Although in many ways the grotesque lumps under her blouse confined her in their own world. She knew that well enough.

"So what do you make of the boy now that you've seen what he can do?" he asked.

"I think he's the same boy who fled the monastery with us a week ago. Even beyond this power of his there's something special."

Jason nodded. "He's nearly irresistible, isn't he? A perfect package of goodness. I can't get over his eyes."

Leiah turned to him and smiled. "He has a way of stealing your heart, doesn't he?"

Jason nodded. "I had a son once. Stephen. He died from ALS—Lou Gehrig's disease—when he was four. If he had lived, he'd be about Caleb's age."

"I'm so sorry."

"It's okay." Jason cleared his throat. "Funny thing is we took him to faith healers, you know. We were desperate and turned to the church. It was all nonsense, of course. Scared him half to death, all those fools yelling their prayers over him. But it also raised his hopes and that was the worst of it. They even had me going for a few months."

"I can't imagine. Someone once suggested I find someone to pray for me.

I don't think I ever could. I've learned to accept myself; wanting to be some-one else again could ruin me."

"Caleb makes you think, though."

"Yes, he does that, doesn't he?"

"It's amazing. Not so long ago the world was flat. Until we discovered that it was round. So now what are we discovering through Caleb? That the human mind is far more powerful than once imagined."

They'd come to the park and Jason piloted the Bronco through its arching entrance. Cars lined the street; pedestrians loitered on the grass; ahead a crowd gathered around a commotion Jason assumed would be the press conference.

"You were married?" Leiah asked.

"Yes."

"And what became of your wife?"

"Ailsa? She left me a month after Stephen died. Ran off with someone who managed to distract her from her hell."

"And you, too, found Africa."

"Yes. I guess I did."

He glanced at her and saw that her eyes were on him, blue and soft. He smiled and they drove on in silence.

∞

They followed Nikolous into a side parking lot with reserved space beside a white news van sporting the NBC peacock.

"I thought this was supposed to be a quiet, comfortable setting for him," Leiah said, looking at the crowd already gathered. "What time is that press conference supposed to start?"

"She said twelve and it's eleven-thirty now."

Leiah humphed and hurried out. She reached Caleb's door before the Greek had climbed out and she quickly took the boy under her wing. They approached the crowd from the rear, looking for Donna. Nikolous strutted forward in his tailored black suit with the three of them in tow as if their allegiance to him was without question. And he wasn't so wrong—although they could have bolted at any time, it would be a futile run from the law.

Where was Donna? This news conference of hers looked as if it was about to start.

Caleb walked along in his typical posture, gliding on his feet, hardly moving his upper torso or his arms. His belt looked cinched too tight, but only because the new shorts he wore were several sizes too large.

The boy looked at the crowd in a dumb silence, and it occurred to Jason that this was the first time he'd been in public since their first visit to the Orthodox church. Since then he'd spent every waking minute in his new prison. There was the visit to UCLA, but he'd met no one except the doctor there. And prior to the first church meeting, he'd seen nothing that could not be seen from the window of a speeding car—either a taxi or his Bronco. Watching him, Jason wondered how much of Dr. Caldwell's prognosis would bear true.

They skirted the crowd toward the front. For the most part this was a news crowd, maybe a hundred strong with all of their support staff. The candidate's people had erected a podium on a small platform. Behind it a huge vinyl backdrop showed a vivid red sunset. A life-size man and woman had been imprinted on the sunset, standing side by side, each staring intensely at their own knotted fists raised to the sky, as if in those hands lay some deep mysterious secret. Crandal's slogan, presumably that secret, was splashed in a bright blue across their waists: *Power to the People.* The setup looked more like something you'd find at a revolution rally in Russia than at a candidate's news conference.

A very large man with a perfectly bald head strode out to the podium, and applause pattered across the lawn. Charles Crandal's face split to a wide grin, and he immediately became a man who looked pleased with his surroundings. He carried himself lightly, despite his enormous size, and he wore his suit as if he'd been born in the thing. Crandal put both hands on the podium without acknowledging the accolades cast his way from supporters encroaching on the perimeter of the news groups. He scanned the crowd carefully, nodded slowly—as if he approved of this particular group, but just barely—and started to speak.

"Thank you. Thank you for your interest. Thank you for coming." So this was the man Donna suggested might very well be the next president.

A young man wearing a headset had found Nikolous and now led them quickly to the right of the pack, where Donna stood directing a cameraman.

She looked up apologetically. "I'm sorry, but they moved the press conference up and it started even earlier. If you don't mind, we can shoot him after. It shouldn't be long."

Nikolous frowned and gazed around. He nodded once.

Donna caught Jason's eye and winked. Aware of Leiah beside him he smiled but just barely.

Donna returned her attention to the stage, where Crandal was making an adamant statement about some budget proposal he assured them would revolutionize American politics.

"It's a plan the American people have deserved for a century but haven't gathered the stomach to insist upon. Until now, that is. Now they insist, and so must I, ladies and gentlemen." The man's jowls shook when he spoke, but not enough to distract from the force of his words. His voice was low and it crackled, drawing Jason in with the first few syllables. A silence had settled over the gathering, and the words engaged their attention like a bullwhip over the heads of sluggard oxen.

"Mediocrity has taken the teeth out of our lives. Make no mistake about it, I will beg the people to demand their power back, and I will give the people what they demand."

He delivered his diatribe with precision, like a laser beam that dispensed with the mind and went straight for the spine. His eyes cut across the crowd, deep-set and knowing. They settled on Jason for a moment, and when they moved on, he felt oddly relieved. An uncanny power possessed this man. Politics had never interested Jason much, but standing eight feet from the stage now, listening to this large man demanding their allegiance, he couldn't help wanting to give it. It was more than good sense that flowed from him; it was a raw brilliance that insisted on being honored, if not revered.

A tall man with eyes as black as coal stood in a blue pinstripe suit in front of the stage to Crandal's left, his legs spread and his arms gripped behind his back. He was the kind you might expect from the Mafia—a hatchet man who was clearly more interested in security than kissing the hands of old ladies.

The reporters scribbled notes and listened with rapt attention, and when Crandal ended his three-minute speech, they blurted their questions almost as one. Crandal let them ask, ignoring them as if he hadn't heard them at all. He turned to face the NBC camera and invited Donna with an open palm. "I'll start with you, Donna."

Donna asked her question, but Jason hardly heard it. He watched her staring at Crandal—the way she carried herself, the movement of her jaw— and it occurred to him that she spoke with an authority that nearly matched Crandal's. He was witness to the making of power. This was how it was done in the greatest of nations. This was how a person rose to command the largest and most powerful army in the world: by engaging a brilliant young reporter with smiling eyes and capturing her heart. Not in a romantic sense, of course, but in a way perhaps far more compelling.

"Well then, we'll just have to see if the people can remember what it means to be American, won't we, Donna?" Crandal said. A few chuckles rippled through the crowd.

"And if you wouldn't mind, sir, what exactly does it mean to be American?" Donna redirected.

Crandal's smile faded and he spoke as if lecturing. "It means we demand freedom. It means we will die for that freedom if need be. And in the event some of you might have misplaced your memory, freedom is a state of existence unrestrained by slavery, regardless of the master, whether he be armed with a hammer and a sickle or a document called the law." He let the comment sink in and then removed his eyes from her. A dozen questions filled the air.

Yes indeed, the making of power.

Jason remembered the boy and he glanced to his right. The Greek was fixated on the stage, big nose matched by a jutting chin. Leiah stood watching the exchange between Crandal and another reporter. She caught Jason's eye and smiled. The boy was by her side, his hand in hers. He stood stiff like a board and his eyes were glued to the candidate. Yes, of course, Caleb was why they had come in the first place. He looked like an awe-struck child gazing in at a circus for the first time.

For ten minutes Crandal handled the media's questions as if he were in a jousting match and he the repeated victor. The media seemed to sense it too. They knew they were watching a man of destiny, and their eyes were bright with the knowledge.

"And how would you characterize the current administration's proposal to trim the fifth fleet?" a question came.

"I would say that Murdock should spend more time trimming his waistline and less time tinkering with toys he knows nothing about," the former director of the National Security Agency responded. Now there, only a man who had them on their knees already could get away with a statement like that. Any other political pundit would be beheaded by the press for the comment.

"How do you respond to critics who say your experience with the NSA casts shadows on your political integrity?"

"I suggest they go for a long walk and study our beautiful skies. If they happen to see a MiG screaming out of the sky, releasing a string of nuclear weapons, then I would tell them to vote for the opposition. But if by chance they find the skies clear, then I would invite them to vote for the man who granted them this gift." They chuckled.

The event felt more like a stage show that topped the best Hollywood could offer than a political rally. According to Donna, the show was scheduled to last thirty minutes today.

But the boy changed that.

It came in a moment of unusual silence that Caleb's soft voice spoke to Jason's right. "He is the Tempest."

Jason raised his brow. The words were barely loud enough for Jason to hear, much less Crandal, but the man's eyes flickered and blinked three or four times very rapidly. He turned his head and stared at the NBC camera as if lost for the moment. Then his eyes searched each of their faces. Caleb stood wooden, unblinking, placid, except for the trembling in his fingers.

"This man will bring a new tempest to the earth."

Several reporters, oblivious to the small distraction, resumed their questioning, but Jason doubted Crandal even heard them. His eyes were on the boy now, deadlocked and unwavering. Caleb soaked in his stare without flinching.

Donna looked quickly between the statesman and the boy; she had seen that connection too.

Crandal broke his gaze and faced the crowd. "Well, ladies and gentlemen . . ." He paused, at a loss for words, Jason thought. But he quickly recovered. "All good things must come to an end. Your understanding of the issues we face in this election has once again been stunning for a mob of journalists. For that I thank you. We'll meet again, I am sure."

With that he turned on his heels and strode from the platform. The tall man Jason had pegged as a Mafia type bolted around the stage, glanced back toward Caleb one last time, and was gone. Immediately the crowd began to disperse.

"What in God's name was that?" Donna asked.

Leiah stared up at the empty stage. "You should ask? That was what you brought him here for." She pulled the boy to her and turned to leave. "We don't belong here," she said and walked for the car with Caleb in hand.

∞

Blane Roberts slid into the limousine next to Crandal, his mind churning incomprehensibly. The boy had said Tempest, hadn't he? He had actually identified Crandal as *the* Tempest, which made no sense. Then again, any comment even associating Crandal with Tempest made perfect sense. If he was not Tempest, he had certainly created Tempest. And now a small half-breed had said so. Which was a problem. Not only because no one in this hemisphere could possibly know about Tempest, but because a small boy who seemed to be able to read minds had done so in public. The NBC reporter had heard, he thought.

Roberts closed the car door with a thump.

"I'm not even going to ask for an explanation," Crandal said without turning. "But unless I'm missing something here, we've got a problem."

"Yes sir, it seems that way. I'll take care of it."

"I'm sure you will."

Encouraged by a red face, a bead of sweat snaked down the candidate's temple. Crandal rarely yelled, at least not with his mouth. But he did wear his anger, and right now it clothed him like a king. His left hand held a tremor, and his jaw muscles tensed as if they were kneading bread. The rear of the limousine was insulated; the statesman could scream bloody murder without a single syllable being heard by even the driver. But for all practical purposes, he *was* screaming bloody murder and Roberts diverted his eyes.

"Give me a day or two—"

"And you'll what? Kill the kid? Abduct him? Steal him from his sorry parents and slit his throat? Of course that's what you'll do because that's what you do best, isn't it, Roberts?"

Roberts blinked. "He's a problem. I'll take care of him."

"Do it quickly."

The large man put a finger under his collar and stretched his neck. The smell of Old Spice stung Roberts's nose. Crandal breathed heavily, uncharacteristic for the seasoned veteran of high drama. Roberts knew what he was going to say before he spoke.

"I thought there were no leaks on Tempest."

"There aren't."

"And I suppose you're going to suggest the boy just happened to look up at me and pull the word out of thin air."

"I don't know, but it doesn't necessarily mean he knows we orchestrated the invasion of Ethiopia. He couldn't. He's a kid, for goodness' sake!"

"I don't care if he's a dog; he knows more than you think he knows! He stood there and stared me down, and I'm telling you this kid knows something!"

"And I'll take care of him."

"How could a kid come across this? He didn't just grab a word like *Tempest* out of thin air. So who else knows? Find out. I don't need to tell you what this could do to our mission. We just launched a war over there to keep Tempest quiet. And now a kid waltzes into one of our press conferences and fingers us? He could be Ethiopian for all we know, straight from the war zone!"

Roberts wanted to tell Crandal that the boy looked about as Ethiopian as Mickey Mouse, but his employer's bone-rattling tone made him reconsider. And the questions were valid. He ground his teeth and took a deep breath. "I'll take care of it," he said.

Crandal paused, taking the time to breathe through his nostrils. "If it happens again, I may begin to doubt."

"I said I'll take care of it."

12

Day 6

CALEB SAT IN THE CORNER OF THE BED and ran an open palm over the wool blanket. It felt lumpy, which meant the sheet underneath was probably messed up. He slipped to the floor, reached under the blanket, jerked the sheet straight, and jumped back onto the bed.

There was a small room attached with a toilet and a shower in it, and he'd used the toilet more than the shower. Besides the bed itself, the only other piece of furniture was the shiny box in the corner, which he'd examined once without any understanding. Being here in the dark for so many hours felt kind of like a long meditation, although one with a twist to be sure.

In the monastery his daily meditation had lasted two or three hours, or sometimes four hours if he got "lost," as one of the priests once called it. They all meditated, but he suspected that none of the others enjoyed it as much as he did. Dadda did, of course, but then Dadda was the one who'd shown him in the first place.

"Be still, Caleb. Just be still and wait. Like it says, *Be still, and know that I am God. Wait upon the Lord.*"

"And what if I get tired of being still?"

"Then it means you haven't waited long enough."

"Did Jesus meditate?"

"He went away every night. Once for forty days."

That was at age four, and forty days sounded like forever. What his father probably didn't know was that Caleb had been meditating for over a year already, ever since that first time he'd poked his eye and seen the light. He didn't call it meditation; he just shut his eyes like Dadda did and thought about the kingdom of heaven and about Jesus. Usually nothing happened. Unless you count falling asleep as something, because he'd done plenty of sleeping.

For all its fancy sounding, meditation was really nothing more than resting your mind and then walking into the light. Into the kingdom. At least that's how he thought of it. By the time he was five, Caleb had decided that there could be nothing as pleasing as walking in God's kingdom.

Now in this dark room he had all the time in the world to fill his mind with God and that was good. The twist was that he was being locked in the room by the witch.

He closed his eyes and hummed softly to himself.

This was one thing Dadda had not told him about clearly enough, he'd decided. This strange world with all of these odd people. It felt like a story-book land, full of bigger-than-life characters. Everything they did seemed awkward and backward. For starters, he hadn't seen any of them sit still for more than a few minutes. Maybe they meditated while he remained locked in the room, but somehow he doubted it. They ran about with frowns and scrunched brows and seemed much too bothered to have come from having waited on anything, much less God.

Leiah loved him. If Father Nikolous would allow it, she would spend all day with him, he thought. She and Jason only came for about an hour each day so far, but it was a wonderful hour. They made him think of Dadda.

And Dadda was gone, wasn't he? Dadda was with God. That made him sad, not because his father was with God but because he missed him.

"Take care of him," Caleb whispered. "I miss you, Dadda."

I will be your Father, Caleb. Just like I am Dadda's Father.

Caleb blinked in the darkness and nodded at the familiar nudge. He smiled and cleared his throat.

"And I will be your son," he whispered.

We will walk through the kingdom together.

"We will walk through the kingdom together."

My kingdom.

"Your kingdom."

Caleb waited for a moment and then lay down on his side, feeling warm now. For a long time he just rested there, lingering in the peace. Gradually his mind drifted through the world outside of his door.

What was *Tempest?* He wasn't sure, but he did know that it was a very bad thing. The kind of evil that had filled Saul when he'd tried to kill David. He knew that and he knew that the big man speaking in the park was Tempest. He wasn't even sure how his mind had formed the word, but it had, and he thought he should tell someone about it. They'd nearly fainted when he said it; that's for sure.

They also seemed surprised when he made things right, as if he were doing something he really shouldn't be doing. But actually he was doing what anybody would do, wasn't he?

That man who'd died in the canyon, for example. How could they just stand by with the poor man dying on the sand? He hadn't understood all their yelling and their popping sticks in the first place—it really seemed quite silly to him. But then the man had died and Caleb just couldn't sit by and watch. He'd asked God for the man's life and God had given it, which was a good thing.

Samuel, the boy in the church, had been blind, like the blind man that Jesus had healed with mud. He'd never seen a blind person before, and he decided right then that Samuel would want to see the cross. The memory of the boy jumping up and down made him chuckle in the darkness. Caleb had almost started jumping up and down with the boy, right there in front of the priest.

Now that woman who thought he was a psychic or whatever, that was different. She clearly needed to see better. She hadn't yet, but she would soon enough, he thought. The breaking glasses had been maybe a little much, but then Jesus had used mud, hadn't he? And he'd cursed a fig tree. He'd also turned water into wine. The glass wasn't a mountain, but when he told it to move, it sure did.

Caleb smiled. The pillow was soft under his cheek and he snuggled into it. *Thank you, Father. You are so good to me.*

A click suddenly sounded at the latch and the door swung in. A wedge of light parted the room; Caleb sat up and swung his legs over the bed. The witch walked in. He called her "the witch" in his mind because she reminded him of the time he'd asked Dadda what a witch was after reading about them in the Scripture. Martha was the first person he'd met that didn't seem out of place with Dadda's description.

She stood in the doorway with her hands on her hips, casting a long shadow into the room. If she owned any clothes besides the dark dresses that made her look fat, she didn't wear them. He couldn't see her eyes because of the shadow that swallowed her face, but he imagined them, and a small chill shot down his spine.

Usually Father Nikolous visited with her once a day, and she was always much kinder when he was with her. Now he was not.

"How's our little prince?"

She always asked questions without waiting for an answer. He wondered if all witches were like that. Not that she was a real witch.

Martha looked about the room, saw that nothing was out of place, and walked to the bathroom. She looked in, humphed, and pulled her head out. Caleb couldn't help thinking that if he'd have left a drop of water on the floor, she would be scolding him about it. It wasn't a pigpen after all.

Martha walked back to the door and turned around, still surrounded by shadows, so that she looked like a black snowman in the doorframe.

"Father Nikolous wants you to go with him to a meeting tomorrow. Which means it's my job to make sure you do just that without causing any trouble."

Again she paused as if he should say something.

"Are you deaf, boy?"

"No, Auntie."

"Then you answer me when I speak to you. You don't fool me; you're a troublemaker, boy. And if there's one thing I detest in this world, it's trouble-makers. Now you may think the world is just one big peachy place filled with people who run at your every beck and call, but believe me, boy, you're going to learn different."

She walked farther in and the light caught her eyes now. He wanted to tell her that he'd never thought of the world as one big peachy place, but the words seemed to stick in his throat.

"If it were up to me, I'd have given you at least one good whipping by now. If for nothing but your snotty attitude. Now, if you get Nikolous upset, I don't think he'd mind me giving you a good whipping. So tomorrow you go with him, you understand?"

"I will go with Leiah and Jason."

She wagged her head and repeated in a mocking tone, "I will go with Leiah and Jason." She took a deep, disgusted breath. "You'll go because I said so, and Leiah and Jason can crawl up and die for all I care." But she didn't push the issue, and he wasn't about to either. Not now.

Martha looked at him for some time, and then scanned the room, as if searching for a violation of some kind. "You like this quiet, don't you, boy? Of course you do. It reminds you of your precious monastery."

She dropped her arms to her sides and turned back to him. "You're actually a happy little fool in this dungeon, aren't you? You are one sick child!"

Martha suddenly walked to the glassy box in the corner, did something to it, and stepped back. The box lit up. It was a light of some kind.

The witch turned, faced him for a few long seconds, and then marched out of the room with a humph. She left the box light on.

Only it was more than a light. Caleb stiffened and caught his breath at the image before him. The glassy part of the box had become a painting. A moving painting full of rich colors and sound.

He scrambled back into the corner of his bed, suddenly panicked. But his alarm passed almost immediately, replaced by fascination at the wonder before his eyes. He'd seen something similar at the airport in England with Jason and Leiah, but it had been far away and his mind had been in a fog. He stared with wide eyes as a painting of a boy with spiked yellow hair and eyes as thin as slits walked across the picture. The boy was not real, but a drawing of a boy. In fact, the whole screen was filled with a drawing, as if someone inside the box were quickly painting this picture and making it move.

Caleb stared at the picture, mouth agape. The pretend boy held a red stick in his hands and he walked over to a sleeping dog. He dropped to his knees, shoved the stick under the dog, and then ran away on his tiptoes, snickering. The scene made the hair on Caleb's neck stand.

A loud boom and a flash of light suddenly filled the room and Caleb started. In the next moment he saw what had happened. The red stick was a weapon and it had exploded. The dog now lay burning on his back with his four legs sticking straight up in the air.

Caleb had never felt the kind of horror that flooded his veins at the sight. He yelped with terror and threw his arms over his head. He curled up tight in the corner of his bed and clenched his eyes. Oh, dear God, what is this? What is this?

He wanted to run to the picture and beg for the dog's life, but he knew he couldn't. It was just a picture. He wanted to run from the room and never see the glass box again. Instead he covered his ears and curled up and began to sing.

∞

It had taken Roberts two days to learn the truth about the boy, Caleb. He would've pieced the information together in a few hours if Colonel Ambozia had shot straight from the start. Instead the Eritrean commander had pretended as though he had no knowledge whatsoever of any living soul escaping the monastery. They had accomplished the mission as agreed and the price had not been cheap. Forty-eight of his soldiers had lost their lives in the invasion, and he personally had suffered more than enough political fallout to threaten his future.

"Then let me be a little more blunt, Commander. The arms are still in my control," Roberts had returned. "You really don't have to pretend that you're in mourning over there. We both know you'd quickly give up a thousand men for this shipment, and for all practical purposes it will *guarantee* your political future. Our agreement was for total silence, and I promise you that as long as there remains any question of that silence, we'll hold the shipment. Now whether you like it or not, we have a boy here who just happens to be walking through our streets talking about Tempest. For your own sake, you'd better find somebody over there who knows who he is."

Colonel Ambozia's right-hand man, a sleazeball who called himself Tony, phoned sixteen hours later, and his news was not what Roberts had been hoping for. He had just delivered that news to his boss.

Crandal blinked and stared, silent for a moment. "So you're telling me this kid, who just happens to show up at one of my press conferences, is not only from Ethiopia, he's the adopted son of our dead priest?"

"Yes."

Roberts took a slug of scotch and set the glass on the meeting table. They were alone in the Hyatt Regency's most expensive private suite, twenty stories above Los Angeles's night traffic. It wasn't the first time they had been in this situation, facing sudden long odds, but this time its gravity felt heavier.

Crandal blinked a few more times, incredulous at the words he'd just heard. He turned to the window and stared off at the stream of lights that lit the 405 freeway. Roberts watched the man: the flare of his nostrils, the slow closing of his eyes, the deep calming breath. And then Crandal's eyes opened and he spoke calmly.

"How old is he?"

A less-disciplined man would be fuming now. Crandal was past that. He'd already moved on to problem solving.

"Ten. Maybe eleven."

"So he was alive in 1991. He was in Ethiopia during Tempest."

"Very young, but yes, alive. We have ourselves a genuine product of our own war, come back to haunt us."

"And the father?"

"Unknown. Father Matthew raised the kid as his own."

"Which would explain the boy's knowledge."

"Except for his use of the name. Tempest. Our sources insist Father Matthew never referred to the 1991 invasion by its given name. Only that the invasion was supported by the NSA."

"Then your sources are wrong. The kid knows about Tempest."

Roberts nodded and took another drink. The liquor burned its way down his throat. He replaced the glass. "They say this kid's psychic."

Crandal ignored the comment. "So we know who he is. How are we taking care of him? And who are the others?"

"The others are caretakers. He's been granted refugee status in the care of an orphanage run by an Orthodox church and directed by a Father Nikolous. Their presence at the park was incidental."

"Incidental? We're five thousand miles from Ethiopia, and you want me to believe that the one person who managed to escape an operation ordered by me just *incidentally* wanders up to one of my press conferences? Don't be an idiot."

"Unlikely, I agree. But I believe that's exactly what happened. Which is why I want to step carefully on this one."

Crandal looked at him, and for just a moment his eyes fell to slits, but otherwise he remained expressionless. "Tell me."

"For starters, I really don't believe he's said anything. And if he has, there's no sign of it."

"There's no guarantee he won't say something tomorrow. For all we know, he's spilling his guts right now."

"You don't think they asked him what he meant by Tempest after the press conference? Sure they did. And he told them nothing. Which can only mean he knows nothing."

"He knows about Tempest. We both heard him."

"No, he knows Tempest, but he doesn't necessarily know anything *about* Tempest. Or he no longer remembers anything about Tempest. For all we know, the old priest in Ethiopia had your picture plastered on his bedroom wall, and when this kid asked him who that man was, he told him that man is Tempest. Who knows? The point is he isn't remembering anything."

"We can't risk a jog in his memory."

"Of course. But on balance we have to weigh the risks. The kid goes; we agree on that. But I don't think we can afford to take him out with conventional means. Donna Blair not only knows of him, she heard him at the press conference. We can't just pop a slug in his head without raising questions that will inevitably lead back to the press conference."

Crandal closed his eyes and stretched his neck.

Roberts continued. "The Orthodox church he's holed up in is a virtual fortress. This Father Nikolous character likes his privacy. A hit-and-run or any other accident will be nearly impossible in this situation. His environment is too protective."

"Then have him removed from his environment," Crandal said, eyes still closed.

"Removed? He's in the custody of the orphanage by order of the court. Removing him may not be so easy. But I believe we may have found another way. A way to deal with him from the inside. Through natural causes."

"Yes, of course. But you're wrong about his removal."

"How?"

"He's a refugee."

"He is."

And then it hit Roberts. He shifted in his seat. Of course! It was brilliant.

"Call the NSA," Crandal said. "Have Jack take the case over on national security grounds. The invasion should give him plenty of reasons to do that. Then have him contact immigration. They've never been a problem; I don't see why they would be one now."

"We have the kid deported."

"Yes."

A wave of relief swept down Roberts's back. He threw back the last of his scotch. "And we terminate the kid the minute he sets foot on foreign soil."

"Yes, of course."

"And if immigration does put up resistance?"

Crandal shoved his bulk from the chair and strode for the bar. "If they do, we use your natural causes, Roberts. But they won't."

13

JASON SAT ON THE WOOD BENCH near the entrance to the L.A. convention hall, watching the scattered traffic of conventioneers coming and going midmorning. Leiah sat beside him, unhappy at being here, he thought. Unhappy because she was a doer, and there was clearly nothing she could do here except watch.

It had been three days since Caleb's last outing to the park, and in that time they had entered a kind of stalemate. They'd visited him each afternoon for an hour without learning more or reshaping the boy's situation. Leiah clearly lived each of the other twenty-three hours for that one with Caleb.

A boy maybe twelve purred by in an electric Everest and Jennings wheelchair, his head tilted and his lips loose. A paperback novel jostled on his lap— Orson Scott Card's *Ender's Game.* Jason wondered how the boy managed to lift the book for reading. Some new contraption would service it, no doubt. A woman, presumably his mother, walked beside him confidently, with her chin lifted and her left hand resting on the back of the chair. They passed by, maneuvered easily around the large junipers growing from their holes in the concrete, and disappeared into the hall.

For every visibly handicapped person, there were at least two professional attendees to the convention, dressed in suits, come to scope out how the latest in technology might fatten their wallets, no doubt. Others walked by as well, caretakers, but they were dressed more casually and generally lacked the hawk eyes of those in suits. The scene rolled past in stark contrast to what Jason had become accustomed to on the streets of Addis Ababa. The lame were no fewer in number in Ethiopia to be sure, and more often than not, they were victims of leprosy or some such illness. But they were simply cast into the pot with hordes of outcasts rather than cared for as they were here. This alone was a reason to love this bastion of capitalism called America, Jason thought.

Jason glanced up, thinking it would be another hot day, even though it was already October. The sun had come out in regular Southern California fashion, diffused by a haze that hung over the city. You'd think having lived in Africa all these years he'd be accustomed to the heat, but in reality he'd spent most of his time above five thousand feet, where the air was usually clear and cool.

"You'd think if the old buzzard insisted we be here by ten, he'd be here by ten," Jason said.

Leiah glanced at him and nodded, and then returned her gaze to a small child hobbling past on forearm crutches thirty yards away.

"You know what he has in mind, don't you?"

"I think I have it pretty much figured out. And if this isn't exploitation, I don't know what is."

"You're right." Leiah had taken to wearing scarves or wide chokers when she wasn't wearing a turtleneck, and she wore them with style, he thought. Today she wore a yellow scarf to accent a white blouse and her standard-fare jeans. Even her choice of black work boots blended with style. Her look was less cowboy and more steelworker, but then again, they weren't in Texas. If they had been in Texas, he had no doubt she'd be wearing cowboy boots and looking like a regular ranch hand. Although regular was not a word that did any justice to Leiah.

She faced him with flashing blue eyes. "Is it just me, Jason, or does this not feel right?"

"No, it's not just you. This doesn't feel right."

"Then why are we sitting by while this maniac drags Caleb around?"

She did have her way with words. No confusion permitted. "We're not just sitting here, Leiah. We're doing what we can."

"And you know as well as I do that it's not enough."

"Maybe not. But you have to look at the bright side. He seems happy, doesn't he? If there were things going on that should concern us, Caleb would tell us, wouldn't he? And I don't know about you, but on both of our last two visits he seemed just plain happy."

"Come on, Jason. What do you expect from a child in his situation? He's lost. He doesn't know any better. All he knows is happy because that's who Caleb is."

"You're saying he's too stupid to know that if someone beats him it's not a good thing?"

"No! Of course not. And I didn't say the old bat is beating him. But he's good to the bone, and part of being good is seeing the best in others. If he's happy, it's because he finds contentment where most ordinary people never would. But that doesn't mean it's healthy for him. They have him locked up in his room all day—you think that's reasonable?"

"No."

"And when will it end?"

"Nikolous is isolating—"

"I know what Nikolous is doing. And today he's going to march Caleb out here to see if he can pull off a few more tricks. He's turning the child into a circus attraction," she said.

Jason considered her argument. The simple fact was Nikolous hadn't damaged the boy in any visible way. Unless or until he did, their hands were tied by the court order. He understood Leiah's love for Caleb; he felt it himself. They had talked of little else for hours on end over this last week. But this was not Africa, for goodness' sakes. You couldn't just muscle your way past the system if you expected to stay a free man.

"Look, I swore to both Caleb and his father that I wouldn't let any harm come to him. I intend to keep that promise." He met her eyes and was struck by the impulse to reach out and brush her hair from her face. "I'll do whatever is reasonable. But doing something halfcocked won't necessarily do Caleb any favors, right?"

She kept her eyes on his, searching his soul, it seemed. Truthfully he felt exposed.

"Whatever is reasonable? How about whatever's *necessary?*"

He thought about it and then nodded. "Whatever's necessary."

She smiled gently, and it seemed to seal more than he had promised.

They waited another five minutes before Jason saw Donna. She approached them from the street, wearing a wide smile. Nikolous had said nothing about her coming.

"Well, well look who's here," Jason said, nodding in her direction.

Leiah looked at the news correspondent and then glanced back at Jason. He shrugged. "Trust me, I didn't invite her."

Donna walked up smiling. "Hello, Jason. Leiah. Are they here yet?"

Jason stood instinctively; he did so alone.

"No."

"We're early anyway. He said he'd be here at ten-thirty."

"And what brings you here?" Leiah asked. She crossed her legs and folded her arms. "Here to make Caleb famous, is that it?"

"Maybe. That really depends on him."

"Maybe it depends more on you. You're the one with the camera."

"What camera? I don't see a camera. Not today," Donna shot back. "Listen, I know you don't approve of the whole idea of bringing the boy into the public eye; for that matter it's quite obvious you don't approve of me either. But like it or not, this isn't your private little party. You have no idea how much good the boy might bring the world. Try to think beyond yourself on this one, will you?"

Jason felt the sting from her words himself. Leiah didn't have a selfish bone in her body. But neither was she spineless.

"It was the boy I had in mind," she said.

Donna looked at her, nearly said something in response, but chose to dismiss Leiah with a nod and turn to Jason instead.

"So what did you make of his statement at the press conference?" she asked. Before them the number of attendees entering or leaving the building had dwindled to sporadic bunches. Donna hardly seemed to notice them.

"I agree with Leiah, Donna. Caleb is our first concern here, not what he can or cannot do. He's a child. And as for Crandal, the man makes me cringe."

Donna smiled. "Point taken. He makes you cringe, huh? That's power for you. And believe me, he's got more than the rest combined."

"It's more than power," Leiah said. "The man is dangerous. I think Caleb saw that."

"Maybe. I ran a search on Tempest and found nothing. But that doesn't mean much, considering where the man's been. Either way, you can't ignore his power. He's pulling away in the polls, and I can't see anything getting in his way. Won't be long and we'll be calling him Mr. President. So what does the boy say?"

"About Tempest? Nothing. He doesn't know. But he obviously spooked Crandal. Tempest is more than some incidental trinket from his past. Did you get it on camera?"

She shook her head. "We were using directional mikes to cut crowd noise."

Leiah suddenly stood and Jason followed her eyes. They were forty feet away, the Greek and the boy, stopped on the concrete. Nikolous had his eyes on the boy, and Caleb was fixed on a blond-headed girl all dressed for Sunday, wheeling past him in a wheelchair.

Leiah walked toward Caleb and Jason followed, but he saw that something had already changed about the boy. It was what had stopped Nikolous. The sight of the girl passing by in the wheelchair hadn't just diverted Caleb's attention; it had frozen him stiff.

Leiah pulled up five feet from the boy—she'd seen it too. "Caleb?"

The boy glanced at her and then looked toward a young man, maybe twenty, who hobbled along with the aid of an aluminum walker to his left. One of his legs appeared bent below the knee.

Jason pulled up behind Leiah. A quiet settled on them. Moving closer to the boy somehow felt pretentious.

Leiah had one hand reaching out to Caleb, but he ignored it and jerked his eyes to another attendee, this one a very old woman in an ancient wheelchair. She had removed the leg rests and slowly eased herself along, using her feet to inch the wheelchair forward. Her skin sagged from her bones as if it were slowly melting. She turned a baggy face toward Jason. Her lower lip drooped to her chin, and the bags under her eyes hung impossibly low. She looked as if she were about to cry, and Jason knew it was how she always looked.

He faced Caleb. An expression of anguish gripped the boy's face now. Near panic. Glistening tears slid down his cheeks and he was breathing quickly. It struck Jason that the boy's sheltering had prevented him from ever seeing such a scene. He swallowed. Leiah was crying beside him now, softly, under her breath, but the sound of it made Jason's knees weak.

Caleb suddenly whirled to the young girl in the wheelchair, now rolling away from him. His little hands knotted into fists and he tore after her. When he reached the wheelchair, he grabbed the armrest and spun around it to face the girl. She uttered a sharp cry of surprise. For a moment their eyes locked, and Caleb's face wrinkled with grief. He began to speak quickly in a high-pitched voice. Jason recognized the familiar Ge'ez dialect. The boy was praying.

He reached out as if to pluck a flower from the girl's hair, and he touched her lightly on the cheek. An endearing touch that lingered and then was gone.

Caleb whirled, acquired sight of the young man with the bent leg, and ran for him.

But their eyes were on the blond girl; Jason knew they were because he himself couldn't remove his eyes from her. The girl's legs hung a foot off the ground, supported by two leg rests. She turned her head and looked after Caleb dumbly. Then she looked into her lap. She turned to him again, just as he ran in front of the young man with the bad leg. Then it was back to her knees again.

Her back was toward them, so Jason couldn't see exactly what was happening to her legs, but clearly they had arrested her attention. She seemed confused and looked to Caleb once more for clarity. But the boy was gazing into the eyes of the young man who'd stopped as a matter of necessity.

Something about her legs made the little blond girl decide to try standing. She couldn't have understood a word Caleb had spoken over her; not even Jason could understand but a word or two. She suddenly leaned forward, pushed a lever that allowed the leg rests to swing free, and slipped out of her seat.

A shriek ripped through the air. A woman raced toward them in high heels, an ice-cream cone wobbling in each hand. The girl's mother had returned from the ice-cream stand behind her to find her daughter collapsed on the ground.

But she hadn't collapsed. She was standing on the concrete looking at her toes, with her hands hanging by her sides. The mother dropped the cones and rushed toward her daughter in a full shriek. And then suddenly she swallowed the scream, because her little girl took one quiet step forward.

The mother slid to a stop, bug-eyed.

The blond girl stood for a few moments, eyes still glued on her feet, and then took another step forward. She wore spotless white shoes with white lace ties, and she placed both feet together and looked up. Her body began to tremble all over. Jason stopped breathing.

The girl stood with her arms neatly at her side and her feet together at the heels, shaking from head to foot. And then it all burst from her and she shrieked. A higher-pitched, slightly quieter version of her mother's shriek, but no less intense. She lifted her arms above her head and began to turn in circles with short shuffle steps. Her mother approached now, her hands spread wide, palms out. Her mouth hung open and she began to circle her daughter, as though grappling for a thread of reason.

Jason jerked his eyes to Caleb, who was grinning now, running for the old woman, who had stopped her pedaling in favor of watching the commotion. Her face still looked like something from the grave.

But the young man—the young man was trembling over his walker. This time Jason saw the changing before his own eyes. It was quite simple really. The young man's leg had become rubber, and now it slowly straightened. The man was watching it and yelping at the same time. A short *"Iap! Iap!"* sound, like someone caught between fear and desire.

He was still trembling when the violent shakes of his body pushed the walker beyond his grasp. Jason doubted it was intended, because the man staggered and caught himself with a giant step forward. Like the girl, he remained fixated on his toes. But only for a few moments. Then he began to hoot and dance a strange dance that reminded Jason of an old Fred Astaire movie he'd seen once.

The little girl was jumping up and down now. Jumping up and down and watching her own legs and crying with delight. Her mother was doing short vertical hops with her, crying buckets.

A faint whoop came from the direction of the baggy lady, and Jason spun to face her. She was out of her wheelchair, wearing a great toothless grin. Her cheeks bunched under bright gray eyes. It was the last straw for Jason. A flood seemed to rise through his chest and he began to cry. Not for sorrow, heavens no. Looking at the old lady baring her gums with such joy, he could not help but join her.

Caleb had run off, to find another perhaps. By now several dozen curious onlookers had run to the scene attracted by the mother's screams. A middle-aged man still clinging to an old cane skipped through the gathering, silent and stunned. Another recipient of Caleb's touch. The three who had been healed first were all hopping, and now the girl's mother had her arms raised to the sky, crying, "Thank you, Jesus. Thank you, Jesus!"

Whistles suddenly shrilled, and three white-clothed security officers angled through the crowd, waving their hands.

"Okay, let's break this up, folks. What seems to be the problem here?"

Nikolous moved for the first time. He swooped down on Caleb, who'd just approached a lady in red with a Seeing Eye dog. The large man grabbed Caleb's shoulder, spun him around, and snatched up his hand.

The wide smile on Caleb's face faded, and he stumbled after Nikolous. The Greek led the boy quickly toward his black Mercedes, still parked in a handicapped-loading zone on the front apron. Leiah cried and ran after them but too late; Nikolous shoved the boy into the car, slammed the door, and was striding back before she reached him. She grabbed his arm, demanding to talk to the boy, but he just shrugged her off.

"Excuse me."

Jason spun to face the baggy woman who'd walked up to him. Behind her the crowd was beginning to disperse, but a number of them cried uncontrollably, maybe relatives and friends of the little girl who skipped around with fists still raised above her head.

"Did you see where the boy went?" the old lady asked. Her skin seemed twice what her face required, but it curved in infectious arcs now.

"I'm sorry; he's gone," Jason said.

She closed the flaps that were her lips and then smiled uncontrollably, showing her gums. "I haven't walked in ten years, you know?"

Jason didn't know what to say.

"He has the breath of God. That boy has God's breath." A tear broke from her left eye and then she turned from him and sauntered off aimlessly on thin legs.

Jason and Donna were left standing like innocent bystanders caught on the perimeter. Small pockets still gathered around the girl and the young man, but they'd drifted toward the edge at the officer's encouragement. Behind Jason, Nikolous's shoes clacked on the cement and he turned. But it was Donna the Greek approached, not him. A grin split his face.

"So you will agree to do it?" he asked.

Donna stared at him and blinked. "How could I not?"

"You will come, then?"

"I'll be there with lights blazing, sir."

He nodded, glanced at Jason, and then turned about. He took in a stern glare from Leiah and strode for his car.

∞

"You'll be where?" Jason asked Donna. His head had cleared quickly, and he wasn't sure he wanted to hear what she would say.

"I'm going to shoot an event he's putting together for national broadcast."

"You're *what?*" Leiah demanded, stepping up from behind.

"Did you just see what happened here? It was incredible! You can't hide this from the world!"

"Maybe, but you're moving a bit fast, aren't you?" Jason asked. "Television? When's the event?"

"One week."

"One week."

"Next Saturday night in the Old Theater on Figueroa Street."

They both stared at her without responding.

"Oh, lighten up. You can't favor a single boy over the lives he can touch. Look at what he just did for that little girl, for goodness' sake. And that man! Go tell them it was all a bit fast." She shook her head and glanced at her watch. "I've gotta run. I'm sure I'll see you soon enough. Please, Jason, don't take this personally. I work for the people; it's my job. He'll be fine; you'll see."

With that she turned from them, and they watched her walk to her car.

They left the convention hall in a kind of dull shock. It took them an hour to dissect in detail what they'd seen. The boy's power was seemingly at his whim. And now it was clear that Nikolous wasn't finished.

It took them another hour of discussing the matter to agree that they should put a stop to Nikolous now before he hurt Caleb. Dragging a boy into public like a dog to perform tricks and then throwing him back in his cage until the next act could easily be interpreted as abuse. Or at the very least exploitation.

The situation was spiraling out of control. It had to be stopped. Jason agreed to go to the court first thing Monday and ask for a temporary restraining order until a child psychiatrist had the opportunity to examine Caleb and offer an informed opinion on the effect Nikolous's scheme would have on him.

And if they weren't granted a restraining order?

Then they would go back to the Immigration Service.

Whatever is necessary, Leiah reminded him.

Jason only nodded. In reality he didn't need reminding, but he let her play the mother. She was born for it.

14

Stewart Long sat across from his wife, forking mashed potatoes into his mouth, thinking that despite his wife's altercation with the doctor, on balance his day had been pretty decent.

"Well, I don't care what Dr. Franklin says," Barbara said. "I'm not going to let them take a knife to Peter's legs. And that's final. They can experiment on someone else's legs." She said it with a firm jaw, and Stewart knew that it was the end of the matter.

To say that the Longs were just an ordinary mother-father-and-son family who lived on an ordinary suburban street in an ordinary Southern Californian town like Altadena would miss the true flavor of the matter entirely. Not that any of this was untrue, no. But no amount of ordinary detail could strip away the extraordinary nature of walking through life with muscular dystrophy.

Or in little Peter's case *not* walking through life with muscular dystrophy.

They lived about fifteen minutes from the Rose Bowl, just ten minutes north of the 210 freeway, and not more than eight minutes from Brookside Memorial Hospital, but in their hearts the Longs lived a thousand miles from the rest of the world. It hardly mattered that Stewart spent his days minding the streets as a bona fide policeman, saving humanity from itself in every way imaginable. It mattered even less in some ways that Barbara carried the credentials of a registered nurse around in her purse. Peter had come into their lives ten years ago and made such facts subservient to this other one—the one that had pushed them into their own personal hell. The one called muscular dystrophy.

At least that's how Stewart saw it. But then that was unfair, because they had actually started to make some sense of life this last year, hadn't they?

"He's been through too much as it is," Barbara added after some silence.

Stewart looked at his son. Apart from the braces on either leg, his body looked slight and perhaps even frail, but otherwise he looked quite normal. "Is that how you feel, Peter?"

The boy lifted his eyes. "Our most important thoughts are those which contradict our emotions," he said. "What do my feelings have to do with it?" Stewart recognized it as a quote he'd heard from his son before. Peter's body might be frail, but his mind was far from it, and he had no problem retreating there at the flip of some invisible switch. He often showed his genius through these quotes of his, memorized and put into perfect context at will.

"Who's that one from?" Stewart asked, testing.

"Knowledge can be communicated, Father, but not wisdom," his son responded.

"Please, dear . . ."

"It's okay, Barbara. Indulge him."

"Yes, indulge me, Mom. We've all had a hard day. Let's give ourselves a break."

For a moment Stewart thought the conversation could go either way: to heaven or to hell. And in truth he could hardly influence its course. It was Barbara and Peter who had suffered the most—she in forfeiting not only her career but most of the last decade, and he in his disability—and through their suffering they had earned certain rights, it seemed. Engaging each other as they saw fit was one of them.

Then with a smile Barbara averted their descent into hell.

Stewart grinned and Barbara chuckled.

"You see, a wise man knows everything; a shrewd one, everybody. I know you, Mother. You need sympathy as much as I."

"Don't get a big head, Peter," Barbara chided. "You think you know so much." She was smiling wide now, and that was a good sign, because there really was no humor. Yes, it was heaven for sure.

Peter grinned, delighted with her. "I am not young enough to know everything," he said. That one Stewart recognized as Oscar Wilde.

"No. Neither are you old enough to know half as much as you do."

"Up to a certain point every man is what he thinks he is," Peter returned.

"And what do you think you are, Peter?"

The grin suddenly faded from his son's face. He looked from one to the other as though lost. Not lost in a strange way, just lost in a ten-year-old-boy sort of way.

"What is it, Son?" Barbara asked.

Peter shifted his eyes and then lowered them to his pants. Stewart followed his son's gaze and saw the dark stain spreading on his jeans. It was the latest development in his disease, this lack of bladder control. By the look of it, Peter had refused his "idiotic" diapers again.

Stewart glanced at his wife and saw that she'd seen the accident. A look of empathy wrinkled the skin around her eyes.

Peter turned beet red. For a moment none of them spoke.

"Mom . . ."

"It's okay, dear," Barbara said, standing. She ran her hand through his hair and kissed his head. "It's okay."

A tear dribbled down Peter's cheek. He might be a genius, but he was still a ten-year-old boy who'd been through hell. And now in a moment of grace from heaven, this reminder that hell was still very much with them.

Peter slumped helpless in his bright blue wheelchair and fought a losing battle for his dignity.

For the millionth time in ten years Stewart swallowed hard, cursed the gods that had delivered this disease to them, and lifted his son from his wheelchair.

∞

It was noon Monday when Jason whipped the Ford Bronco to the curb in front of Leiah's new apartment and shoved the gearshift into park. The windshield wipers jerked noisily against a light rain. He shifted the cell phone to his right ear.

"They can do that!? File a challenge!"

The World Relief director responded quickly. "Not a chance. My hands are tied on this one, Jason."

"That's ridiculous! I don't care who the INS thinks they are; even they have checks and balances on things like this!"

"Maybe. But the INS got their orders from the National Security Administration. And you don't mess with them."

"This is impossible!" Movement to his right caught his attention, and he turned to see Leiah running for the car with a hand lifted as if to fight off the rain. A ringing lingered in his head. He faced the windshield.

"So when? When is all this supposed to happen?"

"Twenty-four hours. Maybe a little longer."

The passenger door opened and Leiah hopped in.

"Give me forty-eight."

"Come on, Jason. You know I don't have any—"

"Just forty-eight hours. I'm telling you, John, there's more here than you think. We're talking about an innocent ten-year-old orphan here, not some terrorist."

"And we're also talking the NSA here, not some family member who's debating custody."

"Then just stall them. Pull in a favor. Anything. Look . . . please."

"What's up?" Leiah demanded. Jason ignored her.

"I'll do what I can," John said. "But trust me, it won't mean a thing. You've got twenty-four hours."

"Call me if anything changes. You can do that, right?"

"Jason, what's going on?" Leiah cut in again. He stopped her with an open hand.

"Sure," John said.

"Thank you."

Jason heard the line click and he snapped the cell phone shut.

"What's—"

"They're deporting Caleb," Jason said without turning.

The Bronco fell quiet except for the patter of rain on the shell. Leiah stared at him, not comprehending.

"Deporting? As in sending him back?"

"Yes."

"That's impossible! They can't do that! He's a refugee!"

"Evidently the NSA seems to think he may pose a national security risk. They've ordered immigration to deport him."

"Give me a break! He's a kid! It's Crandal, isn't it? This has something to do with the press conference."

"Probably. And I'm not saying it's a good thing, but it's a problem we have to face."

"Caleb's more than some *problem* we have to face! He's a lost child desperate for understanding. We can't let them take him away! You know as well as I do that he's not safe in Ethiopia. They tried to kill him once; you don't think they'll try again?"

Jason looked at her, suddenly angry. "You think I don't know that? I'm not the enemy here"—he jabbed out the window—"they are! I'm on Caleb's side, remember? Quit taking your frustration out on me!"

They locked stares.

Leiah's eyes misted and she looked away.

Jason immediately regretted his tone. He wanted to reach a hand to her shoulder and beg an apology. The bandana on her neck had slipped, and ugly scars rose above the white pullover she wore. A picture of scars covering her belly flashed through his mind and he swallowed. *Leiah, Leiah, what did you do to deserve such a tragedy?*

It occurred to him again that she and the boy weren't so different. It was her unique connection to Caleb. She saw herself in him, and her frustration was perhaps as much for herself as for him.

But could *he*, Jason, love such a wounded spirit? He did love the boy. Maybe not in the same way as she, but he did love Caleb. And in a strange way, he cared for her as well.

To think of his caring in any other terms, especially ones laced with romance, felt wrong. Like an unspoken taboo. A perversion even. Heaven help him, but he could never yield to such an impossibility. She was out of reach. An untouchable.

He discarded his impulse to lay his hand on her shoulder.

"We should hear on the Temporary Restraining Order this afternoon," he said.

She looked at him and gathered herself. "Of course that doesn't mean anything now, does it?"

He shrugged. "No. I guess it doesn't."

"So why did you ask John for forty-eight hours?"

"I don't know. I don't like the idea of Caleb going back any more than you. I care for him too." His words struck him and he turned from her.

The touch of her hand on his shoulder took him by surprise. Heat washed through his spine, and suddenly he was fighting tears. The madness of it all was catching him too, he thought.

"I'm sorry. I know you do," she said.

Jason nodded and she removed her hand.

There was nothing to say. It was all ending. The government's most powerful hand had reached in and trumped them all. Nikolous, Donna, an unsuspecting national audience—they were all having the world's eighth wonder plucked from under their noses.

He slid the stick into drive and pulled the Bronco into the street. This visit with Caleb could be their last, a notion that resonated like a slanderous joke. He drove in an awkward silence.

The idea ignited in Jason's mind on the 210 on-ramp, like an unusually large burst at a Fourth of July fireworks extravaganza. He even jerked the wheel enough to get a look from Leiah.

"What?"

He stared ahead, spinning the idea through his mind again. It was staring them down like a challenging bull.

"What?"

"Remember Elian Gonzalez?"

"The Cuban kid? Why?"

"What made the INS move so slowly in deporting him?"

She looked ahead. "The media?"

"Yes. The cameras. Or more to the point, his popularity."

He ignored her stare and spoke his mind quickly. "What would the INS do if Caleb were a nationally known figure instead of a lost orphan?"

"I don't know—"

"They would back off! At least until they could explain themselves!"

"I thought the National Security Administration was pulling the strings."

"Yes, but through the Immigration Service." Jason powered the Bronco down the freeway seized by the simplicity of the idea. "It could work! Think about it."

"I am and it scares me to death."

"And the idea of him being hauled back to Ethiopia doesn't? Let's face it, he goes and he'll last a day if he's lucky. At least here he has us. He has you."

"Okay. You're right. But Caleb isn't a national figure. And we've got what, twenty-four hours? How?"

They exchanged glances. "Nikolous?" she asked.

"Nikolous," he said.

Jason pulled off the freeway and roared toward the Greek Orthodox church. He snatched up his cell phone with the intent to call the man. "You remember the office number?"

"No."

He grunted and tossed the phone down.

"I don't know, Jason. Nikolous isn't exactly a friend."

"He's crookeder than a saw blade. Granted. And he's a greedy slime-ball. Which is exactly why he'll be on our side."

She was quiet for a moment. "So you're saying we join forces with the devil to save Caleb's soul."

"I'm saying we do whatever we can to keep Caleb in the United States. Remember? Whatever is necessary? And unless you have a better idea, yes, siding with the devil fits my understanding of 'whatever.'"

Leiah set her jaw and stared ahead, but she didn't object.

∞

Jason dispensed with the parking routine and screeched to a halt before the double glass door that led to the Holy Ascension Greek Orthodox Church's office suites. He hurried Leiah through the doors and cut straight for the back offices without bothering a confused receptionist. He heard her "Excuse me, sir," and ignored it as he turned the corner to Nikolous's grand suite. Leiah ran to catch him, ten feet behind when he rapped on the heavy oak door.

Jason pushed the door in without waiting for a response.

Father Nikolous sat behind his mammoth desk, his mustache down-turned and his hair slicked back in customary style. Martha, the wench who fancied herself an appropriate caretaker, sat in a Queen Anne chair opposite him, bulging at her seams. They both glared with steely stares. He would have expected a startled look, but their stone hearts were beyond the response, he thought wryly.

The thought strengthened his resolve. If they were going to dive in with the fellow, they might as well do it on their terms and win back a little ground.

"Well, well, the masters of the house are conspiring to wreck the world, is that it?"

They did not flinch. Neither saw his humor.

"Tell the lady to see to her daily beatings, Nikolous. We need to talk."

"Don't be a fool," Nikolous said. "Please leave. I'll be with you in due time."

"I'm afraid due time won't do. We have a problem."

"We all have our problems. Right now mine is your uninvited presence. If you do not—"

"They're deporting Caleb tomorrow," Jason said.

That snatched the sound from the room.

Martha's left eyelid quivered and closed halfway, as if a nerve had shorted in her skull. The great black bags under Nikolous's eyes lifted and he squinted. This all for a brief second, and then they were staring at him again, unmoved.

"Leave us, Martha," Nikolous said without turning to her.

She hefted herself up and frowned at Jason. The caretaker walked out only when Jason and Leiah stepped aside to avoid her ample frame.

Jason closed the door. "You find her at a Halloween party, Nikolous?"

The Greek ignored the comment. "Who says they're deporting the boy? Why haven't I been told?"

"You are being told. Frankly I don't think the responsible party wants you to know."

"Tell me."

Jason looked at Leiah and saw why the Father chose to avoid her stare; to say there was anger cast his way would trivialize her expression. She glanced at Jason as if to offer her agreement, and they sat in the two chairs facing his desk.

He told Nikolous of his conversation with John Gardner from World Relief, who called out of courtesy, only because he'd been incidentally informed by a friend at the INS that the deportation would go down. "So before you carry on with indignation, you should keep in mind that it's thanks to me you're learning of this at all."

That seemed to temper the Greek long enough for Jason to explain that for all practical purposes, they were pretty much in a headlock. Caleb would be gone within twenty-four hours. Forty-eight if they were lucky.

Nikolous heard it all wearing his stately air of disapproval and then stood and walked for the window. He crossed his arms and stroked his mustache.

"There is one thing we might try," Jason said.

Nikolous half turned and eyed him.

Jason could almost feel Leiah cringe beside him. "If we could get Caleb into the public eye, the INS might hesitate."

Nikolous turned slowly and dropped his arms.

Jason continued. "It would have to be in a real big way, I think, but it would make them explain themselves."

"And we have only forty-eight hours?"

"Or less."

"The first meeting is not scheduled until Saturday," Nikolous said.

"The first?" Leiah said.

Nikolous ignored her. "We would have to move it up."

"And you'd need to have it well attended and well publicized. The networks would have to be persuaded to carry the event."

"Tomorrow night?"

Jason nodded. Understanding lit the Greek's eyes. He was walking toward his phone already. Jason gave Leiah a reassuring smile. She managed to return it.

Nikolous punched in a string of numbers and swiveled toward towering bookcases. He was clearly in his element.

"Hello, Donna. I'm afraid we have a problem. What does your schedule look like tomorrow evening?"

He listened and then quickly highlighted the situation. In under three minutes it was done. The Greek dropped the phone ceremoniously in its cradle and looked at them.

"We will have our meeting tomorrow night."

"Where?"

"If we can't reschedule the Old Theater, I will find a suitable location. In the worst case we will use our auditorium."

"How will you find enough people to attend by then?" Leiah asked.

Nikolous grinned at her. "Don't worry, my dear. I'll deliver the people and the media. And you would do well to encourage our boy's participation, yes?"

Jason spoke before she could. "Let's hope the INS doesn't show up before tomorrow night."

"Yes, let's hope," Nikolous said.

The matter was settled, then. The Greek was reaching for his phone as they left; he had a meeting to plan. Perhaps the biggest meeting of his life.

∞

Martha made them wait twenty minutes until the one-o'clock hour before she called them to cross the play yard and enter the West Wing, as she called Caleb's prison.

Caleb was there, sitting on one of the large gray couches when they entered, and Leiah's pulse surged. They kept him dressed in shorts that came to his knees and high socks, like a schoolboy all dressed up for his visits. His aqua eyes shone round, and he cracked a wide grin the moment he saw them.

Martha stood near the wall, her arms crossed, looking disinterested but hawkish nonetheless.

Caleb swung from the couch and ran for them. Leiah dipped to one knee and met him with open arms.

"Hello, Caleb."

She hugged him tight, and truth be told, she did not want to let go. His long curls swept across her chin and she kissed his head. "Oh boy, do I love you." Leiah rubbed his back and then pushed him back to look at him. "I'm so proud of you. Do you know that?"

He grinned and looked up at Jason, who ruffled his hair and then lifted him for a hug. They were like a small family. An impossible, disjointed one without the blessing of union, but a family anyway.

Jason carried Caleb over to the couches and plopped him down with a bounce. Caleb giggled, rolled onto his seat, and pushed himself back between them. He spoke very rarely, and then only in short sentences, often in Amharic. Although he possessed a decent enough command of the English language, he shied from it, as he did from nearly all things Western.

"So how are they treating you, son?" Jason asked, gripping the boy's knee gently.

Caleb smiled and his eyes skipped to Martha.

Jason turned to the caretaker. "Don't you have some laundry to do or something?"

She glared at him and then marched off with a humph. But she didn't leave the room. The kitchen, forty feet off, was as far as she would remove herself during their visits.

Satisfied, Jason faced Caleb again. He winked. "Don't worry; she can't hear if we talk quiet. So are you okay?"

He nodded. "Yes."

He tilted his head down. "Really good?"

"Yes." He looked at them, self-conscious perhaps. But then he reached forward and put his small hands on top of each of theirs. They took his hands and he grinned, but he didn't elaborate.

Leiah felt her heart melt as it always did in the boy's company. At first, back on the road in Ethiopia, she'd guessed that her unique bond with Caleb came compliments of their shared isolation. He as a prodigy locked in a monastery; she as an outcast wrapped in scars. But in the nine days since their coming to California, she'd seen something else in the boy. Caleb wasn't isolated at all. He was simply living in another world somewhere. A world very different from the one she saw. A world that held him in full contentment, like a child curled up in his mother's lap, smiling and asleep.

She'd told Jason that Caleb was too wounded to know the difference between an abusive situation and a healthy one. In reality she suspected that he was too healthy to feel the difference. And she knew that whatever the boy believed, she craved. Because in many ways they were very much alike; their difference lay in their maturity. She wondered what it would take for her to rise to the boy's level.

The thought of going further, of maybe even mothering the child, made her bones feel wobbly.

Leiah took his hand in both of hers and rubbed it. "Are they feeding you well?"

"Yes."

"What do they feed you?"

He thought about that. "Milk. Bread. Porridge." He flashed pearly white teeth.

"That sounds good. Milk, huh?" She looked down the hall and asked the same question she'd asked every visit. "And you're sure you're comfortable in your room?"

"Yes."

"Okay. Because if there's any problem you would tell us, right?"

"Yes."

Why Nikolous had banned any person but Martha from visiting his room, she could hardly fathom. The thought gave her a headache. But the Greek had promised a restraining order if they violated the terms of their visits. Jason had sneaked down the hall on the second day, during a moment when Martha had waddled off to fetch a screaming child in the yard. He'd poked his head in and returned to announce that it was simple but clean enough.

Still, the restriction alone was enough to fill her with doubts.

"And what about the . . . what about Martha?" Jason asked.

Caleb looked at him without answering.

"Is she good to you?"

"Not always."

His answer took Leiah off guard. *Not always?* It was the first time he'd said anything less than glowing.

"What do you mean? She's hurting you?" she demanded in a hushed tone.

"No. She is leaving the moving pictures on all the time."

"What moving pictures?"

"The television?" Jason asked.

"The box with pictures that move." Caleb lifted questioning brows.

"The television!" Jason said, smiling.

Caleb smiled with him. "Yes. The tele . . . vision."

"They have a television in his room and he doesn't like it," Jason explained to Leiah.

"I think I got that," she said. And then to the boy, "We'll tell her to turn off the television, Caleb. I promise."

He rattled off something in Ge'ez and then grinned wide.

They talked for another ten minutes in the same short spurts. Unless addressed directly, Caleb seemed content to sit by them, as if their presence alone brought great satisfaction.

"Caleb, there's something I need to tell you," Jason finally said. "There are some people who want to send you back to Ethiopia."

"Yes?"

"But your father didn't want you to be in Ethiopia. He wanted you to be here, with us."

The boy nodded.

"Well, we may be able to keep you here, but we need your help. Tomorrow there'll be a meeting. You should go to the meeting and . . ." He was obviously stumbling over how to describe what it was Caleb did. The boy just stared at him, and Leiah suppressed the urge to lean over and kiss his forehead. She smiled without thinking. " . . . do your . . . use your power. You should show the people that you can do many strange, wonderful things. Very good things." He stopped there and let his analysis rest.

He seemed bothered even by the simple description of Caleb's power, she thought. Regardless of its source, you could hardly deny that feats like straightening crooked legs and opening blind eyes were miraculous.

"They want you to do lots of miracles," Leiah said. "Can you do that?"

Caleb looked up at her with big eyes and then seemed to understand. "Maybe," he said with a small smile.

Jason shifted on the couch. "That's good." He paused. "Caleb, I know we haven't talked a lot about, you know, your miracles, as Leiah says. But it would be helpful to know how you do them. They say that it's psychic, a power of your mind, but how? How do you make a blind boy see?"

They had agreed not to probe Caleb about the matter.

"Jason—"

The boy cut her off with a long string of words in Ge'ez. He sounded confident and strong but not angry. It was a diatribe neither of them could possibly begin to understand. Caleb ended, took a short breath, and then spoke in English. "Why is the way of God so unknown to you?"

Jason's face flushed red and he turned away. "Well, I don't really know the *way* of God, but if he does have a way with man, it makes about as much sense as the dialect of Ge'ez you insist on speaking."

"Jason!"

He turned to her, unable to hide his frustration. "Come on, Leiah. He can heal people, for heaven's sakes! I for one want to know how."

"I'm sure we all do. But we agreed not to go there."

"Well, now we are there. And frankly I wouldn't mind knowing for myself why a little girl minding her own business at a convention hall is granted a full life, while my son lies six feet under."

It was a frustration that seemed completely out of context to her. Had he lost his senses? "Get ahold of yourself, Jason!"

He closed his eyes and turned away.

A soft, high-pitched note suddenly filled her ears.

Leiah looked down at Caleb. He had pulled his knees up under his chin and was rocking back and forth with his eyes closed. He'd clamped his hands firmly over his ears, and his small lips quivered with wordless song.

Leiah didn't understand what happened next; she only knew that one moment she and Jason (although mostly Jason) were venting frustration that had built for a week, and the next they were both crying inexplicably.

The notes from Caleb's lips seemed to sweep through her like a drug, incapacitating her will to restrain the sorrow already hiding in her veins. That's how it felt. And suddenly she was weeping.

It was an impossible moment; one that terrified her at first. She scrambled for understanding, and for a few seconds she tried desperately to recheck her emotion, but then with one loud sob she let herself go.

What anger she'd felt for Jason melted with the next few tears. She wept for the boy. No, she wept for herself. For her own wounded spirit that begged to find peace.

Leiah put a hand on Caleb's head and stroked his hair. Her tears blurred her vision, but she saw that Jason's shoulders were shaking under great silent sobs, and it made her put aside her last wedge of restraint. She pulled the boy to her chest and rocked with him, weeping. He stopped singing and let her hold him, and the sorrow flowed from her eyes like a tide.

Leiah didn't know how long they held each other, only that when she looked up, Jason was leaning back on the cushions with red eyes and Martha was gone.

They sat dumbly in an afterglow for ten minutes, smiling and speaking little. But Leiah couldn't remember what was said. When they stood to leave, she thought she saw Martha peering out at them from down the dark hall, but she couldn't be sure.

They left Caleb sitting alone on the couch as they'd found him. She still had no clue what had happened. By the looks of it, neither did Jason. He blushed when she made direct eye contact, and his smile made her swallow.

Maybe they'd been touched by God, if there even was a God—she didn't know. But she did know one thing: as long as she had breath to live and strength to fight, she would never, ever let them take away Caleb. Never.

It wasn't until three o'clock that they remembered to call Martha and insist she get rid of the television. She grunted and then snapped a "Fine" before hanging up on them.

15

Tʜᴇʏ ᴄᴀʟʟᴇᴅ ɪᴛ ᴛʜᴇ Oʟᴅ Tʜᴇᴀᴛᴇʀ because when they'd expanded the monster in the late seventies, they'd kept the stage area intact for the-atrical events instead of replacing it with seats as in some renovated theaters. But in reality the brick building was more an arena than a theater, complete with facilities to accommodate any large-venue meeting as well as a variety of sporting events.

If you packed the main floor with folding chairs, the building sat ten thousand: three thousand on the wood floor, four thousand on the first tier of orange seats ringing the auditorium, and another three thousand on the upper tier, the latter referred to as the red seats, evidently the cheap seats. The seats ran in sections, each marked by lighted signs mounted above passage-ways that opened to the outer walkway. Except for the stage at the north end, it was a typical arena layout.

The stage stood five feet above the floor, cocooned in massive purple cur-tains that swept to either side, reminiscent of the oldest theaters. A gray carpet covered the floor, but it creaked when you walked on it, evidence of its age. An old upright piano sat alone on the west side of the stage, but otherwise it was bare tonight. Unless you counted the single mike stand, of course. It stood in the middle, facing the dim expanse like a lost tin soldier. On either side, stage exits, draped with the same purple cloth as the curtains, led backstage.

Jason stood on the large platform and scanned the auditorium, thinking that his part in this impossible show was not unlike a secret service agent, checking out a venue before the dignitaries arrived, in this case Caleb. He wasn't sure exactly what he was checking the place for; maybe the odd char-acter who might be an INS agent, although any INS agent he'd ever seen could as easily be any Joe Blow as an immigration agent. The authorities hadn't come for Caleb yet, and for that Jason assumed he had either plain old bureaucracy or John Gardner to thank. But he wouldn't put it past the agency to march in at any moment and demand custody of the boy.

The Greek knew how to crank up an event; that much was clear. It was no mistake that he had worked his way into one of the largest Greek Orthodox churches this side of the Atlantic. He was a businessman to the core, and Jason couldn't help thinking the man was clearly misplaced. He belonged on Wall Street perhaps. Or in Hollywood. Then again, some churches weren't so different from Wall Street or Hollywood.

At any rate, the Greek had done in twenty-four hours what should have taken two weeks. It had cost, of course, an entire Sunday's offering at least. The facility alone ran five thousand dollars, and so little only because Nikolous had pulled out his nonprofit tricks and made some other undisclosed guarantees. Then there were the short-take radio ads that had played nonstop on a dozen Los Angeles stations, announcing a "free magic show guaranteed to blow the mind" at the Old Theater on Figueroa Street in downtown L.A. The ad mentioned healings, but only as a side note. They'd plastered a thousand neon orange posters up and down the surrounding streets, each with the caption *A mind-blowing look at the impossible!* stamped below a black-and-white shot of Caleb looking innocent and somewhat mysterious. In all, the costs had to have exceeded fifteen thousand dollars.

The fact sat in Jason's skull like an undiagnosed tumor. It was fine that the Greek had gone to such lengths in an attempt to save Caleb, but the greedy snake wouldn't have coughed up a single penny unless he expected returns. Big returns.

By the looks of it, Nikolous's one-day advertising blitz had attracted a few thousand lost souls in search of something either free or spectacular on this Tuesday evening. The facility was about a third full.

They were from all walks of life, all ages, both genders, mostly seated on the main floor but scattered through the tiers as well. People in shorts, people in jeans, people in suits, people in dresses—the fans of magic. A scattering of physically handicapped in wheelchairs and walkers as well. And as far as Jason could tell they *all* had lizard eyes. Maybe because he was the only one on the stage right now, and they were trying to decide if this man dressed in blue jeans and a white pullover was the magic man who would blow their minds.

The center front row was occupied by the full mix. An older woman in a yellow dress who fanned herself with a folded neon poster sat beside a young girl in pigtails—her granddaughter perhaps. A man in his forties with toothpicks for arms and legs and jeans two inches too short sat by them. Two empty seats and then two teenagers with pants hanging a good foot below their crotches. The row was capped by a middle-aged man engrossed in a novel angled for optimum lighting. If any on the row were INS, it would be he.

Nikolous had taped off a thirty-by-sixty section on the left for the media. A half-dozen local reporters sat with recorders and notebooks, staring up at the competition and probably wondering what on earth NBC knew that they didn't. Donna's three-man crew had set up shop on a small step-up platform that elevated the camera tripod above any possible interference. A single camera-man sat behind the gaping lens aiming his contraption at Donna, who was speaking into a mike clipped to her blouse.

Her voice rose just above the cacophony of background voices. "That was my interview with Dr. Patricia Caldwell earlier this afternoon. As you may have gathered, the incident at UCLA occurred over a week ago and it wasn't taped, but let me assure you, it was most remarkable. Tonight for the first time we will see little Caleb on camera, and if the past is any indication, we may be in for a mind-bending ride. Let me assure you, there are no secret wires or hidden cameras or trick boxes that we've all associated with illusion-ists. There is only Caleb. But then Caleb is not so ordinary; I think you'll see that. Trust me, this is one show you don't want to miss. Jeff, back to you."

So they had decided to shoot the event live? Nikolous had told them it would be taped and shown on the late news if the producers gave it a thumbs-up. Jason saw the small dish mounted behind the camera and he had his answer. They were at least prepared to go live, if events warranted. Donna had her clout, no doubt about that.

He quickly stepped to his right and ducked behind the curtains back-stage. Nikolous stood by some huge canvas backdrops (presumably left over from a production) talking to one of the stagehands he'd assembled from his church.

Caleb sat on a folding chair beside Leiah, who stood over him like a pro-tective hen. She had one hand on his shoulder and the other one at her mouth, biting nervously on a fingernail. She saw Jason and he watched the relief settle over her like a cool shower.

They'd dressed Caleb in long black slacks and a white short-sleeve dress shirt, complete with a brass-buckled belt and a red bow tie. His shoes were new too—black leather tie-ups. His hair fell to his shoulders, and his eyes peered up at Jason like pools of deep ocean water.

A thin sheen of sweat glistened on his upper lip; otherwise there was no sign that the boy was nervous.

"You ready for this, Caleb?"

The boy didn't respond, and Jason looked up at Leiah. "It looks like they're shooting it live," he said quietly.

"Live? But what if—"

"I'm sure they'll only go to it if . . . things work out." He noted a tremor in his right hand, and he shoved his hands in his pockets. "Don't worry; it's all going to work out."

"It feels insane," she said. "What if the Immigration Service is out there waiting for him?"

"I think they'd come back here, don't you? We're okay," he said with as much confidence as he could muster. In truth the INS was completely unpredictable. The NSA was even worse.

"So basically it comes down to whether or not he . . ." She let the statement trail off, and he gave her a reassuring smile.

"Pretty much."

They'd both had their worlds rocked yesterday, sitting on the couch with Caleb, and neither one quite knew what to do with the experience, he thought. They had talked about it briefly and agreed on one thing: what they had felt was not a figment of their imagination. Caleb's simple song had somehow infected them. It hadn't overpowered them; it wasn't as if they had wept without the power to walk away. But it had been very persuasive to say the least.

If either of them had harbored any lingering doubt about the boy's power, they'd dismissed it yesterday. The only question that remained was whether Caleb really could turn the power on and off at will, as if it were a fire hose.

By the looks of it they were about to find out.

"Prepare the boy," Nikolous said, approaching, hands clasped behind his back. He would emcee the event in grand style, and he obviously fancied the part. He was all black. Shiny black hair, black mustache, black double-breasted suit, black shoes . . . *and if you got in there with the right instrument, you would find a heart to match,* Jason thought.

"And I don't have to remind you what this evening means," he said, and then turned to his right-hand man—the tall, skinny butler-type from the offices who now shadowed Nikolous, radio in hand. "Tell them to start the music and dim the lights."

The man spoke quickly into his walkie-talkie, and within seconds the lights eased down. A low-pitched note rumbled through the auditorium. The ambient noise beyond the stage walls fell as those gathered took their seats. He heard someone cough in the direction of NBC's setup, and he wondered if it was Donna.

Nikolous pulled the side curtain open and hooked it on the wall. From where they stood, Jason had a clear view of the stage and roughly half of the auditorium, including the camera now under power and winking green. The low, sustained note grew to a bone-trembling volume, and a hush settled over them all.

Nikolous pulled at his lapels, hiked up his shoulders one last time, and strode out onto the stage. Immediately a white circle of light popped on him and followed him to the mike stand. The stand was set low, to Caleb's height, and Nikolous lifted the cordless microphone out of its stand.

"Ladies and gentlemen, I thank you for joining us on this fine evening. You are the few brave enough to believe, and for that you will see what few have ever witnessed. I promise you." Nikolous had already decided that the boy was going to perform; that much was obvious.

"You will see no magic tonight." A few objections peppered the auditorium. "No, no magic. What you will see is a psychic phenomenon never before seen, much less caught on camera. There will be no mastery of illusion or sleight of hand. There will only be real flesh and blood, doing what real flesh and blood could not possibly do. Unless of course you are a small boy with exceptional powers. Unless you are Caleb. Or unless you are *with* Caleb. Because if you are with Caleb, the rules change."

The air felt charged with static. Caleb stared at the Greek and the sweat had spread to his forehead. A flash of doubt shot through Jason's mind. What if he did fail? What if he walked out there and just froze up? It would be a death sentence. Perhaps in more ways than they imagined.

"So then, let me present to you for the first time"—Nikolous lifted a hand toward the side entrance, and Jason's stomach cinched to a knot—"a boy who will destroy your sense of reason . . ." He paused and then announced in full volume, "Caleb."

The audience hesitated as the name reverberated around the arena. A smattering of applause broke out.

Leiah led Caleb forward to the side curtain and knelt beside him.

Nikolous approached from the microphone. They were to send him out after Nikolous had cleared the stage.

"Listen to me, Caleb," Leiah said. "They won't hurt you. When I tell you, go out like we talked about, okay? Don't be afraid." She ran a hand through his hair and kissed his cheek. "Jason and I will be right here."

Nikolous arrived. "Go," he whispered.

Leiah aimed Caleb for the microphone and let him go.

At first the boy did not move, and Jason thought his fears were being realized; the boy had frozen. But then Caleb took a step, albeit a slow one on legs that were now quivering. His hands hung loosely by his sides, and he quaked like a willow in the wind.

Leiah reached for him, but Jason grabbed her arm.

The boy walked toward the single chrome mike stand, and they held their collective breath. The spotlight blazed, and he hesitated for just a moment before completing the long walk to the microphone. The applause had died, and now only the atmospheric organ music throbbed in a low bass.

Caleb reached the microphone and faced it. He stood stock-still. Nothing happened. He shifted uneasily on his feet and stared out.

"What's he doing?" Nikolous rumbled quietly.

Caleb looked at them once, looked back at the audience, and then simply walked back toward them without uttering a word.

He had frozen.

Leiah rushed out and guided the boy the last few feet. "What's wrong, dear?"

"What are you doing?" Nikolous whispered harshly. They huddled around him in near panic. Soft rumbles rippled through the audience.

Jason took Caleb by the shoulders. "It's okay, Caleb. You only need to do what you can do, okay? What happened?"

"He froze!" Nikolous said. "Holy—"

"Shut up!"

Jason turned back to the boy. "Caleb, remember what we—"

"They're gone," Caleb said.

"They're gone? Who's gone?"

"The people are gone," he said.

"He can't see past the spotlight!" Leiah said.

Nikolous bolted up and snapped at the butler. "The lights! Tell the fools to shut down the spotlight! He can't see past the lights. Use backlights!"

The skinny man snapped the order into his radio.

A loud clunk sounded and the lights died. A soft amber light swelled from above and cast golden hues over the stage.

Nikolous patted his forehead with a folded napkin, smoothed his mustache, and marched out to the microphone. "Ladies and gentlemen, pardon us, but it seems the boy could not see with the bright lights. Thank you for your patience." He walked back with long strides.

"Are you okay, Caleb?" Leiah asked. "You really don't have—"

"You'll be fine, Caleb," Jason interrupted, kneeling by him. What was Leiah thinking? The boy's own survival depended on this. "Go on," he said, but the encouragement fell flat.

Caleb turned from them and started the long trek out to the microphone a second time. He was putting on a brave front, but he could neither hide the sweat that beaded his little face, nor the tremor that clung stubbornly to his bones. He reached center stage and faced the crowd. Three thousand sets of lizard eyes held him in their stares. The organ drew long, low, eerie notes.

And nothing happened.

Caleb had been at the microphone twenty uneventful seconds, staring dumbly at the crowds, when the music suddenly stopped, midrefrain, as if someone had bumped the needle on a record. A loud static sounded for a moment and then total silence. Someone snickered in the crowd. Things were not proceeding as planned.

Nikolous cursed in Greek under his breath, grabbed the butler by the arm, and jerked him toward the deeper shadows. The skinny man stumbled and would have fallen but for the other's grip. "Get someone in a wheelchair up there!" Nikolous snapped. "Tell them to grab one of the ill ones and get them on the stage immediately!"

The butler barked his order into the radio, loudly enough for at least the first dozen rows to hear. Fortunately he spoke in Greek.

Caleb looked their way, clearly at a loss. Leiah paced and gnawed at her fingers, and Jason thought she might run out and collect the boy at any moment. He glanced toward the NBC crew and saw that they'd crossed their arms and were shifting uneasily. The camera's green light blinked steadily; they were still on camera, though he doubted very much that they were live. Back at the studios, the anchor, presumably a good-looking fellow named Jeff, was probably talking about the smog alert that day or some other tidbit that preempted this fiasco.

Jason felt the drumming of his own heart, and he wiped his palms. It could be his own son, Stephen, out there, dying in front of the crowd. He and Ailsa had ignored their better judgment and agreed to put little Stephen onstage at the church once. It was before ALS had crippled him beyond standing; before the saints had decided they would rid his little boy of the disease if they had to beat it out of him. The pastor had interviewed him, and Stephen had frozen.

Like Caleb.

A surge of remorse swept through Jason's chest, and he ground his molars. If the stakes were not what they were, he would go out there and tell them all what they could do with their lizard eyes.

Then again, for the most part the crowd stared quietly at this small boy, who stood innocently on the stage before them. He wasn't blowing their minds, to be sure, but he was pulling at their sympathies, Jason thought. Otherwise there would be catcalls and whistles.

A commotion on the far side caught his attention. Three stagehands had a wheelchair-bound man in his midtwenties hoisted shoulder-high and were jogging him down the left side at a frightening clip. They'd evidently found a willing participant in response to Nikolous's demand. He was paraplegic by the look of his spindly legs that flopped about uncontrolled as they ran. If the man agreed to a trip up front, Jason doubted he'd bargained for the route his bearers had chosen.

The young man began to protest loudly ten yards from the stage, but by then it was already too late. The three men hoisted the red sports chair over the lip of the stage and pushed the paraplegic out onto the floor without aim. The chair rolled across the stage and stopped with its back to Caleb, twenty feet from where Jason and Leiah stood.

The man's left leg had fallen out of its rest and hung like a loose wire capped with its black shoe. His face turned white with mortification, and his lips wrinkled in a sudden fit of anger. He grabbed at his wheels and spun his chair around to face the boy, ignoring his loose leg for the moment.

Silence swept through the arena, until Jason could hear only his own pulse and the gentle murmur of the air units high above. The crowd shifted forward on their seats or raised on their tiptoes for a better view. Jason felt

Leiah's hand circle his elbow and squeeze. She was trembling. Maybe it was just his arm trembling.

For a moment he thought the paraplegic might rush Caleb, but he didn't. He just faced him, like a gunfighter with his hands on either wheel. The boy looked back, but he didn't turn. Beyond them the television camera flashed a steady green, and Donna had a mike to her unmoving lips. For an eternity it stayed just like that.

And then Caleb turned to face the man in the wheelchair. Neither moved. From the back of the arena it might have looked like a confrontation, a standoff of some kind. But up close it was a melding, Jason thought. They were looking into each other's eyes, and what they saw was slowly making the rest of their surroundings fall away.

If the boy had been frozen a minute ago, he was now thawed. Jason watched him for a few seconds before realizing that Caleb was actually crying. The amber light glinted off thin trails that ran down each cheek. His wide eyes seemed to droop, and he tilted his head ever so slightly. Caleb stared at the man with a kindness and empathy Jason had never seen. He swallowed and fought to control his emotions.

The young man's hair was short, standing straight up an inch, and it was suddenly quivering. His entire body began to shake. A single restrained sob escaped him, and it echoed through the auditorium like a gunshot. Heat washed down Jason's spine. The lady on the front row with the fan whispered a teary, "Lord, have mercy on him."

The paraplegic's hands fell off his wheels and hung limply. His whole body began to convulse with sobs and the boy just stared at him, weeping silently. The man suddenly dropped his head back and sagged in his chair. His mouth gaped, and he wept without air in a torturous silence. When he came to the end of himself, he gasped loudly and sobbed again, long and silent.

Caleb closed his eyes, spread his arms out, and tilted his head to face the ceiling. His mouth opened in a silent cry. And then he closed his mouth and spoke a single word in his mother tongue. *"Hara."*

Yes.

Jason felt a pulse rush through his body with that word. As if the boy had detonated a small bomb on stage and its concussion had slammed through his body. He caught his breath. Then it was gone.

Gasps and cries of alarm filled the auditorium. The NBC crew were looking around in a stupor. Donna was frantically mouthing something to the man behind the camera, and he ducked his head back to the eyepiece. They were going live. Beside him Leiah released a sob.

The boy lowered his head and strode purposefully to the man, a grin splitting his face now. He had that look, the one of desperate eagerness that Jason had seen at the convention hall. The paraplegic met the boy's onrush as if they'd agreed it was a good thing. By the time Caleb reached the man, he'd picked up good speed. He slid a good four feet on his shiny new black shoes before coming to a stop and grasping the man's hands.

They clasped each other's hands, and Caleb was speaking in Ge'ez. Their bodies shook as if an electric current had juiced them up. The man suddenly gasped and held his breath. His left leg—the loose one without a shred of muscle—shot straight out and stuck there with the shoe flopped to one side. The man took his eyes off Caleb and stared at it, aghast.

They all watched that leg, and there could be no mistaking the matter— it was changing. Growing. Getting fatter. The blue slacks lost their stick look and swelled. The shoe snapped straight, and in a span of ten seconds the paraplegic's leg looked like any leg outfitted in blue slacks.

Caleb was laughing. A child at play.

The cheap seats had nearly emptied, and the audience flooded the floor now. Mutters of exclamation and astonishment rippled through the arena.

Caleb began to hop up and down with excitement. He suddenly yanked on the man's arm and pulled him from the chair.

But the man did not stand.

Jason watched in horror as they fell together—Caleb backward and the man on top of him, sprawling like tangled newborn colts.

Cries of alarm erupted about the stadium. Angry shouts of protest.

Caleb and the man rolled over once and then the boy sprang to his feet. He began to hop again as if it were all part of a great game. The man looked up at him, drew his feet under his body, and stood slowly on wobbly legs.

That shut the crowd up.

A grin cracked the young man's face. A chuckle. He took a step forward. Then another. He gripped his legs and felt through the cloth, and they watched like hound dogs, in breathless silence.

The man suddenly threw back his head and let out a bloodcurdling scream. "Yaaaahoooo!"

Even Jason jumped.

The jubilant man, now with full use of his legs, began to yell and jump with Caleb. "My legs, my legs, my legs!" he repeated over and over. He picked the boy up and squeezed him tight and then spun in circles. Caleb giggled in high pitch and Jason laughed with them. It was infectious.

Suddenly the boy was on his seat and the man leapt for his red chair. He picked it up, swung it around once, and hurled it through the air. It smashed into the back wall and clattered noisily to the floor. Caleb leapt to his feet and began to hop again.

They were like two children. They *were* two children, for all meaningful purposes, dancing this dance of theirs while three thousand people gaped in awe. A general roar filled the place. Voices of praise, voices of amazement, voices of doubt, voices of outrage—the voice of humanity all mixed together in one messy ball.

"Praise the Lord! Praise the blessed Lord!" the old woman in the front row cried.

"It's a sham! That's nothin' but a sham," the skinny nerd next to her said, but he was staring nonetheless. The two teenagers watched the stage with wide eyes. The whole place was on its feet and shouting in confusion.

But the boy was ecstatic.

He ran around the healed man, who was bouncing like a pogo stick, and the volume of outcry rose.

What had happened this far was enough to spawn a thousand interesting debates over coffee, but what happened next made *Caleb* a household name.

Jason didn't know if it was all the noise or simply the boy's enthusiasm that triggered his next move, but one second Caleb was rounding the man, and the next he was rushing the front of the stage. His aqua eyes were fired with excitement, and he still grinned mischievously.

He slid to a stop at the edge of the stage, scanned the audience with a single sweep of his head, and then threw his head back and sang to the sky.

The note that broke from his throat was pure and high, and it pierced the air like an arrow slicing though the fog.

It's Ge'ez, Jason thought.

But it was all he thought, because the boy's song seemed to spin his mind backward. The world fell into slow motion about him. Caleb was there, head jutted out to the crowd, eyes closed, singing with lips round like a Cheerio.

The camera was winking green at him, and a thousand onlookers had their mouths open, but all of it seemed to have slowed to a crawl.

And the sound was gone.

Except for the song. Caleb's notes filled his soul.

For a brief moment everything froze. And then something hit Jason's chest and he crumpled to his knees, dazed and numb. He slumped against the stage entrance, fighting against a thick sea of energy. But his strength was gone. That was all.

But it wasn't only him. Leiah lay facedown beside him, as though she were dead. A body nudged his heel, and he saw that it was Nikolous. The Greek was on his back.

Jason forced his head up. The man who'd tossed his wheelchair lay on his back, facing the ceiling for the second time. And the audience . . .

The audience was collapsing before his eyes!

Jason's mind screamed with alarm, but his body didn't flinch. He simply watched the madness unfold. It was like an invisible wave of raw power that started on the left and rolled across the auditorium, tossing whatever stood in its path to the floor. If they were standing, as many of them were, they crashed to their seats or crumpled to the floor. If they were seated, they slumped in their chairs. The wave approached the NBC camera, which had spun to face it. Donna staggered and then fell to her side as if unable to hold a large weight that had been dropped on her back. The cameraman slumped in his seat, jerking the camera badly. Jason watched as he slipped out of his seat and thumped to the floor. The wave took no more than two seconds to cover the auditorium.

And then there was absolute stillness.

From the corner of his eye, Jason saw the yellow light on the NBC dish and he knew they were live. The world was watching.

Caleb looked over the crowd and spoke in English. "You should not doubt the power of God." Then he grinned again.

They heard it. Sure they did, because Jason heard it, clear as day.

∞

Jason stood to his feet slowly. The world was still woozy; a warm contentment had settled in his mind. He thought it would be good to sit, so he eased himself out on the stage and sat. He swung his legs over the lip and faced the mess.

And it was that. A mess. Bodies lay strewn over each other where they had fallen. Half had pushed themselves to their feet, but few had found the resolve to stand. The old woman up front lay flat on her back, wearing a huge grin that made Jason smile. Her granddaughter sat at her feet staring up at Caleb with round eyes. The vocal nerd to their right had his face planted on the floor, and his hands and legs spread wide to either side. The two teenagers lay next to each other like twins, still oblivious to the world. And the businessman at the end of the row had somehow ended up with his feet on his chair and his back on the floor. He didn't seem in a hurry to reverse the arrangement.

It was a mess. But it wasn't a bad mess.

A woman had stood and was picking her way to the front. In her arms lay a young boy, perhaps three or four years of age. Even from where he was, Jason could see that the child's legs were crippled. He'd seen legs like those before. A vise seemed to squeeze Jason's chest.

She brought the child to the floor directly in front of Caleb, who watched her silently. The cameraman had managed to climb back on his stool, and he swung the camera back to the boy. Donna had pulled herself into a seat and was talking into a mike, dazed. She was telling them what had happened. Of course that was absurd, because she knew no more than Jason did about what had just happened.

Either way it *had* happened. That was the point. It had really happened, right in front of a camera hot-wired into twenty million homes.

And now another thing was happening. Now the mother was laying her child at the feet of Caleb, and the boy was looking desperate again. Caleb dropped to his knees, placed his hands on the child's face, and muttered excitedly in Ge'ez.

Then he stood, stepped to one side adjacent to the child, and faced the crowd. Beside him the young child stirred and sat up, dazed. His mother began to wail. If Caleb noticed, he didn't show it. He raised his hands to the crowd and spoke a long string of words in his own language.

Beside him the four-year-old stood up on quaking legs. Caleb lowered his hands and began to skip across the stage. The cries came from all across the auditorium, then sudden exclamations of surprise as those who had come with illness discovered that they were no longer ill. And those who came with debilitating handicaps were no more handicapped than the young man who'd thrown his wheelchair across the stage, or the young child who now walked in small circles while his mother wept uncontrollably.

16

THE MEETING LASTED ANOTHER HOUR, but mostly it was over ten minutes later, when Nikolous strode out and ushered Caleb offstage without any further words. The rest was aftermath.

Donna made her way through the crowd interviewing those interested in telling their tale. As far as they could tell, ninety-eight people had come to the meeting suffering from some sort of ailment, and all ninety-eight left totally whole. A dozen theories were offered as to the cause of the wave that knocked them all over, and a dozen more as to the source of the boy's power. And that on the floor of the arena, before the talking heads on television had a chance to sink their teeth into what they saw.

The spectacular footage captured by NBC's crew was broadcast live on over two hundred affiliates, and then picked up and rebroadcast on all the other major networks and cable channels before the ten-o'clock hour. By midnight Eastern time over forty million households had either seen the small boy named Caleb or heard his story.

As it turned out, it wasn't the paraplegic who'd thrown his chair, or even the sudden inexplicable crumpling of the entire audience (cameraman included), that captured the greatest attention. Although mind-numbing enough, both could have been staged, a dozen commentators quickly pointed out. But it was the small boy who'd been laid at Caleb's feet that pretty much shut the commentators up. The camera had zoomed in on his naked, twisted legs after Caleb had touched him. They all saw the bones twist and straighten and grow, close up, as if it were a special effect from a science-fiction flick.

Only it wasn't a special effect. It was live footage shot by a high-definition camera manned by a card-carrying NBC cameraman named Phillip Strantz, who'd been working for the network a good twelve years.

Shown together with the young man hurling his red chair and the wave knocking them all into a definitive silence, the footage took the country by storm.

Jason and Leiah left the Old Theater at ten that night.

It occurred to Jason that Leiah hadn't been healed of her scars. But then she'd insisted before that she didn't need anybody's help. She really didn't need to be healed, did she? No, she did not.

∞

Stewart Long was in the garage messing with a stripped socket wrench at ten o'clock Tuesday night when Barbara hollered through the kitchen.

"Stew! Stew get in here . . . you have to see this."

"Hold on. I'm almost finished."

"You'll miss it! Get in here!"

"Okay . . . okay." Stewart threw the wrench back in the toolbox with a grunt. At least it was a Craftsman, which meant he could replace it at no charge. He grabbed an old T-shirt rag and walked through the kitchen wiping his hands.

Barbara and Peter both had their eyes glued to the big Sony television in the living room. "What is it?"

They didn't respond, and he walked behind his son. Three facts settled in his mind at once—not necessarily critical facts, just the kind that police officers learn to mind. Fact one, they were watching NBC news with that Donna chick. Fact two, the Donna chick was at a meeting of some kind—a convention or a religious gathering—and she was definitely worked up. Fact three, both Peter and Barbara looked like they were watching news of a bomb's detonation or the president's assassination rather than coverage of a convention.

It struck him only then that many of the people in the picture behind Donna were on the floor. "I know this looks unusual . . ." Donna was saying. "Well, it looks impossible actually, and to be honest, I might not believe it if I wasn't here myself, but something very dramatic did indeed happen, ladies and gentlemen. And not just to the people you see behind me, but to me." Her eyes glinted with eagerness. "We can't necessarily explain what we're seeing, but we can assure you that it is real. No tricks, no gimmicks, no wires. Just a little boy's power. Let's watch the footage again and let you experience for yourselves what we experienced."

The picture suddenly cut to a screen with white words "recorded earlier" flashing at the upper left.

"Watch this, Stew," Barbara said.

"I'm watching."

He watched a little boy walk out onto the stage, stupefied, it seemed. Then he saw a teenage boy in a red wheelchair shoved onto the stage, and immediately Stewart's heart began to thump. He glanced down at Peter. His son had pursed his lips in frustration or anger.

The scene rolled on and then suddenly Stewart began to sweat because suddenly things were happening that had no business happening. When the boy took his first step, a buzz lit in Stewart's ear, and he thought that Donna was wrong. What they were watching wasn't real.

When the child began to sing and the people slumped to the floor, he knew it was fake. It had to be. He very nearly leapt up to the box and snapped it off. But then the camera wavered and showed a shot of Donna lying on the concrete, and Stewart ground his teeth. A thousand conflicting emotions collided in his mind.

They watched in stunned silence, the three of them, and then they watched the small child's leg twist and straighten before the camera. The child couldn't have been older than four. One look into his wide eyes and Stewart knew that this was real.

The screen cut back to Donna, and she continued her rambling, but Stewart wasn't hearing her. He was replaying that last scene in his mind, and he was thinking that the world had just changed. His heart was slamming in his chest, and sweat was snaking past his temples, and he knew that somehow nothing was ever going to be the same.

Peter suddenly whirled around in his wheelchair and sped down the hall to his bedroom.

17

I DON'T CARE IF THE NETWORKS HAVE DUBBED HIM Boy Wonder! I don't care if he flies around in a red cape; I want him out of the country!" Crandal sounded like a bulldog on the phone.

"I know he's a problem. And it's not just the networks calling him Boy Wonder. The whole country's talking about him. Immigration's requesting clarification."

"Then give them clarification."

"We could do that. But not without accepting significant risks. The last thing we need is the media digging into this and going on some crusade to keep the boy in the country. You think we have problems now . . ."

The phone went silent except for the sound of steady breathing.

"How in the blazes does a punk kid go from being unknown one day to being a national buzzword the next, anyway?"

"I don't know. Maybe you should look at the footage. It's pretty . . . unusual."

"I'm sure it is. And what do you suggest we do?"

"I suggest we go back to natural causes."

A pause.

"That'll take a week. At least."

"It's safe. They'll have no clue what happened to him."

"You sure you can pull it off?"

"I'm positive. I've already set it in motion."

"Okay. But I want a plausible plan for immediate resolution in the event the kid starts saying things. And I want that kid trailed twenty-four/seven."

"It's already done, sir."

∞

Jim's Fish House buzzed with a late-lunch crowd, just enough noise to mask their own conversation without obstructing it, Jason thought. A huge blue marlin glared down at the tables from its perch above the bar, as if daring him to take a bite. The marlin obviously had, and for his appetite he'd been rewarded with a hook through the lip. Somehow Jason doubted that was the display's point. He wondered if the owner had actually caught the fish or simply bought it from the same catalog he'd bought the talking perch at the front door.

He stared at his swordfish dish and tapped his fingers on the inch-thick varnish that covered the square table. Donna was due to join them for coffee in fifteen minutes.

"Look at the bright side, Leiah. Four days ago we were losing sleep over whether he'd be snatched away and sent back to Ethiopia. We have to take this a step at a time. I mean, obviously things have gone nuts on us here, but we have to remember where this started."

"Sure. But isn't it sorta like from the frying pan into the fire?"

"Not necessarily. Nikolous may not be an angel, but trust me, neither are the good folks down at the NSA. I guarantee you that if we remove him from Nikolous through any kind of agency he gets sent back to Ethiopia. And that would be a mistake. At least for now we have some breathing room."

"*We* might, but meanwhile Caleb's suffocating."

"He's alive, isn't he?"

"We should at least file a report with the state."

"Human services? Take a month to get any response from them. No, getting an injunction was really our only short-term option, and now an injunction would harm Caleb more than help him."

She looked at him. The light was low and her eyes were blue and bright, despite her concern. Maybe because of it. Today a black choker hid the scars on her neck, and to the person who didn't know better, she was looking very pretty. Not just her face but her whole . . . being. She had caught him looking at her white blouse once already, and he'd quickly sipped some iced tea to cover.

He'd actually spent a good hour last night tossing and turning over this very matter. This issue of his awkward interest in her. The tossing resulted in a concerted attempt to persuade himself that it wasn't more than interest. That she was clearly in some sort of a pot labeled *Untouchable*. Problem was, he was having more and more difficulty remembering exactly why having a bodysuit of scars put someone in the *Untouchable* pot.

And at the moment, sitting across the table at Jim's Fish House, with

Leiah's eyes boring into his own, Jason couldn't see the scars. He couldn't even imagine what they looked like. He just saw this stunning woman before him.

She smiled softly and nodded. "You're right. I'm just worried for him. The INS may have backed off, but if anything, Nikolous has tightened the noose."

She was right there. The Greek was going batso.

"Well, for now at least, Nikolous isn't the enemy," Jason said.

"Don't you kid yourself. He's as much an enemy as the devil himself. There's no telling what they're doing to Caleb behind closed doors."

"They're doing nothing. They're doing exactly what Dr. Caldwell insisted should be done with the boy. Nothing. If she's right and Caleb loses his power due to the world's influence, Nikolous loses. If anything, that plays to our advantage."

"Having Caleb with us would play to our advantage. Not having him locked in some hole like a prize pigeon."

"Of course, but he's not with us. We've been over this a hundred times. In the real world—the one in which his life is obviously being threatened, the one in which Nikolous *does* have custody of him—the fact that Nikolous doesn't want him to change works to our advantage. And Caleb's continued popularity also works to our advantage. Which, if you really think about it, means Nikolous is our ally, not our enemy. At least for the time being."

She drilled him with a sharp stare and turned away. Maybe he should've been less forceful. A week ago her reaction wouldn't have bothered him; today it did.

"But you're right," he said. "In some ways Nikolous is the enemy. Just not one we want to take on right now."

"He's charging this time," she said. "Twenty-five dollars a ticket."

"He's charging? When did you hear that? Is that even legal?"

"The radio this morning. Next Tuesday night at the Old Theater—twenty-five bucks a shot. Supposedly to be put in a fund for the boy's care. The man makes me sick."

Jason whistled. "The place holds what, ten thousand? So he's looking at two hundred fifty thousand dollars. The man's no idiot."

"But he is the devil. He's in this for whatever he can skim, and we both know it, Jason. We may need to go along with the man for now, but we have to stop him at some point. For all we know what he's doing is illegal."

Jason wiped at the condensation on his tea glass. "He's too smart to do something illegal unless he was sure he could get away with it."

"So let me ask you a question, Jason."

"What?"

"I'm not trying to be insensitive, but just to put this in perspective, how much would you have paid for Stephen's life?"

It was as if someone had hit Jason's head with a sledgehammer.

"Ten thousand? A hundred thousand? A million?" she asked.

He blinked and stared at her. He had a photo of Stephen taken on the day before he'd died. He was lying in bed with a green oxygen tube taped to his nose and he was smiling. He'd shriveled to twenty-five pounds on that hospital bed and he was smiling. Smiling, for goodness' sake! How much would he have paid? Everything. Anything. And anything he could have stolen. He might have killed another man for his son's life.

"You see my point?" she asked softly.

"Yes." He cleared his throat. "But Nikolous wouldn't really . . . do that."

"He *will* do that. And you're right about one thing: as long as Caleb keeps performing, the Greek will do anything, and I mean anything, to keep him performing. And when he's done with the boy, there'll be nothing left."

"Maybe. And maybe you're overreacting just a tad."

"Or maybe I'm not. Think about it, Jason."

He tried to, but his mind kept wandering back to that picture of Stephen's smiling face. It was the one part of Caleb he disliked, the memories he brought back. The irony of it all. He ate a piece of cold swordfish and washed it down with a swig of tea.

"Do you mind if I ask you another question?" Leiah asked.

"Sure."

"What's *really* happening here, Jason?"

"What do you mean?" Jason fought to check his own frustration at her line of questioning.

"It's not every day you're knocked from your feet by a boy twenty feet away."

"He's psychic; that's what's happening."

"Yes, I know, he's psychic. He's a freak."

"That's not what I said."

"No, but that's what they're all thinking. I know that because sometimes even I think it. But he's still just a boy; no one knows that better than I do. He's a simple boy with a heart as big as the sky. So then where does a simple, lovable boy really find the power to make crooked legs straight?"

"You heard Dr. Caldwell. It's not impossible."

"Yeah, I know. But somehow getting knocked from my feet didn't feel like Dr. Caldwell's explanation to me."

"So what did it feel like?"

"Like something . . . someone went through me. Something that touched my emotions, not just my nerves."

He grinned. "We're talking Casper here? Actually, I think the good doctor's theory is slightly more plausible."

"I'm serious, Jason."

"I was there too, Leiah. Trust me. What we felt was definitely physical. It wasn't a flock of ghosts conjured from the past, and it certainly wasn't the invisible hand of God come down to knock us all from our feet. Please, get real."

She turned a shade of pink, and he knew that he'd hit on something.

"You're not serious, are you? You can't actually believe this was spiritual?" In reality he'd had similar thoughts just last evening, but now those thoughts seemed distant and absurd. "I've seen what a band of Holy Ghosters can do, and believe me, in the end it all adds up to *nada*. Absolute zero."

She nodded and pursed her lips defiantly. "Well, we're not exactly in tune with the fundamentals of mathematics here, in case you hadn't noticed. Maybe your little run-in with the hallelujah folks at the Holy Ghost church didn't add up to much, but neither is anything else right now. Nobody—and that includes your Dr. Caldwell—knows what's going on here except Caleb. And Caleb isn't rambling on about what a joy it is being a psychic."

"Caleb? What Caleb thinks he is and what he actually is are probably two very different things. You have to at least see that."

"I don't see anything."

"Exactly."

They locked stares and then each took a drink. Leiah sighed heavily and ran a gentle hand over her temple. "He says his power comes from God," she said. "It may be that no one really knows who God is. Maybe the Buddhists have it wrong, maybe the Muslims have it wrong, maybe the Hindus have it wrong, maybe the Christians have it wrong, and maybe even the God-is-in-the-trees people have it wrong. Who knows? But Caleb seems to think this power comes from outside of him, and I'm not so sure that I disagree any-more. It sure felt like something from the outside to me. That's all."

"Well then, you can join the local 'It's God' group, 'cause believe me, they'll be coming out of the woodwork. The lines are being drawn as we speak. All I can say is that if some higher power is responsible for all this, he's sure got a sick sense of humor."

"Meaning?"

"Meaning any God who could do what Caleb does and yet chooses not to is no God at all. If God empowered any one of your religious groups, including Christians, we would see that power all the time, wouldn't we? Supposedly Jesus walked the shores of Galilee healing the sick. He left prom-ising his followers would do even greater things. But when you're the one in need of a miracle, he's conspicuously absent, isn't he? That's why I know Caleb's power is specifically *not* from God."

"And this from who? A man who wants to fit God into a mathematical equation?"

"No. This from a man who lost his son after spending weeks begging your God to heal him," Jason said.

Leiah stared at him directly for a moment. And then she sat back, soft-ening. "I didn't say he was *my* God," she said.

He had shed some light on the matter, he thought. What he said next came almost without his thinking. "You should know how that feels," he said.

She tensed, and he hoped she didn't think he was referring to what he was. Unfortunately she did.

"Really? And why's that?"

"I don't know—"

"Because I know what it's like to suffer, is that it?"

She wielded an unreasonable tone that betrayed bitterness. He didn't know what to say.

"Because poor Leiah is covered from head to toe in nasty scars? Because anyone confined to the gutter with the lepers should know how it feels? Does that about sum it up?"

"No."

She leaned forward, and he saw a fire in her eyes that frightened him. "No? You don't find my scars ugly, Jason? You don't look at me and wonder how I can stand to take my clothes off at night? It doesn't make your stomach turn?"

Her lips held a slight quiver. It felt like a spike had been driven through Jason's chest, and he was suddenly finding it hard to breathe. Heat washed down his spine, and he looked at his glass, immobilized.

"Oh, so now you can't even look at me, is that it!" She bit the words off, mocking. She slapped her hand on the table, palm down, and yanked on her sleeve.

"Well, look! Look at me! Like it or not, *this* is me!"

She had gone over some cliff in her mind, and Jason suddenly wanted to cry. He looked up at her arm because not to would have been like slapping her backhanded.

She'd pulled her sleeve up to her elbow, and in the very first instant he didn't recognize her arm as an arm, because it didn't look like an arm. It looked like a root from an oak tree, gnarled and discolored and rough like bark. But he knew it was her arm because he'd come to know her surgically repaired hands, and one of them was stuck on the end. He blinked and caught his breath, and he knew that she had seen that. But he couldn't help it. Nothing could have prepared him for the horror embedded in that strip of flesh she called her arm.

Almost immediately another sentiment flooded his belly. The empathy rose through his chest, and suddenly his throat was aching badly. He wanted to scream. He wanted to fall on his forehead and blubber like a baby. He wanted to beg her forgiveness and tell her that it would be all right.

But he could do nothing except stare at that arm and fight for breath.

When he tore his eyes away from it and lifted his head, Leiah's eyes were swimming in tears. Her face wrinkled in shame, and she slowly pulled her sleeve down.

"I'm sorry, Leiah. I'm so sorry," he whispered. The words sounded silly and, in their own way, mocking. She shook her head and lowered her head. The moment was impossibly awkward, the kind woven into nightmares.

"Listen to me. Listen to me, Leiah. I don't care what your skin looks like. You hear me?"

If she did, she wasn't responding.

"Listen . . . please . . ."

And what could he possibly say that would mean anything to a woman with scars so deep? Her scars went past her skin to her heart. She'd bared herself to him, and now she hated herself for doing so. It had left her with a hemorrhaging heart. She sniffed and lowered her left hand to the table. It sat there trembling.

Jason moved almost without thinking. He reached across the table and placed his hand over the back of hers. She flinched and he closed his fingers around her fingers.

For endless seconds he just held her hand. Although her hand hardly showed any sign of the burning, certainly not the damage evident on her arm, it was the first time he'd touched her. And in that moment he wanted to touch her scars. To somehow identify with her. She touched her scars all day long; they were grafted onto her. And now he had joined her in a small way.

She relaxed her hand, and he pulled it to the center of the table and softened his grip.

"Look at me."

She looked up slowly. She hardly resembled the fiery fighter he'd come to know. Now she was Leiah, the wounded girl who would cry if you looked at her too long.

"Now I'm going to say something that comes from my heart, and I guess it's up to you whether or not you believe it. I look at you and I see nothing but goodness. Your heart is as big as the ocean, and I know where all the love in this world has gone to. But it's more. It's not just on the inside. You are one of the most beautiful women I have ever seen."

He paused. It was a bit sensational, but the moment begged for it. And he wanted to give it.

"Do you hear me? You have eyes that most women would kill for. Your face is as smooth as cream and your hair's as shiny as the sea. That's what I see, soft and smooth. And if this all seems a bit melodramatic, you'll just have to forgive me. I see you on the street and you make me blink, because I forget how stunning this woman who I met in an obscure monastery in Ethiopia really is."

She searched his eyes for a few long seconds, and then a small sheepish grin curved her lips.

They were like that, their hands together, when Jason saw Donna out of the corner of his eye. He smiled at Leiah, suddenly shy. "It's the truth. Tell me you believe me."

She'd seen Donna walking their way as well, and for a second she looked panicked. But she recovered quickly.

"I'll give it some thought," she said.

He released her hand.

∞

Donna saw them pull their hands apart, and she approached wearing a wide grin. So then he was interested in her. She was being beaten out by a woman covered in scars. You see what happens when you get lost in this career of yours, Donna? You let the best ones go and they get snatched up right in front of your nose.

Actually there was something about Leiah that she admired. She had a fire that blazed true. And truth be told, with the scars covered she was quite attractive. Jason had always been a sap for a sad sack. It was no surprise he was attracted to a beautiful woman who was obviously hurting. By the looks of them, they may very well have just shared an emotional moment.

"Well, well. Forgive the intrusion, my dear lovebirds, but I was invited to this party, right?"

She pulled out a seat adjacent to them and sat. "Am I right?"

"Of course," Jason said. "Thank you for coming. We were just talking about what a job you've done, Donna. My goodness, it's been what, three days, and you've managed to make our little boy the center of attention, coast to coast. Would you like some coffee?"

"Thank you. I try to do my best. That was the point, wasn't it? And I would love some coffee."

Jason motioned at a waitress, who nodded and went off for a coffeepot.

"Actually you should be thanking Caleb for his popularity. All I did was get the camera there and check for hidden wires. He did the rest, although I will say he had me going for a while there. Have you ever seen such an innocent kid?"

"I didn't realize how much power the camera has," Jason said.

"And still there are doubters."

"You'd expect that."

Donna nodded.

"I suppose we owe you our gratitude," Leiah said. She seemed subdued and distant. "Thank you."

"You're welcome."

"Although I will say, you don't seem to be holding back." That was more like her.

"Never. I've always said, if you see something that looks worthwhile, grab it before someone else does." She glanced at Jason. "Unfortunately, I don't always get there first."

"Well, you got there first on this one, didn't you?" he said without batting an eye.

"I guess I did, Jason."

"And how's the view from up front?"

The waitress filled her cup with hot black coffee, and Donna thanked her.

"The view. Well, for starters there's the media. Nikolous told me this morning that they've received interview requests from over two hundred media sources."

"Two hundred? There *are* that many?"

"Are you kidding? Trust me—many more. He's denied them all, of course. There will only be one interview, next week after this has had time to mushroom, and that will be my interview." She smiled and took a sip of coffee.

They didn't look impressed.

"Anyway, if the next meeting is anything like the last one, the media will be slobbering all over itself. This time all the majors will be there, and with any luck, it'll just be the beginning."

"I'm sure Caleb has his critics in all of this," Leiah said.

"Oh, there'll be critics, honey. But so far it's a general scramble to explain exactly what happened. There's your typical wholesale rejection from the most conservative types. Mostly religious pundits."

"Really? I'd think the religious folks would eat this up," Jason said.

"A lot of them are. But it also threatens a ton of dogma. Think of it. How would you react if you were someone who believed that only the powers of darkness pull these sorts of tricks today? You'd have to either discount the event altogether—some kind of optical illusion or something—or you'd have to pal the kid up with the devil. Trust me, the former is much easier. Either way, most aren't so quick to draw conclusions. Rabbis, sheiks, priests, theologians . . . they're picking their way through interviews as if they were caught in the middle of a minefield. Problem is we have an undeniable bona fide occurrence of the paranormal caught on film. They can't deny it, so they're forced to at least consider it. But they're being very cautious." She shook her head thinking of several interviews she'd seen.

"Give them time," Jason said. "Within a week they'll have him labeled as everything from Moses to the Antichrist."

Across the room a television mounted to the wall beside the bar showed images of street fighting in the Middle East. Give them ten minutes and the chances of Caleb's face filling the screen was pretty decent, she thought. There was a momentum building on this one that came along maybe once a decade or so. In this election year where the race was boringly one-sided, the media was jumping.

"And what about in the real world?" Jason asked.

Donna nodded. "There seems to be a consensus that follows Dr. Caldwell's explanation. She's making the rounds. Putting a UCLA professor in front of the camera holding up her old wire-frame glasses comes off quite nicely. Of course there are other theories—all the talking heads seem to have one—but they're pretty much all variations on some sort of psychokinesis."

She smiled. "Wait until the next meeting. It's one thing for one camera to catch something extraordinary. It's something altogether different when fifty cameras catch it." *It would be a zoo,* she thought. Which was fine; she lived for zoos. "It's gonna be one heck of a ride, and pardon me for saying so, kids, but I wouldn't miss it for the world."

"I'm sure it's a dream come true," Jason said.

She grinned. "Close. So really, you can watch the news for a couple hours and know how the world's reacting to Caleb. You didn't ask me out to hear this. What's up?"

Jason glanced at Leiah, but she was staring across the room. Her mind seemed to have drifted. "What's the scoop with Crandal?" he asked.

"The scoop? He's up about fifteen points in the polls; that's the scoop."

"Come on, Donna. You know as well as I do that something passed between Caleb and Crandal at that press conference last week. You also know that the NSA, an organization that Crandal used to head, ordered the boy out of country shortly after. Don't tell me this means nothing to you."

"Okay, so we have two events that could be strung together. But that's all we have. Two separate events. On the one hand, you have a lost boy who walks up to a man, says a few nonsensical words about him, and then offers no further explanation. On the other hand, you have the Immigration Service recalling a boy who came from a war zone for security reasons. We need a lot more than that to spend any time on it, Jason."

"It's not the *what* but the *who*. The *lost boy* is Caleb, no ordinary boy. And the *man* is a presidential candidate who, like I said, used to run the NSA. You don't find that disturbing?"

"You've asked Caleb about it, right?"

"Yes."

"And?"

Jason sighed. "And he doesn't seem to know."

"So now your source is backing out, so to speak."

"He's just a kid!"

"He's just a kid? I thought he was a special kid. Look, you don't just launch an investigation on a man like Crandal without having at least one credible, authenticated source."

Jason shook his head. "I'm not saying there is a link, or that Crandal is anything more than a wonderful president-to-be. I don't even *care* about politics. But Caleb was recalled on orders of the NSA. That's worth more than just a quick scan of the word *Tempest*."

"I've already looked into it, Jason. I am a reporter, remember."

"And?"

"Nothing."

"Then look again. Dig somewhere else. Ask Crandal himself."

"That takes time. I've got my hands full right now."

"With who?" he pushed.

"With Caleb. With Crandal."

"Exactly. This is about both of them."

He was right about that, wasn't he? It might be worth another look. A quick one at least.

"Okay." She set her coffee cup down with a clink and pushed her chair back. "I'll look at it again. Was that it?"

He glanced at Leiah again, but she still seemed uninterested. This was his concern more than hers.

"Yes," Jason said.

"Then I'll see you two lovebirds at the next meeting." She flashed them a grin, turned her back, and strode from the table.

18

Day 16

CALEB SAT AT THE TABLE, swinging his legs under his chair, trying very hard to eat the mush the witch had put before him. It had the consistency of oatmeal, which was okay. But its taste would turn the nose of a goat, which was saying a lot, because everyone knew that goats would eat anything. Anything but mud.

The world here in America was inside out, he thought. Upside down. Like this food. If America was the land of milk and honey, then their honey was bitter and their milk was sour. Martha insisted that if he ate it long enough, he would learn to like it. But he'd been eating it for many days now, and it wasn't tasting any better. If anything it was even more bitter than he remembered. He wished she would go back to alternating between this mud and the cheesy worms, but for three straight days now she had stuck with the mud.

And who said doing something forever made you want it anyway? It wasn't what Dadda had taught. It was the other way around—desire came first.

"You cannot see the kingdom of God unless you first want to, Caleb. Unless you desire it. Do you understand this?"

"Yes. I think so. Do I want to, Dadda?"

"I don't know. Do you?"

"I think so."

"You think so? Thinking so is not wanting. Come, let me tell you a story." He drew Caleb in with one arm and began to walk across the room aimlessly.

"There was a man who discovered something in a field one day. A shiny object that flashed in the sun. When he bent down to examine it, his heart nearly lodged itself in his throat. He jumped up and looked quickly around. Nobody had seen him. His hands began to tremble, and his breathing became short. He could not take the object, because it was not his to take, yet it was very, very valuable. But he had to have it, you see. No matter what else happened, he realized in that moment that he had to own that treasure."

"Gold? Or was it diamonds, Dadda?"

"Maybe a thousand diamonds in a chest. Enough to make him pace frantically as he plotted how he could own it. Now let me ask you a question, Caleb. Does this man *want* this treasure?"

Caleb had nearly jumped with his answer. "Yes!"

"Ahh, yes. If you want to walk into the kingdom, you also must have this kind of desire. Without such desire, the man never would have done what he did next."

"What did he do?"

"He covered the diamonds so that no one would find them, and then he went home in a frenzy and sold his house and everything he owned."

"Why?"

"Because he wanted that field, Caleb. If he owned the field, he would also own the treasure. And he really, really wanted the treasure. So he gave up everything and bought it. It's that way with the kingdom. You must want it like the man wanted the treasure."

"And then you sell your house."

"And then you surrender everything for it," Dadda had said.

Caleb bent over his mush at the table and smiled at the way Dadda's eyes sparkled when he told his stories. Dadda had borrowed that one from Jesus, he later learned. As he did most of them, actually.

Caleb had already been walking in the kingdom, but Dadda was helping him understand how things worked. And that day he'd learned that desire tended to open the eyes as well as the heart.

He pushed another spoonful of the mud into his mouth, swallowed as quickly as possible, and then took a gulp of water. A shiver ran down his back, and he cleared his throat. Three more spoonfuls, maybe. But they would have to be big.

The last one was in his mouth when the witch walked in.

"Every last drop of that had better be gone, boy," she said in her snotty tone. She slammed the door, clacked across the concrete floor, and peered over his shoulder. The bowl was pretty clean, and for a second Caleb found some satisfaction in that. It really wasn't so bad when you were done. Not everything in life was meant to feel good. Things like washing floors and scrubbing pots and washing your hands were just part of what it meant to live in this world in the meantime.

So in the meantime in America, he would eat this oatmeal mud stuff, and that would be like scrubbing the floors. They kinda looked the same anyway.

Martha humphed and pulled at his shirt. "Let's go."

Caleb stood and marched ahead of her. He'd never seen her happy. She was all mixed up, and for that Caleb was sorry for her. But in these last few days, since that meeting in the big theater, she had stomped around like a leaking olive jar, and it wasn't oil that spilled from her seams. It was evil.

Caleb had almost forgotten about the box she called the television, but he heard the sound as they came to the hallway, and a shaft of heat ripped up his spine.

He halted instinctively. For five days now she had left the frightening light box on except for when Father Nikolous visited. And for five days Caleb had shut it out by curling up tight and singing or sleeping. But the moving pictures weren't like scrubbing the floors or eating the mud. They felt like a disease. Not one in his flesh, but one that wanted to eat at his mind.

He'd found a small knob that shut it off the second day. But when she'd walked in and seen what he'd done, she'd screamed at him and fixed it so that he couldn't shut it off.

"What's wrong, boy?" Martha asked behind him. "Get on with it."

He took two steps and then stopped again. Maybe he could persuade her. He turned around and looked up at her large frame.

"Excuse me, Auntie. I really would like it if you could please turn that box in the room off. It would make it much nicer for me."

"Oh, it would, would it? Get!"

He flinched at her tone, turned, and entered the hall. The sound grew louder as they walked. The squealing laughter of the drawn figures. He just had to tell her that this was not good.

Caleb stopped and turned around again. This time she put both fists on her hips.

"But they're not nice pictures. They're cruel and very bad and they frighten me."

"Is that a fact?" She wagged her head like she always did, mocking. "Well, have you ever thought that you needed a little frightening? Huh? No, I suppose not. You're too busy having your life laid out all nice and neat like a bed of roses. Everybody running to serve you. Do you really think you're *that* special? That you deserve to have special comforts? That you should not face the same fears every other boy in this world faces?"

Most of what she said came out in a blaring rush, and all of it came out in English, so he wasn't sure what she meant.

"I don't like it," he said.

The hall was dark and he couldn't see her face well, but he could feel her anger rise. She stepped forward and snatched him by the collar. Then she shoved him up against the wall so that her knuckles pressed into his throat, nearly cutting off his breath.

"Now you listen to me, you little spoiled brat!" She breathed heavily, and Caleb felt his bones tremble.

"You make me sick! What makes you think you have the right to anything? *Anything!* You're nothing but a spoiled child. You know in Turkey, my father used to beat me every day. Every night after he came home from the alehouse. Even when I was a good little girl. So I wouldn't grow up like him, he said. And do you know what, it was a good thing. Because I *didn't* grow up like him!"

She dropped him down and stepped back. Her hand came across his face like a whip. *Smack!*

"So don't you dare talk to me about what you do or don't like! You have no right. Now get in there!" She thrust her finger to the door.

Caleb ducked under her arm and scooted down the hall, his face throbbing with pain.

"I swear, if it weren't for the others, I would take a buckle to you, boy!" she mumbled after him.

He opened the door, ran to the bed, and leapt onto the mattress.

The door slammed, and then she was gone.

He sat shivering in the corner of his bed for several minutes, allowing the sting on his cheek to fade. He'd never been hit. And now that he had been, his mind was not dealing with it well. But she had been beaten every day? What kind of man could do such a thing? The devil could do it.

"Can the devil enter the kingdom of light, Dadda?"

"Never. He is stuck in the kingdom of darkness."

So then if he ever did want to flee the devil, he would only have to enter the kingdom of God? His father said that was right. Yes, that was about the sum of it all.

The television was squawking in the corner, casting pulses of red and blue light against the wall. Caleb ignored it and closed his eyes.

For a moment all he could think about was that big witch, swinging her hand. He began to cry softly, and he wasn't sure why; the pain had already left him. He tried to cleanse his mind, to fix it on good things and on God, but it wasn't cooperating.

He lay down, curled into a ball, and began to hum. That helped.

Half an hour or maybe an hour later, Caleb opened his eyes and found he was facing the television. The colors skipped across the screen in a kind of intoxicating dance. A furry blue animal with jagged teeth was running upright on tiptoes wearing a wide grin. In its right hoof was a red shirt torn in half. The blue animal was laughing.

Caleb gawked at the scene. It was fascinating and terrifying at once. Stunning. The blue animal had torn someone's shirt off his back, it appeared. And it was laughing as if such a thing made his day bright.

Caleb slammed his lids shut and squeezed them tight.

And what happened to such an animal? Having torn the shirt from the back of some sad child, what happened to the animal? Would it simply wander off the screen laughing, or would the boy run after it and take his shirt back? Could such a deed be left uncorrected?

The question grew in Caleb's mind. He tried to put it out, but he had to know what happened to the blue animal. He listened but heard only strange sounds. There was no speech. There was only *whizzing* and *banging* and *popping*. But Caleb could not bring himself to look.

And then there was a loud *boom*, and Caleb simply had to look.

He opened his eyes and saw a small boy tiptoeing the other direction, grinning like the animal had, with large sharp teeth. He held a coat of blue fur in his hand.

It took a moment for Caleb to understand what had happened. But then he did and his mind wailed in protest. He cried out, curled up tight, and rolled away from the television. This time he covered his head with his pillow and begged to see the light.

∞

They were in the San Francisco Hilton Hotel Monday night when the question came to Crandal, right on schedule, as expected.

The six days since the boy had blown the lid off the Old Theater had been quiet. At least on the outside they had been quiet. On the inside things were festering. But the boy had said nothing at all in public, much less anything about Tempest. With due consideration Roberts had decided to join Crandal in San Francisco for a morning of campaigning on the wharf and a string of interviews that evening. They were a good fifteen points up in the polls and coasting.

All the advisors on Crandal's payroll were saying the same thing: "Just don't rock the boat, Charles. Sit tight and play out the clock. Don't go for any fourth-quarter theatrics."

Made sense. Their opponent, James Murdock, looked like a wounded puppy already. Crandal had made his statement, and the American people had bought it. No need to risk another attack only to lose the battle. They had cut their schedule in half and convinced Crandal to stay away from anything that even smelled controversial.

Roberts had sat by and watched three interviews from CNN and two of the majors, but none of those would pose any risks. They were practically on staff. Crandal had answered their questions with the ease of a slick salesman without sounding like one. That was his gift. It was the appearance of power that earned it, Crandal had told him once, and over these last three months Roberts had come to believe it wholesale. In reality Roberts had run the NSA as much as Crandal, but he didn't have the gift. His boss had the gift.

It was this interview with Donna Blair that they had prepared for. If the question came, it would be tonight and it would come from her.

Donna had asked all the basic annoying questions about policy and issues, and Crandal had beat them to death in a gentle sort of way—another one of his gifts. She paused and glanced at her sheet. It would come now, Roberts thought.

And it did.

"As you know, sir, there was an event at the Old Theater in Los Angeles six days ago. I'm sure you're familiar with it. It seems to have captured the country's imagination. But I think the American people would like to know what the man who may very well be their next president makes of such a boy."

"Well, if this boy is all they make him out to be, I'm thinking he should have a spot in my cabinet."

She laughed along with several close by who heard the exchange. Crandal had taken the question and swallowed it whole. Roberts felt his heart surge for the man. Behind closed doors he had called the kid a freak, and in reality they both knew the kid was a freak. But not in front of the camera he wasn't.

"Do you believe he's capable of doing what they say he can do?"

"You were there, Donna. Maybe you could answer that question better than I. All I know is that if he can, then we have a whole lot more to learn about the mind. Which is precisely why my plan to pour 150 billion dollars into developing sciences is so important to the future of our country. I say power to the people, but understanding the source of our power is something we can't afford to forget."

She smiled. "I hadn't thought of it that way. You've seen this boy yourself once, haven't you?"

There it was. Crandal expressed no reservation. He calmly waved at a passing journalist and answered as though slightly distracted.

"I think I would remember it. He seems like quite a striking young fellow."

"You have actually. At your press conference at Frazier Park in Los Angeles. He was there and wandered up to the crowd. I believe he spoke to you. Do you remember?"

"*This* boy? You're sure?"

"I was right beside him."

"And what did he say?"

Roberts held his breath. He was following their script to the letter.

"He said . . . that you would bring a tempest," the reporter said.

"Well, then the boy knows his stuff," Crandal answered with an amused smile. Man, he was good.

"I think I've already brought a tempest to this country, at least I think my opponent would think so. As I'm sure you know all too well, Donna, we politicians are careful to choose the right words. We can't very well scream revolution from the tops of buildings inciting the people. But I think I've made it clear that in more ways than not my presidency will represent a revolution. A tempest if you must, tearing down the strongholds that suck the life out of the American people. Power's good for one thing, and that is freeing the people. And if someone wants to call that a tempest, I'm with them all the way."

Roberts let out a long slow, easy breath. It was brilliant. He should know—he'd written it. All except the part about power freeing the people; that had been Crandal's two bits. He was obsessed with this "giving power to the people" thing. In reality giving power to the people was the farthest thing from his mind.

Donna smiled and nodded. "So you take it as an endorsement?"

"Take if for what you will, Donna. I don't even remember the comment, but I'll take all the help I can get."

And that was that. She moved on to his plans for the military. They could not have hoped for a better resolution to the matter.

Of course the very fact that Tempest had now become a public word did have its consequences.

In a sardonic way the boy's statement actually *could* bring a kind of endorsement, although Roberts wasn't sure how much good an endorsement from a ten-year-old would do. Then again, this was clearly no ordinary ten-year-old.

On a more practical note, the exposure of the statement to the public now sealed the boy's fate. Another nail in the coffin, so to speak.

Not that Roberts thought they needed any more nails; the plan was running without a hitch. In fact, smoother than he could have dreamed. Martha had settled for fifty thousand dollars, and in reality he thought she would've done it for twenty. Her apparent dislike for the boy had been a gift from God himself.

He had set a second plan in motion, of course. A redundant plan that had no dependence whatsoever on the first. Both were on the move. The only question that remained was which would reach the boy first.

Roberts caught Crandal's eye, and the latter didn't show more than the casual glance of someone disinterested.

He was a gifted man, Roberts thought. A man who deserved the power they were about to give him.

19

Day 17

IT WAS ON A TUESDAY NIGHT, exactly one week from the first meeting and just over two weeks from the day Caleb first set foot on American soil that the second meeting took place. The Old Theater held ten thousand seats, and an eager public lined up for ten city blocks for the first-come-first-served tickets. At twenty-five bucks a pop they were a bargain. They had all seen the replay a hundred times of that small child's legs straightening; this was the real thing.

The LAPD had stationed itself at all the intersections and relegated itself to traffic control for most of the day. It wasn't an unruly crowd waiting for a chance to see the boy; if anything it was a subdued, introspective crowd—a far cry from the jostling, snorting, beer-drinking types waiting for a crack at Ozzy Osbourne or the Nine Inch Nails or some other rock band, which was normal fare for a ten-block line.

To walk down the line without knowing of the event, you might think it a convention for the fringe of society. The foreign, the handicapped, the nerds, and the like.

Perhaps a full third were of foreign origin, mostly from the Middle East or Asia. Quite a few had come in traditional clothing: head wraps and white cotton robes or sarongs. Some stood in groups, all dressed identically, like monks or sheiks. Others stood in black robes, unmoving. Still others stood with clear markings on their foreheads or arms that identified their affiliation with a particular sect.

The religious community had come out in all stripes and large numbers to see the boy. Hindus, Muslims, Buddhists, and a scattering of smaller groups—Moonies, and the like. Which made sense. They had all had a week to fester over the boy's power, and now they wanted to know for themselves. The earliest suggestions that the power had somehow been faked had been easily refuted by the media itself. So then the only real question which remained was the source of the boy's power.

It was God, of course. Ah, but was it?

The Eastern religious elite weren't so sure. It could well be psychic, a human's unique connection with the universe that allowed him such power. But even so, what kind of human could connect so purely with the universe? A very great teacher indeed. A god perhaps.

And if the boy's power did come from God, which God? The God of Mohammed? Perhaps Mohammed himself, sent by God?

The Christian community was no more united. Clearly if the boy's power was genuine, and it seemed to be, then it came from either the Holy Spirit, as sent by Jesus Christ, or from Satan. He was either a prophet from God or an antichrist. Some had already decided on the latter, and they identified themselves with placards or picket signs with long verses from the book of Revelation.

Most of the Western world heeded the rhetoric of the parapsychologists, however, and many who waited were everyday folk who'd come to see a psychic with extraordinary powers. Or be healed by him.

Thousands who'd come leaned on crutches or sat in wheelchairs or in a few cases lay on wheeled beds. There was no telling how many others suffered from invisible ailments, but surely thousands.

They opened the doors at five, two full hours before the event was scheduled to begin, and it took all of that to ease the first ten thousand into the auditorium. Three thousand were turned away.

Jason stood on the stage behind the huge purple curtains; they'd lowered them this time, evidently for theatrical impact. It wasn't the only change. The stage itself had been covered in a rich purple carpet. Tall palms, more than twenty of them, ran in a semicircle behind where Caleb was supposed to stand. Tall Greek pillars that looked as if they might have been ripped off from the Parthenon stood on either side. The set reminded Jason of a picture from the *Jesus* movie, or a passion play he'd seen once.

Organ music rumbled in low tones and colored lights cast an atmospheric red hue over the whole stage. Two black boxes—fog machines—sat just behind the curtain. Jason had beat the drums in a rock band during his college days, and they'd played exactly one gig. It was the only other time he'd seen a fog machine close up. The outfit Nikolous had hired to create the set was going Hollywood.

Jason parted the curtain and looked at the crowd. The entire floor section had been set aside for those who might find negotiating the stairs difficult, and by all appearances it wasn't enough room. The media waited in taped sections, their cameras peering at the stage from all angles: CBS, ABC, FOX, CNN, NBC, of course, and a slew he hardly recognized. At least thirty cameras in all.

Every seat in the house was filled, and the quiet, speculative talk created a dull roar that gave the general impression a train was rolling through the station. The air conditioners were having a hard time keeping up with the mass of flesh.

Jason scanned the midtier orange seats. It was mind-boggling to think that just over two weeks ago Caleb had been hidden from the world in a monastery in northern Ethiopia, and here people were coming in droves to see him. Like a rare treasure unearthed in an archeological dig—the Holy Grail with the power of everlasting youth or something. Thinking of it in those terms, this all made sense.

What didn't make sense was why the boy's life had been threatened in the first place. Why had they been chased in Ethiopia? Why had the monastery been leveled? And more to the point here at home, why had the NSA been so eager to have him deported? They had saved Caleb for the moment, but to what end? The NSA didn't do things haphazardly. And for that matter, although the boy's burgeoning popularity may have stalled the threat, the popularity itself seemed to be getting out of control.

Caleb was a lost child, not some holy relic with magical powers. It was the impression that lingered the longest these days. Maybe Leiah's motherly love was rubbing off on him.

His eyes suddenly met with those of a man to the near right not thirty yards away on the midtier balcony. He stood in a hooded black robe beside five other men, all Caucasian and all dressed alike. To a man, they were staring at him from behind their hoods.

Jason started and pulled the curtain closed. And what was that? A cult of reapers holding signs instead of sickles?

He parted the curtain again, barely this time. Several had shifted their attention to the crowd below, but the leader and two others still drilled the stage with their dark stares. They held pickets with the words, "Beware the Antichrist who comes as a wolf in sheep's clothing," scrawled in red on black boards. He blinked. Maniacs like these could be a problem. They could pose a threat, couldn't they? How far would a disciple go to kill the Antichrist?

"It is full?"

Jason jerked back. It was Nikolous.

"Yes. The whole world is out there."

"Good." The Greek pulled on his lapels and rose to his toes once.

"You're pulling out all the stops on this, aren't you?" Jason asked.

"Of course. Anything less would be a disgrace."

"Not to mention a whole lot less money."

"Not everything is about money. There is far more at stake here than a few dollars. To reduce such an appointed time in history to complaints over who is making money would be to miss the point."

"Smooth. That's part of the spiel you plan on feeding the cameras? You actually think they'll believe that you have no interest in the money? You're talking what, $250,000 here, less maybe fifty for expenses? To buy the boy shoes, right?"

"Say what you like." Nikolous glanced at his watch. "The show starts in five minutes."

"The show, huh? And what about you, Nikolous? You're a religious man who believes in the deity of Christ, aren't you? Where do you think the boy's power comes from?"

The Father peered at him over the dark bags under his eyes. "This is not about any particular religious dogma. It's about the power of the mind, which was indeed created by God, though we don't necessarily know how. We have evolved far, and now we have a crowning example of God's accomplishment at our fingertips. And it is appropriate that he's in the hands of God's church. He's God's gift to the church."

"And is God's gift doing miracles from God?"

"Miracles are things we read about in storybooks; they certainly have no place in any thinking man's faith. Now, if you will excuse me, I must prepare."

Nikolous turned and walked to the stage entrance.

Jason wasn't a theologian, but he somehow doubted they were the words the founder of Christianity would have chosen. The man was under a cloud of delusion.

Caleb and Leiah were where he'd left them, behind the stage. Caleb was playing with some marbles on the floor while stagehands walked about barking orders in their walkie-talkies and adding to the general confusion. The boy seemed more comfortable with his surroundings than he had a week earlier.

Leiah looked up and grinned deliberately. The incident at Jim's Fish House had brought an awkwardness to their interaction, Jason thought. She'd pulled back. Not that they were close before, but at least they'd never had trouble speaking their minds. During the last four days their candor had been replaced by a sort of insecurity. A shyness. The kind of feeling you might have returning to a swimming pool the day after having the water suck your trunks off on a particularly spectacular dive that you knew darn well they were all watching.

The feeling was compounded by his budding certainty that she was terrified of his interest and was kindly withdrawing. Which in turn made him wonder if he really was interested. It felt like a nasty downward spiral.

He grinned and dipped his head.

To his right Donna's voice broke his train of thought. "Hello, Jason. You ready for this?" She'd entered from the floor, smiling wide, obviously in her element. He glanced at the door she walked through. A guard stood by biting one of his fingernails. He'd have to talk to Nikolous about security. If Donna could just waltz in, so could the black avengers out there.

"I don't know, Donna. Depends what *this* is. There's gonna be a lot of disappointed people if he decides not to walk on water tonight."

"He won't. I don't think he knows the difference between water and land. By the way, I interviewed Crandal yesterday. If you didn't catch it, the whole thing's being rebroadcast on the late edition tonight."

She winked and walked by.

"And? You asked him?"

She turned back, smiling coy. "I did and he's clean. If anything, the boy might have helped deliver him his presidency."

"What?"

"*Late Edition,* Jason. Eleven o'clock. Watch it." She headed for Nikolous and was gone.

He stared dumbly after her. She was wrong. Crandal was involved like hydrogen was involved with water. They might not see it, but it was there.

The organ music suddenly swelled and the lights dimmed. Nikolous was starting his show.

∞

They started with the fog machines behind the curtain even before Nikolous had finished his upgraded and considerably longer speech of introduction.

Jason couldn't see the crowd, but he could almost hear their rapt silence. The new stage managers had improved the sound system, he noted. He could feel his spine rattling with the sustained note. And the light show was nothing to laugh at either. Ten new banks of lights hung from the high ceiling, shifting colored hues that leaked onto the stage despite the lowered curtain. They had most definitely gone Hollywood.

The Greek strutted offstage, and Leiah reluctantly let Caleb go. The boy did a sweet thing then. At the entrance to the stage he reached up and kissed her on the cheek. A bank of fog about six inches deep covered the stage as he walked out to the microphone, giving the illusion that he was walking on a cloud.

They didn't lift the curtain until he stood still in the center. Then the purple curtain rose on its cables, and for the second time the world looked at the small boy on the stage of the Old Theater.

Caleb just stood there, gazing out at the lights, and Jason wondered if he would walk back again. But he didn't. Instead he put his hands behind his back and walked slowly to his right, away from them.

They had lowered the music to a whisper, and you could hear the collective breathing of the crowd. Caleb reached the end of the stage and then turned and walked back to their end, slowly, like a schoolmaster studying a group of misfits gathered for detention.

He stopped and looked out for a long time—enough time for a few voices to begin whispering. He suddenly turned around and Jason saw his face. Caleb's cheeks were wet with tears. But it was the only sign that he was crying. He was reacting to the crowd in their wheelchairs. Jason swallowed.

The boy suddenly turned and walked back to Leiah, who'd stepped up to the side curtain. She dropped to a knee and took the boy in her arms. But Caleb didn't want consoling; he wanted to talk to her. He put his mouth by her ear and began to whisper.

She stood and looked at Nikolous. "He wants me to go out with him."

The Greek hesitated. He waved her out quickly. "Go then. Go."

Leiah quickly straightened her scarf and, with a final furtive glance at Jason, walked out onto the stage with Caleb.

He led her by the hand, he wearing his red bow tie and she her red scarf, and Jason wondered about the coincidence. They walked through the fog and stopped before the microphone. Caleb looked at her and she bent again. She listened for a few seconds and then stood. Leiah looked back at Jason one last time. He tried to give her an encouraging smile, but his heart was slamming away in his chest and he wasn't sure what his face actually did. Whatever it was it seemed to work. She lifted the microphone from its stand and spoke to the audience.

"Caleb is from Ethiopia, as you know. His mother tongue is Ge'ez, and although he speaks some English he says he would rather that I speak for him, since I am very good at English."

A few chuckled at that, but it was an oh-isn't-that-cute chuckle and Jason found himself joining it.

"Those are his words, of course. He wants me to ask you if you believe in God . . ." Caleb was pulling on her arm and she bent to him, listened, and then straightened again.

"I'm sorry; he wants me to ask you if you believe in the kingdom of God." The room remained silent, and she looked down at him for further instruction, but Caleb seemed satisfied. He looked to the crowd, waiting for some kind of response.

They waited in an awkward silence for about ten seconds. And then Caleb looked up at Leiah again, and he whispered in her ear for a long time.

When she stood, they were leaning forward in their seats to hear her words. The boy's words.

"He says that's what he thought. Because he has seen a lot of anger and meanness and bad things, and he doesn't understand them. There is darkness and there is light, and he doesn't understand why so many people would want to walk in the darkness. He says that when Jesus walked on the earth he walked in the light, and Caleb thinks it would be very good if all of you would start to walk in the light as well."

Caleb was pulling on her arm before she finished. Leiah dipped for his words.

"He wants to know if anyone really wants to walk in the kingdom of God, because anyone who really wants to enter the kingdom of God can. It is a simple matter of belief. Of faith."

Another tug, another whisper, another nugget.

"Whoever follows the Spirit into the kingdom becomes a son of God. His dadda taught him that. It is inside you, and everywhere, through the narrow gate. But it is very nice in that place. He thinks you should all go there and be sons of God."

For what seemed like a full minute, no one spoke. The boy stood very still and Leiah kept looking at him for more, but he just looked at the people. Someone on the front row had a bad chest cold and coughed loudly. Jason imagined he could hear the combined whir of the cameras, but it could just as easily have been the buzz of lights above.

Caleb tilted his head up to Leiah and spoke again, quickly this time.

"He wants to know . . ." She stopped and bent to Caleb for clarification. Leiah started again. "He wants to know who draws the pictures that move."

Still no one responded. They were star-struck, Jason thought. Absolutely flummoxed. It was the first time the boy had spoken of his faith, and no one seemed to know what to make of it. Jason certainly didn't. The kingdom stuff was clearly something out of a storybook or something.

Leiah was bent over Caleb yet again, and now they exchanged whispers several times. Fresh tears wet the boy's face, and he kept looking out to the audience. When Leiah straightened she took a small step away from him. Her voice held a tremble.

"It seems very important to him for you to know that this kingdom is not a matter of eating or drinking or walking or even breathing. His dadda taught him that too. It is about peace and happiness and doing right." She paused and shifted.

"He will ask his Father if he wants to do some things for you now."

It was the boy's way of saying he was going to pray for them, Jason thought. He was tying his power to a faith; that much was clear. God and Jesus and this kingdom of his—Dadda's words for how things worked.

Caleb had closed his eyes and lifted his chin, and it occurred to Jason that something might actually happen now. Oddly he hadn't really prepared himself for a repeat of the last meeting, maybe because it still seemed so far-fetched. He had been thrown from his feet, true enough. But it had been a distant place, like in a dream. Real, but only momentarily real, if that made any sense.

And yet here he was, facing the boy who had his chin lifted, presumably praying to some God in the heavens. He swallowed and instinctively steadied himself with a hand on the wall.

Leiah stared at the boy, and she took another step back. The tears were drying on his small cheeks, and his hands hung loosely by his sides. He stood like a lost child in the middle of the large stage, with wisps of fog floating by his feet and a serene blue stage light illuminating the tall palms and pillars behind him. For a moment the scene was perfectly peaceful and as still as a painting.

For a moment.

The light came first, a jagged finger of white lightning that started above the stage and reached to the back of the arena. Jason jerked back and threw a hand up to his face. The light stuttered above them; silent for a brief blinding moment, it seemed to hang in the air.

The sound followed, a deafening thunderclap, as if a bomb had detonated twenty feet above the stage. With the clap, the lightning blinked to black. Scattered voices cried out, but for the most part, they crouched, frozen.

If Jason wasn't mistaken, lightning had just struck—*in* the building.

From the corner of his eye, he saw that Leiah had dropped to her seat with her legs in front of her. He was aware that the hair on his arms stood out.

Caleb stood unmoved in the blue light. A smile now curved his lips, but his eyes were still closed.

The lightning sputtered again, but not with the same force as the first time. It cracked once, then twice. Jason felt the air feather his face and lift his bangs. A force tickled his skin and brushed through . . .

No, it wasn't a force. It was wind! A warm wind was blowing over them!

Jason looked out to the boy again. He stood with his arms wide now, facing the wind head-on, smiling ear to ear with an open mouth, like a kid on a joyride. And suddenly the wind was more of a gale, rushing through the auditorium on its way to the stage.

The wind whipped at Caleb's shirt and hair, flapping both back. Loose sheets of paper and wrappers spun by him. The wind gathered strength, howling loudly now. One of the camera tripods crashed to the ground. Camera crews were desperately holding on to their equipment, but they dared not interrupt their signals; this was all live. The tall palm trees bent backward and then began to fall, smashing to the plywood floor. Leiah lay flat on her back, arms spread wide. Jason thought she might be laughing.

And then the wind suddenly died.

A large orange poster with Caleb's silhouette on it floated lazily down like a tossed feather.

And then it began again, with a loud roar. Only this time, the wind had reversed direction and rushed from the stage toward the audience.

Caleb was laughing out loud now. His hair flew past his face, and his little shoulders shook in laughter that pealed above the rush.

There were over three thousand people on the main floor, most of them sitting in wheelchairs or holding oxygen bottles or holding their walking devices with white knuckles. The wind blew through them head-on, and nobody really saw exactly what happened to them. Some things, sure. Bodies were falling over backward, and arms were flailing, and pillows and blankets and hair clips and all sorts of loose objects were flying through the air. They all saw that. But no one really saw the healing.

But suddenly the wind was gone again, and the kind of stillness that comes right after a storm settled on them while they cleared their heads. Caleb was hopping on the stage. Laughing and jumping, ecstatic.

It took all of one second for the crowd to understand what had happened. To see and feel their whole bodies. To come to the brutal realization that they had been totally and completely healed. All of them.

∽

Pandemonium had broken out on the floor. The cameras swung and jerked to catch this one and that one, dancing or jumping, mouths screaming and arms lifted. The press lines were swarmed by people eager to try out their limbs. Three of the minitowers toppled, including CNN's.

Caleb began to run back and forth, thrilled, hands raised to the sky, giggling and generally beside himself.

Jason watched the scene with an open jaw. It had all happened in less than sixty seconds. Maybe two minutes if you started from the time Caleb had closed his eyes. Apart from a healthy dose of hair raising, nothing had happened to him. But out there where the people had come to feel the boy's power, they had felt it and their lives had been changed. At least in part.

This time Nikolous let the boy run around on the stage for fifteen minutes while the auditorium went nuts. Then he collected him, ushered him into the protected limousine, and whisked him off to that dungeon they called his home.

The last thing Jason saw before leaving with a grinning but otherwise unaffected Leiah was the black-clad avengers. The wind must have blown their picket signs away, but they still wore their hoods. The CBS crew was interviewing them and they weren't smiling.

20

CALEB LAY ON HIS BED IN THE DARK.

Well, it wasn't really dark because the lights were flashing on his wall in reds and blues and greens. The television lights. But he was trying not to look at that.

A day had passed since the meeting when the wind had come. He knew it was a day, because Jason and Leiah had visited once. Leiah was beginning to see, he thought. Or at least she *wanted* to see, which was just as good, because it all started with wanting. The wanting and then the surrendering.

"Surrendering is like *not* wanting," Dadda said.

"You want and then you *don't* want?"

"You want to enter the kingdom and then you decide it's worth everything in your life. You decide not to want your own kingdom. Like the man who sold all he owned for the field. See?"

He saw, but he'd never really understood why Dadda should call it surrender, because it didn't feel like giving anything up. It had always felt more like gaining.

Until now. Now he was fighting; not watching the moving painting felt like Dadda's surrender. And it was harder than he would have guessed.

He wasn't sure why watching was something he shouldn't do, only that he shouldn't. Well, for one thing, it was mean things and bad people over there on the picture. At least to him it felt bad. And that could not be good.

He rolled onto his side and began to hum softly.

He had been doing well with the witch, he thought. He was eating all of his dinner food, because it seemed to please her. The bitter mush was an every-night thing now, but with enough water, it really wasn't that bad. At least she hadn't hit him again.

Martha had said that he'd go to two more meetings this week. They really liked that, didn't they? Of course, who wouldn't? The wind had been like God's breath. Like something from the life of Elijah or Elisha, who were two of his favorite people. Not that he was really them; for one thing they were a lot older. And for another thing, they spoke to kings, and Caleb didn't think he was really a prophet or anything like that. But when those prophets asked God, fire fell from heaven, and ax heads floated, and all kinds of amazing things happened. Things like God's wind blowing on the faces of the sick and healing them. He chuckled.

Of course there was always Moses. Maybe he was more like Moses, and Moses was one of his favorites too. He didn't speak well in front of people either, did he? He used Aaron instead. But when it came to calling down frogs and turning the sky black with insects and making the rivers red with blood, Moses didn't seem to have a problem. He hit a rock once and water poured out— enough water to flood the monastery, Dadda said. That's how much it would take for them all to drink. Maybe Ethiopia needed a Moses during the droughts.

A shiver ran through Caleb's bones at the thought, and he smiled. Elijah had once been fed by birds. Did that mean he liked birds too?

Caleb had been walking in the kingdom a long time now, five years at least, but never had he seen how easily the kingdom could spill over into this world. Like light into darkness. But then he'd never seen so much darkness either. Definitely not in the monastery. By the way some of the people were acting in the theater, you would think that they no longer believed in people like Elijah and Moses. Or God, really. They no longer believed in God. At least not *God,* God.

The miracles were God's choice, of course. Father Nikolous might think he had something to do with what happened, but really Caleb had done what he'd done because his Father had given him the power to do it. And because his heart felt so heavy at seeing the people. He could have walked off the stage, but why would he? Not with so many hurting. And he knew that it was all a part of God's plot for sure. He wasn't completely sure of the plot, but it was unfolding like a thunderstorm, wasn't it?

An hour later Caleb was still thinking, not in meditation or in the light. Just thinking. In fact, he wasn't really thinking about anything when he suddenly decided to sit up and look at the television.

He watched the colors and the figures running around, and his heart began to pound. It was terrifying and exhilarating at once. And it was only looking. That's all it really was. He wasn't going into the picture and joining them; he was only studying them like he might a book.

He watched them for three minutes before throwing his head into the pillow and wrapping the covers over his ears.

His chest felt like it might explode, and he began to cry softly. Then he began to shake with sobs. He begged his Father for forgiveness, and he soaked his pillow with tears.

21

Day 24

EVERY ONCE IN A WHILE, maybe every hundred years or maybe every five hundred years, something comes along that makes life on earth very different. That's what the talking heads were starting to say on the tube. Things like the Industrial Revolution or the discovery of electricity or Mohammed's penning of the Koran or the death of Jesus Christ. Well, maybe, just maybe we are witnessing another one of those moments. That's what they were saying.

It was no longer just an American phenomenon; the mind-boggling footage said just as much in Arabic, or German, as it did in English. You could be a seven-year-old girl walking down the sidewalk and see the pictures on the television through the shop window in Copenhagen just as easily as in Boston. And either way, if you asked your mother if those legs straightening was a trick or not, she would probably shake her head and say something like, "I don't know. They say it isn't." It took the Beatles years to find worldwide recognition; it took Hitler months; it took the boy two weeks.

Despite the relative autonomy of the Holy Ascension Church, the Archdiocese of the Greek Orthodox Church was beginning to flex its muscles. In a statement made public by Donna, the archbishop was skillfully avoiding any clear position on either the boy or the local parish's dealing with him. It was too soon to draw judgment.

In short, although they weren't enthusiastic about the way Father Nikolous seemed to be thrusting the boy into the spotlight and charging for admittance, they weren't eager to distance themselves from Caleb either. You could not, after all, ignore the boy's power.

Two more meetings had been held since the night the wind rushed through the Old Theater, each two days apart. Nikolous had paid a premium and preempted a big junior-league hockey game and a heavy-metal comeback tour scheduled for the Old Theater.

He had also raised the price to a hundred dollars a ticket in the orange and red seats, and two hundred dollars for the floor. The boy was pulling in well over a million dollars per show.

They operated out of two entrances now, a western one on the street for those who could walk, and a southern one facing the parking structure for those who couldn't. Four thousand people were wheeled in through the southern entrance on the first night, six thousand on the second. It took four hours to get them all situated.

As promised, Donna had her exclusive interview with Nikolous. When she asked him why he held the meetings so close together, Nikolous told the world there was no guarantee that Caleb's powers would last, and he recited Dr. Caldwell's analysis as his reasoning. Either way, as a man of deep humanitarian convictions, he didn't see how he could do any less. The world needed the boy *now,* not a year from now.

Already one consumer advocacy group was making it clear that Nikolous seemed more interested in the ticket price than in humanitarian concerns. A hundred bucks a pop was price gouging. Unfortunately there were no recorded regulations that dealt with the reasonable charge for a boy who could rock an arena with not much more than a nod. At least not yet.

Caleb had come out with more confidence on each night. He walked with more purpose, and he didn't look around as though lost for as long. He appeared to be getting the hang of these gigs, as one commentator put it. During the last event he'd even said a few words into the microphone. They were simple words rebroadcast a thousand times since. "You can walk into the kingdom of God with the power of the Holy Spirit," he said. That was all.

The words only expanded the raging controversy over the true source of the boy's power.

The debate over the authenticity of the phenomenon was already fading. Only the most ardent skeptics (those who had their heads planted so firmly in the sand of their own dogma that they would not accept the existence of the ocean, for example) even questioned the miracles as genuine. And when they did, their arguments came off as silly and embarrassing in the face of what was happening. You can only say the world is flat for so long before even the most common man starts snickering. Evidence has a way of making its own arguments, and in the case of the boy's authenticity, there was gobs of evidence. Nearly as much as that which suggested the world was indeed round.

As Jason had predicted, the antichrist crowd was growing. The black-hooded demonstrators had swelled to occupy four entire rows on the right side. Their leader had made it abundantly clear in a dozen interviews that the world was pandering to a child of the devil. Why Nikolous allowed them in was unclear. They made excellent camera coverage, and in their own way they lent added excitement to the meetings, but they also posed a threat to the boy. Jason confronted Nikolous about them once, but the man seemed to think restricting attendance might impact the boy's popularity. Like all of their discussions, this one proved mostly fruitless. He did persuade the Greek to double stage security, which was something.

Jason kept his eye on the leader of the cult, which was unnerving for the simple reason that the ominous lizard-eyed fellow seemed to be keeping his eye on Jason.

At the third meeting Caleb had hopped off the stage and run through the crowd ecstatic, much like he had at the handicap convention. People's eyes lit up like Christmas lights as he approached, and they leapt from their beds and chairs and danced in the halls after he passed.

At the fourth meeting he prayed a very long prayer in Ge'ez. He began to cry, and he fell to his knees and appeared to be begging his God. Then he fell prone on his face and lay still. An earthquake hit Southern California that night. Magnitude 4.3 on the Richter scale. It shook the entire Los Angeles basin, but its epicenter was later determined to be under the Old Theater on Figueroa Street. There were no broken windows or toppled trees to show for the quake. There was only a mess of wheelchairs scattered about the vicinity of the epicenter, abandoned by their owners in its aftermath.

To say that Caleb had become a national sensation would be a bit of an understatement. And this all in the span of fourteen days since first having his face displayed to the nation through Donna's camera—twenty-four days since first entering the country with Jason and Leiah.

∞

Jason sat in his living room in the corner recliner, nursing a cup of hot coffee. He stared at the television, only half listening to the talking heads beating the issue to death. Leiah sat on the couch adjacent to him, both legs tucked to one side on the cushions, nursing her own cup—a *Tiggers-are-wonderful-things* mug someone had given Jason at Stephen's birth.

It struck him that she'd been here with him at night like this only twice since coming to America. Not that it meant anything, just a thought. She looked comfortable leaning against the corner pillows, studying the picture tube. Her tan work boots stood heel to heel at the door.

Burn scars still covered her skin, head to foot. All around her people were being healed, but her condition hadn't been affected by the boy. Jason had decided that it was because she probably didn't really need healing. Or at the very least, *she* didn't think she needed healing. Plastic surgery was not exactly something someone *needed*. She hadn't asked the boy, of course. She'd probably considered and rejected the notion already. Something along the lines of, "Asking would be like confessing that I have a problem. And I don't have a problem." Case closed. Some would call her brave and principled. He thought of her more as stubborn. It was a trait she would take to her grave, he thought.

It was also a trait that would have saved a marriage. On balance he liked it.

She caught him looking at her. "What?"

He smiled. "Nothing."

"Hmm." She lifted an eyebrow and turned back to the television. But she couldn't hide the smirk on her lips.

Their relationship had slowly warmed after those first few days of cooling in the wake of the unveiling at Jim's Fish House. He was beginning to think that she might not hate his guts after all. And he was also beginning to look for reasons to be in her company. Silly little excuses, like meeting for lunch before their visit to Caleb each day. Antonio's Barrio was on the way, after all. Or like taking a ride together down to World Relief's Garden Grove office to talk to John Gardner about the prospects of removing the boy from Nikolous's custody, when he knew full well there were no such prospects.

Or like watching this round-table discussion on NBC together. At his house. Not that it wasn't an important event, but they both knew she could just as easily have watched it at her apartment. Still, she hadn't hesitated when he'd suggested they watch it together.

Jason rose from his chair. "More coffee?"

"No thanks."

He walked into the kitchen, topped his cup, and returned. He lowered himself onto the couch beside her, set his cup on the end table, and calmly crossed his legs. The move from recliner to couch felt a bit obvious, and he avoided her look. But it was his couch, wasn't it? And he did have a better view of the television from this angle. A little better anyway.

The discussion on the tube was advertised as a summit—the definitive analysis of the boy's power. The guests sat around a gray table very similar to the one Larry King hosted from, a slightly off-center half-moon with Donna Blair at its center and the seven experts in a semicircle. They were the leading authorities from the fields in question—religion and science.

Dr. Caldwell was there on the left. If she hadn't been a leading authority on psychic phenomenon last month, she was one now. Dr. Shester, a well-known physics professor from Cal Tech, sat next to her. The other five were religious leaders: an Islamic imam wearing a turban—Mohammed something or other—a Hindu priest with a shaved head and a long white beard whose smile would not take a break, two Protestant leaders from opposing camps, and a Catholic bishop. Their names kept popping up under their faces as they talked, but between listening to the overlapping diatribes and thinking about Leiah, Jason hardly cared who they were. For all he knew, they were *all* wrong.

Donna was talking to the Hindu holy man. "Yes, of course. But what do you make of the boy's own words? He's referred to either Jesus or the Holy Spirit on two occasions. He's said that the way to walk in what he calls the kingdom is through the power of the Holy Spirit. If you believe he's the incarnation of a higher power, as you say, why would he invoke a Christian message?"

"That is quite simple," the man said with an Indian accent. He would not relax his smile, and Jason found that annoying. "First of all, it is not only a Christian who speaks of God's Spirit. We all believe in God's Holy Spirit. And the boy was raised in a Christian monastery, was he not? He will then use what language he knows. He speaks of Jesus, and so do I; Jesus was an enlightened teacher of great wisdom. The boy speaks of God, and of course, so do I. And he speaks of God's kingdom, which is the Christian way of addressing the greater consciousness."

"You are being too general," the imam interjected.

"Hold on; you'll have your chance to respond," Donna said, cutting off the imam.

She addressed the Hindu priest again. "I know this is all very controversial, sir, but what if the boy were to specifically validate one religion, say Christianity, and denounce another? What would you then say?"

"But I don't think he would, you see."

"But if he did. Hypothetically."

"If he did, then I would say the same thing that a Christian would say. I would say that he's a ten-year-old boy and he is mistaken."

Donna addressed one of the Christian leaders. "And you, Dr. Clark, would you say the same if the shoe were on the other foot?"

The gray-haired man smiled. "If Caleb were to denounce the deity of Christ as some of my friends here would, I'd assume that his power does not come from God at all. But he hasn't done that."

"He hasn't in so many words," the other black-haired theologian cut in. "But for starters, not everyone is convinced these so-called miracles are real. And—"

"Please, sir," Donna interrupted. "You can't seriously be suggesting that the evidence we've all been exposed to is some magic trick. Have you been to one of these meetings?"

"As a matter of fact I have."

"And you honestly question the authenticity of what you saw?"

"Of course. As do many others." The others smiled, obviously embarrassed for the man. He cleared his throat. "But that's not the point. Even if they are authentic, the nature of these events we've seen don't reflect the Spirit set forth in God's Word. For starters, God is a gentleman. He doesn't knock people over for no reason. He deals only with willing participants. He certainly wouldn't knock a cameraman from his feet for the kicks of it. I don't see how any such thing would bring glory to Christ. And he's not the author of confusion. How can you see any one of the meetings and not think of confusion? If, and I say *if*, what I've seen is real, it looks totally beyond the control of God's Spirit."

"But you wouldn't say that Caleb's power comes from his own mind like Dr. Caldwell would?"

"If it's real, no."

"Then what is the boy's source? If it's real."

"I don't know. But it isn't God."

For a moment they all sat in silence. Then the imam spoke up. "You see, this is the kind of bigoted, narrow view of God that is customary with the Christian. The whole world is rejoicing at the works of this prophet from God, and yet the Christian will throw the boy in hell because he does not attend his church."

Three of them broke out in response at once, but Jason couldn't tell which three. He flung an arm out to the television. "You see, they don't have a clue. And if the rest of them think this is God, then why don't they tell us why God doesn't do this more often? Or at all, for that matter. Why do a million prayers for the sick go unanswered?"

"Your lady friend's making the religious ones look like fools," Leiah said softly.

"She's not my lady friend. And she's only asking them questions. They should be able to answer simple questions."

"She's pushing them into disagreement while the two scientists sit by to set them all straight."

Jason didn't dispute her analysis.

The gray-haired evangelical, the boy's defender, Dr. Clark, was speaking again. "I'm not saying that Caleb's incapable of making mistakes. As long as he's human he'll be making mistakes. But to say he's authoring confusion or that God doesn't knock people down because he's a gentleman is to misplace huge sections of the Word of God. Jesus Christ himself had the people in an uproar, confused over his identity, if you will. They ended up killing him to silence his voice of dissent. Several weeks later his own disciples were accused of being drunk at Pentecost. The biblical record is loaded with incidents of God's reaching out to man as dramatically and in many cases more mind-boggling than what we've seen through the boy. Why are we so surprised to find God alive today?"

Donna seemed caught off guard. "More dramatic cases? Such as?" She was obviously no biblical scholar.

"How about the sun standing still? Imagine city walls collapsing on their own, or the parting of the Red Sea, or a woman turning into salt. Need I go on? Jesus fed five thousand with two fish and five loaves. He calmed a storm with a word. And the early church was hardly less dramatic in its demonstration of God's power. Perhaps the biggest difference between then and now is that they didn't have cameras then. They had writers, and those writers gave us the Gospels."

The skeptical evangelical spoke up. "Yes, they gave us the Gospels, but nowhere in the Gospels did Christ knock people over for the fun of it, now did he? Certainly not pagans."

"No, not for the fun of it. But you will remember that the men who came to arrest Jesus—and I will assume they were pagans, given their plans—fell over at Christ's words. It's at the end of John's Gospel. I don't see how this is any different."

The dark-haired man appeared flummoxed. "Please, you can't ask me to believe that a host of believing people sitting in a room would all suddenly be healed with no expectation of it. I don't see the pattern in Scripture, not at all."

"God is not bound by our boxes, my friend. If he can heal one, why not ten? And if ten, why not ten thousand? He frequently healed everyone who came to him, not just those with exceptional faith. He healed from a distance, and he healed in the dark. What faith does a dead man have? Lazarus could not form a thought, much less believe, and yet he was raised."

"But surely miracles were at the least meant to lead one to faith."

"Yes, if you don't believe in me, then at least believe in the evidence of the miracles, Christ said. We will see where the boy's miracles lead men."

The conversation stalled. Donna blinked and faced the physicist. "Well. What about you, Dr. Shester? You've been awfully quiet."

The Cal Tech physicist grinned smugly. "Honestly, I really don't see where this is leading us, Donna. History is strewn with man's foolish attempts to explain the great questions of life with a few cute anecdotes from the local priest. If you couldn't explain something, it was because God did it. The world was flat and at the center of the universe because God made it that way. Man was made in six days from dust, and all kinds of other impossible things happened throughout history because God just did it that way. And if our neighbor disagrees or claims that a different god did it, well then we massacre them in a crusade and set the world right. Forgive me if I don't follow the logic. If we would just apply basic reason to these unique events, I'm sure we would find something very different from God. This is the time to explore new possibilities, not to argue over whose god is responsible. The laws of physics have been redefined a dozen times since Newton first defined gravity. Well, it looks like we're getting ready to redefine them again, and I for one am excited about the prospects."

Caldwell was beaming. So was the Hindu priest, but not because he necessarily agreed. The other four looked bothered by the comments.

The Catholic bishop spoke up in a quiet voice. "I think Dr. Shester is confusing the issue. You may invoke all the examples from history you like, sir, but you must not ignore the evidence that presents itself at the current time. We don't live in the past. The boy clearly draws his power from a higher source. From God. In the same way Elijah did, in the same way Moses did, in the same way the apostle Paul did, and in the same way many God-fearing Christians do today, all over the world. You might be surprised at what an honest look at the evidence from around the world would reveal. God is not dead, my friend. He works in stunning ways every day. Now, if the boy claims that his source is indeed the Holy Spirit, then why must you immediately dismiss it? Perhaps it's time you reconsider your assumptions, beginning with the assumption that there is no God."

"Nonsense," Dr. Caldwell said. "Darwin settled the issue a hundred years ago. We're seeing a new step in evolution here, not some return to the dark ages, where you take everything you don't understand and dump it in a barrel called God."

"Darwin did nothing but propose a theory," the bishop returned with a smile. "A theory that has been progressively unraveling in virtually every scientific circle since the day it was so blindly accepted. And that was before the boy. If evolution survives another month, it'll only be in the minds of fanatics with clogged ears."

The physicist flew off at that, but Jason let his mind drift again. This was like watching a political debate as an undecided. If you pick a side one moment, you might switch the next. In reality the answers were locked in little Caleb, and even if the boy knew how to unlock his mind, he wasn't being as forthcoming as the world wanted.

Which could be a good thing in the end. Even Jesus Christ was a bit elusive at times, if Jason remembered right.

"Doesn't it feel like we're in some Mad Hatter's game, where no one knows the rules, much less how to win?" Jason asked. "Listen to these guys; it's like arguing over whether Mars really is crawling with little green men after all."

Leiah tilted her head and gave him a twisted grin. "He's a little boy, he lives on earth, and the last time I checked, he was brown, not green."

"Yes, of course. And I love him too, Leiah. He's practically family. But that doesn't mean any of us have a clue what's really going on."

"Any of us? So you're no longer subscribing to our psychic professor's doctrine?"

"I didn't say that. She makes more sense than anyone else."

He and Leiah were exchanging jabs, sure enough. But they were smiling through it, instead of blasting each other as they might have two weeks ago.

Jason cleared his throat. "There's more to his predicament than all this nonsense over whether Caleb's a genie out of a bottle or a prophet of God. Things are getting overlooked."

"Such as?"

He looked at her and lifted an eyebrow. "Such as the fact that the remote monastery Caleb spent his first ten years in just happens to get leveled during an invasion that has no business venturing so far south. Such as the fact that you and I are chased even farther south for eight hours with the boy in our custody. Not only was Father Matthew clearly convinced that Caleb's life was in danger, but we left Ethiopia under the same persuasion. Someone wanted the boy dead."

"Well, hopefully when we left Ethiopia, we left the problem behind us. Not that the one we have now is any better."

"They were trying to kill him, Leiah."

"They're killing him now," she said with a firm jaw. "He's changing."

She was right. Neither of them could put their finger on it, but Caleb seemed to be changing a little. Adapting.

Jason shook his head. "I don't know. I just don't buy the threat to his life taking a back seat to all of this sudden popularity."

She looked at him, taken aback. "So because he's a public figure now, you think he's in *more* danger? I thought the idea behind helping him go public was to protect him."

"It was and we did. They were going to deport him, remember? But *why* were they going to deport him? *Why* were they trying to kill him in the first place? *Why* was Father Matthew so concerned for his life? For that matter, why did Charles Crandal react so strongly when Caleb mentioned Tempest? And now we know that Caleb *isn't* just a unique orphan in a spot of trouble. He's a person with unthinkable power. He's a person who maybe could change history. So maybe these 'why's' are bigger 'why's' than we thought they were. Does that make sense?"

"Donna seemed convinced that Tempest was—"

"An endorsement. I still don't buy it. You don't gag when someone endorses you. Donna's star-struck with Crandal. And I'm not necessarily saying Crandal *is* tied up in all of this. I'm just saying that the questions are bothering me more now than when Caleb was just a lost boy."

She shifted her eyes to the window and thought about that. "Nothing like being optimistic," she said. Her tone had resumed the bite he had come to expect from her. So maybe the blasting wasn't a thing of the past after all.

"And you are?" he asked.

"No. I've known from the minute Nikolous gained custody that Caleb would probably be ruined. That they would strip his innocence away and destroy his spirit. And now you want me to believe that someone still wants to kill him as well?"

"I'm just asking questions, Leiah." He crossed his legs so that he faced her. "Seriously, what if the only reason Caleb's still alive now is because of all"—he motioned to the TV—"this?"

"I don't know, Jason. What if? If you knew that to be the case, what would you do? How far will you go to keep your word to him?"

"I'll go as far as I can; you know that. And I've gone as far as I can already."

"You have? I don't see you standing outside on his street with an Uzi, waiting for the big bad guys to come and try. I don't see you taking a two-by-four into Nikolous's office to knock some sense into him."

"Come on! I'm just telling you that I'm concerned here. Not so you can tell me to strap a nuke to my chest and threaten detonation if they don't fork him over!"

She took a swig of coffee and looked absently at the television. "I'm sorry."

"No. You can be downright obstinate at times. Anyone ever told you that?" She didn't answer.

"You walk around with a chip the size of the Empire State Building on your shoulder, and not only do you refuse to let anyone help you with it, you want to make sure anyone near you carries one just as large, is that it?"

Leiah's jaw muscles flexed.

"Well, I've got news for you, Leiah. I care about Caleb, maybe as much as you do. And I care about you. Not because you're some victim either."

He looked away. *And why do you care for her, Jason?*

"I'm sorry," she said. "I'm sorry. Really."

He shook his head slowly. "No, I'm sorry. I don't have the right to talk that way. It's just . . ." He faced her again, and now she was looking at him with her blue eyes. "I do care for you."

"I know you do, Jason." She looked at the floor. "And it scares me."

They sat in silence for a few minutes while the panel went back and forth about the boy. Jason suddenly wanted to reach over and touch her. Just lay his hand on her feet or something. Her feet were right there on the couch, inches from his left hand. But in truth the thought terrified him as well. He wasn't even sure why it terrified him; it just did.

So he didn't.

At least not for a good five minutes.

And then he did, on an impulse that made him swallow. He just moved his hand five inches or so and laid it gently on her white-socked feet. She didn't even look at him. Neither did she move her feet.

"Maybe you're right," he said, fighting for normalcy. "Maybe there is more I can do for him."

She faced him. "Like what?"

"I don't know. Torch the Orthodox church?"

She chuckled.

"Okay, maybe not. The two-by-four sounded like an idea, though."

This time she laughed, and it was good to hear her laugh. It was very good. She still didn't move her feet.

22

WHILE JASON AND LEIAH SAT and tried to make sense of themselves, Blane Roberts was cracking his neck and running through his options while he waited for Crandal's plane to land. The man had insisted he stay in Los Angeles while he made a three-day swing through the Northeast. They had already canceled a dozen campaign stops through the Southwest, but New York, of all places, was lagging in the polls. They'd pulled ahead in California—a welcome sign after two solid weeks marching all over the West. And there was good indication that their momentum was building. If Crandal took both California and New York, they might very well win the election by the largest margin in history.

The DC-9 they'd called home for the past six months was on final approach.

Crandal was growing impatient. The plastic faces forced upon him by the campaign were stretching his limits. That was the only way Roberts knew to make sense of the foul mood that had descended upon the man over the last two weeks.

In a democracy, politics and power always went hand in hand, although not always naturally. Great politicians always got the power, but those made for great power were not always great politicians. Crandal was an exception, a great politician, destined for great power. But as of late, the politician in him was growing thin.

Roberts stood by the black limousine and watched the jet glide over the runway like a hawk settling over its nest. The words "Power to the People" ran down the fuselage above the windows. The slogan had done its job.

Roberts spoke into his radio. "Touchdown. Clear the exit, Barney. Remember, no news vans within a mile. They can ask all the questions they want after the dinner."

Barney's voice crackled in his earphone. "You got it."

There was this little problem of Caleb, of course. The simple fact that the boy wasn't dead. It wasn't helping to ease Crandal's nerves.

Any man who had ingested as much poison as the woman swore she'd fed the boy would be dead by now. Of course, if and when they did get around to an autopsy, the traces of Clostridium they'd laced the rat poison's standard arsenic with would fool them into thinking common food poisoning had done the kid in. It was an old trick rarely used.

But the boy wasn't even showing signs of weakness. The only explanation that made any sense at all was that the wench wasn't administering the poison as he'd prescribed. He'd met with her an hour earlier and she'd nearly bitten his head off in the wake of his accusations. She'd given the kid exactly what he'd prescribed, she insisted. Every night, without fail. And he had better not shake his finger at her or she might think about telling Nikolous.

It took exactly thirty seconds to convince her that if she whispered one word to the Greek, she wouldn't live out the day.

She wouldn't talk. But that still didn't help them with the kid.

The jet whined to a stop, and Crandal followed a small entourage of bodyguards off the plane. He looked at Roberts only when he was within three strides of the limousine. Roberts opened the door.

"Welcome back, sir."

The large man dipped into the cab without acknowledging him. Roberts shut the door, rounded the car, and slid in beside Crandal.

They'd been sealed into silence for maybe three seconds before the candidate spoke. "Why isn't he dead?"

"I don't know. He should be."

"She's giving it to him?"

"I believe so."

"You believe?"

"Short of feeding it to him ourselves, we can't know for sure, can we? But I spoke to her this afternoon, and I have no reason to think differently."

"You should watch your tone." Crandal paused. "And if she is giving it to him, then why is he still breathing?"

Roberts didn't have a good answer, so he didn't give one. Crandal had always respected his right to question aggressively. It's what kept them sharp he'd said once. Now he was demanding a respectful tone?

"I swear, Roberts, if this kid says anything . . ." He didn't finish.

"He *hasn't* said anything. And there's no evidence that he even knows what you did. It was ten years ago. But I won't bore you with probabilities. I deal in certainties as much as you do. I know we need him dead, but we're clearly dealing with a different animal than we first thought. He's a national hero, for heaven's sake!"

"Exactly! Which is *why* we need him dead."

Roberts looked out the window and said what had been gnawing at his mind for three days now. "Have you considered the possibility that the kid's unaffected by the poison because of this . . . this power of his?"

"We're not living in a comic book full of superheroes. Trust me, the kid will bleed as well as any kid."

"Maybe. But he's not bleeding yet."

"Then forget the poison and use Banks. Their cover should be set by now. Take him out."

Roberts shook his head. "I talked to him this morning, and he thinks it's too soon. If you want this to go down without the media coming unglued, we have to set it up right. Another week. Any sooner and you could blow this open."

The large man breathed deeply and slowly closed his eyes. "I don't like it."

"It's a fine line, but we've walked it before."

They rode in silence for a few blocks. Crandal reached a huge hand up and rubbed it over his bald head. "One week?"

"One week," Roberts said.

"Then double his dose. Give him enough to kill an elephant, if you need to. I'm not sure we have a week."

"I already have."

∞

"I really don't care how much you hate religion or how afraid you are of dis-appointing Peter!" Barbara Long said. "Do you think he's not disappointed with life already?"

"He's learning not to be," Stewart returned.

"They're all healed, Stew! Every one of them! They go into those meetings in wheelchairs and on hospital beds, and they come out on their own two feet. I know this is something that you've decided is impossible—I knew the same thing just a couple weeks ago. But now there are a few thousand people who know differently, and every one of them came from a wheelchair!"

Stewart nodded absently. She was right, of course. The lame were flocking to the Old Theater, and they were leaving changed. But that was them and this was Peter, and for some inexplicable reason, the prospect of taking his son to a meeting terrified him.

"How much are they charging now?" he asked, knowing it was a stupid question.

"Who cares what they're charging! If a fifty-thousand-dollar operation held out hope to put Peter back on his feet, would you do it?"

"Of course."

"Exactly. Come on, Stew. I know this makes no sense. But what if Caleb really does have the power in his mind to heal? Listen to me . . . he *does!* We know he does; we just don't know why or how. So let the scientists grapple with that one all they want. All I want is to give Peter a chance to be normal again."

"And you think I don't?"

Movement to his right caught Stewart's attention, and he turned to see the back of his son's blue wheelchair disappear into the hall. He closed his eyes and bit back his frustration. Barbara was right; he had no right to allow his hatred for religion to deprive Peter of the chance to be made normal again. His son had refused to talk about Caleb, but he had watched him at every opportunity, and that was enough for Barbara. Peter still spoke in his riddles, but not so often, and when he did he said very little. He mostly surfed the channels, looking for news about Caleb.

Suddenly Stewart knew that they would go. Of course, they had to go, didn't they? No matter what the cost—no matter what he had to do to get tickets—they would take Peter.

"Okay," he said. "Okay." And then he turned and walked out to his cruiser.

∞

The boy was changing. Jason and Leiah saw it the next day, and it stopped them both by the door. His hair was dirty, his face looked haggard, and there were circles under his eyes. He smiled, but it looked apologetic. He began to chew on his right index fingernail, and they'd never seen him do that. Martha glared at them from her corner post, and even she looked somehow different to Jason.

They spent ten minutes with him, and Caleb seemed distracted. He picked up a *Good Housekeeping* magazine, probably one Martha had left on the table, and glanced at it for a few seconds before softly closing its cover. It was the way his eyes shifted around that bothered Jason the most.

Jason finally stood, announced that he was going to see Nikolous, and left Leiah with the boy.

The Greek met him in his office, grumpy as usual, but not belligerent. He watched Jason sit in the guest chair without comment.

"Have you seen the boy today?" Jason asked.

"No. He's not working tonight. He has a busy weekend coming up."

"Busy? You plan on working him to death, is that it?"

"No. As a matter of fact, you may be pleased to know that I am changing the format for the boy's meetings. There will only be three thousand admitted to the meeting on Friday night."

"Three? In the theater?"

The Greek smiled. "Does that surprise you? I'm not a man beyond reason. In fact, we will soon be moving to even smaller, more exclusive meetings. We have our first one-on-one session on Saturday."

Jason knew immediately what the Greek was up to. "You're after the wealthy, one-on-one now. Who is it?"

"Some people have . . . greater capacity than others. This man is well known. A Paul Thompson. Have you heard of him?"

"Maybe. Sounds familiar. What are you charging him?"

Nikolous chuckled. "Nothing. Not everything is about money, my friend. Dr. Thompson's practically an evangelical icon with an enormous amount of goodwill. There are few names as well known as his in religious circles. He's also terminally ill. I'm not even sure he knows the boy's coming. A group of his friends have made this request. If it goes well, I'm sure others will follow."

"And of course those won't come cheap. I don't suppose you're raising the ticket price for Friday's meeting."

"Smart boy, Jason. It's a simple matter of supply and demand."

"How much?"

"A thousand dollars. A pittance for another crack at life, wouldn't you say?"

Jason shook his head. "It's extortion. And you're not going to stop there, are you? Maybe you ought to hire a few salesmen to sell the sessions to the highest bidders. For that matter, why not charge a hundred thousand a head?"

"Not a bad idea. Radiation therapy is nearly as expensive and not half as effective." The Greek was grinning and Jason wanted to yell at him.

"You're going to wake up one day and find that this whole scam of yours has crashed around your ears," he said. "Doesn't the Orthodox Church have anything to say about this?"

Nikolous frowned. "As a matter of fact, my change in strategy is in part a response to the bishop. Evidently the San Francisco diocese isn't seeing eye to eye with my progressive nature. To be honest, I think the archbishop sides with them. They will apply more pressure as time goes by, but it is I, not them, who runs this parish. I have more autonomy than you might think. All the more reason to maximize the boy's value now."

"You're dealing with a child's life here!" Jason forced himself to ease up. "What makes you think Caleb will continue to perform for you?"

"He hasn't complained yet."

"That's because he's too innocent to know that you're abusing him. He's too trusting to know that you're his worst enemy."

"What? You've not told him that Uncle Nikolous is a beast?"

"Of course we've told him. And he tells us that you're just a sorry sad sack who needs sympathy. Imagine that! You need sympathy."

"He calls me a sad sack, does he?" Nikolous seemed amused.

"Close enough." Jason sat back and breathed deliberately. "He's changing, Nikolous. He's losing his innocence."

A fire lit the Greek's eyes. "Nonsense! He's isolated for good reason!"

"Sure he is. But you can't isolate him from the crowds at the meetings, can you? Look at him. He's tired."

"You're right, but I can reduce his exposure to the crowds, and I am doing that by eliminating the poor."

"Listen to you! You're a priest and you're shutting out the poor so that you can line your own pockets! You're a fraud."

What good grace Nikolous had maintained until then fell away. He slammed his fist on his desk and stood abruptly. Jason started.

"I am *managing* him!" the Greek thundered. "I am a steward of God's gift, and I will manage that gift as I see fit! Now get out, before I have you thrown out."

Jason stood. "Thrown out? By who, the butler?" He walked for the door, hot from the exchange. "Caleb isn't a gift," he said, turning. "He's a child. You don't manage him like an investment. And if you believe in God, you return him to God and let God use him as he sees fit. But silly me, I'd forgotten: you're one of those priests who don't really believe in God, aren't you?"

"And you do?"

Jason blinked and stared the man down. But an intelligent response was not coming. He stepped out, slammed the door, and stormed down the hall.

23

Day 27

IT WAS NIGHTTIME WHEN CALEB WOKE UP with the gut-ache. It had to be nighttime, or at the very least early Friday morning, because he had just eaten and gone to bed a few hours ago, it seemed. The bitter taste of the gross gunk the nasty witch was forcing down his throat still lingered on his tongue.

He rolled over and rubbed his eyes, thinking that his mind was being more creative these days. He was discovering this new life, and it was opening up some doors in his mind.

It was also making him sick in his heart.

He sat up and put a hand on his stomach. The pain felt like gas pain or something, only it throbbed. A gurgling sound rumbled through his belly. Across the room the television blinked its pictures noiselessly. He'd figured out how to turn the sound down, but the box stayed on all the time. And he was watching it more than he should. Maybe quite a bit more.

He plopped back on the pillow and sighed heavily. A shaft of pain swept through his heart, but it wasn't from his gut. He rolled away from the TV and curled up.

"Dadda, what is happening to me?"

The night answered him with silence.

For the first time in a very long time Caleb felt confusion. Not the kind that wonders what this is or why that happens. But the kind that sits in your heart, makes you feel nothing, and refuses to budge. When you finally do feel, it's only pain. He wasn't really confused about why he felt confusion; that much he knew. He felt confusion because the kingdom was growing fuzzy. And the kingdom was growing fuzzy because the light had dimmed. And the light had dimmed because he was drinking in this other light. Which was really darkness and not light, wasn't it?

Dadda always used to say that the human heart only has the capacity for so much. He once put a large glass vase on the hearth before a crackling fire. He handed Caleb a bottle of olive oil.

"Pour it into the vase, Caleb. To the very top." When he did, Dadda asked him what he saw.

"I see the firelight coming through the oil. It's like . . . gold," Caleb had answered.

His father produced a glass of black water, and Caleb didn't know what it was except that it smelled sour, like brine maybe. "If I want to put some of this into the vase, what must I do?" Dadda asked.

"The vase is full."

"Yes, it is. So what must I do?"

"Pour some of the olive oil out."

"Then do that for me."

Caleb had poured some of the oil back into its bottle, spilling a little on his hand. They had a little chuckle about that. Then Dadda handed him the black brine water and told him to fill up the vase again. He did.

"What do you see?"

Together they knelt and looked at the glass. Caleb would never forget the image. The firelight still glowed in the olive oil, but now fingers of black brine reached down into the vase. The two did not mix; they just swirled around each other.

"Your heart is like this vase, Caleb," his father said. "It can only hold so much. You will have to decide what goes in it—the oil of the Spirit or the blackness of evil. But make no mistake; one will displace the other. They do not mix."

That was three years ago, maybe. A tear came to Caleb's eye as he lay there on the bed. He swallowed and prayed. "Oh God, I am falling into a darkness and it frightens me. Father, do you hear me? I am feeling sick in my heart. What should I do? What should I do to make this end?"

Usually he would hear that small faint voice answer him, but right now it didn't. He knew the answer already.

He blinked. Dadda had once told him that those close to God can hear his still small voice, like a son can hear and understand a father's whisper. God always answers, and he never answers with silence. He is eager for us to hear. But many people cannot hear because their hearts are too far away. Then sometimes God will shout, or use a prophet, for the weak.

But Caleb didn't really need a prophet now, because he already knew the answer to his question. It was very simple, of course. He should not be allowing the blackness into his heart. Into his eyes.

Actually, he already knew that from before. Nikolous had taken him to four large meetings now, and on the last one, something had changed a little. The light wasn't there, and it had confused him and terrified him. He had dropped to his knees and begged to see and then he'd lain down and cried on the stage. Only then did the brightness of day come. An earthquake came as well, but in his mind it was God's voice reassuring him, whispering words of love that shook his body. He had vowed then, lying on the stage, to never look at the glass box again, because he knew it was not for him.

The next day he had looked again. Just a peek, for maybe ten seconds. And then it had stretched into an hour, and he found it fascinating.

Caleb fell into a fitful sleep, trying very hard to ignore the pain. He dreamed of a blue tiger chasing a little boy. They ran for a long time. When the tiger caught the boy, it ate him.

∞

Caleb bolted up in bed, breathing hard. He stared at the television screen. It had colored stripes on it. No pictures.

He'd never seen it without pictures before. A twinge of panic tickled his spine. Maybe it would change. But he watched it for thirty seconds and it didn't change.

On impulse Caleb scrambled from the bed, bounded to the set, and dropped to his knees. He started to push the little buttons, suddenly frantic. Nothing happened. The witch had removed one of the buttons, and Caleb found himself very angry with her.

Suddenly the picture lit up with something new. A full picture, but it wasn't a drawing. Caleb jumped back to the bed. The picture was of a real man, talking from the tube. And it wasn't just any man.

Caleb caught his breath. The man was very large and he had a bald head on top. This was the man from the park. Crandal. *Tempest!*

A light ignited in Caleb's mind. He was watching the man smile and talk, but he did not see smiling and talking. He saw a string of frightening images that made no sense. Women crying and babies dying. Fields burning and gray skies. A picture of a monastery standing alone with smoke rising from its entry. From the monastery a woman walked, slowly. He knew her!

He knew the woman!

But then he didn't know her. Only that he knew her, but not who she was.

Caleb closed his eyes and sat on the bed, but the image didn't stop. His heart beat heavily in his chest. The woman was looking at him with wide eyes. Suddenly a very large bird swooped from the sky toward the woman. Fire blasted from its beak and its mouth gaped wide. It was going to eat the woman!

The room suddenly went dark and Caleb sat dumbfounded. He opened his eyes. Crandal was gone from the screen. A picture of a flag waved, and he watched it for a minute before it too vanished and colored lines ran across the television.

He rose unsteadily and climbed under his covers. What the images meant he didn't really know, only that the man was a very bad man. He had killed many babies and women and burned many fields and made the sky gray. He knew that without question. But the image of the bird and the woman did not mean anything to him.

Pain swelled in his gut again and he burped. The bitter taste of the nasty food the witch made him eat filled his mouth and for a moment he felt like throwing up. But it passed.

An idea flashed through his mind. Martha had told him that Nikolous wanted him at another meeting the coming night. Friday night. He would tell the people that this Crandal man was a bad man.

Yes, he should do that. Of course he would. And he would stop watching the television.

Yes, he should really do that.

∞

Roberts received the call at eleven o'clock Friday night. He was alone at Calypso's Bar and Grill, trying to settle his stomach with a thick New York strip when his cell phone changed all that. It was Banks. There was a problem.

He listened to the whole spiel without speaking. When he did speak, his voice sounded unnatural. "I'll get back to you."

He snapped the phone shut and glanced around. No one was looking his way. He abandoned the half-eaten steak and a full glass of white zinfandel and eased out of the booth. He left through the front door and made his way to the alley behind the restaurant, ignoring the faint ring in his skull. For ten years he'd walked a tightrope in this business, and every other day it felt like a fall. But the safety net had been there. Every time. You got used to it. But even after so many years, the rush of adrenaline that came when you suddenly realized your feet were no longer on the rope was enough to make your pulse pound.

His pulse was pounding now. Because he was clearly falling now.

He jabbed Crandal's private cell line. The man answered after three rings, and he was laughing, at someone's joke by the background noise.

"Yes."

"We've got a problem."

The laugh faded. Silence. "Hold on." He was excusing himself.

Roberts never smoked. Unless he was falling. He fished a pack of menthols from his coat pocket, dug for a book of matches, and lit up a cigarette.

"This better be good, Roberts. I'm in the middle of—"

"The boy talked."

That shut the big man up. Roberts took a long draw on the cigarette and flicked it into the alley.

"The boy talked," Crandal said. "And what did he say?"

"Not too much, but enough. He said that you were a bad man, and he thought you hurt a lot of people in his country."

The phone went silent for a moment.

"Where did he say this?" Crandal asked calmly.

"At a meeting in the Old Theater. Over thirty cameras filmed the statement."

"What else did he say?"

"I haven't seen any footage, but according to Banks, that was it."

"Banks was there?"

"Banks is always there."

Crandal paused for a second, spinning through the information. "Okay, Roberts. I want that kid popped, you understand me? Go with whatever cover Banks has and kill the kid."

"We can control this," Roberts said. "If that's all he said, we have a plausible cover." Crandal didn't object, so he pushed on.

"We did support the Ethiopian Liberation Army in its fight against communism in '91. The whole world knows that. A lot of people got killed in that conflict. Regrettably. For the sake of freedom, of course. So in a very plausible way the boy's right, and it's understandable that he'd say what he said after hearing locals talk about the conflict. As far as him not liking you—"

"Fine. Spin it. But only God knows what he'll say the next time. This is getting out of control, Roberts!" Crandal's jowls were shaking with his frustration—Roberts could see the man in his mind's eye. "Just kill him. I don't care if Banks wants another week to lay his cover; do it now. Our future's at stake here."

"The next meeting's Tuesday."

"Then I want him dead Tuesday night."

"She said he was complaining of a gut-ache today. The poison may be kicking in."

The phone just clicked in his ear.

Roberts grunted, snapped it shut, and turned for the street. Crandal knew as well as he that poison would be much safer. And they both knew that the lack of patience was the single greatest cause for failure in any covert operation. President-to-be or not, Crandal needed to lighten up. They'd been here before.

Then again the stakes had never been as high. He punched in Banks's number and lifted the phone to his ear. Maybe Crandal was right. Maybe they should have done this two weeks ago.

24

Day 28

D R. PAUL THOMPSON LIVED ON THE COAST, fifty miles north of Santa Monica off the Pacific Coast Highway. He convalesced in a two-story Spanish-style house overlooking the slow roll of blue waves as they swept in from the west. It was a serene setting in which to end one's life.

Jason and Leiah had followed the black-shrouded Mercedes up the coast and had been ushered into the home with Caleb and Nikolous. A plump Swedish nurse named Heidi had emerged from the back hall and asked them to wait in the living room for a few minutes while Paul spoke with the boy alone.

That had been over an hour ago.

Nikolous sat cross-legged and silent for thirty minutes before rising and asking the nurse what was happening with Caleb. She'd simply smiled, brought him another soft drink, and told him to show a little patience. Dr. Thompson would spend only as much time alone with the boy as fit his judgment, and he was not a careless man.

Leiah had joined the nurse in her smile and offered to help in any way she could. They disappeared into the kitchen and talked quietly. Fifteen minutes later Leiah had come out and asked Jason if he wanted to wait on the deck with her.

They sat at a small glass-topped wrought-iron table overlooking the bay. A sea breeze cooled their faces.

"I had no idea our host was such a heavy hitter," Leiah said. "Do you realize who he is?"

"Only what Nikolous told me. Big man in evangelical circles."

"If the evangelicals had a pope, it would be Dr. Paul Thompson. His opinion will weigh heavily in the minds of a lot of people."

The trip had been gnawing at Jason from the beginning, and he decided to speak his mind. "Well, frankly, I don't see that it'll make any difference. He could be the Dalai Lama, the pope, Mohammed himself. In my mind he's tainted by religion, and he'll see what he wants to see."

"Have a heart. He's also dying of leukemia."

"And that's why we're here. Not to hear his wisdom on Caleb."

She looked out to sea. "Caleb's tainted by religion as well. You hold that against him?"

"Caleb's different. For one thing, he's a child who doesn't know any better. For another, he's actually doing something, not just pretending. If his power came from some Hindu god, then we oughta see a few other people accessing that same god and walking around doing these kinds of things. The same goes for every other religion's gods. Dr. Thompson may be the cat's meow among his buddies, but he's only one religious zealot among a thousand, and as far as I'm concerned, they're all missing the point."

"And what is the point?"

"The point is he's complaining of a gut-ache this morning, an ulcer for all we know; the point is Caleb's *life's* in danger. The point is that he's being ruined by this circus."

"Of course that's the point; I've been saying that for weeks. But you can't ignore what he does. How many people do you know who can do what he does?"

Jason looked at her, surprised at her defensiveness. "So suddenly we've flipped sides on this?"

"No. I'll give anything for his safety. But I've also been coming to the realization that what Caleb does is part of who he is. We can't just separate the two. Why does his power bother you so much?"

It was a good question and he couldn't answer. His own son's death entered into the picture somehow, but thinking of it gave him a headache.

"I don't know. It doesn't," he said.

They sat staring out to the wind for a few minutes, he with his right arm on the glass tabletop, she with her left. The waves washed back and forth far below.

She faced him without speaking; he could feel her eyes on him. But a heaviness had settled on him and he just looked forward.

It *was* his son, wasn't it? Caleb's powers angered him because what seemed so effortless for the boy had been withheld from his son. They'd done everything they knew to do; they had begged God and made fools of themselves and in the end a fool of Stephen. And then he'd died.

He swallowed.

Her hand touched his. A light, cool pressure on the top of his fingers. But it made him immediately warm.

"It's okay, Jason. I know how it feels, believe me. It doesn't seem fair."

Jason looked at her. She was speaking of her burns. Caleb's power had been withheld from her as well. He had assumed that she ignored it with a stiff upper lip, but now he knew differently.

She was holding his hand. He had touched her in the restaurant; he'd touched her feet on the couch. But this was the first time she had touched him. He glanced down and saw her fingers resting gracefully on his own. The rumpled flesh began at her wrists and then disappeared under a light windbreaker.

Jason lifted his head and stared into her eyes. They were blue, like the sea; they were tender like her hand. But they were swimming with fear as well.

He tried to smile, but he wasn't sure how it came off. "I know."

She looked away. Her fingers moved, and he grasped her hand to stop her from withdrawing. Now it was she who was swallowing.

"I know it's hard," he said. "Maybe you should ask him."

The muscles in her jaw flexed.

Poor, dear Leiah, you're so wounded. And have I told you that I think I might be falling in love with you?

Goodness! What was he thinking?

She looked back at him and her eyes were misted. "I'm afraid," she said.

Afraid of what? Of loving me or of asking the boy?

The door opened and Heidi stuck her head out. "He'll see you now."

Jason released her hand and cleared his throat. His mind was jumping rail, he thought. Going places it had no business going.

∞

Dr. Paul Thompson sat in a wheelchair by a large picture window overlooking the bay when the nurse ushered Nikolous and company into the room. A liquid oxygen tank stood beside the bed to their right, and an IV pole suspended a bag of solution over the electric bed's elevated head. The smell of alcohol hung lightly in the air. The large suite was the quarters of a dying man.

But to look at the tall man slumped in the chair, there was no sense of death at all.

Thompson's hair was white and his face was pale, but the brightness of his baby blues and the infectious curve of his lips had him glowing nonetheless. His flesh hung loose on a large frame. A nasal tube rested on his lap and snaked to a portable tank on the back of the chair.

Caleb stood beside the evangelical heavy hitter with his back to them, drawing imaginary lines on the window.

"Good morning," Thompson beamed. He coughed once, but the smile did not leave his face. "Jason and Leiah, I presume. And you must be Father Nikolous."

"Yes," they each answered with a nod.

It struck Jason then that Dr. Thompson wasn't standing. He was not healed. So what had they been doing for the last hour?

"So you're the people responsible for Caleb?"

"Yes," Nikolous said. A frown had found his face. "So are we . . . successful?" he asked.

Right to the point.

Thompson folded his hands and looked up at the Greek. "Successful?"

"Has the boy attempted . . . anything?"

"Well no, I wouldn't say that. We've been talking, haven't we, Caleb?"

The boy looked over from his drawing and nodded with a smile.

"Talking," Nikolous said. "Is there a problem?"

"No. No problem." Thompson looked at the Greek, inviting him to pursue the matter. But Nikolous was flummoxed. There was tension in the air, and Thompson seemed to relish it.

"He can't do it?" Nikolous asked.

"Do what?"

"Please, Doctor. I brought the boy here to heal you as requested by your associates. Surely you are aware of the boy's power. And I will say that private sessions do not come cheap."

For a few seconds Thompson just looked at the Greek, smiling. Then he turned to the boy. "Caleb, how would you like a chocolate shake?"

Caleb turned without responding.

"Have you ever had a chocolate shake?"

"No."

"Well, well, you are in for a treat. Heidi—"

"I'm sorry, but I can't allow that," Nikolous objected.

"No? And why not?"

"We are monitoring every—"

"Lighten up, Nikolous," Jason interrupted. "A shake isn't going to ruin your precious money machine. He's a boy, for heaven's sake. Let him have a snack."

Nikolous glanced at the three of them, obviously outnumbered. He finally nodded.

"Wonderful!" Thompson said. "Go on, Caleb. You have to try a chocolate shake. Heidi will make one for you. And if you ask the right way, you might be able to talk her into a banana split."

Nikolous looked as though he might object again, but he thought better of it. Heidi led Caleb from the room and shut the door.

They stood in a semicircle around Thompson, who motioned to several armchairs beside him. "Please, join me. I don't want to be the only one seated in comfort."

They each took a chair, and Thompson wheeled around to face them, coughing again. Jason liked this man. He carried himself with the kind of gentle authority you might expect from a leader.

Thompson studied them for a moment and then turned to face the blue sky beyond the window.

"It's always amazed me how so many of my fellow humans manage to live their entire lives without ever seeing the vacation by the sea."

He faced them. "That was how C. S. Lewis put it, and I can hardly do better. He compared us to children busily making mud pies in the slums, unaware that just beyond the horizon there waited a stunning vacation by the sea. But the children never go to this paradise by the sea, because they either don't know about it, or they don't believe it's possible."

Nikolous shifted in his seat. "I'm not sure it was made clear, but I do have an appointment—"

"Do you know what the mud pies represent, Father?"

The Greek didn't respond.

"The mud pies are this world. The vacation by the sea is the kingdom of God. I have lived seventy years among the mud pies with only glimpses of the kingdom. Now I ask you, why would I want to postpone my vacation by the sea?"

The audacity of his perspective hit Jason like a hammer to the chest. But Thompson was smiling and a twinkle flashed through his eyes.

"Why would I put off for one day what I have eagerly awaited my whole life?" He faced the window again, and a mist covered his eyes. "All of creation groans for the day I will soon face, my friends. The doctor tells me that I may have a couple months, and I can hardly stand the wait."

He chuckled. "Two months seems rather long, don't you think? Although I'm sure my heavenly Father knows what he's doing. I feel like my work is done; perhaps I'm wrong."

Nikolous just stared at Thompson with round eyes. Leiah was smiling in awe. And Jason was thinking that the old man had lost his marbles.

Thompson faced them. "I knew the instant that I saw Caleb that he could ask the Father for my health, and his request would be honored—God has given him that unique gift. And I'm sure my associates mean well; I don't blame them. It's not every day that a Caleb walks our streets. But I simply can't. You understand."

"So Caleb didn't pray for you?" Leiah asked.

"I asked him not to. And he agreed."

"So what did you talk about for an hour?"

"Mostly about how fortunate I was."

"That's it?" Jason asked. "You spent an hour talking about how lucky you were to be dying?"

"No, not dying, son. Living."

Leiah cut in. "So you think that Caleb's power really does come from God?"

Thompson coughed raggedly. "Excuse me. Contrary to what some of my colleagues in high places might think, I have no doubt."

Jason checked his earlier attraction to the man. He wasn't sounding reasonable. "You can't just say that without hearing the arguments," he said. "Everyone sees what they want to see through their own bias. And you're different?"

"I may be confined to this chair, my friend. But neither my eyes nor my ears have failed me yet. As you might guess, my schedule is not very full these days; I've followed Caleb like a hawk and I've heard every argument cast. More importantly I've just spent an hour with the boy, and I really don't see the great mystery that surrounds him."

"And you say that his power comes from God?" Leiah asked again.

"It isn't his power. He will tell you that. It's the power of the Holy Spirit."

"Which comes from God?"

"Yes. And which is God himself."

Leiah might be enamored with the old man, but Jason wasn't ready to let him off the hook.

"The scientific community is saying that his power's from his mind, and they have documented cases of other psychokinesis."

"Yes, they do say that, don't they? And do they have cases of man parting the Red Sea? Or multiplying a loaf of bread to feed five thousand? Or knocking five thousand men and women from their feet with a song? Really, it stretches the imagination, don't you think?"

"No more than saying that the parting of the Red Sea and the feeding of the five thousand and knocking people over comes from some spirit. Both explanations are completely immeasurable. What makes you think one's better than the other?"

"I've experienced one," Thompson said with a raised brow. "The other's only hearsay."

"You've knocked people over too?"

"No. That I haven't. But I've felt the power of God's Spirit in other ways just as real."

Nikolous looked at his watch. Leiah stared at Jason, but he ignored her for the moment. He wanted to make a point here.

"Okay, if you don't mind, Dr. Thompson. I don't mean to be argumentative, but even within Christian circles, there's no consensus that Caleb's power comes from God. One says that God is a gentleman and would never create such confusion, and the next says that men of God take the world by force. One says that God only works miracles that lead people to Christ—which incidentally hasn't happened—and the next says that God's sovereign; he'll do whatever he likes. These are theologians, for heaven's sake, and they can't even begin to agree!"

"People may not have come to Christ yet, but the boy's ministry isn't over. I think there's much more to come. There is a purpose here, my friend, and in the end the reconciliation of man to God will make the rest of this look like child's play, no pun intended. You seriously can't think that Caleb is simply a pawn being used for man's whim! He is no more being manipulated by his circumstances than Christ was manipulated by Pilate at his trial. It all has a greater purpose. You'll see that one day, if you look for it."

Thompson closed his eyes and sighed. "And to be honest, I don't understand the bickering among the denominations myself. I suspect they all would do well to take a deep breath." He opened his eyes and stared directly at Jason.

"Good people often make mistakes, Jason. But if my brothers would spend a few hours with Caleb, they would have to rethink their positions.

Who can know the mind of the Lord? You know he's always confounded the wise. He had a fish swallow Jonah—you don't think he could have arrested the man's attention in a more conventional way? He spoke through a donkey, and he wrote on a wall. Sounds a little like showing off to me, but I suppose it's his right. He turned water into wine and cursed a fig tree. Tell me how these are any different than knocking people over? Just because God doesn't part a Red Sea every year, doesn't mean that he never did or can't again."

"They're not different. And I'm not sure God did any of those things."

A silence settled in the room.

"This is all fine and well," Nikolous said, "but we do have to be leaving."

Leiah ignored him and spoke. "Actually, I think the one question we all have more than any other is why? If this is God, then why don't we see the miraculous more often? Can't all Christians access this Holy Spirit?"

"Please. The miraculous is much more common than you might think. Travel through the churches in South America and the Far East as I have, and you'll find it run of the mill."

"Then why not here, in America?"

"It is common here in America, as well. But the Spirit of God doesn't frequent places where he is not eagerly sought. Like the pearl of great price Jesus talked about—if you want it, you seek it. And you must remember that the Holy Spirit's greatest power is not necessarily miraculous as you think of it."

Leiah had a raised brow, and Jason thought she wasn't buying his simplistic explanation.

"Miraculous or not, walking in the Spirit means stepping into the kingdom of God, and most Christians aren't willing to walk there. They enter the kingdom at their rebirth but they take few steps." Dr. Thompson grinned and faced them. "At least that's the way Caleb puts it, and I think I like his perspective. Those who do walk in the kingdom have far more power than you would ever guess. It might not be the straightening of bent spines; you may not even see it here among the mud pies, but believe me, the power of the Spirit-filled man is quite stunning. Whoever said that a straightened hand was more dramatic than a healed heart anyway? Caleb may be a vessel of God's spectacular power, but he's not as unique as you think. Not at all. You're just not seeing the rest of it with your eyes—the fruits of the Spirit, the power of love, the color of peace. What you need is to have your eyes opened."

"That's a cop-out," Jason said. "If you can't explain it, you just throw it off to the unseen. But meanwhile here in the real world people are dying by the bucket load, and I don't see how any rational man can see that and believe that some good God just stands by to watch it all."

"Some would say that I am suffering, Jason."

Jason blinked. And what did that mean?

"Maybe we have it all backward. Maybe the suffering in this world pales beside the glory of the next. Maybe it even defines it in some ways. I can't speak for everyone, and I certainly don't know the mind of the Lord, but for me this suffering is a temporary distraction. I would gladly give my life for a few moments with him."

"Wonderful. I'm glad for you. But my son wasn't ready to go spend a few moments with your God." A wave of heat washed over Jason's head. He had come to the crux of the matter, hadn't he?

Thompson just looked at him, reading him. Jason glanced at Leiah, who was staring off to the ocean.

Thompson broke the silence with a coughing fit.

"Excuse me. I should really hook my tubes up soon." He picked up the translucent tube on his lap. "Heidi tells me they make me look like an alien," he said with a grin. "Which is fine, because I'm headed out soon enough."

He wheeled around and rolled toward his bed.

"You know, Jason, your problem is that you've never seen into the kingdom." He spun his chair around. "I've known a lot of people in my days. Pastors, evangelists, devout men of God. But I don't think I've seen anyone as pure as Caleb. He's as innocent as they come in this world. And he knows the reality of the kingdom of God like he knows his hands each have five fingers. Jesus said that if you have as much faith as a mustard seed, you can say to this mountain move, and it will move. Caleb is simple enough to believe it. And he's pure enough to do it. His theology may not come in the nice neat boxes we love in the church, but then again, he's just a ten-year-old boy. You certainly can't fault his heart. I'm not even sure you can fault his mind."

He spun back around and wheeled to an over-the-bed table.

"Maybe he can help you open your eyes," he said, lifting a bottle of pills from the table.

It was Leiah who asked, "How?"

A mischievous glint swept Thompson's face. "By entering the kingdom, of course. By surrendering yourself to God's forgiveness. You know you need to be forgiven, don't you, Leiah?"

Jason felt his chest constrict. He wanted to yell at the old man in that moment, and he wasn't entirely sure why.

Thompson spoke after a moment. "Tomorrow's Sunday. Take Caleb to the Coastview Fellowship in Huntington Beach. I believe their service begins at ten. Or take him to any church where the people are seeking the touch of God. I think you might see some things."

"We've seen plenty already," Jason said.

"You've seen a few acts of God's power. But you haven't begun to see the power of the healed heart. Not with the eyes of faith, you haven't. Whoever said that a straightened hand was more spectacular than a healed heart?"

It was the second time he'd asked the question.

Thompson looked out the window. "If God were to open our eyes the way he did Elijah's servant, it might just fry our minds. You ever wonder what a chariot of fire really looks like? Hmm? Or how about tongues of fire, floating over someone's head? Both have happened, you know." He faced them. "But then that's another matter altogether."

"We'll take him," Leiah said.

"You'll do no such thing," Nikolous said, standing.

"It's a church, Father," Thompson said. "Surely you wouldn't prohibit the boy from attending a church."

"He *lives* at a church! My church."

"Which is why he cannot attend your service. Your own congregation would ignore you for the boy. He would upstage you in your own church. But surely no caring shepherd would deny a child of God the right to attend worship."

Thompson was no idiot.

"I will give it some thought," Nikolous said. "But now we have to go. Thank you for your time, Dr. Thompson. I'm sorry the boy was not able to perform." The Greek dipped his head, headed for the door, and stepped out.

"I'll pray that he opens your eyes, Jason," Thompson said. "From where I'm looking, life could not be better. It would be a pleasure to meet you again on the other side." He flashed a mischievous grin and tossed two pills in his mouth.

Jason thanked him and left the house, trying his best to ignore a bad headache.

25

Day 29

COASTVIEW FELLOWSHIP WAS BURIED in a warehouse district five miles from Huntington Harbor, an hour south of Pasadena off the 405 freeway. It had been four weeks to the day since Jason and Leiah had first taken Caleb to the Orthodox church. They had lost the boy that day, to Nikolous and his machinery. But today represented a reunion of sorts. Because today there was no Nikolous or Martha or even the Mercedes, for that matter. It hadn't been a pleasant task, but they'd finally persuaded Nikolous to allow them to take the boy without him, on the one condition that they hang sheets on the inside of the Bronco to protect him. They had agreed.

Jason pulled onto the freeway and smiled at Leiah beside him. She winked and peeked over the sheet they'd wrapped between the front seats to keep little Caleb from seeing out the front.

"So Caleb," Jason said, eyeing the boy in the rearview mirror, "what do you say this beautiful morning?"

"I say that I have a monster gut-ache and it's the pits!" he said.

At first Jason wasn't sure he'd heard correctly. *It's the pits?* He caught Leiah's raised brow.

"It's the pits?" she said. "Where did you hear that, Caleb?"

He shrugged and fingered the pink sheets in an attempt to see out. "On the television."

The television? They had asked Martha to remove it once when the boy first complained, and she had humphed off. Caleb hadn't mentioned it since. But now the matter was plain: he was watching television in his room.

"What do you see on television, Caleb?" Jason asked.

The boy looked forward and grinned. "The drawings that move and talk. They are very funny."

Cartoons.

"I see other things too, but I like the drawings mostly."

The boy had found some entertainment under their noses. He was spending his days locked in the room with a television, and Jason doubted that Nikolous was even aware of it. And by the sounds of it, he was getting a bit of an education.

Jason grinned at the thought. "You're learning some things on the television, are you?"

"Yes. Very much."

"Do you really think that's the best thing for him?" Leiah asked.

"Why not? They can't hide the world from him forever. He's been confined to either the room or the Mercedes for four weeks now. Except the Old Theater. And yet he has a window to the world right there in his room. Nikolous would have a fit!"

Behind them Caleb chuckled. "Father Nikolous would drop dead."

Jason looked over at Leiah, unable to hide his smile. "Yes, he would. Nikolous would drop dead." The boy was a quick study. Cartoon talk had expanded his vocabulary.

"What else have you seen on the television?"

"I saw the man who spoke in the park and I had a vision."

Crandal? Caleb's comments two nights earlier about Crandal being a bad person had raised some interesting discussion, but the media spun it as a sort of right-wing reaction to Crandal's NSA affiliations. Jason had asked him about the comment that night, and Caleb had only repeated himself.

"He must have seen a political commercial," Leiah said.

"What was the vision?" Jason asked.

"A big bird flew out of the sky and attacked a woman. The bird could breathe fire. And I also saw babies and people dying."

"And that's why you think Crandal is a bad man?"

"Yes."

"What does the vision mean?"

"I don't know."

"But it's bad?"

"Yes."

The threat Jason had connected to Crandal had faded over the past week. The INS was no longer breathing down Caleb's neck; there was no mention of the NSA. But what if the threat really was still there? What if this vision of Caleb's really meant something about Crandal?

He glanced in the mirror. "What do you say we pull those sheets off the window, Caleb?"

"Yes?"

Leiah looked from one to the other and then nodded. "Why not? Why not?" She jumped into the back, cracked the windows, and tore the pink sheets down. Light flooded the cab.

Caleb immediately pressed himself up against his window and stared at the world for the first time in nearly a month.

∞

They pulled into the church's parking lot at a quarter past ten. Without specific instructions they never would have found the square converted warehouse with the words *Coastview Fellowship* splashed above wide white doors.

"Here we go," Jason said, stepping up to the door. "I hate these places." He pulled the door open and followed them in.

Jason had been in two churches in the last seven years: Greater Life Community, where his son had been practically prayed to death, and the Greek Orthodox church that had stolen Caleb.

Coastview Fellowship was patently different from either.

The service had started, evident by the team of musicians on the stage, singing and playing with their faces lifted to the ceiling and their eyes closed. A thousand or so men, women, and children of all dress and stripes sang in unison.

You are mighty,
You are holy,
You are awesome in your power.

They stepped into a row of folding seats. Although the open ceiling was somewhat reminiscent of a warehouse with its large hanging lights, nothing else about the interior of the building was. Hundreds of flags hung from the rafters; maybe every flag of the world. Large twin screens flashed the words of the song they were singing from a huge console above the stage. A twenty-member choir sang behind the song leader.

You are mighty,
You are holy,
You are awesome in your power.

So many people, ordinary people, giving themselves to this God of theirs. The air felt thick and a chill ran down Jason's back.

Beside them a woman stood with her chin raised, her face aglow as she sang. Directly in front of them, a family stood with hands folded and heads bowed. On all sides the people looked as though they had really stepped into a king's courtyard. Jason had never seen anything quite like it. An odd concoction of reverence and open expression. At least there were no charismatic elements hopping and shouting or any such obnoxious thing, Jason thought. It was all quite orderly.

The worship leader suddenly sank to his knees and continued to sing with one hand raised. Jason glanced down at Caleb in the aisle seat. The boy stared ahead, slack-jawed. He'd undoubtedly never seen anything like it either. Jason looked ahead and studied the words on the screens as they thundered their song.

You have risen,
You have conquered,
You have beaten the power of death.

A tightness suddenly gripped his throat. And what if that were really true? What if the boy wasn't speaking only from his own past, but from the truth? What if Dr. Paul Thompson really was headed for a better place? Thompson hadn't pretended to understand it all. Instead he assumed something as simple as having one's eyes opened would settle the matter.

So what did these simple people presume that having one's eyes opened felt like?

The tightness spread to Jason's chest. There was something here that seemed to be touching him. So many people together with one mind, like at a Hitler rally—maybe that was it. Group consciousness.

Jason wanted to cry. The impulse terrified him. He should get out, go to the bathroom maybe. Beside him Leiah sniffed. He glanced over. Dear God, she was starting to cry!

A slice of panic slipped through Jason's mind. He really didn't belong here. He really should . . .

Movement to his left caught his eye and he turned.

Caleb's seat was empty. The boy was five feet up the aisle. This time he was running.

Jason froze. Leiah still had her eyes closed, trying not to lose control of herself. And the boy was running for the stage as if this were a fifty-yard dash instead of a church service. The music was so loud that yelling for him would be pointless.

He nudged Leiah, and when she opened her eyes he nodded forward. She looked.

Caleb reached the front row and threw himself at the foot of a wood altar that ran across the front. He literally left the ground parallel to it and landed prone. Nobody seemed to mind. The prospect of a single small child racing to the front and throwing himself prone was evidently not unheard of here. The singing swelled.

Jason swallowed hard. His throat muscles felt as if they were choking him.

For a few seconds Caleb just lay still. And then he rolled on his back and covered his face with both hands and his crying rose with the song. It was the weepy wailing sound so common in African countries.

The kneeling worship leader, a young man with short-cropped sandy hair, lowered his mike. His shoulders began to shake. The choir softened behind him, but they sang on. Now Caleb's voice rose above them all, crying in Ge'ez. Jason had no idea what was going on—nothing spectacular, no rushing wind, no earthquakes—but his heart was hammering and his head was throbbing. Beside him Leiah was crying.

Slowly, ever so slowly, the music quieted. The percussion faded, the singing stopped, and only the keyboard played on, a soft organ tone. Sniffles and soft sobs rippled through the auditorium. The worship leader dropped the mike, lifted both hands to the sky, sat back on his haunches, and wept openly. Behind him several members of the choir had dropped to their knees. The rest stood swaying slightly. It was suddenly all very quiet except for the crying.

And above it all Caleb wailed.

He writhed on the floor, turning from one side to the other, and he brought his knees up to his chin. The keyboard player removed his hands from the keys, covered his face, and began to cry.

Whispers of "Thank you, Lord" and "Touch him, Lord" carried through the crowd. No one seemed to know what to do. A boy running up to the altar and crying might not be unheard of, but this display had them at an absolute standstill. Jason doubted if any of them knew who the prone boy in the front of their church was. A few in the front row might have seen enough to recognize him, but if they did, they didn't show any signs.

A blond man of medium build wearing a sharp blue suit walked from a side row, paused to look at Caleb, and then took the two steps up to the platform. He put one hand in his pocket, the other on the podium, and looked out at the congregation.

Caleb stopped his crying and lay facedown.

"God is here," the leader said by the podium. He looked as if he wanted to say something else. But then he lowered his head and stood very still. His shoulders began to shake. The air in the auditorium did not move. The man Jason assumed to be the pastor just stood there with one hand in his pocket and the other on the podium, shaking with silent sobs. Then he released the pulpit and sank to his knees.

Jason felt hot, wet trails leak down his cheek, and he quickly wiped his eyes with the back of his hand.

The worship leader behind the pastor suddenly began to groan aloud in indistinguishable words. Then his voice grew, and Jason heard his cry.

"Forgive me. Oh, God, forgive me . . . Forgive me!"

The sentiment swept across the stage. Now the pastor was groaning the same. "Forgive me. Father, forgive me . . ."

Half of the choir members and four of the five band members, including the drummer, fell to the ground begging for forgiveness.

But it didn't stop there. The groaning that Caleb had started spread into the audience, as if carried on a wave beginning at the front row and sweeping backward. Back toward where Jason stood, slowly unraveling. He watched through watery eyes as they fell to their knees and cried out for forgiveness. Repentance had seized the place.

It wasn't a rational argument, it wasn't carbon-dated, and it really made no sense at all. But it was plain, and it was obvious, and the evidence of its truth swept up through Jason's throat like a burning iron. He had rejected God, and for the first time in his life he knew the terrible sin of it.

Whoever said that a straightened hand was more dramatic than a healed heart anyway? Dr. Thompson had asked. *You need your eyes opened, Jason.*

Maybe this was how it felt to have your eyes opened. The eyes of the heart.

An older woman with a yellow hat three rows in front of him suddenly cried out and sat back heavily. "Oh, God, forgive me." All around her, people slumped to their knees.

When it hit Jason he thought he would explode. A fireball of bitter sorrow rolled up his chest and swelled in his mind. And in that moment he knew that he had committed an appalling crime. He had done it in front of the whole world, and he could hardly stand the shame of it all. He'd slapped the swollen face of a leper; he'd kicked a dying man and walked away; he'd spit in the face of Christ.

He'd spit in the face of Christ.

"Oh, God," he muttered. His legs weakened and he sat to his seat hard. "Oh, God. Oh, dear God, forgive me . . ." Jason slid from his chair, suddenly desperate to bow to his face. It was that kind of sorrow. He was on the floor, lying in the aisle before he had time to reconsider.

The sentiment that flooded his body was the most painful emotion he'd ever experienced. It was also the sweetest. He was dying on the floor at the back of Coastview Fellowship in Huntington Beach. And he was coming to life.

∞

It took a good five minutes for the sounds of repentance that filled the auditorium to soften. Jason lay with his left cheek pushed into the blue carpet. He opened his eyes and saw that Leiah was sobbing beside him. The aisle was strewn with bodies, softly repenting. A few people sat quietly in their seats, but most were either kneeling over their chairs or between them. The musicians were all on the floor; the pastor lay prone with one hand hanging limply over the edge of the stage. Not a soul stood in the entire building.

And then one did stand.

The boy.

Caleb stood and looked around as though lost. Jason lifted his head. Waves of sorrow still washed through his chest, but now another sentiment joined it. The impulse to run up there and hug that boy. To beg his forgiveness.

Jason pushed himself to his seat, crying once again.

The boy suddenly jumped up on the stage, and Jason stared at him dumbly. Caleb spun around to face the people. He had that look Jason had come to know, that mischievous glint of delight.

The boy whirled around, jumped over the body of the worship leader, and pulled at the arms of the drummer. The young man looked up, dazed.

Caleb grabbed the drumsticks, lifted them over his head, and beat down on the tom drum with both hands.

Boom.

The sound echoed against the walls. The drummer rolled to his knees. Caleb grinned wide and hit the drums again, this time twice, *boom, boom.*

And then he began to beat the drums, out of rhythm, wearing a white-toothed smile. The people began to rise from the floor.

The drummer stood and Caleb shoved a stick at him. He took it, looked around wearing a crooked grin, and hit the tom once with the boy. Then twice and three times.

Caleb shoved the other stick to the drummer, gave a little hoot, and jumped out from behind the set. The musician slid onto his seat and began beating out a steady rhythm. *Boom—rapatat, bada boom—rapatat.*

Caleb skipped across the stage, ecstatic, and Jason stood thinking he would join him. It was all very foolish, but somehow it felt just right. To be a child again.

Boom—rapatat, bada boom—rapatat!

The boy hopped over to the guitar player and pulled him up. The man needed no encouragement. He slung the instrument over his neck and began to strum. He lifted his head and began to hop up and down, and he strummed in perfect rhythm. The people began to clap now.

Boom—rapatat, bada boom—rapatat!

Caleb threw both fists into the air and hollered to the ceiling in Ge'ez. His voice cut across the room, and he yelled the same thing again. He'd repeated it seven or eight times before Jason managed to piece the words together.

"The lamb who was slain is worthy! The lamb who was slain is worthy!"

Jason wanted to jump with the boy. He wanted to shout and jump and say that same thing. He began to bob up and down back there in the aisle, and it must have looked terribly awkward, because he had never done such a thing. Leiah was climbing to her feet.

Caleb was skipping across the stage, waving the people to their feet, beside himself with excitement. The sandy-haired worship leader needed no encouragement. He was on his feet, hopping vertically like a pogo stick. The other musicians joined in, and the music swelled to a thunder.

The worship leader snatched the mike up to his mouth and began to sing with one hand stretched to the sky.

You are mighty.

Then again, this time with the choir.

You are mighty!

Then again, with a thundering cry from the congregation.

You are mighty!

Jason couldn't stand it any longer. He ran for the platform, nearly oblivious to his surroundings. He flew over a middle-aged man still in the aisle, raced to the altar, and was up on the stage before having time to consider his rash move.

The boy was jumping up and down, singing full throated to the sky. Jason took three large steps forward, swept the boy from his feet in a bear hug, and swung him around.

The band boomed in full volume, and suddenly a thousand normally reasoned citizens of Southern California broke out in a spontaneous dance of celebration.

Jason dropped the boy to his feet and glanced out to the crowd. Leiah was running for them. Behind her, a sea of people bounced with uplifted hands and twirled into the aisles and thundered in unison:

You have risen,

You have conquered,

You have beaten the power of death!

Then Leiah was onstage jumping with Caleb, tears still wet on her face. The pastor was still on his knees, but his hands clawed for the ceiling and he wailed the song.

The entire scene was surreal. No one had urged them into such an uninhibited state. The pastor himself, a conservative-looking fellow, seemed as stricken as any of them. The wordless repentance and now this exuberant dance were completely unsolicited and spontaneous.

A thought whispered through Jason's mind. The notion that this was all absurd. But it was quickly overpowered by the strange desire to worship this same God that the rest were worshiping in such abandon. To fall at the feet of this God. This Christ.

His God.

He fell to his knees, lowered his head, and sobbed breathlessly.

They sang the song for fifteen minutes while Caleb, Leiah, the worship leader, and now the pastor as well skipped from one end of the stage to the other. In the end Jason joined them, and the place became a madhouse of wild celebration. No brilliant words were spoken—no pulpit message to bend their ears—only this uncommon display of repentance and passion. Twice the pastor walked up to the podium to say something. Twice he walked away without speaking.

And then the auditorium quieted, and they knelt among whispers of reverence to God for several very heavy minutes, before the drummer started again and a new song broke from the worship leader's lips. Dancing erupted across the auditorium once again. The celebration went on like that for two hours, and Jason felt as though he just might have crossed over into heaven.

They knew who the boy was now, because several had yelled out his name and the rest had roared their approval. Caleb left the stage and began running through the crowd, tireless in his delight. He touched a deaf woman, and she began to scream with praise. He pulled a paraplegic from his chair and then danced with him across the floor. For two hours the party went on.

Jason had never seen the boy in such a state of joy, and it occurred to him that this was what Dr. Paul Thompson had counted on. This free flow of the spirit among a throng of believers.

Countless members of the congregation came up and hugged Caleb. He was small and cute and full of the Holy Spirit, and they could barely resist him. Jason moved through the hours in a daze, stunned at the emotions rolling through his own heart.

It made little sense, but he no longer cared. His eyes had been opened. For the first time since meeting little Caleb he had seen the boy's treasure; he had seen the kingdom of heaven. At least a small part of it. And he knew without question that he wanted to walk in that kingdom.

∞

They would have stayed longer if it weren't for their promise to return the boy by three. They reluctantly climbed into the Bronco at two and left Coastview Fellowship.

They rode for ten minutes in silence, and Caleb seemed content to lie down in the back seat to sleep.

"Well," Jason finally said, exhaling.

"Well," Leiah repeated with a grin.

"So, I guess Dr. Thompson wasn't such a fool after all."

"I guess not."

They rode on, and Jason wasn't sure there was much else to say. They just sat there wearing silly grins and rode in silence for another ten minutes.

"I think I'm a Christian now," Leiah said.

"Yeah." Jason chuckled. "And what's that mean?"

"I'm not sure. But I met him. He forgave me. Does that make sense?"

"Yeah." It made sense because he knew the same thing.

"It was like I felt his breath on me and I could hardly stand it," she said. "I knew that I desperately needed his forgiveness and he gave it to me. He smothered me with it." She turned and looked out her window. "I never would've imagined such a love."

"I know."

"I think I know what Dr. Thompson meant," Leiah said. "I think I know the power of a healed heart."

"Yeah, wow."

Then they fell back into silence and eventually small talk. But Jason's mind was buzzing all the way to Pasadena.

It wasn't until after they had dropped Caleb off that the snide whispers about his son's death began slinking through Jason's mind. They had prayed for Stephen, hadn't they? So why was his son dead? If Caleb's power really did come from God, why had God passed Stephen over?

Why couldn't other Christians be like Caleb?

Was all of heaven somehow captured in this one boy, relegating the rest of the world to slog through a powerless existence? So he had seen the kingdom, but what did it mean to *walk* in that kingdom with the kind of power so easily at the fingertips of the ten-year-old boy back there?

It was a good question. And it was gnawing at his mind already.

26

Day 30

"H ONEY!" STEWART LONG STRODE through the front door grinning from ear to ear. "Peter!"

It had taken a week, but he had done what they all knew had to be done. The last seven days had drifted by in a surreal haze for all three of them. It was a kind of "the train's at the station now but may be leaving at any minute" feeling that hung over them at the dinner table each night. That's what more than a few talk-show hosts were saying anyway. They were debating over this "noble savage" theory of Caleb and saying that once culture got ahold of him it might be all over. So then the Longs had to get tickets fast.

But getting tickets proved far more difficult a chore than deciding to get them. Not because they'd jacked the price to a thousand bucks a head, but because Nikolous the Greek had trimmed the audience down to three thousand. From what Stewart could dig up, two thousand of those weren't even traded on market but sold to a class of people beyond his reach. That left a thousand and at least half of those were snatched up by scalpers, who then resold them for an ungodly sum within hours. It wasn't the money—Stewart would have paid any price now. But simply put, tickets were as scarce as fossils from Mars.

This morning his luck had changed. He'd pulled a Jack Burns over for speeding and discovered a warrant out for twenty unpaid speeding violations. That was when Jack flashed five tickets for the show downtown at Stewart. He had caught himself a scalper.

He even paid Jack for three of the tickets, two grand apiece. That was six grand he gave Jack—a lawbreaker whom he should be hauling down to the station rather than making rich. Instead Stewart wrote him a check, told him to slow down, and then broke every posted speed limit on his way home to display the spoils.

But then he was a cop; he could do that. And Jack would get his due soon enough.

"Peter!"

His son spun out of the kitchen, leading Barbara.

"What is it?" his wife demanded.

Stewart waved the large green tickets. "Guess what these are?"

"Tickets?" Peter asked, leaning so far forward Stewart thought he might tumble out of his chair.

He paused for effect. "Tuesday night. The Old Theater. Three—"

"You're kidding!" His wife flew at him and snatched the tickets from his hand before he had a chance to finish. She studied them, mouth open.

"We . . . we're going?" Peter asked. He'd turned white.

"What do you think of that?" Stewart asked, grinning wide.

Peter looked from his dad to his mom, and then back to his dad. "What does it matter what one thinks as longs as . . ." He let the quote trail off and sat in silence for a moment. Then he whirled around and wheeled for the kitchen.

"I think that's good," he said. "I trust Caleb."

∞

Something was wrong with Caleb. One glance and Leiah knew that something was terribly wrong.

He slouched on the couch, pale as dough, with his hands on his gut. He'd been looking a bit peaked these last few days, but she'd assumed it was nothing more than the lack of sunlight. The poor child had hardly seen a ray of natural light in a month. He'd complained of his stomach, but never adamantly. The food was new; it was to be expected.

But looking at the dark circles under his eyes now, she knew that he was a sick boy.

Jason picked her up at noon, boiling with questions and eager to ask Caleb about something that had kept him up half the night. He'd changed somehow, and his demeanor had made Leiah laugh. But Caleb had changed too, and that had wiped the smile from her face.

They'd tried to coax him into talk, but the boy was disconnected this morning. Honestly it looked like he'd taken a whipping back in that room of his, and Leiah wondered if Martha had taken it to him. Jason had given it about ten minutes and then ran out to fetch Nikolous. Martha was out tending to her duties. Leiah sat alone with Caleb who stared blankly at the far wall.

"Caleb, honey." She brushed his bangs from his forehead. His head felt hot. "You're scaring me."

He just sat there like a lump of clay.

"We'll get you to a doctor, okay? I don't know what this is, but we'll get you to a doctor right away, okay?"

Caleb closed his eyes.

The door suddenly banged open and Nikolous strode in, followed by Jason. The Greek stormed up to the couch, snorting like a bull.

"What do you mean he's sick? He can't be sick!"

Leiah took Caleb's hand. It felt clammy. She looked up at Nikolous. "We need to get him to a doctor right away. He has a fever and whether you like it or not, he *is* sick."

Nikolous scowled at the boy. He stepped up, pulled the flesh below Caleb's eyes down, looked into each eye, and stood up.

"He's not sick. He's tired, and what do you expect after your keeping him out so late yesterday!"

Jason spoke quietly. "He's sick, and it has nothing to do with taking him to church for a few hours yesterday morning. We have to get him to the doctor."

"He can't go to the doctor, you idiots!"

"Why not?" Leiah asked.

"How would that look? He's a faith healer, for heaven's sake!"

"I don't care how it looks," Jason said, more sternly now. "He looks like death warmed over."

"And he has a meeting tomorrow night. Three thousand people have paid a thousand dollars each to come, and they did not pay to see a boy in a hospital!"

Leiah stood, suddenly furious. "There's no way he can go out onstage in this condition. He's sick, you big oaf!"

"He doesn't look sick to me, and as it stands I'm his caretaker, not you. If you think he's sick, then tell him to heal himself. If he can fuse spines, he can certainly bring a little color to his own face."

"Please, Nikolous," Jason said in an even tone. "He's really not looking his best. Could you at least bring a doctor here to have a look at him?"

The Greek lifted a hand to stop them. "You don't think I see through your silly plot to have him removed from me. You're pretending he's sick to destroy his reputation. Do you take me for a fool?" He turned for the side door.

"Martha!"

The door opened and Martha clacked in.

"Take the boy to his room and see that he's ready for tomorrow evening's meeting. Give him some water."

The Greek faced them and pointed to the door. "Now please leave us. You are not helping the boy."

"Our hour isn't up! You can't just throw us out," Leiah said.

"I am doing just that. Now leave."

"But you can't!"

Jason stepped over to the boy and kissed him on the head. "We'll be here tomorrow," he said. "Don't worry; we'll take care of you."

He stood and faced the Greek. "You'd better hope you're right about this, Nikolous. If anything happens to him . . ." He ground his molars and let the statement stand.

"Come on, Leiah."

She leaned over and kissed Caleb on the cheek. "I love you, Caleb," she whispered. "Don't let them hurt you."

He looked into her eyes for the first time that day and he grinned barely. "I won't," he said.

She nodded and smiled back. There was some hope.

Leiah faced Martha. "At least give him some aspirin and some Pepto-Bismol. His stomach's bothered him for three days now; you'd think a caring person would notice."

Martha blinked and Leiah thought her look odd. It was surprise that crossed her face, not the anger Leiah would have expected. But the nursemaid ended it in predictable fashion, with a *humph*.

They left Caleb sitting under the towering figure of the Greek, who watched them out the door.

∞

Neither Jason nor Leiah managed to bring any understanding to Caleb's illness on the drive back to Pasadena. It simply made no sense. Nikolous was right. The boy had the power to heal a thousand people in one fell swoop. How could he be sick?

Unless he wasn't really sick. Or unless he couldn't heal his own body, or ask God to heal his own body or however that worked.

Or unless he was losing his power altogether.

But how could that be possible? They'd both felt the power of God run rampant through the church just yesterday. They'd seen it with their own eyes. They had both met God, and they'd come away changed, knowing that Caleb's source of power was indeed Christ. This they agreed to as they left the freeway and headed for Jason's house.

So then how could Caleb be either sick or losing his power only a day later? It made no sense. Unless he wasn't sick.

Jason drove straight to his house and parked the Bronco without dropping her off. She wondered if he'd intended that.

He suddenly turned to her. "Whoops. Sorry. We're at my house."

Obviously. She smiled. "I was wondering."

"Do you want a Coke?"

"Sure."

He may not have meant to bring her here, but he'd asked her in quickly enough. And she'd answered as quickly.

They'd spent a lot of time together over the last month, but almost all of it either in the car or in the coffee shop. The last time they'd been alone in his house he had put a hand on her foot.

And it had terrified her.

He led her into the kitchen, tossed his keys on the table, and opened the refrigerator.

"Let's see, we've got Coke; we've got root beer; we've got water."

"Water's fine," she said.

He poured the drinks and lifted his own glass of cola. "To Caleb," he said.

She touched his glass in a toast. "To Caleb."

She walked into the living room and sat on the couch. Jason walked past her and eased himself into the armchair. The armchair was a good ten feet away, and she wasn't sure how she felt about that. It was just as well.

"So what was the question?" she asked.

"What question?"

"The question that kept you up all night. The one you were going to ask Caleb."

"Yeah." He looked absently at the carpet. And then back up at her.

"I still don't understand this power of his, Leiah. I mean I understand that it must be from God . . ."

"That it is from God. You said you met him yesterday."

"Yes, I know. And I did. I met God. But exactly who is God?"

She wasn't sure where he was going with the question. "God's God. The all-powerful Creator. I don't know; look it up in the dictionary."

"That's not what I mean. I know God is God. In fact I don't really doubt that Christ was God. I prayed to him yesterday, kneeling on the platform, and it seemed totally self-evident. Jesus was—is—God. But what I'm asking is, what's God like?"

"I suppose you'd need to ask a preacher or read the Bible," she said.

"I did. I read the Bible last night. The whole Gospel of John." He jumped up, grabbed an old black Gideon Bible off the television, and flipped through the pages.

"Here, listen to this," he said, settling back in his chair. "John fourteen. He, Jesus, says: 'Believe me when I say that I am in the Father and the Father is in me.' Okay, good enough, but then he continues. 'Or at least believe on the evidence of the miracles themselves. I tell you the truth, anyone who has faith in me will do what I have been doing. He will do even greater things than these . . .'"

Jason slapped the book closed.

"So where's all the miracles? Where are all the believers with faith doing what Christ did? Or for that matter doing even greater things? I don't see them in the church. You think I should ask a preacher what God is like? How do I know he has a clue what he's talking about? Especially if he's not doing what Christ did." He shrugged. "Just a question."

He had a point. "You ask Caleb. He's doing what Christ did."

"Exactly."

"Or you ask Dr. Paul Thompson. I can't believe he doesn't know what God's like," Leiah said.

He nodded.

"Or the people from the church yesterday. You can't believe they don't know God."

"They think they know him. They know a part of him. But do they do what he did? Did the people that prayed for Stephen do what Christ would have done? Where was their power? They were nothing more than a bunch of rednecks jumping around, hooting and hollering."

He had come back to his son.

"Hooting and hollering? Sounds kind of like what we did yesterday."

"I know. I became a hooting and hollering redneck Christian yesterday, and it makes me cringe. I don't have a clue what that means."

"It means you will follow Christ."

"And what does following Christ look like? That's the point: most Christians I've seen do their thing in the church maybe, but they don't follow the teachings of Christ. Do they?" He shook the Bible. "They don't do what he did."

She thought about that. He was right, but his line of reasoning bothered her. She'd spent the day yesterday releasing all the voices that questioned God, and he was bringing them back.

"So not all people who call themselves Christians follow the teachings of Christ. So every movement has its pretenders. I'll give you that. Are you saying that just because a person doesn't walk around healing everyone they touch like Caleb does, they aren't a true believer?"

"Of course not. Dr. Thompson doesn't walk around like Caleb, and I have no doubt he follows Christ. But how many Christians have you met that show any power at all? I mean *any?*"

"Depends what you mean by power. Dr. Thompson seemed to suggest that what we see with our eyes isn't the half of it. Whoever said that a straightened hand—"

"—is any greater than a healed heart," he finished for her. "I know."

"And yesterday we saw some of that, didn't we?"

"Yesterday was just a bit unique." He cocked his head, challenging.

"I've seen other good people who call themselves Christians."

"Some. In a nation supposedly half filled with them. And how many of those showed any power at all that couldn't be explained by a third grader?"

She didn't have an answer for that.

"All I'm saying is that it casts questions on the whole crowd. God is real, and I've met him. He's Christ. But who is he? And where are all his followers? Besides Caleb and Dr. Thompson and a few dozen others?"

"It all comes back to your son, doesn't it?"

He sat back and sighed. "Maybe."

His face looked haggard in that moment, as if a load still hung around his neck. He diverted his eyes and took another sip of cola. It occurred to her that she had become quite used to his company over this past month. She almost enjoyed a good argument from him. He was as sharp as she, and they complemented each other well. And in these last two weeks his bright blue eyes had been speaking a language that was totally unfamiliar to her.

Well, not totally. She'd nearly married once, before the accident. But it had been long enough ago that she hardly remembered. And the thought of being intimate with anyone now brought a shiver to her spine.

If there ever were a person, though, it would be someone like Jason.

"I'm surprised you don't feel the same way," he said.

At first she didn't know what that meant. And then she did. *He's talking about your burns, Leiah.* She stiffened.

"Not just you, of course, but anyone who's felt pain or suffering." He had seen her stiffen and was digging himself out. Leiah picked up her glass and crossed her legs. Heat washed down her back, and she wasn't sure why. What he said wasn't wrong.

"I mean especially people like you and me who've faced pain." He followed her lead by picking up his glass.

Leiah felt herself slide into a place she hated being. A cocoon that made no sense. A place of anger and fear and strange comfort.

"Don't you agree?"

She wanted to turn to him and answer, but her mind was suddenly swimming in its own brew of self-pity. Because he was telling her that she was no different than Stephen, wasn't he? She, too, had been passed over.

"Leiah, please. I didn't mean anything offensive."

"I didn't say I was offended."

"No, but you are. Either offended or scared or both."

"I wasn't aware you knew me so well."

"I don't. You won't let me get that close, remember?"

Oh, Jason. Dear Jason, what are you saying? "Please let's not take this any further," she said.

He unfolded his legs and leaned forward. "Why not? I feel different, you know. Ever since yesterday. Pretending isn't sitting so well anymore. I feel like saying what's really on my mind."

Leiah wanted to leave then. She'd never seen him so open and it did scare her. Not that it should scare her—it should have her laughing. But it didn't.

"You know what's really on my mind?" he asked. "Well, let's start with the fact that I don't know how in the world this happened, but I think that maybe, just maybe, I've fallen in love with you. And I'm tired of pretending that I haven't. Because now that I've said it, I know it's a fact. I'm in love with you. And it scares me to death."

A chill snaked down Leiah's back. For years she had secretly hoped for just this. For a strong, independent man to love her for who she was, burns and all. She'd dreamed his face a thousand times, smiling tenderly and saying those words: *I love you, Leiah.*

And in the last three weeks that face had blue eyes and blond hair and spoke like Jason. Not in a hundred years had she dared to dream her independent man would be so handsome and so kind.

Yet now, hearing him say it, she wanted to shrivel up and vanish. But she wasn't the kind to cower; she was the kind to snap. It came without warning.

"How dare you play with me?" she snapped.

"Playing? I'm not—"

"Do you have any idea how cruel you can be?" She was beyond reason now, and by his wide eyes he knew it as well. "You don't just take salt and dump it into a wounded heart for the sport of it!"

"I . . . this isn't just sport."

"And you don't toss a woman's heart around as if it were a ball!" She was fairly spitting the words. "How dare you?"

Jason stood and threw both hands up like a policeman. "Stop it! Just stop it. I love you! Do you hear me? I love you, Leiah!"

He was breathing hard. They were both breathing hard. And Leiah had no idea how they'd gotten here, only that they were indeed, right here, in the most uncomfortable place imaginable. Her skin was crawling, and the thought that it was burned and wrinkled strung through her mind.

A tear slipped from one of his eyes. He was crying.

She closed her eyes and tried to grab for reason. *What on earth are you doing, Leiah? He's pouring his heart out for you, and you're screaming at him! You're a fool!*

A hand touched her arm and she started. He was sitting beside her now.

"Listen to me, Leiah. I know this is new territory. For both of us. But I'm crazy about you." His eyes searched hers, and she stared at the black television screen. His hand was on her arm.

"I'm in love with you! Not your arms or your legs or your body. You."

He couldn't have meant it the way it sounded. He could never be so dense. But it was the fact of the matter, wasn't it? He could never love her for her body. Who could possibly love such a twisted mess of flesh?

Leiah lowered her head and began to cry. All the grief and self-pity she'd stored for so long oozed to the surface and she couldn't contain it. She let her arms go limp in her lap and she started to sob.

"Leiah?"

The poor man had no idea. He might think that he loved her now, but one touch of her flesh and he would be swallowing. One accidental peek at her rippled belly and he would be running for the door.

The sorrow racked her body, and it felt good. In a way it was her only friend. This and God now.

But even God had passed her over.

"Leiah, please." He was crying as he said it.

She had been in meeting after meeting where thousands around her were made whole. But she? No, not Leiah. Leiah is strong enough. She doesn't need normal flesh. She doesn't need soft, tender skin to make a man melt in her hands, because she will never have a man in her hands. Ha! Leave her with the bark for her skin. God was mocking her. Even Caleb, in his power to heal or not to heal, was mocking her. She was the brunt of their cruel joke. Her skin was.

Leiah suddenly stood, furious. She took three steps and whirled back to him. "You have no idea what it's like to live in my skin! Let me tell you. It's hell! It's hell every minute, every day! I wake up feeling like a monster, and it takes every bit of strength I have to walk out the door to face the world."

She reached up and ripped off her scarf. She popped the top two buttons of her shirt and exposed her collarbone. She did it in fury, without thinking. And the moment she realized what she'd just done, she felt the deep pain of humiliation ripple through her body.

"Nobody can love this." Her voice was failing her, and her face wrinkled with anguish. "Nobody!"

Jason stood slowly. She was suddenly sobbing, staring at him, and he stepped forward. Tears streaked his face, but it wasn't sorrow that flooded his face. It was empathy. And love. Tender love.

Which was not humanly possible.

He walked slowly up to her. He stopped within arm's reach and shifted his eyes to her chest. To Leiah it felt like someone had opened her skull and poured boiling water over her mind. His eyes were as scalding, fixed on the flaps of skin that covered her breastbone. She swallowed. He just looked at her, and she just let him, powerless to move.

Oh, dear Jason, I'm sorry. I'm so sorry. You didn't ask for this. I don't mean to hurt you. You can do what you want and I won't be angry. I won't blame you.

Jason lifted his eyes, and they had stopped their watering. He looked at her simply, neither with empathy nor with sorrow now.

"I love you," he said. "And I love you the way you are. I think you're beautiful the way you are."

Leiah could barely breathe. How could he stand there and say such a thing? She closed her eyes. *I love you too, Jason. I love you so much.*

"I'm scared," she whispered. She dared not open her eyes. "I'm so—"

Warm lips covered hers and she gasped.

She froze, desperate and terrified at once. His lips pressed hers lightly, and they did not release her.

His right hand touched her side lightly, and he pulled her to himself. His other hand encircled her back and held her gently.

It wasn't until that moment, when his fingers felt through her thin blouse to the scarred flesh beneath that she began to believe him. And then she abandoned herself to that belief in a sort of mad desperation.

She groaned and kissed him back, surprising herself. She threw her arms around his neck and pulled him tight against her body. He kissed her with an equal passion.

It was like being dehydrated bone dry and then diving into a pool of crystal-clear water. She drank deeply, and for a moment she thought she would spend the rest of her life here, in this embrace.

But then she remembered where she was, and she pulled back, breathing heavily.

They stood staring at each other, dumbstruck.

A grin cracked his lips. "Wow."

Slowly a smile settled on her own lips, and she felt heat wash over her face. She put her hands together and fiddled with her fingers, unsure what she should do.

"Wow," he said again.

Wow. He'd kissed her and said *Wow.*

"Wow," she said.

Jason laughed like a child and reached for her hand. "Come here." He pulled her to him and put both arms around her. She rested her cheek on his chest.

Leiah wasn't exactly sure what had just happened, but she did know a few things.

She knew that she was in the arms of a man.

She knew the man was Jason, a man too good for even her dreams.

She knew her face couldn't seem to relax the dumb smile that curved her lips.

And she knew that her heart was beating like a tom-tom.

It was enough knowledge for the moment.

27

Day 31

THE GUN WAS A SILENCED RUGER MINI-14, and Banks could pick a cherry off the nose of a rabbit at one hundred yards in his sleep with it. Not an assassin's most obvious choice, but it was light, reliable, and at close ranges, deadly accurate. In some settings the rifle was a perfect killing tool. Settings like the Old Theater in downtown Los Angeles.

The plan Banks had suggested to Roberts was brilliant, not in its execution, but in its preparation. In some kills you had to pull off the perfect hit, in others you had to set up the perfect hit, and in the case of the ten-year-old kid they wanted to knock off, it was definitely the latter.

The plan was almost identical to the one he'd pulled in Rome four years earlier. Then it was a bishop meddling in the wrong affairs, tonight it was Boy Wonder here, but both were cut from the same playbook. The trick was to place motive squarely in one corner and then pop the subject from another corner. Simple. It was the setup that counted.

Banks stood in the shadows behind the last row of cheap seats and gazed past his hood to the auditorium below. Several thousand people waited eagerly on the main floor, but the upper tiers were nearly empty. Starks and his gang stood exactly where they always stood on the opposite side of the auditorium, dressed in black robes just like his own, staring like maniacal religious fools at the stage. It had taken a few weeks, but Starks had delivered as promised. His mug was on the tube nearly as often as the kid's, spewing his nonsense about how the Antichrist had come. His group had grown to over a hundred unsuspecting souls, but tonight they'd come only with the original dozen. At a thousand bucks a pop, Banks wasn't about to pay for the whole load.

Of those twelve standing at the rail with their antichrist signs, only Starks knew the true purpose here, and he'd been paid handsomely for his part. Ten others were rabble-rousers who would do anything to get some airtime. And one—the one who stood nearest the exit now—was a true believer. Some junior who'd joined the group of black-robed avengers because he really believed this trash about the kid being the Antichrist.

Well, tonight Junior would get his due. On cue he would be sent out the back and over to where a black-robed Banks stood in the far bleachers. Purpose? To deliver a note. By the time he got here, Banks would be gone, and the kid would be dead, and Junior would be left holding the bag. They even had his fingerprints on the gun, compliments of the kid's curiosity at a party a week earlier. And the note in his hands would seal the case.

Good enough.

Banks ran his hand along the rifle under his robe and fingered the safety. The minute this went down, he was out of here. He would take the two hundred K and spend some time in the East. Bangkok. They went for skinny rednecks like him in places like that. They even went ape over the red hair. And two hundred thousand would go a few rounds in Bangkok. Not as far as three million, which is what he figured the Reverend Greek running this show would pull down tonight. Now, there was some quick thinking. But then the Reverend Greek had a little surprise coming tonight. It would be his last three million. And maybe he oughta pop the Greek while he was . . .

The lights suddenly dimmed. Organ music began to throb.

That was the cue; the kid was coming out. Banks pulled farther into the shadows and glanced around quickly. Not a soul sat in his section. The exit to the main hall waited ten feet to his left. He rehearsed his escape one last time, eased the rifle to his right side, and looked at Starks and his flock. As soon as Junior left to deliver his note . . .

His cell phone suddenly vibrated. He snatched it off his belt, saw that it was Roberts, and flipped the phone open. What was the fool doing calling him now?

"Yes?"

"Is it done?"

"No."

"New plan. We have reason to believe he's dying. We would rather let him die than kill him," Roberts said.

"The poison? It's been two weeks—"

"And now it's working. You take him only if he begins to talk about anything that sounds even remotely threatening. Follow?"

Banks glanced down at the antichrist flock. Junior still hadn't left. "That's complicated," he said.

"So is covering up an assassination. If we can help it, we let the poison work, you got that?"

He would have to risk Junior getting to him early. Banks closed the phone without answering. It was a scrambled signal, but he didn't like talk much anyway.

The curtains suddenly parted below, and a faint gasp ran through the crowd. Three thousand people fortunate enough to get their hands on the pricey tickets, many of them in wheelchairs or hospital beds, waited in breathless anticipation for the prospect that they would leave tonight forever changed. And Banks held the instrument under his robe that would dash their hopes.

It was almost enough to evoke pity. Almost. But when you'd spent fifteen years in his profession, slicing a couple dozen throats, the pity was hard in coming. He knew that and he didn't care.

Junior still hadn't left his post by Starks.

The wonder kid stepped from the side stage entrance. Banks's pulse quickened. He'd been here that first night when they had all been knocked over, and it had taken him a day to get over the feeling. Just went to show how powerful the human mind could be. He'd always thought his own mind was stronger than most; it allowed him to take life without weak knees. But knocking someone over with your mind . . .

The boy walked out onto the stage. Correction: the boy dragged himself out onto the stage. Something was wrong. Maybe Roberts was right.

The kid's shoulders drooped and his chin hung low, like a vulture. He took four slow steps and then stopped. Then he made what looked to Banks like a death march out to the microphone. All around him palm trees stood tall and stately, but the kid wavered on his feet, thin and weak. The whole auditorium seemed to sense that something wasn't right with their wonder boy.

Caleb stood for a full minute without moving. A man to the right of the stage suddenly wheeled a blue chair forward, hoisted a boy about Caleb's size out of it, and set the child on the edge of the stage. Both of the boy's legs were in braces.

"This is Peter," the man said. "He watches you whenever he can." The man backed up. "Please, I'm asking you to heal him."

The child was struggling to sit—maybe his balance was off. He suddenly rolled to his side and lay down. He coughed and the sound echoed through the arena.

"It's okay, Peter." It was a woman, stepping out from the seat next to where the child's father had come. The boy's mother. "Peter, it's okay, honey. Just remember, he's going to help you." She tried to sound reassuring, but her voice cracked.

Caleb looked at the small boy, his hands loose by his sides. He was undecided, Banks thought. Something was definitely wrong. He glanced across the room: Junior still hadn't left. The scene had stalled them all.

Caleb walked to the boy. He stood over him and reached a hand out. This would be it, then. The boy would stand and the place would go nuts.

But the boy didn't stand. He tried to sit again, but his arms must not have been strong enough. He lay on his back, helpless on the stage.

Caleb brought a limp hand to his forehead.

None of this was totally out of the ordinary; the boy had done stranger things in the theatrics of the preceding weeks. It wasn't even so strange when he began to cry.

But the two words Caleb said next were out of the ordinary, and they cut across the auditorium like the Grim Reaper's sickle.

"I . . . I . . . can't."

He wavered on his feet for a few endless seconds. Then he turned around, took one step away from the terrified child, and collapsed in a heap.

For two seconds nobody seemed willing to accept what had just happened. They just left the two boys onstage as if it must surely all be part of some elaborate show. A wind would begin to blow or an earthquake would hit. But they didn't.

Instead the small child with leg braces began to moan, panicked. Then everyone was moving at once. The child's mother flew to the stage, crying out frantically, "Peter? Peter?" The father crashed into the CBS camera in his rush, toppling it to the ground with a great crash.

The wonder boy's blond-haired protector, Jason, rushed out, scooped him into his arms, and ran from the stage.

The lights dimmed and cries of protest filled the building.

Banks humphed and slipped out the exit. It was over, he thought. Roberts was right; the kid was dying. Maybe he was dead.

∞

Both Jason and Leiah demanded they rush Caleb to the hospital, but Nikolous insisted on the visiting physician. The boy had revived backstage, but his face was covered in a cold sweat, and he only wanted to curl into a ball and hold his stomach.

The physician, who looked as though he could easily be Nikolous's brother, was waiting for them when they pulled up to the dorm. He inspected Caleb, decreed that it was nothing more than a stomach flu, fed him a strong sedative, and left him sleeping on the couch.

"You're killing him," Leiah said, stroking Caleb's cheek.

"How can I kill someone who raises the dead?" Nikolous asked, standing over them.

"I don't know. But he's obviously sick, isn't he?"

"And I wonder *why* he's sick. I told you that taking him out into the world was a bad idea."

Jason sat in the chair opposite them. "Come on, you can't honestly think our taking him to church had anything to do with this."

"No? And why can't he heal himself? Because he's had too much exposure to the world, that is why! Dr. Caldwell warned us about this. His mind is becoming confused with all this madness"—he flung his hand about—"and it's messing with his power." The Greek was red in the face.

"If anything's messing with his head, it's the way you have him caged up like an animal," Leiah snapped. "And now you're so concerned with your big stage show that you're denying him the medical attention he needs."

"The world's hopes rest on this *stage* show of mine! And you heard the doctor—he has a stomach flu. If there is a problem here, it's that he's seen too much of the world."

"Wake up, Nikolous," Jason said. "He's a child. You can't keep him in your cage forever. And for the record, his power doesn't come from his mind. It comes from the Spirit of God."

Nikolous looked at him with a raised brow. "You have decided this, have you? Our Dr. Thompson's pathetic little talk has persuaded you? Fine. But I know of God as well, and I can assure you that this boy's psychic abilities have nothing to do with a ghost floating through the earth. They have to do with the fact that he's accessed the power of his mind, and his isolation has allowed him to sharpen those powers. He's nothing more than a noble savage, and the minute you put him into circulation he loses that nobility!"

"And either way that's his choice," Jason returned, hot now.

"Not as long as he's under my care it isn't. In two days we have our first exclusive engagement. A hundred upper-class citizens will be there seeking the boy's power. We're asking for donations of fifty thousand dollars per party. And I'll tell you what"—he jabbed a finger at Caleb—"he'd better perform."

"Or what? You're threatening now?!"

Nikolous ignored him. He turned his head and yelled toward the kitchen. "Martha!"

Martha hustled over to them.

"Put the boy in the boiler room under the church. No one will disturb him. That includes you. He must be isolated at all costs. Do you understand?"

"Yes, sir. Of course. I will bring his food to him there."

"No. I will have the physician prepare a special diet and monitor him. Take him."

Martha looked at the boy uneasily. "He . . . he's sleeping, sir."

"Then carry him! Take him!"

A look of horror crossed her face. She poked him lightly and he stirred. She poked him again and Caleb pushed himself up.

"Up, boy!" she said. "Come with me."

Leiah reached for him, but Nikolous put his hand out and stopped her arm. "No. You two may not see him until the meeting."

"What do you mean we can't see him? We have an agreement!"

"He's to see no one! No one!" He said it with such force that even Jason blinked.

The boy followed Martha through a side door, sagging on his feet.

Nikolous snorted like a bull, turned from them, and marched toward the main entrance. He stopped at the door. "Do *not* try my patience on this one," he said and shut the door firmly.

∞

Silence surrounded Jason and Leiah.

"Jason . . ."

"It's not the end of the world, Leiah. In fact it may be the beginning. Nikolous is starting to unravel."

She lifted her head and her blue eyes flashed with concern. "And so is Caleb."

She was right. They might have argued with Nikolous, but they couldn't dispute the fact that Caleb had been unable to heal the child on the stage. His power was slipping. Or had slipped.

"I won't let him hurt Caleb again, Leiah. That's a promise. I don't care what the Immigration Service has to say about it; I'll take him away from this mess myself." He had an inkling to chase Martha down right now and take the boy.

"Whatever it takes?" Leiah said.

He stood and reached for her hand. She gave it to him, and he rubbed the back with his thumb. The scars were faint there, but they were still visible.

"Whatever it takes."

28

THE WITCH LED CALEB THROUGH THE BACK of the church and down a dark staircase that ended in a big room full of pipes and a large metal box that sounded like a car. She opened a pale blue door and pointed in. He shuffled past her into a small room with one bare cot and a folded gray blanket. She glared at him, and he thought she was going to yell, but she slammed the door and walked off.

The room was black. He felt for the bed and collapsed onto a thin mattress. His stomach felt like someone was in there twisting it into knots. But the pills the doctor had given him helped a little. Mostly they made his eyes heavy. Tonight had been a very bad night. The light had disappeared from his world and he felt like maybe he was dying. He curled into a ball and drifted into sleep.

∞

It was still dark when Caleb awoke. He lay on his back, wet with sweat, and he stared hard at the ceiling. But he saw only black. Where was he?

Oh yes. The small room.

The terrible meeting.

Desperation hit him like a hammer. What was happening to him? Images of that small child with metal braces on his legs skipped through his mind. The Father had his hands out begging, and the child was crying.

He did not heal the boy because he could not heal the boy. There was no light. Not even a small glimmer.

"Dadda," he whispered. "I am falling, Dadda."

The old familiar voice from so many years remained silent. Funny how he had come home from the church just two days ago, full of light after begging forgiveness, and yet already the light was gone.

On Sunday he'd decided with simple clarity that watching the television was doing bad things to his spirit. Maybe he should have smashed the glass box then. There was no other way to shut it off since the witch had stolen the knob.

But he hadn't. Then later at night he'd grown bored with the silence and taken the pillow off his ears, just to hear. An hour later he was sitting in bed laughing at the behavior of a crazy fox chasing a chicken. And an hour after that he was turning the dial to find other pictures. Not only the drawn kind either. For the first time in his life he watched in stunned disbelief as a young woman kissed a young man on his mouth. They were not united in marriage. He thought of Adam and Eve walking naked through the garden, but it felt different. It felt dark. And it also felt exciting.

Caleb lay still on the cot and blinked in the darkness. "Dadda, please what's happening to me?"

But he knew what was happening to him. At least he knew a little bit. He closed his eyes and cried himself back to sleep.

∞

"Wake up, son."

Caleb heard the distant voice twice before opening his eyes.

The light was on and a man sat on the edge of his bed. It was the doctor. He smiled. "You were tired, I see."

Caleb blinked the sleep from his eyes and pushed himself to his elbows. "Don't get up."

Caleb lay back. The doctor was tall and had a mustache like the Greek Father. He had bags under his eyes too. He put his palm on Caleb's cheek, then pulled an instrument from his pocket and touched the shiny cold end to his chest and stomach.

"Stomach's still going to war. How are you feeling?"

"My whole body hurts." It was the truth: a dull pain ran through his whole body, and he thought it was worse than yesterday.

The doctor smiled. "Well, the flu will do that." He reached for the floor and put a tray of food on the bed. "I brought you some chicken soup and crackers. When you're done, take both tablets with the water," he said, pointing to two white pills.

Then he stood and walked to the door. "I'll leave the light on. See you tonight." He left.

The soup tasted very good, and it seemed to soothe the pain in his stomach. He drank the last drop, finished the last of the crackers, and took the pills with the water. But a half-hour later the pain in his stomach began to flare up so badly that he couldn't straighten his legs. He used the toilet in the corner, hoping that would help, but it didn't.

He broke out in a cold sweat. What if there was something very wrong with his body? What if he was dying? Oh, dear God, don't let me die!

If God was talking, Caleb couldn't hear him.

He thought about going out and finding the doctor, but the thought of the witch catching him out of the room effectively pushed the idea from his mind. Instead he curled up very tight and began to rock. He sang an old Ge'ez song about the goodness of God.

∞

When Caleb woke again the room was dark. Someone had turned off the light. So it was the next night?

He tried to sit up. Pain shot through his head and he dropped back, moaning. His gut throbbed and his bones felt on fire.

You're dying, Caleb.

The truth of the statement struck him as odd. It was true, though. Somehow he was dying, and he was dying all alone. Dr. Thompson was dying over by the ocean, but not alone.

Caleb began to cry. This was all happening because he had let the black brine into his cup of olive oil. He'd let some of the pure oil spill out and had poured in some black brine. Or maybe a whole bunch of black brine.

I beg you for your mercy, Father. I have sinned and fallen away and I beg you to forgive me.

He sobbed and prayed it again, and then again. Not because he doubted that God had heard him, but because he wanted to. It was becoming his mantra, this prayer. He'd prayed it at the church and several times before that.

He had to urinate, but his stomach hurt so bad that he could not climb from bed. He was dying.

Step into the kingdom, Caleb. Dadda's old voice ran through his memory.

How?

Do you desire to?

Yes.

Have you confessed?

Yes. I confess. I do confess!

Then surrender. You will give yourself back to your Father?

Yes. Yes, I do. I will do anything, Father.

Then believe.

Believe?

Of course he knew what belief was. It was the faith that had lived in his mind every hour of his life. The simple knowledge that the kingdom of God was here for the discovering, just behind the skin of this world. That in the kingdom the rules were different. He had known so without doubt. Until just these last couple days, of course. Now the truth of it felt distant.

A small sputter of light lit his mind and then faded.

He blinked. Distant but not gone. He smiled and his heart surged with comfort.

"I believe," he said aloud. "Of course I believe. I have always believed."

The light in his mind's eye stuttered again. And then again.

He rolled to his back, wide-eyed. "Yes! I do believe! I really do believe!"

Suddenly the world turned white and his heart began to float. It felt like that anyway, like he was suddenly floating off the bed, when he knew very well that he was lying on the mattress.

He rolled onto his stomach and began to sob, but this time with joy. *My Father, forgive me. You are so tender and kind; I don't deserve your love.*

The light lapped at his mind and spread warmth through his bones. He lay for a long time just resting in the light. He was home again, and now that he thought about it, he no longer really cared if he died. In fact, it would be lovely to see Dadda again.

It wasn't until a couple of hours later that he decided dying might not be the best thing right now. His stomach still hurt very badly. But that wasn't a problem now, was it?

No, it wasn't.

He touched his belly and asked God to take away the pain. Like a vapor rising into the air, the pain vanished.

Caleb smiled. Yes, that was really no problem at all.

Thank you, Father. Thank you.

A light ignited in Caleb's mind and he gasped.

He was seeing the woman again. The one who looked so familiar from his vision. The woman was looking at him with wide eyes. Caleb watched in horror as again a very large bird swooped from the sky toward the woman. Fire blasted from its beak and its mouth gaped wide. It was going to eat the woman! It was, it was!

But then the vision vanished.

29

Day 34

Thex were two weeks away from the election and all of the national polls had them twenty points up in the race. It was an unstoppable tide, and Crandal was swimming in it.

The modified DC-9 was over St. Louis on its way to Washington when Roberts answered the phone call that changed the mood of the morning.

It was Banks. Did they know that the kid had another meeting last night? Roberts jerked in his seat and politely excused himself from the entourage who were chatting amiably with Crandal. He slid into the last row.

"What do you mean? What meeting? He was practically dead!"

"Not unless you call practically dead attending a private party with a bunch of rich snots and dazzling them with healing tricks," Banks said. "From what I hear he made a bundle too."

"Caleb did this? Last night? She said he was practically dead. Why didn't she call?"

"Because she's an amateur, Roberts. For an extra fifty I'll do her too." Banks chuckled. "Actually she said that a doctor took the kid off her hands. She said she thinks the kid healed himself. Can you get a load of that?"

This was impossible! Roberts glanced up the aisle where Crandal's booming voice laughed loudly.

"He said some things," Banks said.

Roberts spun to the window. "What?!"

"Don't worry. It was only a handful of people without media. But she said that he talked about a bird eating a woman, and he thought it might have something to do with Crandal. The people there weren't laughing."

"Okay, listen, I want you to go to the orphanage and end him. This is crazy. Just go in there and kill him!"

"No," Banks shot back. "It's too risky. I've got my cover set at the Old Theater. It's big, it's public, and I've got the bases covered. Don't overreact here."

"Overreact? You've been telling me you've got things covered for two weeks now! Now he's talking and you're telling me not to overreact? My head's on the line here."

"And mine's not? I told you, there were no cameras."

"Where's the kid now?"

"He's back in her care."

"And she's back on the poison."

"I told her to double it again. He's getting enough to turn him purple by tomorrow night."

"The next meeting?"

"Yup. And his last. No calls this time, Roberts. I'm not going through this again. If he walks onstage, I take him."

"And there's no way to take him before?"

"There's reasons why I've made it this far, and I'm not messing with those reasons. The Old Theater's all set."

Roberts took a deep breath and thought about not telling Crandal.

"Don't worry, Roberts. I've seen my share, and I don't see how this turns bad. By eight o'clock tomorrow this deal's done. Get some rest."

"I hope you're right, Banks."

His phone went dead.

∽

Jason sat with Leiah in the coffee shop at four on Friday afternoon, only half interested in Donna's latest interview with Nikolous on national television. The Greek was saying nothing new, and Donna was asking the same old questions. They only skirted the real facts, and the real facts were these.

An estimated twenty-three million people watched Caleb's failed attempt at healing the small child in leg braces on Tuesday night. It was by all accounts a pathetic scene. Caleb's collapse had the spinsters talking late into the night. The religious folk took it the hardest. Understanding why a person with psychic power might fail was easy enough. A whole range of factors could be accounted for. Fatigue, stress, even something as simple as a bad hair day. But trying to explain why God could falter so dramatically had more than a few pundits stuttering.

The event was the boy's sixth nationally televised appearance, not a career by any stretch. But the previous five consecutive events brimmed with stunning power had already made believers out of half the world. They could not agree on exactly *what* they believed—every religion had their own take on the boy, and within each religion there were a half-dozen major positions on the phenomenon. But for the most part, everybody agreed that Caleb's power was undeniable. He had become an instant icon for their particular belief system.

During the five events, the boy had not spoken very much, except through Leiah on one occasion, and she refused to comment on camera. It was clear by what he did say that Caleb was a devout follower of Christ, but this didn't deter the Hindus or the New Agers or even the Muslims. He was a ten-year-old child who had been raised Christian; of course he would sound Christian. That did not mean Jesus Christ was God alone, as most Christians claimed. It only meant that Caleb was exceptionally gifted by God, whoever God was.

In a strange way the boy had brought unity rather than division among the people of faith. Unity and hope. God, whoever he was, did care and was reaching out to humanity.

Of course, you always had your kooks, in this case those who simply didn't believe—the *I'm-an-atheist-despite-the-facts* crowd. They still hung on to the absurd notion that it was all somehow a conspiracy to reinvent God, the sham of all shams. And if you looked real close, you would find wires and rubber legs and all sorts of devices that made what they all saw on television possible.

In any event, Caleb's failure during that sixth meeting on Tuesday night sent ripples throughout the world. It was either *See, I told you so,* or somber stares of disbelief.

Which was why when Mary Sue Elsworth stood before the cameras on Friday morning and told the world that she'd been healed by young Caleb at a private dinner Thursday night, the media went into a feeding frenzy. Mary Sue was a well-known Hollywood actress who'd broken her leg in a Sunday skiing accident, and she stood free as a bird. She even did a little jig for the cameras. And she wasn't the only one; there were about a hundred people there, and as far as she knew, they all got healed.

It wasn't surprising that when three thousand tickets for a Saturday-night event went on sale for a thousand dollars each that afternoon, they were sold out within the hour.

Caleb was back.

But none of them knew what Jason and Leiah both knew as they silently watched the madness on television: Caleb's gut-ache was back as well.

Leiah turned to Jason, shaking her head. "They don't know how to lighten up, do they?"

"If he fails again, they'll lighten up. Although I'm not sure that would do us any good."

"Well, it can't go on forever."

"You're right, but I'm having trouble seeing how it ends. It looks more and more like a no-win scenario."

"What do you mean? Eventually we need to get Caleb out of this mess. That's a win scenario."

Jason glanced back at the television, where Donna had just concluded an exclusive, and then turned back to Leiah. "Maybe. But not if someone really is still trying to harm him. Especially if it's NSA related. Let's say all this goes away and Caleb becomes just another ordinary child. Chances are they'll still ship him back to Ethiopia, and as far as we know his life is endangered there."

"No, we fight to keep him here," Leiah said.

"And even here he may be in danger."

"From the NSA? Based on what?"

"Crandal," Jason said. "He's talked about Crandal in association with his vision three times now. And people are starting to listen. You could hear a pin drop in that room last night when he talked about the vision. I guarantee you Crandal's wetting his pants about now. Caleb could throw his whole campaign a curve."

"He wouldn't hurt Caleb over an election."

"Probably not. But this has to go beyond the election. This goes back to Ethiopia and the EPLF's attack on the monastery."

"You think Crandal's behind that?" she asked with a raised brow. "Seems like a stretch to me."

"Maybe. But we can't just ignore Caleb's vision. He doesn't like Crandal, and if it were anybody else, I would shrug it off. But Caleb's not anybody."

She didn't respond.

"Even if Crandal isn't a threat, Caleb's got this gut-ache . . ."

He stopped midsentence with his mouth still open. It was the first time he had even thought to connect the two—Crandal and Caleb's gut-ache. Not that they were actually connected, but . . .

"What is it?" Leiah demanded.

"I don't know. I just thought . . ."

"Thought what?"

He glanced around the coffee shop. "It's probably crazy, but what if Crandal's somehow responsible for this illness of Caleb's?"

"He's got the flu—the doctor said so himself."

Suddenly the pieces fell in his mind like dominoes. He sat up, intent. "That would explain his recovery!"

"From the flu?"

"No. Okay, listen. Caleb can heal anybody, right? Jesus said that with the faith of a mustard seed you can move mountains, and Caleb really believes it. He's never been exposed to anything contrary. In that sense Dr. Caldwell at UCLA is right. He's a sort of spiritual noble savage. But then he's isolated in a room with a television. I know this might sound strange, but follow me." He lifted his hand.

"Suppose his delicate mind-set is assaulted with these crazy images day and night. He's filling his mind with cops and robbers and who knows what else."

"What does that have to do with his illness?"

"Nothing at first. But then say he begins to lose his . . . I don't know, his faith or something. He starts to lose his healing power. Remember he came out on the fourth meeting, and he lay on the floor like he was repenting before anything happened. Then again in the church, only even more so. Finally he comes out onstage and just collapses."

"Maybe. But I still don't see how his illness . . ."

"What if it wasn't an illness? What if it's something that's building up in his system? As long as his faith is strong it doesn't affect him. He's healing himself, so to speak. But as his faith fails, the effect grows."

"Something like what?"

"Something like poison."

"Come on! You can't be serious!"

"I'm not saying it is, but think about it. It would be the perfect way to eliminate him. And who else has the flu? No one."

Leiah wasn't buying the explanation entirely, but her face was wrinkled with concern nonetheless. "That's hard to believe."

"Maybe. Depends on what Crandal's hiding."

She grabbed her purse and began to stand. "Then we have to do something! We have to get him out of there!"

Jason reached for her arm. "Hold on. We have to think this through. We don't even know if I'm right."

"No, but if you are, we don't have time to think this through. We have to tell Nikolous."

"And Nikolous will laugh us down if we don't have more evidence. He was forced to refund a bundle on Tuesday. I don't think he's in any mood to do anything until after tomorrow's meeting anyway. His whole reputation's at stake."

She eased back.

"It's only two hours until we pick him up anyway. If he fails tonight, we take him to the hospital."

"Based on your theory, it won't matter," she said.

"The hospital should be able to tell if he's been poisoned."

"But if he's full of poison and he loses his power for lack of faith, what can save him?"

"What saved him last time?"

"Renewed faith?"

"And then he lost it again after they moved him back to his room."

Jason shrugged. It was all quite confusing, this meddling in faith. Jason wasn't even sure where his own faith rested. In Christ as God, yes. But this matter of the powerless church would not let him free.

He took a gulp of cold coffee.

"We should be prepared to do whatever we need to tomorrow night. He looked pretty gray this afternoon. If need be we take him to the hospital without Nikolous's permission."

"He'll fry you," Leiah said.

"So be it. And I know Donna's already talked to Crandal about this latest accusation of Caleb's, but I think she might be up to pushing it. His answers were too pat and I could be misjudging her, but I don't think she was entirely satisfied. Maybe she can put some pressure on him."

He threw back the last from his cup.

Leiah slid her hand across the table, palm up. He put his hand in it, and she closed her fingers around his. Her sleeve rode up her arm enough to show the scars. He still wasn't sure how to deal with her skin. He only knew that he loved her. She calmly reached forward and pulled the sleeve back down.

"I love you, Jason."

He looked up into her blue eyes. "And I love you, Leiah."

"You won't let anything happen to Caleb, will you?"

She was asking him to be strong for her. For Caleb. To be her man.

"No, I won't. I promise."

∞

"No way." Stewart Long turned away from Barbara, grinding his teeth. "You're crazy. I can't believe you'd want that after what we put him through."

"Put him through? What did we put him through, Stew? It happened, sure. He was mortified, we were all mortified, but how can one night of mortification compare to ten years of muscular dystrophy? How many diapers does it take to balance out one night of embarrassment?"

Stewart swung around. "Look, I'm the one who bought the tickets, remember? I paid six grand for that shot—six grand we don't have, incidentally. I'm the one who got us front-row seats by securing a place in line ten hours before the event started. I'm the one who wheeled Peter up there and put him on the stage in front of the whole world. Don't patronize me!" He breathed deep through his nostrils. "This has nothing to do with my embarrassment. We're talking about Peter's dignity here. Let's not strip away what little he has."

"I agree, Stew." She spoke softly but firmly. "But we're also talking about his life. He has to live with the diapers and the wheelchair. And so do we. If there is a possibility of changing his life forever, isn't it worth the loss of a little dignity?"

"*If.* And what if there isn't a possibility?"

"They say Caleb has his power back. He healed a hundred people in a private meeting."

"Good for him."

"There's a meeting tomorrow."

"And we're not going," he said. And then added, "Even if we could find tickets, I wouldn't want to go."

"I want you to think about it, Stew. Maybe not for tomorrow but for the next time. I want you to put yourself in Peter's shoes and pretend you wear braces on your legs and think about going to see Caleb no matter what the 'if's' are." She walked into the kitchen, then turned on the checkered linoleum. "He wants to go. Did you know that? Now you do."

30

JASON STOOD BEHIND THE CURTAIN, sweating, his stomach in knots. In the side wings Caleb waited with Leiah, trying to be as brave as possible, but he couldn't hide the thin film of sweat that shone on his forehead. They asked him how he felt, and he told them fine, but neither Jason nor Leiah believed him. He was discovering denial.

Most of the three thousand ticket holders sat or lay on the main floor. A few hundred sat in the orange seats. A dozen of the black-clad antichrist club stood at the railing in their customary place. The leader stood perfectly still and held his eyes on the curtain as he always did. Behind him several members held their "Beware the Antichrist who comes as a wolf in sheep's clothing" signs and imitated the posture of their leader. Only the one on the end did not stare forward.

Why would a group of protesters clearly in need of no healing pay a thousand dollars a head to attend the meetings? It made for some awful serious protesters, but at whose expense? Jason had brought the matter up with Nikolous again at the last meeting, but the Greek only shrugged and said that they were ticket holders.

Jason shivered. He was about to turn away when the small one at the end caught his attention again. The black-hooded fellow was looking toward the back, and Jason followed his stare. The red seats were empty and the lights along the back wall were off, perhaps to discourage anyone from sitting there. But the man seemed to be studying something up in the bleachers.

Jason released the curtain and returned to where Leiah waited with Caleb. The boy sat on a chair, his legs hanging limp and his shoulders hunched. Jason ruffled his hair.

"You ready for this Caleb?"

The boy stared ahead with glassy eyes. Jason exchanged a concerned look with Leiah and knelt down. The boy looked as sad as Jason could remember seeing him. He put a hand on his shoulder.

"You sure you want to do this, Caleb? We can go, you know. We can call this off and go home."

"No," Caleb said in a near whisper.

Jason bit his lip and nodded. He stood and walked to the side stage door, feeling disturbed without being able to corner the emotion. True, Caleb was obviously not himself again, but there was more to worry about here than his health. The notion crawled along his spine like a burrowing tick. Maybe as a result of all the talk about Crandal.

"God, help me," he muttered, opening the door. He found himself praying naturally these days, almost as if God was right beside him. That's how it had felt in the church last Sunday, and the closeness hadn't entirely left him. "Give me wisdom. Protect us."

Jason scanned the crowd from the shadows of the side entrance. Atmospheric music that he recognized as the theme from the movie *Platoon* swelled to fill the auditorium. "God help us." His praying was not colorful or even proper, but he didn't really give a flip. Colorful and proper had put Stephen in the grave.

That small man with the black hood was still studying the bleachers. Jason looked across the arena and saw that he divided his attention between the stage and the same section of red bleachers.

Jason followed his line of sight again. But there were only shadows.

"Ladies and gentlemen," Nikolous's deep voice boomed over the speakers. "Welcome . . ." The word reverberated and the already quiet crowd fell motionless. Two dozen cameras focused on the curtains.

Jason pulled the door closed and joined Leiah. Nikolous insisted that the boy go out before the curtain went up tonight and Leiah intended to walk him out. She stood and helped him to his feet.

"Okay, Caleb?" she whispered.

Nikolous's voice boomed again. "We are here to witness history."

Caleb nodded.

"After tonight, your life will never be the same," the Greek's voice echoed.

Leiah led a weak Caleb out onto the stage, stood him before the microphone, and smoothed his hair. She knelt and whispered in his ear. Then she kissed his cheek and walked back to Jason.

Nikolous said a few more things, but Jason's attention was on the boy, wavering on his feet with his hands limp by his sides. Such a brave boy. He was sick; you could see it even at this distance. So why were they allowing Nikolous to exploit him in such a state? Maybe they'd become so used to this odd arrangement that they no longer took exception to it.

Something is wrong.

Jason felt the impulse, like a hot iron at the base of his skull.

He stepped up to the stage entrance just as Leiah returned.

Something was very wrong. His pulse thumped in his ears. Nikolous had said his last and the music was building up in eerie volume. They should take the boy now. Just take him and run.

"What's wrong?" Leiah asked.

"I don't know."

Jason almost ran for the boy then. Everything in his body was telling him to run for Caleb. He'd never felt such a strong compulsion in all of his life.

The curtain suddenly began to rise and Jason pulled back slightly. Too late. He couldn't run out now. The show had started.

Leiah stood at his elbow. "Jason, what's wrong? You're scaring me."

He shook his head and held up a finger to silence her.

The curtain rose slowly, exposing Caleb to the crowd. Thundering applause filled the arena. The black-hooded antichrist protesters came into view diagonally from Jason. Their leader glared directly at him. At *him!* Not at Caleb, but at him, like a devil from hell peeking through that hood. *We've got our eyes on you; yes we do.*

Jason felt a chill rip up his spine. He jerked his eyes to the small one at the end. The one who'd been looking up at . . .

He was gone!

∞

Banks eased the rifle out as soon as the houselights dimmed.

He saw Junior leave his spot and nodded in satisfaction. *That's right, Junior; we're about to make you famous.* As soon as Starks had given the punk his mission, Junior had started that idiotic staring of his. The price of setting up an amateur.

The mini-14 felt good in his hands. The perfect kid killer.

The curtain began to rise and Banks knelt behind the last row of seats. It would take Junior four minutes to get up here, assuming he didn't stop at the john. But he'd been instructed not to. No running, no stopping off even to take a leak. Just walk calmly up to section 63 and give the note to a brother in black robes. The same walk had taken Banks between three minutes, forty seconds and four minutes, two seconds on his three trials.

Banks would take the kid out at three minutes, thirty seconds.

Applause filled the auditorium and he smiled. The kid was there, under the white glare of a bright spotlight. Banks lifted the rifle to the back of the chair. He snugged his cheek on its butt and peered through the scope. The boy's face filled the glass, then moved out. Banks adjusted the rifle, but the kid had moved again. He was wavering back and forth on his feet.

He let the face wander around his scope. Beads of sweat stood out on the boy's forehead. His eyes were round; blue-green, like the ocean. *Pop goes the weasel, kid. Pop!*

Except for the music, which droned on in eerie tones, the arena grew quiet. The silencer would kill most of the shell's report, and what was left would be swallowed by the music. The suppressed muzzle flash presented the only real risk of detection. But then all eyes were on the kid, weren't they? By the time they realized what had happened, Banks would be long gone.

He glanced at his watch. Three minutes, fifteen seconds. The kid hadn't done squat yet. Banks moved the cross hairs over his forehead. Right between the eyebrows. The movement was annoying, and he thought about going for the heart.

The kid still hadn't done anything. He just stood there looking as if he were about to drop.

And then he did drop.

Banks watched dumbfounded through the round glass as the kid's eyes rolled back into his head and he slumped out of his scope.

He jerked his head back, saw the kid in a lump down on the floor, and quickly reacquired him. He was gonna finish this. He found the body in his glass, looked for a good shot, and finally decided to go for the body.

He pulled the trigger.

The rifle jerked in his arms. *Whap!*

His breathing came faster now. He lingered on the body for a second. It didn't move. Yeah, he got him.

Banks slid the gun under the seat and ran through the exit just in time to see Junior rounding the corner. Then he was gone.

∞

Jason had bolted for Caleb before the boy's body hit the ground.

He was halfway across the stage when the small flash lit the corner of his eye. *Someone's taking a picture of me,* he thought.

Shouts of outrage rose from the crowd, but he ignored them. He ran up to Caleb, scooped him in both arms, and lifted his frail body. He had the limp body close to his chest before he saw the blood.

He froze. All around him cries rang, but his ears had shut them out. Caleb's white shirt was red with blood nine inches from Jason's face. A ragged little hole had been torn in the boy's shirt.

He'd been shot!

Jason gulped and spun around, panicked. Someone had shot Caleb!

He stumbled across the stage toward Leiah, but he glanced up to the red seats as he ran. That's where the flash had come from. He was certain of it now.

Jason crashed right past a stunned Leiah.

"Follow me!"

"Is he okay? What's—"

"Just follow me to the car. Quickly!"

He ran for the rear stage entrance.

"Stop! Stop it!" Nikolous had rounded the corner and was yelling at them. Jason ran on.

"Where are you taking him?" Suddenly the Greek seemed to sense what Jason intended.

"Stop them! Stop them now! They're stealing him!"

Two stagehands near the rear door stared at Jason with wide eyes. He ran right up to them before they broke out of their stupor and grabbed at him. He shoved a boot into the first man's midsection and was rewarded with a grunt. Caleb's body flopped in his arms.

"Get the door! Get the door, Leiah!"

The second man had grabbed the boy's foot and was tugging. Leiah swerved, slapped the man's face hard with an open palm and then shoved him. He released the foot and back-pedaled into the wall.

She shoved the door open and Jason ran past her into the night. Then she was running beside him, tearing for the parking lot with as much speed as he could gather with the boy in his arms.

The door crashed open behind them and shouts cut through the night. "Stop! You're breaking a court order. You're kidnapping!"

It was Nikolous and he was right. Feet pounded the pavement to their rear. They had to hurry. The Bronco loomed and Jason spun to Leiah.

"Here, take him. Quick!"

She slid her arms under Caleb and Jason grabbed for the keys in his pocket. He yanked them out and shoved them into the door lock.

"He's bleeding!" Leiah said.

Jason opened the door and punched the electronic locks. "Get in the back!"

She clambered into the back seat with the boy and he slammed the door shut. Jason had just jumped into the driver's seat and locked his door when the first thug slammed into the side of the Bronco.

He fired the engine, rammed the stick into gear, and roared forward. An angry cry sounded outside, and he wondered absently if he'd taken the man's arm off. But then he was past the gate and only one thought strung through his mind.

Somebody shot Caleb.

III

THE UNVEILING

When [Elisha] got up and went out
early the next morning, an army with horses and
chariots had surrounded the city.
"Oh, my lord, what shall we do?" the servant asked.
And Elisha prayed,
"O LORD, open his eyes so he may see."
Then the LORD opened the servant's eyes,
and he looked and saw the hills full
of horses and chariots of fire
all around Elisha.

2 KINGS 6:15, 17

31

THEY SPED UP THE 5 FREEWAY pushing the speed limit, frantic and very low on options.

Leiah insisted they take him to a hospital immediately.

"Where's he bleeding from?" Jason demanded, glancing in the rearview mirror. "Is it critical?"

"It doesn't matter if it's critical—we need to get to a hospital now!"

"We can't. That's the first place they'll look."

"Who cares? He's dying!"

"And if they find him, they'll kill him! So take his shirt off and tell me what you see."

She was a nurse from the war zone; surely she would be able to make some sense of Caleb's condition. She tore his shirt and examined him quickly.

"It's in his side. I can't tell." She looked up, frightened. "Jason, he really needs some care."

"Turn the light on. We don't have a lot of options here. If whoever shot him discovers that he's still alive, we're toast. You hear me? Toast. A hospital is our last option."

The light turned on and she examined him closer. "I think if I can stop this bleeding he'll be okay for a while. Looks like the bullet passed through the muscle on his right side. As long as infection doesn't . . . You have a first-aid kit?"

"In the back. What about his illness? I'm not sure it was the bullet that made him faint."

"Why not?"

"I saw a flash of light from the red seats as I was running to him. At the time I thought it was a flashbulb, but I'm not so sure anymore. He was shot; it could have been the gun. And what if he really was poisoned?"

"There's nothing I can do for poison here. I don't like this, Jason."

"Okay, if his condition hasn't improved by morning, we'll get him to a doctor. But we have to think this through."

"Where are we going?"

"To the hills."

She was silent for a few moments. "We should pray for him."

"Yes, we should."

Jason drove the Bronco north, out of the L.A. basin over the San Fernando Pass toward Gorman, praying softly under his breath most of the way. It was an unusual impulse for him, but the simple prayers felt completely natural now. They reached a small road that cut west from the freeway. Within a mile they passed a lone Texaco station, turned south, and headed out on a dirt road. He'd been back in here a dozen times riding dirt bikes, but it had been some time ago. Headlights glared behind him a couple times and he sped to lose the car. He didn't need the locals wondering who had driven the white Ford Bronco up the logging road so late at night. Especially once the media got ahold of the fact that Caleb had been kidnapped in a white Ford Bronco.

Leiah had bandaged the boy to her satisfaction. The first-aid kit was a large box with more than most doctors carried in the Third World. Caleb had stirred, awoken for a few minutes—enough time for Leiah to feed him some aspirin—and then promptly fallen back into a deep sleep.

They drove down the rough road for ten minutes before Jason turned onto another much rougher road that snaked up a valley. The Bronco bucked over potholes and rocks to objections from Leiah. Jason eased up and picked his way deeper into the valley.

"It's pitch black and we're in the middle of nowhere," Leiah said. "You're sure about this place?"

"No. It was here five years ago. Do you have any better ideas?"

She didn't respond.

He drove over a knoll and the trees gave way to a rolling, sandy meadow. He pulled into the clearing and swung the headlights to his right. The cabin stood in the white glare of the lights, grayed by time but still standing. He breathed a sigh of relief and angled for the structure.

"There we go. Thank God."

Jason parked the car and shut down the engine. The silence brought a ringing to his ears. "Wait here." He climbed out, walked to the back, found the flashlight from the roadside kit, and walked toward the cabin.

Stars blinked in the dark sky; it was odd to be in the country again.

Depending on how enthusiastic the authorities got, there could be heli-copters in those skies tomorrow.

The shack's rotting door creaked on its hinges when he pushed it open. He played the light on the interior, saw that it was empty, and returned to the Bronco.

"It's not a hotel, but it'll do. There's a couple of blankets in the back."

She helped him take Caleb from the back seat and followed him with two large blankets. The shack was a one-room affair with a wooden bed along one wall and an old rusted stove along the other. Leiah threw a blanket over the bed and Jason laid Caleb down gently. The boy groaned, rolled over, and lay still.

They sat on the bed and looked at his small frame. The flashlight cast a large circle on the wall. It struck Jason then for the first time that what they were doing was madness. He had rushed out here on impulse, driven by the urge to get away. To free the boy and clear their heads and remove Nikolous from their lives. To protect the boy from whoever had attempted his killing.

But the night was silent and the boy was sick and a quiet desperation fil-tered through his bones. Caleb and Leiah were depending on him now, and his plan did not extend beyond this moment. He didn't even know where he and Leiah would sleep. On the hard wood floor he supposed. Maybe outside.

Jason stood and walked to the door.

"Where are you going?"

"I'm going to hide the car under the trees. Might as well be safe."

"Don't you need the light?" she asked softly.

"No. I can see."

He left them and it felt very lonely in the night. *Dear Father, please help me. Please, I beg you.*

∞

"No, I'm not saying that we confirmed his death. I'm saying Banks shot the kid and he fell. But Jason took him and ran before anyone could react." Roberts coughed once and cleared his throat, avoiding Crandal's glare. "He wasn't taken to the hospital. We don't have a confirmation."

"You're saying he was shot, collapsed onstage, and then was what? Kidnapped?"

"That's about it. Yes, sir."

"So as far as we know, he's alive and holding a press conference as we speak."

"That would be highly unlikely. The poison was getting to him again. And he was shot. In all probability he's dead. We just can't confirm it."

They'd been in here before, three stories underground in Crandal's study discussing death. But for the first time in Roberts's memory, it was feeling more like their own death than some remote target's death. Crandal stood from his desk and walked toward a large raised relief map of the United States. He looked at the picturesque map for an inordinate amount of time, silent in thought.

"He's probably dead," Roberts said again. "Banks isn't the kind to slip up."

The man did not turn. "Roberts, do you know how much power the president of the United States has? The most powerful nation on earth, and he holds the reins. The most powerful person in the world. I used to feel that way about directing the NSA, but in reality I always had to tiptoe around the executive and legislative branches. Now I'm less than two weeks away from owning those branches."

He turned around and set his jaw. His voice sounded like a tuba in the enclosed space.

"The only thing in my way is a 'probably.' And in this business probablies might as well be headstones."

"We are working to remove the ambiguity from the situation," Roberts said. "Banks is on their tail. I've offered to double his fee if he can confirm his death within three days. Triple if he eliminates all three of them."

Crandal frowned. "He knows where they went?"

"He followed them from the theater but lost them in the foothills."

"How does someone like Banks lose a couple civilians?"

"Simple. They're in a four-wheel-drive Bronco, he's in a sedan, and they ended up on rough roads."

"And yet you talk as though you're confident."

"Yes, I am. Like you said, Banks is no idiot. Most men wouldn't have had the sense to follow them in the first place. In addition they've removed themselves from protection. They've run from the only system that was watching their backs. When he finds them they'll be easy game."

"If he finds them," Crandal said.

"He'll find them."

"For your sake, I hope so." Crandal eased himself into a large armchair and crossed his legs. "There is something we should understand, should this not go well."

A small buzz ran through Roberts's brain. They'd had a talk like this once before, when the fiasco in Colombia nearly blew up in their faces.

"We're entering new territory, Roberts. You know that, don't you?" He gripped his hand to a fist and gently bumped the wooden arm. "We're on the verge of taking power—real power—for the first time. Nothing can be permitted to stop that." He paused.

Roberts sat still.

"This includes an abstract rumor about what might have happened a lifetime ago in Ethiopia. We may have made some mistakes in our past, but this cannot preclude us from running the board now. Agreed?"

"Agreed."

"But if there is blame to lay, someone will have to take it."

"I think you're overreacting," Roberts said.

"Maybe. But in the event I'm not. If something were to come out of this nonsense that sounded ugly—something that could snatch this victory from our grasps at the last moment—then I would expect you to step forward."

There it was. Roberts blinked. He wasn't sure how to take the directive. "If I can be candid, sir, I had very little to do with the plan."

"With which plan, Roberts? This particular one? Colombia? How about Indonesia in '87?"

Roberts knew where Crandal was heading, but he wanted to make his point. "With the plan to pay off Colonel Ambozia's army to stir up border disputes with Ethiopia on the heels of their liberation from the Mengistu regime in 1991. That plan. The plan to divert over a billion dollars of arms to the EPLF in return for their invasion along the border, all in the name of some cockamamie treasure hunt."

Crandal's face grew red. "And how does this plan differ from any other you were involved in? You break one law; you might as well break them all. And for the record, this second invasion *was* your plan."

"And the first one was yours. The EPLF slaughtered over three thousand men, women, and children on your crusade. You want me to put my name on that?"

"Don't be a fool, man! This is no time to find morality. There's no need for both of us to take the fall. We've fought too hard for this moment."

Roberts took a deep breath and crossed his legs. None of this changed the matters at hand. It was clearly understood that he would take a fall if anything ugly surfaced. Insulating Crandal might not be possible, but they would all swear to their graves that he had nothing to do with it. Still, Roberts wasn't the kind who would lay his neck on the guillotine for the big man without a good argument at the least.

Either way it was all moot.

"This is premature," Roberts said. "The kid's as good as dead. We're talking abstractions that have no basis in reality."

"I hope you're right. Like I said, for your sake."

"I am right."

∞

Donna had never seen Father Nikolous as furious as he was in the wake of Jason's flight. Not that it wasn't a significant event; the media had swarmed like hornets themselves. But the Greek was presumably a religious man and his actions hardly came off as pontifical. She leaned back and watched him across his desk near midnight, and she wondered if Jason didn't know some things that she did not.

Caleb had failed twice before a national television audience now, although, as a dozen talking heads were quick to point out, this second episode could not be clearly seen as a failure, because he hadn't tried anything. He'd fainted before having the chance to perform.

The theories for this latest incident were clearly overshadowed by the general outrage that he'd been kidnapped. True enough, Jason and Leiah were not your typical criminal-looking types, and Donna had gone out of her way to ease the suspicion that surrounded them. But her role in this story was that of an impartial reporter, and Nikolous more than offset her voice of reason with his ranting and raving.

He looked at her with a set jaw. "They have no legal right to take the boy, and I promise you that I will see them behind bars for this."

"I'm sure kidnapping is looked at very seriously by the law, but I hardly think you're dealing with a typical case here," Donna returned.

"Of course not. We're dealing with something much worse. The world has an interest in this boy. And he's ill. Perhaps even bleeding. He belongs in a hospital, not in some fleabag motel or wherever—"

"Bleeding?" Donna jerked her head to him. "That wasn't in any report."

"We found a few drops of blood where he collapsed. He may have bitten his tongue when he fell, but this is not for the media."

The news intrigued her. She could not escape the gnawing notion that there was more to this story than met the eye.

"Both you and I know that Jason and Leiah couldn't hurt Caleb if they wanted to. Please, Father Nikolous, you must see that. If there were any real danger to the boy, they would have gotten him medical attention. For all we know he's in some vet's clinic right now, under medication and having his tongue sewed up."

Nikolous frowned deeply, and Donna thought he looked like a clown she'd once seen. "I do not share your optimism," he said. "They've willfully and knowingly violated the laws of the state. If they are capable of this, there's no telling what else they're capable of."

"Or they have taken the boy out of a situation they see as dangerous to him, and they're willing to pay the consequences."

The Father studied her for a few long moments, obviously taken aback by her insinuation. But she hadn't accused him of anything.

"I'm not sure many people would sympathize with such a rash statement," he said.

"Maybe. But surely, you don't think that the world will just stand by and let the boy live under such restraint for long. At some point they will want him to just be a boy. Maybe Jason and Leiah just came to that realization faster than the rest of us."

"You may not approve of restraint, Donna, but it is my restraint that maintains his innocence. And believe me, whether or not his power comes from God, only his innocence keeps him from becoming just another boy. If that were to happen, the world would scream for the Caleb I give them now."

Donna smiled and nodded, not wanting to push him too far, but curious still. "I'm curious, Nikolous. Do you care for the boy?"

His eyebrow arched. "Care?"

"Yes. I mean do you find him appealing?"

"My dear, if you were to turn on the television right now, you would find a dozen stations featuring discussion on the boy's disappearance. The world is in an uproar tonight because of one boy. Why? Because I made him a boy worth caring for. Do you not see this? I made Caleb who he is. Tomorrow morning over three hundred law enforcement officers will go looking for the boy, and by nightfall I am sure we will have found him. And you ask if I care for him?"

"Okay. But you know I've had to ask myself that question these last few days because I'm not sure any longer whether I'm more interested in Caleb or the story Caleb has dropped in my lap."

"Well, he's brought all of us a little something. Which is another reason we have to find him. Hiding him away like Jason would choose is an immensely selfish approach."

It was his own use of the word *selfish* that pushed Donna to her next question. "A little something? How much money have you made off him, Father Nikolous?"

He squinted and stared at her. "Money is not the point. The point is that Caleb has done more good than we can possibly measure with a few dollar signs. And unless we find him, it may be lost. *Even* if we find him, it may be lost."

She nodded. No need to push the point at this late hour. In a perverted way his reasoning made some sense even to her. And yet she knew by simple calculation that he had made in excess of ten million dollars off the boy already. If Caleb were to lose his power, no one would pay as dearly as Nikolous.

Donna sat up and stood to leave. "With the effort under way I'm sure they'll be picked up before long. They've got every cruiser this side of Las Vegas looking for the Bronco." She chuckled. "I always knew Jason was a character, but I never would have expected him to go this far. You might want to lighten up on him, Father. He's got a good heart, and when this is all over, people are going to see that. If you sound off too much, it could come down awkwardly for you later, if you catch my drift."

He just stared at her, wearing that great frown of his.

"I'll see you tomorrow. We have an interview at ten, remember? And don't worry, I promise I won't pry. Just the basics. We can't let our fans down, you know."

She smiled and left him, still frowning.

32

JASON AND LEIAH SAT WITH THEIR BACKS TO THE CABIN, staring out at the night in the wee hours. Inside, Leiah had dressed Caleb's gunshot wound with antibiotic ointment and fresh bandages. His bleeding had stopped, and under the bright flashlight she determined that the bullet had entered at his belly but exited harmlessly out his side. A nasty wound, but only his skin and exterior muscle had been harmed. She'd cared for him tenderly and covered him with the blanket.

"I think we should assume it was the same people who destroyed the monastery," Jason said.

Leiah looked at him and then laid her head back on the wood without responding.

"You okay?" he asked.

"Should I be okay?"

"No, I guess not."

She lifted her head. "I mean here we are nursing a sick boy who belongs in a hospital, stranded in the middle of the forest, and you think it's all courtesy of the same maniac who chased us across the seas. How would you expect me to feel?"

"Afraid?"

"Yes."

She sighed and leaned back again. "It could have been the antichrist group. They've lost no love on Caleb."

"The antichrist group wasn't in Ethiopia, taking potshots at us," he said.

"Neither was the NSA."

"No, but the NSA was behind the attempt to deport Caleb, we know that. I'm not saying it was the NSA, but I am saying we should assume it is unless we learn differently. And I say that because I really do think Crandal is somehow behind this. Caleb's practically implicated him, for goodness' sakes. Can you think of anyone else who would want to kill Caleb?"

"Not besides the antichrist group."

"If it is Crandal and his NSA connections, believe me, they won't stop now."

"So why did we run? If they'll come after us anyway?"

"Because back there we didn't stand a chance. At least this way we have the chance to think things through. If we have to we can surrender ourselves up tomorrow."

She shook her head. "Listen to us, Jason. You're talking like we're Bonnie and Clyde. When I said whatever is necessary, I'm not sure I had this in mind."

"No, you suggested I take a two-by-four to Nikolous's head."

Leiah chuckled, more from stress than from the humor of it, he guessed. She laid her head against his shoulder, and he put his arm around her. "Dear Father, help us," she prayed aloud.

They sat in the cool night for a few minutes and Jason couldn't help thinking how insane this was all turning out. Five weeks ago he'd dragged an angry woman and a boy from a besieged monastery and fled the EPLF. They'd narrowly escaped and then taken the boy to safety as promised. Who would have guessed that he would still be on the run with that same boy, now dying, and holding that same angry woman in his arms?

"Jason?"

"Hmm?"

"What will happen to us when this is all over?"

Her question shortened his breath. He'd wondered the same a dozen times. "I don't know," he said. "What would you like to do?"

She shrugged. "You have a unique reason to love me now, right? But when all this is past and I'm just an ordinary girl who isn't bossing you around about Caleb—then when you see only me, how do you know what you'll feel?"

Heat washed over his skull. He'd asked the very question of himself earlier. He answered her the way he'd answered himself. "I love you as you are." He sat up and turned her shoulders with both hands. "Look at me. I fell in love with a beautiful woman from Canada with the backbone of a tiger and the wit of a scholar. She has blue eyes and black hair and her body is scarred from head to toe. This is who I fell in love with. Are you telling me that you're going to suddenly change?"

Leiah smiled in the moonlight. It was the truth too, he realized. It was exactly how he felt.

She lifted a finger and ran it over his lips. "And I fell in love with a man with a heart the size of Africa and skin so soft you could polish silver with it. Will you change?"

"Never," he said.

She leaned forward slowly and kissed him on the lips. "Never let me go, Jason," she whispered into his ear. "Promise me."

"I promise," he said, and a lump filled his throat. "I swear it with my life."

∞

It was barely light when Caleb awoke.

He stared at a wooden wall and blinked. Images of a prophet with a long white beard holding his arms over a valley strung through his mind. It was Moses. He'd dreamed of Moses.

Caleb turned his head and was rewarded by a sharp pain through his temples. He groaned.

Slowly the room came into dim focus. This wasn't his room. He'd never been here before. And why was his stomach hurting so . . .

It came to him then: he was ill. He had collapsed at the theater. He had failed again! A pang of sorrow shot through his chest.

"Oh, Father, what have I done?!"

Caleb pushed himself up, wincing at the pain in his body. He swung his feet to the floor and sat still for a long time, trying to orientate himself to the spinning room. He felt his stomach and was surprised to find no shirt. A bandage was wrapped around his bare side. It was white and blotched with some red spots. He'd been hurt! He had fallen or something. Or maybe someone had cut him.

The world slowly settled and Caleb saw that two people slept on the floor to his right. Jason and Leiah. They must have brought him to this place. He tried to stand, but he was afraid that he would fall, so he sat back down. Instead he sank to his knees and crawled toward the door. His dream strung through his mind. Moses.

Caleb managed to get out of the cabin and crawl twenty feet from the cabin where the ground began its slope down to the east. The sky was just beginning to gray. Stars still blinked overhead, tiny pinpricks of light scattered over the heavens. He fell to his face, panting from the exertion.

It seemed so simple now, this falling of his. He'd seen it clearly in his dream. There was a time when Moses had stood over the children of Israel as they fought the Amalekites. As long as he was strong and held up his hands they won. But when his arms grew tired and he lowered them, they were beaten. So Moses had two men hold his tired arms up until the Amalekites were beaten.

He was like Moses. When he lowered his shield—his faith—the sickness overtook him. And when he reclaimed his faith, the sickness left him. He'd never had to fight so hard before, because he'd never faced this world.

How had he missed it before? The world had pulled him into its trap. Yes, that's what had happened to him these last two weeks. He had come to this country and lowered his shield to the world. Not that the whole world was bad, but lots of it was, and he had opened his heart to bad parts as well as the good parts. Bad parts that were like the brine he poured into his vessel to replace the clean oil.

And most of it was through that silly television box in the corner of his room. He had soaked it into his spirit. Not that the box was evil by itself, but it had been his window into the world, a world that had taken him by storm.

Well, now he knew all of that, and it made him feel sick. He rolled to his side and coughed. He had known most of this three days ago in the basement when he'd repented. And now already he was here, dying on the ground like an animal because he had looked just a little.

"Jesus, forgive me," he said softly. "My dear heavenly Father who has given me life, please, beat me if you want! I deserve much worse!"

But I don't want to, Caleb.

Caleb caught his breath and lifted his head, half expecting to see Moses standing over him in a long white robe. But there was no one and the night was quiet.

He began to cry. "I have been so bad. And I can't take two steps without falling on my face. What is happening to me?!"

You are fighting the fight that all my children fight. Hear me, Caleb. You are my light. You are my smile. You make butterflies fly through my belly. Do you know why, Caleb?

Caleb did and he began to blubber like a baby.

Because I love you more than words can say.

He wasn't sure why, but the soft voice in his heart made Caleb want to weep, so he did. He begged forgiveness and he cried into the dirt and he loved his Father with everything in his own little body.

The eastern sky had grown light and Caleb lay on his back, suddenly warm all over. He wanted to wrap his arms around the clouds and scream his love for God to the sky. He was changing; he knew that. The simple belief he'd once had as a matter of habit was not as instinctive any longer. He'd fallen and tasted the dirt and its memory lingered. But he still knew how to walk in the kingdom. Any child could walk in the kingdom of his Father.

He smiled. "Father, will you heal me?"

Immediately warmth spread through his bones and Caleb began to laugh. It was almost as if the Father were tickling him. He rolled over on his belly, laughing. The nausea and pain from the illness had left him. A sharp pain from the bandage remained. He turned to his side and felt the bandage. The pain from the wound was still there.

"Caleb?"

He spun to the voice. It was Jason. Caleb sat up, grinning.

Leiah walked from the shack, wide-eyed. "Caleb? Are you okay, dear?" She rushed up to him and knelt.

"Yes. I am okay."

They must have thought his reaction strange because they exchanged an odd look. "How is your bandage?" Leiah asked, glancing at the white strapping.

"It's okay."

"I should change it. Does it hurt?"

"Yes. But I feel better. God has taken my illness."

Jason lowered himself to the ground, and Leiah followed his lead. They sat on the knoll facing the rising sun.

"So you still have your power?" Jason asked.

"It never was my power. But yes, God has healed me." Caleb scrambled to his knees, ignoring the pain at his side. "I have learned some things, Jason. I'm fighting the same fight that you fight, like Moses holding his hands up to beat the Amalekites. Do you know this story?"

"The Amalekites? No. God didn't heal your gunshot wound?"

Caleb blinked. "Gunshot? I . . . I was shot?"

"Yes, but it's only a flesh wound," Leiah said. "We need to keep it clean and dress it, but thankfully it isn't deep."

Caleb looked at the shack and then scanned the meadow, for the first time really. He saw Jason's white truck under the trees nearby. "Where are we?"

"We're in the hills north of the city," Jason said. "You fell last night and someone shot you. We thought you might be in some danger, and we didn't want to take you back to the Orthodox church with Nikolous, so we brought you here until we decide what to do."

Caleb grinned. "I like it here. Thank you, Jason."

An amused smile crossed Jason's face, and he exchanged another odd glance with Leiah. "You're welcome, Caleb."

"And to be honest, I didn't care for the witch's food anyway."

Jason laughed at his reference to Martha. "You have her pegged. What was wrong with the food?"

"It was bitter."

Jason sat up attentively. "Bitter?"

Caleb nodded. "More bitter every day it seemed."

Jason jumped to his feet. "So he was poisoned! I knew it! And that witch was in on it!"

"I was poisoned by the witch?"

Leiah held her hand out and touched his shoulder. "Not necessarily. If you were poisoned, it would build up in your system—"

"Think about it," Jason interrupted. "Both times he's gotten sick he's been removed from her food, and both times he's gotten well."

"No," Caleb said, shaking his head. "That's not why I got well."

Leiah faced Jason. "You see? Besides, the poison would have built up in his system. It wouldn't just disappear when he stopped ingesting it."

"I was healed by God," Caleb said. They turned to him. "Both times. And the poison could've been in my body all the time because the food has been bitter for a long time. When my faith remained strong, the poison didn't work. But when I began to fail, it made me sick. Like Moses."

They looked at him with raised brows. "Your power comes from your faith?" Jason asked. "So if you lose your faith, you lose your power and you get sick?"

Caleb chuckled. "I told you that I learned some things today. I'm only a boy and I don't know all his ways. Really I know only a very little, like how to walk in the kingdom. But I do know that it's God's power and not mine. But yes, it's faith. How can you walk in the kingdom unless you believe?"

Jason didn't seem completely satisfied with the answer, but Caleb wasn't sure how to make him understand. Walking in the Spirit was a very simple thing that people in this country wanted to make very complicated. But not even he knew how to describe it in their terms. In fact, he wasn't even sure he had it all right. Not even Dadda knew all the answers. He used to say that all those smart people who knew exactly how it all worked usually had it all wrong.

"Why didn't God heal your gunshot wound?" Leiah asked.

Caleb shrugged. "Maybe I need it as a reminder. It's okay."

That seemed the end of it.

"Well, we really need to change the bandage. But I guess getting him to a hospital isn't the first priority. That settles that question." She turned to Jason. "So what do we do?"

"We sit tight," Jason said.

"For how long? We have no food; we have nothing."

"I'll have to get some food. But if we go back, Caleb will be taken back to Nikolous, and we'll be taken into custody. I'm not sure I'm ready for either."

"Yes," Caleb said. "I would not like to go back to Father Nikolous."

Leiah stood. "Couldn't we just tell the media what's going on? Or tell the police?"

"Tell them what? That we believe there's a conspiracy to assassinate Caleb? One maybe led by Charles Crandal, the presidential candidate? That although we have no evidence of it, we know the boy's been poisoned? Without hard evidence, we'll sound like two kidnappers who've done some fast thinking to cover their tracks."

"We have hard evidence. His wound."

"Something they might accuse *us* of," he said. "And even if there's evidence at the Old Theater, I doubt very much it points to Crandal. And there's still the real possibility that whoever shot Caleb isn't finished with us. Going public could be the worst move now. No, we need to let this cool down a little."

She put a hand on Caleb's head and smoothed his hair. He liked it when she did that. Their discussion about media and police required a better understanding of this country than he had, but it was clear that they didn't know what to do.

"We should ask the Father for his help," he said.

"I agree," Leiah said. "God knows we need it."

Jason nodded. "You're right." There was still a shadow of doubt that darkened his face, Caleb thought. Maybe he could help him see.

33

Banks had followed the Bronco onto the dirt road before losing it in a cloud of dust that was itself lost to the night. Jason and company had disappeared into the wooded hills. That could be good and that could be bad, depending. But in this case it had been good.

According to the map, Banks had doubled back to the Texaco, for the road Jason had headed down forked three miles up, and both forks were dead ends—one within five miles, the other in seven. Unless that Bronco could climb trees, it was going nowhere but back. Which is why Banks spent the night parked on the road, at the fork, with his .308 on his lap. If they planned on retracing their way tonight, they would have to ram their way through.

But there had been no ramming. There had been nothing but black silence. Enough for him to sleep. And now it was morning.

Banks started the Monte Carlo, pulled it off the road, and stepped out. He walked up to where the road forked and opened the map. The fork to the right had the name *Canyon Crossing* scrawled in italics beside a wiggly line that ended in the hills five miles up. The other followed a dry creek for a few miles before heading into the same forested area under the name *Canyon End.*

He slid the map into his belt, plucked a stalk of grass, and walked across both forks, studying the gravel. These were not well-traveled roads, but there was no way to tell which had been used last night. Dried potholes spotted both; some molded mud or splashed water would have been the most obvious indication, but the roads were powder dry.

Banks stuck the grass in his mouth and looked south. The kid was probably dead. He should've taken another shot, for the head. Junior might have walked in on him with the delay, but at least he wouldn't be in this mess.

On the other hand, this mess was going to pay well. And in truth he could hardly ask for a better setup. Jason might be more resourceful than the average pinhead, but he was stranded up one of these two deserted roads with a woman and a wounded child. They would have to come out sooner or later. It was either that or shrivel up and die in the hills, and Jason didn't strike him as the shriveling-up type.

Banks walked back to the car and backed it into the bush beside the road. If he knew which road they'd taken, he would drive in and pop 'em. But as it was, he couldn't risk being up one while they doubled back on the other. No, this would be a simple waiting game.

Good enough.

He took out his rifle and his binoculars, locked the car, and climbed the twenty-foot rock outcropping that rose to the north of the fork. He settled behind a large boulder and studied the road below. He could see half a mile either way on each fork.

He rested his rifle on the rock and sighted down the road. *Pop!* He could take the driver of a car out at three hundred yards with this thing.

And that would be that.

∞

Donna watched the sea of bodies march down Figueroa Street, waving their banners of protest overhead. The mob was well over a thousand now, and growing by the minute. The eclectic group wielded signs that read everything from *His blood will be on your hands* to the slogan from Charles Crandal's presidential bid *Power to the People.* But they all seemed to agree on one thing: the boy's abduction was part of some conspiracy involving the authorities, and they wanted him back.

Donna slapped the side of the news van. "Let's go. We have an exclusive with Nikolous in an hour."

Her cameraman, Bill, jumped behind the wheel and fired the engine. A large white man with a red beard and bright blue eyes walked by with a girl who looked to be about seven or eight. They held signs that read simply, *We love Caleb, not Uncle Sam.* Donna smiled. She'd already sent the studio enough live footage to fill a dozen newscasts, and this was no longer her gig.

She climbed into the front of the van, and Bill pulled into the street, honking to clear a path. "This is nuts," he said, inching the van onto a side street. "Plain nuts."

"They're not as crazy as they look," Donna said. "If you had a daughter with Down's syndrome you might be out there with a sign too."

"I wouldn't be marching in a parade with a sign that accused Uncle Sam. I can't believe they organized this thing so quickly."

"It's nearly ten. Floor it, will you?"

"Am I ever late?"

She smiled. Bill might be surprised at how the people were reacting to Caleb's disappearance, but she wasn't. If they were in a different country, a predominately Muslim or Hindu one, for example, the crowds would be ten times the size. As it was, their own phone lines were burning up with overseas calls for information. At last count, over five hundred overseas networks had called NBC alone. Half of those had asked for her by name. She had broken the story and they figured she knew more than most, which in some way she did. She knew that Jason was no criminal.

Teheran had issued a public statement condemning the United States for allowing such harm to come to what they called "a chosen instrument of God's grace." Evidently they figured that if God had seen fit to deposit the boy in Iran, they would have never been so flippant as to allow such an absurd thing as a kidnapping to occur.

Pakistan had issued a similar statement, blasting the president of the United States for not protecting the boy. In all honesty, Donna was sure the outrage expressed by the international community was taking the administration off guard. Separation of church and state might be a good thing, but it did not play well into the current situation. The White House had remained quiet about Caleb over the last four weeks, clearly uneasy about political fallout, regardless of their statement. Well, now the matter was in their lap, whether the administration liked it or not. Kidnapping was a federal offense.

Some were saying that it was already the largest manhunt in L.A. County in a hundred years. If you included the Feds, they might be right. They were sweeping the cities by category. Hospitals first, hotels and motels next, and so on. City police and highway patrol had cruisers on the streets of course, checking the roads and alleys for a white Ford Bronco.

The boy would resurface, and when he did she intended on being there. Jason couldn't keep him hidden forever. She understood why he'd taken Caleb—if her own child were being manipulated by the Greek, she might do the same. And Jason was seeing Caleb more as a son these days, she thought.

But there might have been better ways to deal with the matter. Why go into hiding? He should be coming out into the public with this protest. She would be the first to paste his face on a few million screens. Heck, she could probably get a worldwide audience for him if he wanted it.

There was always the possibility Caleb was as ill as Nikolous said he was. But if so, why had the Greek allowed the boy onstage in the first place? To restore his reputation. Either way, it looked like the Greek was whipping up public opinion against Jason for the event any such question was asked once the boy was found. The Father was no idiot, and he saw opportunity even in this. If it was determined the boy was ill, Nikolous would easily pin the blame on Jason. In fact, no matter what the boy's condition when he was found, Nikolous had Jason in the cross hairs.

"Jason, Jason," she muttered. "You have no idea what you've done."

"What?" Bill asked.

"Nothing. When was the last time we saw a day like this?" she asked.

"Not for a while. Oklahoma City bombing?"

"Maybe all the way back to Kennedy's assassination," she said.

"Wouldn't know. I wasn't around at the time," Bill said, smiling. He maneuvered the van onto 405, heading north.

"And you think I look like I was?"

"Didn't say that."

"Sure."

Her phone tweeped and she unfolded it. "Donna."

"Donna, thank goodness." It was Beck from the studio. "I just got off the phone with Sergeant Macky at the downtown precinct. You'll never guess what they found."

"What?"

"A gun."

"They found a gun. Where? On a demonstrator?"

"No. They found a gun in the Old Theater. Upper seats, left side. A rifle. And they believe that someone might have taken a shot at the boy."

Donna jerked upright. "What?! Did he actually say that?"

"Not in so many words. But they did find a silenced rifle that he thought had been discharged—"

"How'd he know that?"

"Shell casing on the ground. They found blood on the ground where the boy fell."

"I know. Any signs of a bullet anywhere?"

"Wouldn't tell me. The FBI are down there now. It's yours if you want it. We have enough of Nikolous."

Donna turned to Bill. "Change of plans. Get us back to the theater."

He swerved for the nearest exit.

"They have any ideas who might have done it?" Donna asked into her phone.

"Off the record, they have some ideas, but they're not saying." Beck paused. "You can bet the antichrist crowd is on the top of their list."

"Is Macky down there now?"

"Yes."

"I'll get back to you as soon as I have something."

Donna snapped the phone closed. So the boy had been shot! This changed everything! For starters, it cast a whole new light on Jason's flight.

"Move it," she said.

"I'm moving it."

34

J ASON LEANED ON THE DOORPOST of the old shack and watched Leiah with Caleb. The boy sat cross-legged, talking to her in sweet tones. It was the most Caleb had talked since they'd first met him. He seemed to have broken out of his distant seclusion and found common ground with them. Or at least with Leiah. She sat with her legs folded to one side, listening to him intently.

The meadow had remained perfectly still through the morning. It was amazing how many jets and helicopters took to the air around the L.A. basin. There was hardly a minute when their sound could not be identified with a careful listen. But none of them came swooping in over the treetops with megaphones blaring. If they were doing a search, they were sticking primarily to the city, which made sense, considering the fact that they were probably operating under the assumption that Caleb was sick and required medical attention.

Caleb had spent most of the morning sitting on the grass overlooking the forest that fell away below them, content in the solitude. Leiah had changed his bandage twice. From what she saw, the bullet had struck his belt buckle and been deflected. The resulting superficial cut ran from his bellybutton to his right side.

Despite their growing hunger, Leiah had agreed that they should at least wait out the day before making a move. Jason would go into the Texaco for information and food if nothing happened before five. How to get in and out without being recognized was still under consideration. For all they knew, their pictures were plastered all over the newspapers and television. He couldn't very well walk up and make conversation with the store clerk.

Jason walked up and eased himself into the grass beside Caleb. A bird chirped noisily on the edge of the meadow.

Caleb turned and smiled and then continued his discussion with Leiah.

"It's not like really stepping into a kingdom with your feet, but with your heart. So this is why it's done with faith. Because faith's like the feet of your heart. That's what Dadda used to say."

"And by kingdom you mean the realm? Like it's a different dimension?" Leiah asked.

"Dimension?" Caleb stumbled over the word. "It's a place, but a place your heart goes to. Where God rules. A kingdom."

"But it's real? I mean real like this world."

"Yes."

"And you walk into it with faith, like just opening a door and walking in?"

Caleb chuckled. "I think you're already in this place, Leiah. You entered it on Sunday. Dadda used to call it being born into the kingdom. But to *walk* in the kingdom . . ." He scissored his fingers on his knee in a walking motion. "To walk in the Spirit—that's a different thing. Dadda called it stepping past the skin of this world. You find a new world."

Jason listened, leaning back on his hands. The distant midday smog hung over Los Angeles in gray streaks, but here a pure breeze rustled through the trees, uncaring. Two worlds: the distant one where Nikolous was undoubtedly climbing the walls in search of them, and this one where the meadow lay peacefully under the sun. Like Caleb's two kingdoms.

"And what about me, Caleb?" Jason asked, facing the boy. He doubted Caleb's theology could be easily reduced to a book, but in a simple, childlike way it had the ring of truth. Dr. Thompson had a sharper understanding of proper theology than most, and what had he said about Caleb? *"He knows the reality of the kingdom of God like he knows his hands each have five fingers."* More importantly, Caleb was clearly walking places few Christians Jason had ever known walked. Places Christ walked.

"I was a Christian a long time ago, I think. At least I made a profession of faith—when Stephen was sick. You think I was in this kingdom you speak about then?"

Caleb looked at him with round aqua eyes. "I don't know. Did you love God? Did you follow his Son? Then you were his child, but only you really know."

"So you're saying that maybe I was born into the kingdom, but didn't have enough faith to walk where the real power exists? If I would've walked there, my son would have been healed?"

"The real power? Do you think that real power is found in the miracles? God does them, of course, but other things like loving are much more power-ful than healing. That's what Dadda taught me, and I've seen it too. God can form a world and straighten a crooked hand with a whisper, but to lure a black heart—that's the amazing thing. Did I tell you about the brine and the oil?"

"No. You sound like Dr. Thompson now. And where are all the black hearts you've lured?"

"God lures."

"Either way, the fact of the matter is that if my son were here under the influence of your faith, he would be healed. But under my faith, or whatever you want to call it, he wasn't healed. That's a fact."

The boy shrugged. "I don't know exactly how it works. I don't know why he didn't heal your son's body. But that's a small thing; the small things that happen in this life aren't really so important." Caleb smiled wide. "We all die, Dadda used to say. Some a moment sooner than others. The moment works out to fifty years here on earth, but it's really only a blink of an eye and it comes for everyone." Caleb looked down the valley. "I think that one of us will die soon."

Jason blinked. Die? Leiah was staring at the boy. "What do you mean? You can't mean that! Why do you say that?"

The boy shrugged. "I don't know for sure. It's just a feeling I have."

For a long time they sat in silence, staring at the horizon over Los Angeles.

Jason was the first to speak again. "My son was *everything* to me."

"I think you're missing his point," Leiah said. She leaned forward and studied him. "He's saying that the things we think are so important in this world aren't really that important at all! It's the heart that matters. The healing of the heart, not the body."

Caleb didn't agree or disagree. He just looked down-valley.

Leiah was saying it, but watching her swallow, Jason knew that she was struggling. "And I think that makes sense," she said. "What happens to this silly body of ours isn't the point. A person may be beautiful in this life—they may be given shiny hair and silky smooth skin—but it all means very little. It's gone in a flash. Like Dr. Thompson said: 'Whoever said that a straightened hand was more dramatic than a healed heart anyway?'"

She was talking about her scars, which it seemed God had seen fit to leave her with. The comment brought another stillness to the knoll. Jason felt the impulse to rise and sit by her, but he sat still, awkward.

A strand of her dark hair played along her cheek, bent by the breeze. He saw her throat move with a swallow. And below, just below that blue collar, began the rumpled skin that she was relegated to hauling through this life—her skin of this world. One which she couldn't step past if she tried.

"Would you like to walk in the kingdom?"

Caleb asked the question, and it sounded odd on that lonely hill.

Jason joined them in looking down-valley. "What do you mean walk?"

"Would you like to empty your heart and let the Spirit of God give you the strength to walk in the kingdom?"

"Yes," Leiah said.

Caleb turned to her. "Then you should first want it like you'd desire a treasure. More than anything you could own. It's your desire that will guide you, not your intention." He spun back to Jason, excited. "Do you understand?"

Jason thought about that. In all honesty the things that once seemed so important to him felt like crumbs next to the peace he'd felt last Sunday. He was being a fool about his son's death, letting it hold him in this impossible place. What he would give to be free from it all—to walk where Caleb walked.

" . . . give it up," Caleb was saying. "Surrender it all for the treasure. Even your life. It's not worth anything anyway!"

The boy scrambled to his knees. "Then you ask and trust him," he said.

Just ask and trust? Easier said than done. Jason glanced over at Leiah. She sat cross-legged and her face rested in her hands as if she were praying.

He looked to the horizon and closed his eyes. *Dear Father, I'm a fool. I feel like an ant down here.* He paused, thinking on the truth of that. This kingdom Caleb talked about seemed so far beyond him.

But I will set it all aside to walk with you. With your Spirit. Fill me with your Spirit, Father.

He paused. In all honesty he would give up everything to walk with the Spirit. He would soon die anyway—another fifty years maybe. But to live with Caleb's simple joy, now that would be something. Just ask and believe? And why not? If Caleb could walk in this kingdom, why couldn't he?

Father . . . fill me with your kingdom, your Spirit. Open my eyes—the eyes of my heart. Maybe he should put it like a relationship, he thought. *I will leave everything for you.*

For a few moments the silence continued. Jason opened his eyes and looked over at Caleb and Leiah. Leiah had lifted her head and was staring ahead without expression. Caleb knelt between them wearing an open-mouthed smile.

Jason grinned patently. "Is that it?"

Caleb didn't speak. He bounced his head a little and looked at Leiah.

That was it, then. And what had happened? Jason looked back to the tree line. He felt peaceful enough; the breeze tickled his neck and the sun was warm. But had he just been somehow changed again?

"I don't feel anything," he said.

Caleb giggled and Jason faced him again. "I'm sorry, but I just don't feel any power or anything. I just don't—"

Caleb's hand suddenly covered Jason's eyes. The boy's high-pitched voice rattled off a short string in Ge'ez. Then he stopped and Jason could hear the boy's quick breaths.

"Open the eyes of his heart," Caleb said softly in English. He removed his hands.

A high-pitched ringing filled Jason's ears, but otherwise nothing happened. Nothing at all. The field grass still faced the same sun; the breeze still rustled through the nearby trees; the sky was still lined with that distant gray haze. A voice came to Jason's mind. It was Dr. Thompson and he was repeating himself— *"Maybe the boy can help you see some things. Whoever said . . ."*

Whoever said.

Jason was about to turn to the boy when that gray sky exploded.

He caught his breath and jerked back. White light streamed from a round hole cut from the clouds, as if a bomb had detonated over Los Angeles. Nothing else around him had changed (unless you count the boy's sudden laughter a change), but that hole in the sky hung there, glowing white like a small sun. A low roar filled the air. The thought that it really might be a nuclear bomb flashed through Jason's mind.

He glanced quickly toward Leiah and saw that her mouth hung open. She saw it too.

The hole in the sky suddenly rushed them, widening with a transparent blue throat, as if it intended to swallow them. The roar grew louder.

Jason threw his arms up instinctively. The hole smashed into them, and Jason clenched his eyes and cried out.

Only it didn't really smash them. It swallowed them, and then it was gone, leaving pitch blackness and absolute silence in its wake.

Jason heard a soft rushing and it occurred to him that it was his own breathing. He let his eyes flutter open. The blackness was as thick as cotton.

He could be in the void of a black hole and see more, he thought. A thumping drummed in the background, but he quickly realized that it was only his heart. Had he gone blind?

"Caleb?" he called out.

Nothing.

"Leiah!"

Not even his own voice echoed back.

I've died! I've died!

A pinprick of light suddenly poked through the blackness. A tiny spot of white, like a star a hundred miles off. He blinked and steadied himself on the grass. Yes, the grass was still there, at his fingertips. He glanced down but saw nothing. When he lifted his head again, the pinprick had become a hole. And it was widening, slowly. There was something in it.

Jason pulled back instinctively. His first thought was to run. To jump up and scramble for safety. But to where? And who said that hole there, growing by the second, wasn't safety?

It was the size of a headlight now, like a train heading toward him in the dark. The hole in the black sky swelled to the size of a three-story house just over where the trees had been a moment ago, nearly close enough to touch, it seemed. And then it hung there, motionless: a tunnel of light.

Jason recognized the shape in the light: the silhouette of a man. A tall, strong man walking directly toward him with a deliberate step. Footsteps echoed through the sky. *Clack—clack—clack—clack.*

It was the sound of Florsheims on a marble floor and they came louder. *Clack—clack—clack,* right toward him with hands swinging at the waist and shoulders square.

The sound of the man's footfall joined the pounding of his pulse to fill the black sky. And then it was only his pounding pulse, because the silhouette had stopped at the tunnel's mouth, standing much taller than an ordinary man and gazing faceless at Jason.

"Do you believe?"

Jason jerked at the rumbling voice. The man had said that! The man had talked!

Thump—thump—thump. Only his heart answered. The man stood still. He was waiting! Did he believe? Yes! Yes, he did believe, didn't he? Yes, he did! He scrambled to his knees.

"Yes," Jason said, but it came out scratchy and breathy. He tried again, with more power. "Y—"

"Then I will show you something," the man interrupted. The silhouette whirled around to leave, as if he'd done what he intended to do here. Jason saw his cloak swirl around his body, like a bold musketeer.

What happened with the sweep of that cloak could only be described as a detonation in his mind, because it was too large to have occurred over the trees. The horizons of his skull blinked to a brilliant white and Jason gasped. He clenched his eyes tight.

When he opened them three seconds later he stared at a new world.

The first thing he saw was blue. Not only above them in the sky, but all around them, as if they were submerged in a warm, transparent blue sea. But he could still see the sky and it was even brighter blue. Wisps of red and yellow swirled through the air, as if carried on a breeze that drifted lazily about the meadow. The distant smog was gone, but the meadow remained, surrounded by trees greener than they had been a moment ago.

He turned slowly, stunned. Leiah was there, where he'd last seen her, looking around, fascinated. Their eyes met.

There was something strange about those beautiful eyes of hers. A very faint blue light was streaming from them. He looked down at his chest and saw that the light played on his shirt. If he wasn't off the deep end here, he could actually feel it, warm and numbing.

Then I will show you something.

And what was he seeing?

Jason smiled and looked up at her, filled with a strange intoxicating love. He felt the impulse to shout out to her. Something like, *Hey, Leiah, did you see what I saw? Are you catching this?* But actually it sounded . . . crazy. Childish.

Leiah smiled sheepishly, and a green light spilled from her lips.

Jason rose to his feet. Dear God, they were in heaven!

Caleb skipped up to them from the direction of the cabin. He was pumping both arms into the sky, laughing. How had he gotten over there? He skipped around Leiah, and a red hue rose from his skin like colored steam. His eyes shone bright green and a yellow light glowed around his mouth.

Leiah stood and stared at her fingers and then touched her mouth with them. If Jason hadn't been firmly rooted to the ground, he might have run over to her and swung her from her feet and given her a great big bear hug. But his feet seemed unable to move.

They had entered a world of impossibilities.

Light was everywhere. Yellow light, red light, green light, blue light. Oozing from their dumb smiles and streaming from their eyes.

Caleb started to giggle again. "Say something, Leiah," he said. "Tell me what you think of me."

She faced him and spoke immediately. "I love you, Caleb."

A shaft of red light rushed from her mouth with those words. Jason's heart jumped. The thick beam was laced with wisps of smoke like at a laser-light show. It struck Caleb in his chest, cascaded over his body, and was gone.

The boy threw his head back and laughed as if tickled by some great unseen hand. Leiah stared ahead, mouth still open, dumbfounded.

Caleb dropped his head and looked past his eyebrows at Jason. "Now how's that for power?" he asked with a smirk. "And don't think it comes from your own heart."

"What's . . ." Jason's skin tingled with anticipation. "What's happening?" he asked.

"He's showing you! Do you see it? This is what it's like! The kingdom of God is among you. It's like Elijah's servant! You're seeing some things. You think he still uses chariots today? I've never seen it like this. Have you read John's Revelation? This makes me think of John's Revelation." He laughed, delighted at the idea.

"This?"

Jason looked at Leiah, who was breathing into her palm and watching it as if she expected fire to consume her fingers. She suddenly faced Jason and smiled.

"I love you, Jason."

The shaft was bright red, but it was laced with gold. It struck Jason's chest like a battering ram and took away his breath. It didn't physically hit his flesh. But it slammed through his heart, and it might as well have been a real shaft made of raw energy, because his whole body buzzed with it. Maybe it was real energy.

His knees felt weak. He loved her desperately, but it was a new kind of love. Suddenly everything in him wanted to say that back to her. He did.

"I love you, Leiah," he said, and it came out like a shout.

A red shaft of light from his mouth smashed into her, and she took a step backward, gasping.

"See? See?" Caleb shouted, jumping up and down now. He suddenly ran over the knoll and tumbled from his feet. He somersaulted through the grass once and sprang to his feet again.

Jason's head swam in the mind-numbing intoxication of the moment. Leiah was still staring at him, wide-eyed at his last statement.

"I love you," he said again, and the light shot out again.

This time she stepped into the shaft and walked to him as if she were walking upstream. "Say it again," she said, locked on his eyes.

"I love you, Leiah." He stepped toward her.

"And I love you, Jason."

His body trembled with her words, and he loped the last three steps. They collided there on the meadow, lost to the world, swimming in this mad passionate love spun from words made flesh. This love born of the Spirit.

Leiah broke away, laughing with Caleb, who still skipped around, delighted at their display of love. She danced, twirling, like that shot of Maria spinning on the hills in *The Sound of Music*. She began to sing, and despite the silliness of it all, Jason joined her twirling.

They were children on the meadow. Ha! The air felt heavy with anticipation and pleasure all bundled into one. It was like a surreal version of Hansel and Gretel's candy land.

The boy ran up to them, panting. "Do you know what's happening now?"

"Our eyes have been opened?" Leiah said.

"It's . . . it's like a picture. Today it's his picture," Caleb said.

"The kingdom of God?" Jason asked. "It's full of colors?"

"Today it is! You're seeing the power of the Spirit. Dadda called it the fruit. The greatest power." Caleb grinned. "Love, joy, peace. Pretty neat, huh?"

Jason blinked at the revelation. God was showing them the stunning power of the simplest things born of the Spirit. Love. *Whoever said that a straightened hand was more dramatic than a healed heart?*

"Thank you, Father," he breathed.

The swirling colors suddenly stopped their drifting as if they had taken note of his words. Silence engulfed them. All except for Caleb, who'd rolled to his back and faced the sky spread-eagle, still giggling, as if he knew something they did not.

Jason spoke again in the quiet. "Thank you, Jesus."

The ground began to tremble.

Leiah lifted both hands and whispered to the sky. "I love you, Father." White light streaked from her mouth toward the heavens.

Jason lifted his chin and joined her. "I worship you, Father. I love you."

Three blazing shafts of light fell from the sky, like supercharged spotlights illuminating each of their heads. The light pounded through Jason's skull and numbed his bones with a love so pure and raw that he thought he might die. He dropped to his knees and then collapsed to his back, trembling from head to foot.

God was responding.

I love you.

Jason could barely breathe. An ache rose through his chest and he began to weep.

"I love you, Jesus."

The light washed through his body, like an airborne intoxicant, and he lay there quaking and begging forgiveness and loving his Creator in a way he did not think humanly possible. Beside him Leiah and Caleb lay on the grass, receiving this kiss from heaven.

And then, like tractor beams pulled in on themselves, the shafts from heaven were gone.

Jason lay still for a while before rolling to his belly and pushing himself to his knees, dazed. The colored lights had not gone. Caleb was already on his feet dancing around. Jason dropped back to his belly and rolled through the grass. He bumped into Leiah and their eyes met, wild and zany.

They burst into laughter simultaneously. Gut-wrenching peals of laughter that refused to let them go. It took them a full minute to find enough control to stand.

"I saw something," Leiah said.

"I did too," Jason returned, and for some inexplicable reason, that made them bend in laughter.

"No, I mean I saw a vision," Leiah said.

"Oh."

Caleb suddenly grabbed both of their hands and began to jump up and down in his customary form of dance. Without a word and smiling like a chimpanzee, Leiah peeled his hand off theirs and put it through the crook of her elbow. She winked at Jason, bent her other arm for him to take, and then led them in a circle dance.

They laughed and danced as if this were a fairy tale and they were the children, expected to live happily ever after. But it wasn't a fairy tale. It was somehow more real than life itself. Jason knew that. *Unless you become like a child, you cannot enter the kingdom of God.* Caleb said Jesus had said that. Did that mean you couldn't be in the kingdom of God without being like a child?

They were mid-dance when it occurred to Jason that Leiah hadn't told them her vision. They'd become distracted.

He pulled up. "What was your vision?" he asked.

Leiah was showing Caleb a chorus kick and giggling with him. She turned to him. "My what?"

"Your vision."

"Oh, yeah. The vision." She stopped. "Yes, I should tell you the vision. It was important."

Caleb found a little humor even in that statement. It was like that. The importance of anything but this display of Dadda's *fruit,* as Caleb put it, seemed to pale in comparison.

Leiah continued, still smiling. "I saw a small fledgling bird in a nest. And at first it looked okay, like any innocent little bird. But then it began to grow big. Very big, and black too." Her smile softened as the details came back to her.

"Then it cried and flew into the sky, growing even bigger. It circled, screeching." The smile left Leiah's lips. She turned from them, suddenly serious.

"Suddenly the bird dove to the earth, breathing fire and looking very angry. It was headed for a woman."

"That was my vision!" Caleb said.

"I know what it means too," Leiah said.

They looked at her, expectant. She stared back with wide eyes.

"Well? Tell us," Jason said.

"The woman was me. But it was also you, Jason. And you, Caleb. It was the whole . . . church. The bird wanted to destroy the church."

"Really?" Jason asked.

"Really. And the bird is Crandal. He's the fledgling bird. But when he gets into power he's going to grow." She became excited and grabbed Jason's arm. "Do you see it? He may not even know it yet, but if he gets in power, then someday he's going to try to destroy the church."

Jason looked at Caleb, who didn't seem too concerned. "How?" Jason asked.

"I don't know. It doesn't matter. He's an evil man who'll grow worse in power. Much worse."

Jason looked around. The blue light covered the field, and he suddenly felt like running through it. Oddly enough this revelation of Leiah's seemed perfectly natural. Incidental information.

"So, what do we do?"

"I don't know," Leiah said. She turned to the boy. "Do you know, Caleb?"

"No." He was watching some yellow wisps to his right.

They stood silent for a few moments. The notion of fledgling Crandal growing into a monster began to feel distant.

A mischievous grin spread over Leiah's face. "I know what I want to do."

"What?"

She looked first at Jason and then at Caleb, and then back at Jason, tantalizing him. And then she tapped Caleb on the shoulder. "You're it!" She tore off, laughing hysterically and looking over her shoulder.

Caleb looked at Jason, not understanding.

"It's tag! You have to chase her and touch her!" Jason cried.

"And when you catch me you have to hug me!" Leiah called back, circling to her left.

"Yeeehaaaa!" The boy leapt into the air and tore after Leiah with Jason on his heels.

They were playing tag. They were jumping and running and laughing and playing tag. And it might as well have been skydiving or zooming through space.

That's how this strange, wonderful world made them feel.

This fruit.

∞

Sometime during the jubilance Leiah's left sleeve was inadvertently pulled up to her elbow and left there, unminded. Jason remembered thinking to himself that he could see her flesh, wrinkled up to her elbow. But time seemed to have stalled, and the realization drifted in and out like a distant, inconsequential snippet. Leiah evidently liked the feel of air on her skin because she pulled the other sleeve up as well and waved both arms above her head in the kind of victory dance you might expect from someone whose team has just won a very important game.

It suddenly occurred to Jason that they should try some things. If the light responded so strongly to simple words like, *I love you,* what would happen if they tried other things?

"Leiah. Leiah?"

She smiled. "Yes, Jason? What would you like, my love?"

For a moment he forgot what he wanted, because when she spoke, blue light from her mouth washed over him and he began giggling. Then she got to giggling, and it took them a few minutes to calm themselves.

She stood there with both arms bared, delighted and finally stilled. "What were you saying?"

"What was I saying? I was saying that we should try some things."

"Things like what?"

Caleb stood ten feet away and answered them. "Try praying."

They looked at each other. "What kind of praying?" Leiah asked.

"I don't know. Pray for India."

"India? How do you pray for India?"

The boy walked toward them. "Ask the Father to protect the orphans in India."

Leiah looked at him and then back to Jason. "Do I close my eyes?"

Caleb found it funny and he began to laugh.

"I guess that's a no," Leiah said, grinning.

She turned down-valley and spoke aloud. "Dear Father . . ." She paused and turned to Jason. "I'm going to close my eyes," she said.

He just shrugged.

Leiah faced the valley again, closed her eyes, spread her palms at her waist, and spoke again. "Dear Father." She paused again, and blue light spilled from her lips as if she were speaking with dry ice in her mouth. "Father, please show mercy to the poor orphan children in India. You are their Father . . ."

She kept speaking, but Jason didn't hear any more. Blue light had erupted from her face and blazed toward the horizon. Jason took a step back, stunned. She prayed on, evidently unaware of the light that engulfed her whole face so that he could no longer see her eyes.

" . . . I know you will, Father, because you must love them very much and . . ."

"Leiah, open your eyes," Jason said quietly.

She stopped praying and opened her eyes. The light vanished.

"No, keep praying. Open your eyes and pray."

She faced the valley. "Father, I ask that you will . . ." The light bolted from her face and her words froze in her throat. She trembled and then sank to her knees, overcome.

She continued in a whisper now. "Dear Jesus, please show them your love." The light crackled as if it were charged with electricity. Leiah began to weep. Beside her Caleb smiled, delighted.

Jason turned and opened his mouth. "Dear Jesus, Son of God, I ask that you show your love . . ." His eyes were open and he saw the light leap off his face and shoot to the sky. " . . . to the children of Ethiopia who have lost their mothers and fathers." It was as though he were speaking through a tunnel of light.

A lump rose into his throat. This by a few words of prayer? For how long had he considered the prayers of Christians foolish blabberings? And all the while they had wielded such power?

Jason looked at the rippling sky, and suddenly the gravity of this entire magnificent display boiled over in his chest, as if it had outgrown his capacity to contain it. It was all so very real—God's ever-present power streaming over the earth it had created, awesome above the ants who marched in defiance below, blind to it.

And he had been one of those ants, hadn't he?

The sorrow hit him like a sledgehammer dropped from heaven. How could he have doubted such a loving God? He who had fashioned man swirled passionately around him still.

Jason groaned, suddenly overcome by desperation. He sank to his knees. Sorrow unlike any he had known rolled up his chest, and he begged God to forgive him. A minute ago he had been dancing before his Father with delight. Now he could do nothing but bow at his feet in a state very near agony. But it was a kind of agony that felt pure, like a cleansing fire. His bones trembled under its weight and he began to sob softly.

Oh, Lord my God, when I in awesome wonder
Consider all the worlds thy hands have . . .

Now the emotion poured out of him and he could not finish the thought, much less kneel upright. He bowed to the ground and worshiped his Creator.

Beside him he could barely hear Leiah praying through tears now—praying for forgiveness as much as for anyone in India. Caleb was praying as well. They knelt on the knoll, swept away by the majesty of their Creator, desperate in his presence, overcome by their dependence upon his love.

Jason wasn't sure exactly what happened to the light that streamed to the horizon as they prayed, but it was real and it was crackling with static. Somewhere a little boy in India with a runny nose was having his heart warmed; somewhere a little girl with round eyes had just found food for another day. The notion made him desperate to pray.

He did that. He stood and prayed, stunned that God would use him as a conduit for such power.

∞

Somehow Jason and Leiah ended side by side, hand in hand, humbled by God's presence, silent in the wake of his power. Jason looked into her eyes and then at their hands. She lifted her hand, clasped around his, and they both looked at her arm.

"That's my arm," she said.

"Yeah."

"Doesn't seem so bad now, does it?"

It was twisted and lumpy and looked like the bark of a pine tree. But at the moment it didn't bother Jason.

"No," he said.

"It seems stupid that it used to bother me so much."

"Yeah."

"I ran away from Canada because of it. I mean it looks pretty ugly, but who cares? Seems kinda minor when you compare it to this."

Jason lifted his free hand. "Can I touch it?"

"Yes."

He lowered his index finger and ran it along her skin. It felt like rubber. He rested all of his fingers on her arm and drew them up toward her elbow. The gnarled skin covered her entire body; he knew that and he even imagined what it must look like: her back and her chest and her thighs, pitted and rough. But it did seem silly right now. Like a woman worrying about the shade of her lipstick before a party, but hardly more.

"Does it feel strange?" she asked.

"Yes, it does. But it doesn't bother me." He turned her around to face him and held each of her elbows.

"I love you, Leiah." Light spread over her face. "I love you more than words can say." He leaned forward and kissed her lips.

She pulled back a fraction of an inch. "And I love you, Jason." Her hot breath mixed with light and washed over his lips. He held her, overwhelmed with the impulse to squeeze her as tight as he could.

"Excuse me."

They parted to find Caleb standing beside them, that wide smile still stuck on his face.

"Do you think you would like to have smooth skin, Leiah?"

Jason's heart bolted. What was he asking? Leiah looked up at Jason and opened her mouth, but she seemed too flummoxed to speak.

"I just wanted to know if you would like to have the burn marks taken away," Caleb clarified.

"Well . . . yes, I . . . I suppose so. I mean, I don't have to have them taken away. I'm okay with the way that I look with them. It's not like I really need to have smooth skin or anything and I . . ."

Caleb gave a short snortlike laugh and touched her hand.

A surge of power crackled through the sky, and for a brief moment Leiah vanished behind a brilliant flash of light, as if she herself had become a strobe light. And then she stood there, as if nothing had happened.

It occurred to Jason that he still held her fingers. He absently wondered if he'd lit up as well. He looked down. The sight of her arms confused him at first, simply because they were not her arms. They couldn't be; they were white and smooth like cream.

Leiah gasped and jerked her hand away. Her mouth gaped and she stared bug-eyed at herself.

"Uhh . . ."

Jason blinked once. Then again.

Leiah lifted trembling fingers to her forearms and touched her skin lightly. Her jaw hung open and she ran her fingers up her arms very slowly, as if afraid they might break. She suddenly reached down with both hands and pulled her blouse from her jeans. Her bellybutton was surrounded by perfectly smooth skin, like the vortex of a whirlpool made of milk.

Leiah stared at it for three full seconds, frozen.

She looked up. "I . . . I have . . . skin." Her round mouth spread into a splitting smile. "Eeeeeiiaa!" She dropped the hem of her blouse and threw both arms around Jason's neck, screeching like a child.

"I have normal skin!"

Jason held her and spun around, laughing and hooting. She had normal skin. What a gift! What a gift! Thank you, Father!

Leiah spun from him and twirled away like a ballerina. She pulled the rest of her blouse out and it rode up her torso, revealing smooth flesh all around her belly and back. She kept stopping and looking at it and pinching it.

She ran over and lifted Caleb high in the air. "Thank you!"

"Thank your Father," he said, but he squealed with laughter.

"Thank you, Father!" She cried it to the skies. "Thank you, Jesus!"

Jason thought his heart would explode.

35

THE SUN WAS DIPPING IN THE WESTERN SKIES when they finally calmed from their exuberant display of delight. It had been five hours and the light had not vacated them.

Now they sat on the top of the hill, three abreast holding their knees, dazed by the unique vision that God had given them. They felt sure that it wasn't necessarily the exact way that things worked, just like Ezekiel's vision of God wasn't necessarily a precise vision of how God looked. But it was an equivalent presentation, and either way the power granted each and every child of God was like this: mind-boggling. They had prayed, they had worshiped, they had played, and they had loved. They had reveled in these fruits of the Spirit. In the love and the peace and the joy. In its own way it overshadowed Leiah's new skin. Not that Leiah wasn't delighted with her new skin, but beyond that skin, beyond the skin of this world was this other world—this kingdom—and here the power was staggering.

Through it all, they had all but forgotten that short of this kingdom there waited a world ready to string them up. That a fledgling bird was about to grow into a monster. But now as the day faded, Jason was remembering.

"How long do you think our eyes will see this?" he asked.

"I don't know," Caleb said. "Until he's finished showing us what he wants to show us."

"It would be nice if he could show us what to do."

Leiah looked at him. "Maybe that's it."

"You think?"

"Why not? Couldn't he show us what to do, Caleb?"

"He could show us whatever he wants to show us."

"But we should ask him, shouldn't we?"

"Yes, we should."

They sat still. Wisps of red and yellow floated through the air all around them. They were growing used to the wonderful new world.

Jason folded his hands, put his elbows on his knees, and rested his chin on his fists. He spoke, hardly thinking. "Dear God, give us wisdom."

The sky flashed, and a single bolt the diameter of a man's thigh fell into Jason's head and then vanished.

Jason jerked upright.

All around them the blue air sputtered once, then twice, and then shut off.

The blue air was gone. The colored wisps had vanished. A sun turned orange by smog was setting on the western horizon. The world had become normal again.

Jason leapt to his feet and whirled to face them. "That's it! What's soft and round and says more than it should?"

They both looked at him dumbly.

"Father Matthew's riddle. The hem of a tunic. Caleb's tunic!"

"The riddle he gave you just before we escaped. Caleb doesn't wear a tunic anymore."

"But he did then. We have to find that tunic!"

Caleb stood. "God told you this?"

"No. Yes! I don't know. I just remembered your father's words. And I think I know what we should do."

"What?"

∞

Banks had made three trips to the car during the day, once for food, and twice to stretch his legs. He had reported in to Roberts, who was still in D.C. with the big man. Evidently the world was hanging in the balance over the kid, although Banks didn't really see what the big deal was. Sure the boy could do some strange stuff, but he was just a kid, who would soon be dead.

Truth be told, he could probably wrestle a full million out of Roberts for the hit. Especially now that the rifle had been found. There was a panic in the air and as long as the boy was alive, the threat he posed to Crandal was alive. The only real way to terminate that threat was to snuff the kid. And while the world went nuts speculating on what might have happened to the boy, he had them pinned up a lone country road with no escape.

Banks smiled and lifted his field glasses to his eyes. The light was failing fast, but he was in no hurry. He would have to pull the car into the inter-section again once darkness hit; couldn't have the foxes sneak past in the middle of the night. The road hadn't been used during the day, which was odd. You'd think a sportsman or a hunter . . .

Banks froze. A low rumble carried through the thin air.

He swung the glasses up the first fork. But it lay empty and brown like it had all day. Somewhere a car was driving, though. He could hear the rush of tires on gravel.

He jerked the binoculars to the second fork. A white Bronco filled the view.

Banks's heart hit the roof of his throat. He grabbed the rifle, popped off the scope cover, and swung it in line with the onrushing vehicle. The Bronco was blitzing over the road, spewing billows of dust from the rear wheels. They were in a rush.

But the rush would end in a head-on with a bullet. *Smack!*

The car was still a good four hundred yards off, and Banks clicked the scope up to full power. The windshield shimmied in his view. The driver sat with both hands on the wheel. He had the same red shirt he'd worn at the meeting. *What's wrong, buckwheat? No shower in the woods?*

The seat beside Jason was empty. And behind him . . .

The low sun splashed light across an empty rear seat. Where were the other two, then? The kid. A finger of panic rode Banks's spine. He had to kill the kid first! He was the primary target. He'd taken out a secondary first in Nicaragua once and lost the primary because of it. Things changed once there was a killing. Just like they were changing now back in the city because someone had found the gun.

The blazing Bronco was within a hundred yards now, and Banks backed the power off on the scope. Jason was coming out alone. For supplies maybe. He couldn't shoot.

The white vehicle approached the fork and then roared by. Banks caught a glimpse of the floorboards as it passed. No low-lying bodies. He pulled up the gun and watched the Bronco disappear in a cloud of dust.

His pulse thumped in his ears. "Gotcha," he muttered.

He rose, gathered up his binoculars, and returned to the car. His wait on the rock was over. The game had just changed. He would have to wait for the Bronco's return, sure. And the Bronco would return, because up there in those cold hills waited the kid and the woman. Jason wouldn't be leaving without them, unless he intended on returning.

But in leaving, he had inadvertently tipped his hand. He had removed a chunk of ambiguity. He had eliminated one of the forks. The kid was some-where up the fork to the left.

Which meant that as soon as the Bronco sped back by, Banks would go on a little hunt.

He chuckled and bit into a day-old sandwich.

A night hunt.

∞

It was a good day to be alive.

Jason approached the Texaco and eased the Bronco to a roll. There was one other car at the pumps: a yellow Volkswagen Bug. The trick here was going to be getting out without being recognized. The fewer people that saw him the better.

He parked the Bronco on the side by a large white cooler that read ICE. His mind still buzzed from the day's exhilarating experience. It was hard to believe that less than an hour ago he'd been spinning through the grass, arms locked with Leiah, who kept commenting on the fact that her skin was smooth. For a tidbit that had hardly seemed important to either of them sev-eral hours earlier, the healing had taken on symbolic importance that tied a bow around the whole experience. One day that bow would come in handy.

Yes, it did happen, Junior. And see Mommy's skin? That proves it happened.

Now there was a thought.

Jason looked in the mirror and pulled his hair forward toward his eyes. The blond curls were short, but long enough to manipulate a little. The day's growth on his chin would've been better if it was black stubble, and he thought about taking some dirt to it. But then, a dirty face might be some-thing that attracted attention more than dispelled it.

His plan was simple. He would walk in with his head turned from the clerk, make for the hatrack, put a cap on his head, grab a few groceries, and make his purchase at the register without removing the hat. He'd discarded the impulse to do the same with dark glasses as the light faded. Sunglasses at night might raise an eyebrow.

"Father, help me," he breathed and stepped from the car. The telephone booth stood at the edge of the lot. He would end his trip there.

Jason got halfway to the front door before stopping midstride, frozen by the stack of newspapers in a white rack labeled *Los Angeles Times*. It was the red shirt that caught his attention. *His* red shirt. The same one he had on right now!

The picture sported him running offstage with Caleb draped in his arms. The headline told the story. *Kidnapped!*

Jason jerked to the window. A large Marlboro sign blocked the view to the store. Thank goodness. He spun back for the car. The yellow Volkswagen gunned its engine and peeled out of the driveway.

A thought spun through his mind: How much of what was happening at this moment was at the behest of swirling colored lights? His seeing that newspaper, for example—if his eyes were still opened to the other world, would he have seen a bolt from heaven turning his head? How much of the mundane was really crowded with the mystical? More than most could imagine, he suspected.

Jason clambered into the Bronco's rear seat and slammed the door shut. He had to get on with this before the clerk came out to see who was slamming doors and wandering around the white Bronco. That would be the end.

He peeled off the red shirt and foraged around the back for the white T-shirt he used on occasion when he messed with the car. He found it rolled up in the corner and pulled it on. A black KNAC ROCKS logo ran diagonally across his chest. It smelled of mildew and it was wrinkled. But none of this mattered. Not unless he wanted to walk into the store bare-chested.

He climbed from the car and straightened the shirt. On last thought, he ran his fingers around the rim of the wheel well and rubbed a couple streaks of grease along his cheekbones. He might as well look the part of his shirt. Just an ordinary guy who'd just finished changing a tire.

Jason exhaled and strode into the store.

The clerk wasn't in sight. He hurried down the aisle and grabbed a loaf of bread and some peanut butter. The hatrack loomed, and he slid a green John Deere hat over his head. So far so good.

Cash! Did he have cash? He couldn't use a credit card! A tremble took to his hands. *Dear Father, please help me.* It was amazing how frail he felt back in this skin.

He approached the counter, slid his rations on the glass, grabbed a two-liter jug of root beer from a side rack, and fished for his wallet. A single twenty sat neatly in the folds. Thank God.

The clerk emerged from the back, wiping her hands. "I'm sorry. Doing inventory. That it tonight?"

"Uh-huh."

She glanced at him. "Hat too?"

"Oh, yeah. Sorry."

"No prob." She rung the groceries up, took the twenty, and handed him eight dollars and change.

"Thank you," he muttered.

"Drive safe." She turned and walked toward the back.

The minute Jason hit the sidewalk, he bolted for the car. No other cars had pulled in. He started the Bronco, drove it away from the lights, shoved it into park, and hurried for the telephone booth. So far so good. The worst of this mission was behind him. Just beyond his eyesight the air was swimming with colored lights, he was sure of it.

He pulled Donna's business card out of his wallet. Leiah had raised an eyebrow when she'd learned he still had it, but she hadn't argued. He punched the number for her cell phone and waited.

"Hello."

Jason adjusted the receiver. "Donna? That you?"

"Yes. Who is this?"

"It's Jason."

"Jason! What are you doing?"

"I'm calling an old friend for some help."

"Hold on."

The line went dead for a few seconds. "Sorry. I was in a bar. Where are you?"

"Never mind that. Listen, I need you to help me. I don't know what you think's going on, but it isn't what it looks like."

"They found a gun, Jason."

He blinked. "They did, huh? Figures. Who did it?"

"Is Caleb okay?"

"This is all off the record, Donna. You'll understand when I tell you. Okay?"

"Sure."

"He's fine. The bullet grazed him. Who did it?"

"Maybe one of the antichrist gang. A black-hooded man was seen walking toward the upper seats a few minutes before the boy fell. They sure had the motivation. Everyone's saying that he was shot and that you took advantage of the confusion to steal him away. Nikolous is climbing the walls. You've got to come out, Jason. It's not looking good."

"It was Crandal." He paused and she didn't object. "I know it sounds crazy, but I think we can put our hands on some solid evidence that might tell us who Crandal really is."

"Please. Crandal may have a problem with a boy who walks around telling the world that he's a bad guy, but that doesn't make him a killer."

"It's more than that. He's . . ." How do you tell someone like Donna that the man about to become the president of the United States is really a monster in waiting? "He's not what he seems. Something happened back in Ethiopia, something that would destroy him, and he's bent on keeping it out of the news. Even if it means killing Caleb."

"Did what in Ethiopia? You can't just throw out accusations like that. Right now it's you who has some explaining to do, not Crandal."

"You know it's not beyond him. Tell me you at least suspect that much."

She paused, thinking. "Maybe."

"So if I could produce some evidence that showed motivation for his threat to Caleb, you would be willing to play along?"

"Depends on what I'm playing along with."

"I want to go public. I want a worldwide exclusive with as much coverage as you can manage. I mean I want every person within reach of a television to be tuned in. I'll bring Caleb out with Leiah. And I want you to guarantee me ten minutes in front of the cameras without obstruction. The cops can haul me off and lock me up when I've said what I need to say."

"I can probably arrange that." An edge had come to her voice.

"And I want Crandal there."

"What!? Come on. Now you're going over the top."

"Am I?"

"Even if I agreed, how do you propose I get him here? He's in D.C. now. When would you want this?"

"Tomorrow. Tomorrow night. If I'm right, he'll come. You ever blackmail someone, Donna?"

"Please."

"You ever tell someone that unless they do so-and-so, you'll go public with a story? You must have. You're a reporter."

"That's not exactly blackmail," she said.

"Call it whatever you like. You interested?"

"I'm all ears."

Jason blew some air out and stretched his neck. "Go to my house. 2445 Hollister. You'll find a key under the planter at the back door. Go in and find the laundry room on your left. In the corner there's a basket, and in that basket you'll find a tunic."

"A tunic? You mean a robe."

"It's the tunic Caleb was wearing when I took him from the monastery. Take it home with you and look through all of the hems. If I'm right, you'll find something in one of the hems."

"What am I looking for? I gotta be honest, Jason. This seems a bit—"

"I don't know. Something that shouldn't be there. A note maybe."

"I take it you haven't actually seen this note or whatever."

"No. But it's there. You wouldn't believe me if I told you how I know. But there's a worldwide exclusive in this. Don't tell me that doesn't get you going."

"And if there is something to all of this, how do I contact you?"

"I'll call you in the morning. Before sunrise. It's safer for me that way. We'll decide what to do then."

"A tunic, huh?"

"A tunic."

"Okay, Jason. You're on. And if it turns out your magic tunic is a sham, you turn yourself in to me anyway?"

"Don't push it, Donna. We have a deal?"

"We have a deal."

Jason hung up and left the Texaco station. Mission accomplished. He was half a mile from the station before he let out his howl of victory. "Yeow! Thank you, Father!" He pumped his fist.

It was indeed a good day to be alive.

36

Day 37

R OBERTS STARED AT CRANDAL across the white linen in the private dining room. A basket of English muffins sat untouched with the rest of
their brunch. An hour ago he'd been a man thoroughly smug, unable to hide
the glow that reddened his cheeks. Now he was having difficulty with a purple
that flushed those same cheeks.

He slammed his huge fist on the table and Roberts blinked. "I'm not
about to let a little piece of trash from Africa influence me! Do you hear me?
I don't care what he says he has. Bury them!"

"We've been trying to bury them for four weeks now," Roberts said softly.
Heat tickled the back of his neck. "But you don't just take out a shovel and
start throwing it on the world's favorite little boy when you're running for
president. We've had to move with caution. Either way this was unantici-
pated. It implicates you directly."

"And you actually believe I would consider flying all the way to California
because some idiotic reporter says she has something I may want to see?"

The heat spread over Roberts's head. "Sir, you'll have to excuse me for
being blunt here, but you're not thinking clearly." He sat back.

"Let me put this in perspective. Imagine waking up tomorrow morning
to a headline in the *New York Times* that reads *Baby Killer!* And imagine the
story going something like this: Ten years ago Charles Crandal, then director
of the NSA and an ardent collector of obscure artifacts, stumbled across compelling information putting the Ark of the Covenant in one of northern
Ethiopia's Orthodox monasteries. So what does the man who may be our next
president do? Does he take a private trip to Africa to interview priests and fer-
ret out the precise location of the elusive artifact like any sane man might do?
No, he goes in with guns blazing, slaughtering priests and pillaging the
monasteries in a sweeping search for an artifact he must have."

Crandal's face whitened. "Don't be a fool! The Ark's not simply an artifact! It's a relic that could shift world power! And I didn't go in there like

some gunslinger. Over a year of preparation went into that mission. It was nearly perfect!"

"I'm just telling you what they'll write. You may not think of it as gunslinging, but they will. They'll make Charles Manson look like a nursemaid next to you."

"They'll never have the chance!" A fleck of spittle rested on Crandal's lip and he made no move to remove it. He was losing himself to this.

Roberts lifted an eyebrow. "Worse still, you rerouted arms to Colonel Ambozia in exchange for his invasion to find your relic. They'll call it treason."

"You know as well as I do that the country was already at war. One that we publicly supported."

"No, it had just *finished* a war. But your plan extended that war with this invasion. And after learning that Ambozia's rogue army was unsuccessful in finding your Ark, despite pillaging eight churches and killing over a thousand civilians, you demanded he push farther south if he wanted his arms. Well, they did push farther south. They didn't find an ark, but they did manage to kill another two thousand civilians."

Crandal breathed deeply and sat back. "You're telling me what I already know."

"But what you *don't* know is what I was just told. One of the civilians they killed was a nurse. A Caucasian nurse. An American nurse. An American nurse who happened to be the mother of a son she'd had with a local."

Crandal blinked. "Caleb?!"

Roberts nodded. "Caleb. It gets worse. It was an EPLF captain under Ambozia who took Caleb's mother's head off with his sword while she huddled over her infant son. The captain stood there and watched the baby scream, but instead of taking its life, he swept it up and fled, suddenly horrified by the carnage his soldiers had left behind them. You'll never guess where he took the child."

"Don't patronize me, Roberts. What are you driving at?"

"I'm preparing you for tomorrow's headline, remember?"

"This is all nonsense!"

"Not anymore it's not. The captain took the boy to an isolated monastery called Debra Damarro and left him at the front gate."

"This is idiotic! How would anybody know any of this?"

"Well, that's precisely the problem." Roberts felt a small surge of power over the man, and it actually gave him goose bumps. "Our EPLF captain was a good Orthodox Christian, you see. And his religion was getting the better of him. Which is why he wrote out a confession begging for absolution and then left the note with the child as a sort of penance. Donna claims that she has the note."

Crandal sat very still for a few moments. When he spoke, his words came with a slight tremor. "A note? Anybody could have written a note."

"That's what I told her. But this note came from the boy's tunic. It was sewed into the hem by his father. It's written on parchment and in Amharic. She had it translated this morning and says the scholar who examined it is quite certain that it is authentic."

"What examiner?"

"Don't worry. He'll be dead by nightfall. But the note is a problem, Charles." *Charles?* He was feeling unusually bold, wasn't he?

Sweat peppered the candidate's face. He looked as if he might be coming down with a case of food poisoning.

"We can't allow that note to surface," Roberts said. "Even if you think you can hold on to your lead once the media starts screaming about the baby killer, there's the issue of treason."

Crandal stood abruptly and slammed both fists on the table. A glass toppled over the edge and shattered noisily. "This is hogwash! It's ancient history!"

Roberts stood with him, allowing his anger to rise. "It's the truth! And whether you like it or not, it's going to come out. Our only option is to meet with her."

"Kill her! Kill them all!"

"By five o'clock tonight? Banks will get the kid and the other two, but you don't just walk up to Donna Blair of NBC and pop a slug in her head. If we're not there by five, she goes public. If we are, we at least have some time to reason with her. Give us another evening, and I think we have a better than even chance of making them all dead. But not cooperating now would be a fatal mistake. We have to show good faith."

Crandal balled his hands into fists and turned from the table, steaming like a bull. His jaw flexed with the grinding of his teeth. "I swear, Roberts, if this goes bad, I'll crucify you."

"Actually, I think it's you they're trying to crucify. I may be your only way out. You should keep that in mind. We've got six hours to get to L.A. We should leave."

Crandal walked away from the table, unable to hide a tremble in his hands. He walked up to the wall and smashed both palms against the green-leafed wallpaper. The entire room shook. It was the first time Roberts had seen the man hit a wall.

∞

The night hunt had gone badly.

For starters Banks had eased his Monte Carlo down the road for less than two miles before coming to the conclusion that he was passing terrain that would have allowed Jason's four-wheel drive to leave the road in a dozen spots, given the right motivation. And that motivation clearly existed.

He had painstakingly covered the first three miles of the seven-mile stretch before deciding to park for the night and resume his hunt at first light. He pulled the sedan out of sight and slipped into a light sleep.

Problem was, first light came at four-thirty, and it wasn't the sun blaring through his windshield; it was two headlights.

A lone driver roared by in the Bronco. Again? Jason was going back out by himself. Banks nearly followed the man before deciding that this actually worked to his advantage. The sport utility would return. And now Jason had inadvertently narrowed his location to the direction from which the Bronco had come.

The vehicle roared back by forty minutes later, and this time Banks followed with his lights out. He made it another mile before the dust had settled enough for him to lose certainty that the Bronco had passed. But that put them in this last three miles of the road.

He had taken up the search again at six, with full light, and he'd run into his first logging trail at eight. The good news was that he was certain that the Bronco hid somewhere in these last two miles of road. The bad news was that the only way to search logging trails was to leave the main road and risk missing a fleeing Bronco.

He decided he would have to accept that risk. He searched the logging trails by foot, keeping the road within earshot. The first trail ended within a hundred yards, and he returned without incident. The second trail was longer, but he came to a large muddy patch under heavy growth that was clearly undisturbed. No vehicle had passed this way. Strike two.

The search proved much slower than he'd anticipated. But slowly he eliminated road. By three o'clock he was down to the last half-mile and his pulse was feeling it. They were probably camped where the road ended.

He pulled out his cell phone and sat on the edge of his seat with the door open. Roberts had called four times. He had the ringer off, of course. Nothing like a shrill beep to warn the world of an approaching thug. *Take a seat, Roberts. I'm on the job, if you didn't know.* He punched in the ten-digit number.

"Banks?"

"Yeah."

"Where in the world have you been?"

"Doing my job."

"We're an hour out of LAX," Roberts said. "There's been a problem. What's the status of the kid?" He sounded panicked.

"Lighten up. I've got them pinned to the next half-mile of road."

"Any chance they'll get away?"

"Nope."

"Okay, listen to me. You take out all three; you got that? The price goes up to one million dollars if they're dead by sunset."

Banks whistled softly. "So they've got you spooked good, huh?" Wasn't surprising, really. At least half of all his hits ended up bringing more than initially promised due to complications. But he'd never pulled down a million dollars before. Not on one hit. He looked up the road. The afternoon was dead quiet.

"What's changed?" he asked.

"The kid knows more than we thought he did. So do the others."

"One point two," he said and wiped a trail of sweat from the bridge of his nose. There was a pause.

"Okay, one point two. Just get it done."

Banks snapped the phone closed and tossed it onto the passenger's seat. Good enough. They were offering double the six hundred thousand he'd agreed to yesterday. Whatever the kid knew, it was worth all the marbles. He checked his 9-mm Browning by habit, left the car half hidden in the side brush, and walked toward a trail that broke to the left twenty meters ahead.

One point two million! His pulse spiked at the thought. *Jiminy Cricket, I'd pop 'em for the fun of it. They got away, didn't they? Nobody gets away.*

The fact that the trees kept heavy shade on the forest trails was his salvation, he thought. It had rained three days ago—he remembered that now—and the mud was still wet in spots. All he had to do was find a spot and see if it showed any tire marks. He'd tracked on less before. The cowboy trackers in them Louis L'Amour novels could supposedly follow a man on horseback for days based on bent grass blades alone. That was the biggest pile of . . .

Banks pulled up and blinked. Shade covered the entrance to the logging trail. A soft layer of dark dirt was bared of grass at his feet. An eight-inch tire track ran right through the wet earth.

The Bronco!

Banks jerked his head up, immediately alert. This was it! They were down this trail. His heart thumped loudly in his ears. Yeah, baby!

He ran back to the car, pulled out the rifle, and cut into the forest at an angle that would meet with the trail. The trees were mostly pines and their growth relatively sparse here. He followed the rise in the terrain, bent low and moving steadily. Somewhere to his right the trees broke for the trail. The Bronco would either be on the forest trail itself or in a clearing.

Banks pulled up behind a pine at the hill's crest and studied the trees. They ended thirty yards ahead. So there was a clearing! Sweat leaked steadily from his pores now. He ran the back of his hand across his upper forehead.

He ran crouched low, squinting his eyes for the Bronco's white paint between the trees. They'd be sitting ducks in a clearing. *Pop! Pop! Pop!* In the middle of nowhere. One point two.

Banks stopped behind a tree ten feet from the edge of the clearing and saw two things in the same moment. The first was the cabin. It sat on the edge of the clearing, less than thirty yards away, overlooking another couple hundred yards of open meadow, and he thought to himself, *Jiminy Cricket, they got themselves a cabin!*

The second thing he saw was the white Bronco tearing away from the cabin, down the meadow to the forest trail that emerged fifty yards to his right. Its engine growled through the mountain air.

Banks stared unbelieving for a split second.

Then he was on one knee with the rifle to his shoulder. White paint flashed in his glass, and he followed the car with a trained eye. If it hadn't been for two trees that momentarily blocked his vision, he would have nailed the right tire then. One shot, *Pop!* and they would have been stranded for the picking.

The Bronco lumbered over the crest and disappeared. Banks cursed and tore down the hill through the trees. He had one more chance before it became a chase. And he almost made it too.

The white truck roared up the dirt road toward his hidden Monte Carlo. He pulled up in the trees twenty feet from the road and dropped to one knee for a shot.

Now was when scopes were in the way. The Bronco roared by full throated, and Banks came very close to pulling the trigger, despite the trees that kept blurring his view.

He swore, jumped to his feet, and ran for his car. They were a good three hundred yards ahead of him by the time he stowed the rifle in its back-seat case, fired the engine, and pulled around in pursuit.

Easy, boy. This ain't over, not by a long shot. It was personal now. A fury that made his eyes feel hot settled over him. *Easy, boy.*

The options ran through his mind with accustomed precision. *This ain't over. Not by a long shot.*

The Bronco was losing him, and he removed his eyes from the potholes and drove straight ahead, ignoring the bucking ride. If he lost them now, there would be no options. His only hope was to follow them. They would stop. They had to stop somewhere. And when they did stop, he would dispense with the cute stuff and do this right. He didn't care if it was in front of the police headquarters itself; they were dead.

Banks suddenly slammed the wheel and roared.

Then he took a deep breath, cleared his throat, and drifted into auto kill.

37

DONNA STOOD AT THE FIELD ENTRANCE in the Rose Bowl Monday afternoon, her stomach bunched in knots, thinking that she'd gone over the edge on this one. Flat off a cliff.

She was a journalist, she kept reminding herself. She lived for stories like this one. The operative word there being lived. She wasn't sure she was ready to die for a story like this—or any story, for that matter.

She'd chosen the Rose Bowl for two reasons. Actually three. One, she knew the head of maintenance, Bob Sardoni, who had agreed to let her use the huge stadium for this test of hers, seeing as how it wasn't booked tonight. Which led to the second reason: the test, a loose term at best. Bill stood hidden in the announcer's booth a hundred yards off, armed with the highest-power zoom lens the studio had. He'd fixed three long-range directional mikes to the nearby seats on three different sides, triangulated on her position. His receiver could supposedly pick up a whisper from anywhere within twenty feet of where she stood. From his one remote uplink Bill could feed the world with as much footage as she could bluff her way into. It was a state-of-the-art setup that Bill insisted was smoother than goat cheese.

And the third reason? The third reason was more of a hunch. Just in case this thing got big in a hurry.

The protests downtown had swelled to over three thousand marchers and they weren't going away. They'd taken on a life of their own. The manhunt for Caleb had escalated as the hours slipped by, broadening to Nevada, Oregon, and Mexico. Well over a thousand officers were sweeping the huge region. The suggestion that Jason had almost assuredly ditched the white Bronco in favor of another vehicle only diluted resources further. It was nonstop coverage on all the stations now, and it had taken every professional trick she knew to keep her knowledge from spilling out. When it was all said and done, she might face legal action for allowing their mad search to continue while she knew the boy's location, but it was something she would have to live with. For the country's sake as well as hers, if Jason was right.

She glanced at her watch. Four-fifty. Crandal was due in ten minutes and Jason still wasn't here. "Check. You read me, Bill? If you read, flash me."

A white strobe ignited from behind the dimmed announcer's glass at the other end of the field.

"Okay, remember, I want you to start filming the second Crandal arrives. Just film and send. Mitchell will decide whether or not to broadcast, but keep the shots clean. If this is good, we've got all the majors lined up to pick up the feed."

The strobe flashed twice. "A-OK."

One hundred two thousand seats sat empty, staring down at the green grass. Football uprights stood bare and alone at each end of the field. The lights were burning already, a favor for which she would pay dearly later. Behind her the north tunnel gaped to deep shadows. She was very much alone, and the thought made her swallow.

A door slammed and she spun around. Jason?!

"Jason! Thank God! You're here!"

He strode out, grinning from ear to ear, with Leiah on one side, black hair lifting in the breeze, and Caleb trotting on the other side.

"I said I'd be here. Thank God *you're* here." He ushered both Leiah and Caleb by the shoulders and looked around the stadium. "You actually did it."

"Believe me, it took some doing." She glanced at her watch again. "We have about five minutes before Crandal shows, assuming he shows."

"So he agreed."

"I'm not sure he had a choice." She pulled the rolled parchment from the pocket of her suit. "Here it is." She handed it to Jason and motioned to a door under the bleachers. "I want you to wait behind that door, out of sight. And I want the boy to come out with the confession when I say. You'll be able to watch us through the cracks."

He glanced at the Amharic text and handed it to Caleb, who read it quickly.

"A bit theatrical, don't you think?" That grin still hadn't left his face, and Donna thought it a bit strange. There was a quality different about him. He wasn't striking her as the kind of person who'd just spent a day on the bad end of a massive manhunt. His blue eyes moved quickly with strung nerves, but otherwise he seemed unusually calm.

"I put my career on the line in exchange for this show. I direct the show; that was the deal. Without Caleb, there's no show; you know that."

"We were followed here," Jason said.

"You're serious? By whom?" She looked around at the seats.

"Don't know. Maybe just a hiker who saw the Bronco. I think we lost them on the freeway. You got the camera magic ready?"

"You're being shot as we speak. If we pull this off, our faces will be simulcast on all the major networks. They've guaranteed open feeds. Five minutes with live footage of Caleb, and I promise the world will tune in. Nothing like this has been done, but then the world has never been so interested in one person before, at least in our day. The audience could top at two hundred million people, so put on your best smile." She looked down at the boy. "Does Caleb still have his power?"

Jason grinned wide. "I guess. More or less."

Donna looked at Leiah, who stood quiet, surprisingly at ease. There was something very different about her. A glow to her cheeks. Something else Donna couldn't place. New makeup or hair, maybe.

"You should go. If we have a show, it starts in three minutes."

"Thank you, Donna," Jason said. He reached forward and touched her shoulder as if he were her father or something. "Thank you for believing."

"You just make sure we turn some heads," she said with a grin.

"If they could see what I've seen, I guarantee you their heads would be spinning," he said.

They turned and walked toward a side entrance that led under the seats. They were already stepping past the door when it dawned on her what was different about Leiah. It was her skin!

Her scars were gone!

∞

The flight had been an impossible ordeal. They were both in crisis-management overdrive, but there was very little to manage. Crandal had climbed back into his professional skin and begun his methodical consideration of alternatives and contingencies, almost as though they were discussing a third party rather than him. For a few minutes there, flying at thirty thousand feet above it all, Roberts actually enjoyed himself. Their exchange came like the old days, when they faced each day with the absolute persuasion that the only thing that might tamper with their invincibility was a lapse in reason. Stupidity in the vernacular.

But today, reason wasn't offering any solutions, and as the flight droned on, their conversation became more sporadic. As long as there existed a piece of paper from Ethiopia bearing the confession of a captain fingering Crandal as the mastermind behind a plan that resulted in the knowing slaughter of thousands, there were no contingencies that offered relief. They could twist arms; they could pull in favors; they could deny until they were blue in the face. But if the confession surfaced it would be the end, at the very least the political end. How a captain under Colonel Ambozia had come into the details of the operation in the first place was another matter. Ambozia had to be silenced; that much was now evident. They should have done it long ago.

And they should have killed the kid day one.

They should have, but they hadn't, and now they had to kill them all in the next twelve hours. Crandal insisted it with a trembling jowl.

They'd left the entourage in D.C. under the understanding that they were flying to L.A. for a private policy meeting and would be back in the morning. Roberts had rented the Grand Am and wheeled it up to the back entrance of the large stadium.

"I talk," Crandal said, patting his face with a napkin. "Our only purpose here is to get the document. This is strictly political. She owes us a favor; we call in that favor and promise her the world, that's all. Your only purpose in there is to make sure we're isolated."

"She agreed to come clean," Roberts said. "I walk around her first. If there's an electronic device within twenty feet of her, I'll know. You get my signal to back off, then you back off."

"We can't leave without the confession."

"We won't."

They exchanged a glance and Crandal nodded. They stepped from the car, straightened their jackets, and walked toward the back door.

∞

Banks had lost them at the intersection of the 5 and the 210 freeways, courtesy of some lamebrain idiot in an old Cadillac who insisted on sitting in the on-ramp merge lane with her turn signal blinking, waiting for traffic to clear—an absurd expectation during the rush hour. No amount of his furious cursing or honking budged her. He'd finally taken to the grass and roared by her, but by then the white Bronco was gone.

They were heading east. He assumed Pasadena—Jason's home.

Banks had driven to Hollister Drive, parked down the street, and searched the house. But the Bronco wasn't there. He returned to his car with nerves wound tight enough to set off a quiver in his bones. He couldn't remember feeling as agitated.

Waiting he could handle. But waiting with images of a white Bronco cruising down the road to Tijuana while he sat here, dead in the water, was enough to turn him bald.

Then again, he had no choice. He couldn't just take off for Mexico without knowing it was their destination. He flipped his police scanner on and closed his eyes. If anybody was going to find the Bronco, it would be the police. And if they did, he was there—police or no police.

38

They walked out of a side door at three minutes past the hour, and Donna felt a chill rip up her spine. Roberts led, dressed in simple black. Crandal's huge bulk followed, dressed in double-breasted black. The latter smiled. The former did not, but then she wasn't sure she'd ever seen Roberts smile.

Donna watched them come and nonchalantly dried her palms on her skirt in a smoothing motion. She cracked a let's-do-an-interview smile and extended her hand. It seemed appropriate. Roberts ignored her and walked to her left. Then around and to her right.

"What's the matter, Roberts? You think I have a shotgun under my skirt?" She forced a laugh and Crandal joined her.

"You know these grunts," he said, dismissing Roberts with a wave of his hand. "They think there's a sniper hiding behind every tree." His voice came low, dripping with authority. She'd forgotten how imposing the man could be. He stretched his hand out. "Good to see you again, Donna."

He looked around the stadium, and Roberts stood behind him with his arms behind his back. The security man scanned the rows of seats, but for the moment he seemed satisfied.

"Thank you for coming, Mr. Crandal. Or should I call you Mr. President?"

He smiled, patently. "Well, it looks like I've earned the confidence of the American people. They want a change and I'm going to give it to them. The people's will is preeminent in this country, don't you think?"

"Yes, I do."

"To the detriment of some, unfortunately. I'm sure my opponent isn't so interested in the will of the people right now." He was smooth. Goodness he was smooth.

"No, I guess not."

"And how about you, Donna? How do you feel about interfering with the will of the people?"

"I just have a few questions, sir. That's all."

"Please."

She took a breath and let it out slowly.

"I told you on the phone that I had a confession from a man who claims that you orchestrated an invasion of Ethiopia. Is it true?"

"Of course not. I can tell you that in my former duties as the director of the National Security Administration, I was involved in many covert operations in this country's national interest, but an invasion of Ethiopia was not one of them."

"How would you suggest that this document came into being?"

"Donna, let's be reasonable. You're too intelligent for this. We're about to change the world, my dear. This country needs a strong leader willing to cross ideological lines for the sake of progress. The American people want me to be that man. Surely you aren't suggesting that a rumor from some forgotten corner of the world should be allowed to stand in the way of that."

"I'm not suggesting anything. But it strikes me as strange that you would agree to meet me in the middle of this vacant stadium over a rumor."

"Does that surprise you? Well, it shouldn't. I know the power of suggestion. Misinformation can ruin a man. It was how we brought Milosevic to his knees. I'm sure my enemies would love to see me destroyed by a piece of paper. But we aren't going to allow that, are we, Donna?"

She cleared her throat. *I hope you're getting this, Bill.* They would never air unsubstantiated accusations. But they would air Caleb. This whole show depended on Caleb, and she had the boy in her pocket.

"What do you suggest?" she asked.

"I suggest you give the document to me and we call it a night. It's the only responsible thing to do. We have a country that's waiting."

"We?"

He grinned and winked. "I'm sure all of our lives will improve under my administration."

"You want the document now?"

"Yes."

Donna's pulse spiked; she turned to the side and nodded. It occurred to her that she hadn't told Jason precisely what the sign was. Bill knew—her nodding—but would Jason follow? She nodded again. *Come on, Caleb.*

The door under the seats behind Donna suddenly opened and Caleb stepped out. He climbed two steps and stepped onto the field.

"I thought it would be appropriate for Caleb to give it to you," Donna said, motioning with her hand.

Crandal's face went white. Roberts dropped both arms, took a step forward, and cursed.

Caleb walked toward them, holding the folded note with both hands. His hair was in tangles, and he smiled at Donna. Unless the studio had been caught flat-footed, Mitchell had already patched the feed through to live coverage. If they were on their toes, this picture was now live on all the majors.

"I thought Banks . . ." Roberts trailed off, red in the face.

The boy stopped by Donna's side. "Hello." He unfolded the note, glanced at the script, and then looked up at Crandal. "This is my father's paper. I recognize it, because he taught me to write on paper just like this when I was even a smaller boy. It says here that you killed many good women and children in my country. And I think it's right because I had a dream where you ate a woman. So it must be that you are a very bad man."

They stared at him, stunned.

We're making history, Donna thought. *The world is watching and we're making history.*

Crandal closed his eyes for a long second and then opened them. He looked at Roberts, and his security chief moved to the right. Roberts scanned the seats quickly. He slipped his hand under his jacket. Donna watched it all, not quite willing to accept the conclusion that blared through her skull.

He was going for a gun. He was actually going to pull his gun!

A pistol flashed in Roberts's hand. To Donna it felt like someone had opened her skull and poured in a bucket of ice water. She stiffened and took a step back.

"We have no option," Roberts said. "The kid's alive."

∞

Jason was watching the scene through a gap around the door, and he bolted as soon as Roberts pulled out the gun. He shoved through the door and pulled up. "You'd better think twice about that, Roberts. You're on live camera."

Roberts spun to him, gun extended.

Jason stepped forward, his heart thumping in his chest. "You fire and a million people will watch you do it," he said.

Roberts blinked rapidly a few times. Leiah ran past him and pulled the boy behind her. Both Roberts and Crandal diverted their eyes and quickly scanned the empty stadium.

"You're lying!" Roberts snapped. "I swept—"

"He's not lying," Donna said. She pointed down the field. "We have a camera in the announcer's box. We're live."

"You're lying," Crandal growled. "We agreed to no cameras!" He was panicking.

Roberts's gun wavered and he lowered it slowly. Somewhere in the distance a horn honked. Then another. Then a chorus of car horns, as if someone were getting married at a nearby church.

"Bill, you know how to turn on the PA?" Donna asked.

A brief silence. Roberts began to lift the gun, his knuckles white. "You're bluffing."

The air squealed with feedback. The public address system crackled with a man's voice. "Am I on?"

"Say hi to Bill," Donna said, wearing a smirk.

Horns blared, closer now. The cameraman's voice echoed through the empty stadium. "We're rolling, Donna. Mitchell has the feed out for the taking. We're live on most stations across the country. And Jason's wrong if he thinks that only a million people are watching this. You better believe that."

A healthy dose of feedback shrilled again.

The goose bumps that spread over Donna's skin were from the thrill of it now. "Did they announce the party?" she asked.

"Yes, ma'am."

"Thank you, Bill."

Donna turned to Crandal. "You see? I'm not bluffing. In fact, my guess is those horns we're hearing are from rush-hour motorists who've heard our open invitation to come down to the Rose Bowl to see the boy. I'd say we have three minutes before they start flooding the stadium."

Crandal took a step backward. "This is nonsense! Absolute nonsense, you hear me?! You'll never get away with this!"

Roberts's gun had disappeared. He stepped up, white as a sheet. "Let's go, sir."

"I think I am getting away with this," Donna said.

The horns were blaring much closer now. It occurred to Jason that they were getting all of this dialogue over their radios. Every word spoken here was being broadcast to millions of cars as well!

Crandal looked directly at the announcer's box and scowled.

"We should leave, sir! Now!" Roberts said.

A man suddenly sprinted through the side entrance at the fifty-yard line. He ran out about twenty feet and pulled up, wide-eyed. Two more ran in behind him. They were here already.

"Sir . . . !"

Crandal spun and strode for the back entrance through which he'd come. Roberts turned back once, still white, and then they left the stadium.

Donna immediately went into action. "Okay, Bill, let's set up the other camera down here. Keep the feed rolling." People were entering the stadium in a sudden stream now. The horns in the parking lot rose over the high walls like a symphony tuning up. Jason watched the unfolding in unbelief. Whatever strings Donna had pulled to bring this together were paying off in grand fashion.

She was facing the booth and talking directly to the television audience now. "What you're witnessing, ladies and gentlemen, is something you're unlikely to ever see again in your lifetime. History is being made before our eyes. We'll leave the speculation about Charles Crandal's comments to the appropriate authorities. But I think we've all learned tonight that not everything is as it seems." She eased over to Caleb and put her hand on his shoulder. "As you can clearly see, Caleb is alive and well. And I'm sure that we can persuade him to tell us what has happened in a few minutes."

She continued, but Jason tuned her out and faced the field. Several people were out in the middle screaming at the top of their lungs, directing traffic, telling the floods of people now entering the stadium to find seats as quickly as possible. Another NBC team had arrived and were running to the front with suitcases of equipment. Four men dressed in T-shirts were wheeling a ten-by-twenty platform on wheels toward them. It looked as if it had come from under the seats.

Jason stepped up behind Leiah and swallowed.

When Donna said show, she meant show.

∞

It was Peter who saw the Rose Bowl coverage first.

He was sitting in his blue wheelchair flipping through the channels, but following his new custom, he peeked in on NBC every five minutes or so. They were the ones who seemed to be on the inside of Caleb's story. The Learning Channel episode on mummies came to a commercial break, and he switched back to NBC.

At first the picture looked like something from a home video—like a football field without any football players or people in the stands. The picture shimmered and then zoomed in to Donna and two other men.

Peter watched with mild interest as they talked. It was the kind of thing his mom and dad probably would go nuts over, but to him it was just a political story, and as far as he saw it, politics was one of those things that would matter one day, but for now . . .

Wait a minute! Who was that? The camera focused on a small boy walking from a side door. It was Caleb! Was it? Yes! Yes, it was Caleb!

"Mom!"

His mother poked her head in from the kitchen. Peter glanced at her and then returned to the picture. Suddenly the one man had a gun out, and it was pointed at Caleb!

"Stew! Stew get in here right now!" His mother sounded frantic, and his dad heard that too, because he bounded in from the garage.

"What? What is it?"

"It's Caleb," Peter said. "That guy has—"

"Is this for real?" Stew demanded.

"Yes! Yes, it's for real," his mom shot back.

His dad bounded for his radio on the kitchen table and flipped it on. The speaker crackled with a man's voice describing what they were seeing right now. The police knew.

The Longs watched for another three minutes in stunned silence. They watched Jason run out, followed by Leiah. They watched Crandal and Roberts leave and then they watched as a tag line appeared across the bottom, inviting anyone who so desired and could to come to the Rose Bowl. Caleb was back.

The black ticker tape scrolled across the bottom for a full thirty seconds, and Peter felt his heart pounding in his chest like it was going to tear loose. Then his mom spoke.

"The Rose Bowl's only fifteen minutes from here."

No one answered her. People were already arriving at the stadium. A helicopter shot showed long bunches of lights suddenly breaking from the three surrounding freeways, heading toward the Rose Bowl. It looked like a blotchy ring of fire moving into its center.

"The roads will be jammed pretty soon," Mom said.

Peter looked up at his dad. "Please, Dad."

His dad hesitated one moment longer and then he was suddenly grabbing for his police jacket. "Okay, in the cruiser. If we're gonna go, we might as well get there in style. Barbara, grab Peter's coat. I'll get him in the car."

They were on the road with their overhead lights flashing five minutes later. The radio was crackling, and the roads were filling up, and Peter couldn't help but think that something was about to happen.

Something very big.

∞

Banks had picked the news up when some rookie cop with a high voice started yelling over the scanner that the kid had been found. In fact, the cop insisted, he was on television right now with that reporter from NBC, his kidnappers, and Charles Crandal, of all people! Where? At the Rose Bowl. And the tag at the bottom of the screen was inviting one and all to the Rose Bowl.

The scanner immediately clogged with cops crackling back and forth.

Crandal was with the kid? Banks had nearly panicked. For a fleeting minute he considered leaving it all. But then the beauty of the situation hit him square in the head, and he fired the Monte Carlo and screamed toward the Rose Bowl.

The kid was there, the kidnappers were there, and most importantly, confusion would be there. You put them all together with a trained killer and you got one point two million out of it.

He arrived with the first few cars, parked on the north side, and waited for more cars to arrive. If he was going to depend upon confusion, he had to let confusion set up.

The cars came in long strings of headlights, sounding their horns like adolescents who thought they had something to celebrate. They rolled in undirected and parked in surprisingly neat rows, considering the spontaneity of it all. There were no attendants with orange vests and flashlights facilitating a smooth process. There were just hordes of people who'd evidently heard the announcements on their radios and pulled off the freeway to see what all the fuss was about. They parked their cars and hustled toward the gaping entrance, which was flooded with light.

According to the police band, the 210 freeway had come to a standstill, and they were scrambling to redirect traffic. To complicate matters, all the freeways leading anywhere near Pasadena were hopelessly clogged. Evidently the whole basin had heard the news and decided en masse to beat a path to the Rose Bowl before their neighbors turned on their televisions and decided to make the drive. The only solution offered was to divert as many exits as possible toward the stadium. According to a police chopper reporting over the band, the region looked like a massive spider web of lights leading to the lighted bowl.

Banks felt a twitch over his left eye. The idiots had no idea what kind of show they were in for. Not even a clue. He might have to give up Jason and the woman—he knew that. It depended on what kind of position he could get in. But then again, maybe he would just pop away.

And what if the game had changed now? What if this exposure of Roberts and Crandal dampened their willingness to pay?

He cursed out loud and shoved the thought from his mind. He couldn't think of that now. Not when he was closing in for the kill. Not when he was about to finish what he'd started.

His wait lasted seven minutes. A sea of cars surrounded his own. He stepped from the vehicle and walked to the back. His getaway lane was clear to the left. Good enough. He popped the trunk.

The Israeli manufactured .308 with its gas-operated blowback recoil system was his workhorse. He could pick the kid off from here if he had the line of sight, and that was with the silencer.

A father and his kid ran by three cars over, jabbering excitedly. If they'd seen him, they showed no sign of it.

Banks pulled out a dark brown trench coat and slid into it. He glanced to either side, saw that he was alone between the cars, and eased the rifle under the coat. Quickly he strapped it in place, using a wide strip of Velcro that fed under the scope and around his waist. The barrel poked at his armpit. Good enough.

Banks closed the trunk and strode toward the side of the stadium, joining the streams of people hurrying to the entrances like ants scurrying for the nest. Horns still blared from a thousand cars that lined the surrounding streets waiting to squeeze in for the show.

Good enough. He was going to steal the show.

39

T HE STADIUM FILLED TO HALF of its 102,000-seat capacity within the
first fifteen minutes before the general clogging of main arteries around
the facility slowed the influx. A dozen news crews had now set up remote
cameras facing the makeshift stage on the north end. A green artificial turf
covered the plywood, and on the turf was a stand with twenty microphones
strapped together with duct tape. The contraption reminded Jason of one of
those porcupine-looking land mines.

They stood off the stage with little to say. It had all happened so quickly,
the flight into the hills, the opening of the heavens, and now this show
thrown together by Donna. His mind was still buzzing.

"I feel like I'm floating on a cloud," he said.

"You feel it?" Caleb asked.

"I feel something."

"I feel it too," Leiah said. "It's like the air is thick with something. Not
just the excitement."

Caleb looked up at Jason with his impossibly round aqua eyes, smiling.
His hair was still disheveled from two nights in the shack. Leiah had insisted
they stop at a trinket shop on their way in; they couldn't walk around in
clothes smeared with blood from Caleb's wound and enough dirt to start a
city garden. The weather was a tad cold for the Magic Mountain T-shirts
she'd bought them, but at least they were clean. It was the first time in seven
years she had worn short sleeves, and she seemed decidedly content baring
her arms.

Caleb's shirt was at least a size too big. "Are you feeling like you did in the
field?" he asked.

"Yeah, sort of."

"The Spirit of God," the boy said. "Maybe something's going to happen."

In all honesty, Jason felt oddly out of place standing here while the
throngs funneled in. As if he were the stranger here, an alien on show. It was

Caleb they had come to see, and he could hardly blame them for that. But he had a part to play as well. It looked as though the boy was mistaken when he'd suggested one of them might die soon. That was good.

The unfolding scene before them felt small and inconsequential to Jason, as if it were just another game to be played, this time in this massive stadium. The real thing had happened in the hills. There the worlds had collided and revealed their real power. Thinking on it, a small chill spread down his spine. *Dear God, I love you dearly. You are my king.*

A quiver ran through his bones.

"You okay?" Leiah asked. Her eyes sparkled. "You've been smiling here for the past ten minutes and I think the cameras are going to wonder if you've lost your mind." She grinned.

"I'm fine." He kissed her forehead. "I think I'm in love."

"I know what you mean. Me too."

He wasn't positive if she meant him or the Father. Maybe both, like him. It didn't matter; they were bound together.

Donna approached them. "Okay, I think now would be a good time. Can you talk to the people, Caleb?"

"It isn't full," Jason said.

"It will be in a few minutes. Either way our audience is staring at us through those cameras out there. We're live in fifty-two countries. By the studio's estimates, we now have the largest audience that's ever witnessed a single event live. Over three hundred million people are staring at us right now." She flashed a deliberate grin with her back to the camera.

"Like I said, now would be a good time to do something. Besides, I understand Nikolous will be here any second. We don't need him calling a halt to all this."

The numbers seemed empty to Jason. The thought of Nikolous storming in felt trivial. Small. That in itself was strange. Maybe Caleb was right; maybe something was about to happen.

"Okay, Caleb," he said. "The world awaits. Go up there and tell them how it is."

The boy paused and looked from Jason to Leiah, and then back. He seemed thrilled with them. He reached both arms up to them, inviting an embrace. Jason glanced at Leiah, and they both bent and hugged the boy.

"I'm very happy," he said.

"We're happy too," Leiah said, hugging him tight. "Thank you."

He released them and drilled them with a stare. "Thank you."

It wasn't until Caleb had mounted the stage that the tone of Caleb's words struck Jason. They felt like a salutation.

Donna ran toward Bill. "We're on!"

The boy walked toward the microphone, and some people at field level began to shout for everyone to shut up. The word spread like wildfire. The boy was taking the stage.

By the time Caleb stopped in front of the wad of mikes, a deafening hush had engulfed the stadium. Only the background symphony of horns, honking in the distance, and the steady backbeat of a chopper's blades sounded high above.

Caleb stood in his large T-shirt and leaned up to the microphones.

"Hello."

The word reverberated loudly. Too loudly. He pulled back and grinned, amused. He glanced over at Jason and Leiah and tried again.

"Hello." This time they had turned him down.

"My name is Caleb."

A young woman in a front-row seat to their left stood, lifted her arms high, and yelled her approval. "Yeaaaa, Caleb! Yeaaaa, Caleb!"

Hundreds rose to their feet around her and joined in her cry. Within seconds the entire place was on its feet, thundering its approval with yells and whistles. Caleb said something into the mike, but it was lost to the roar. The air shook under the power of eighty thousand voices screaming at full volume.

Caleb blinked and stepped back from the mike. It was hard to imagine that a short five weeks ago the small boy they cheered had huddled under his tunic in the back of Jason's bouncing Jeep. Hard to imagine that so many people would drop what they were doing to rush here on the news that Caleb was alive. But then the boy had walked onto the horizon of their worlds and changed everything, hadn't he? They might follow him over a cliff.

A dozen people who evidently fancied themselves as leaders ran onto the field and waved the crowd to silence itself. It took a good thirty seconds, but the din slowly died, to the yelling of a bare-chested man in jeans and long hair who was especially enthusiastic about their quieting.

The boy glanced over at Jason, his smile now gone. Jason nodded encouragement, and Caleb stepped back up to the mike.

"I'm just a boy," he said. "It's frightening to hear all this noise. You should be praising God, not me."

He paused. The hush felt unearthly.

"Because you know that everything you've seen comes from God. All the good things, anyway. Dadda told me that we shouldn't look for the praise of men."

Caleb glanced to the side, and Jason's heart swelled. The boy was speaking like the young educated man he was. It was amazing how his extensive book learning of English had steadily translated to speech over the last month. *You tell them, Caleb.*

The boy faced the mike again. "I'm not a magician. I know that some people think I am, but I'm not. And the power you've seen isn't from my mind like some of you think, either. It's not from me at all. It's from God."

For a boy who had spoken very little publicly in the five weeks he had been in America, he was now forthcoming, gaining confidence with each word, it seemed.

"And when I told you that Jesus Christ is the only power behind what you've seen, it's not because I don't know better. I know Christ because he's saved me. I think I understand sin pretty good now and it isn't very nice. I walk in Jesus' kingdom, the kingdom of God. He is God. The only God."

You could almost hear the swallowing of tongues across the world. The boy's words defied the beliefs of well over half of those watching. But he wasn't finished.

"Some of you believe in stone gods. Some of you worship prophets. I don't understand all your fancy words, but I do know God, and I can tell you that he's only one. He's not Buddha, he's not Mohammed, and he's not man. He's Jesus Christ, and he has made a path to God. To the kingdom of God."

A roar broke out spontaneously. The Christians couldn't contain themselves, and neither could Jason. The stadium shook, and Jason realized that his own voice was among those that made it shake. It hardly mattered that half of those in attendance only stared at the boy with round eyes, shocked at his words. The pronouncement of truth from the rest triumphed, and soon others were joining in. From where he was standing, Jason could actually see the mikes vibrating with the thundering cry.

"And some of you who call yourself Christians . . ."

Jason saw that the stadium was now overflowing. Nikolous had arrived. He stood at the side entrance wide-eyed. The bare-chested man in jeans was running out in the field, vigorously waving the crowd quiet again. The cheers fell off.

"And some of you who call yourself Christians need to learn how to *walk* in the kingdom of God, not just sleep there," Caleb said. "Dadda told me that just because you are born into a palace doesn't mean that you know how to rule. You are children who are blind to the power of God's Spirit. I think you might still be babies in the palace. Maybe you are still playing with mud pies."

Jason laughed loudly enough in the silence to warrant the swing of a few cameras his way. He jerked at Leiah's elbow in his side and swallowed his laughter. But she was chuckling under her breath. Dr. Thompson's words were not lost on the boy.

Caleb looked their way and grinned. "Jason and Leiah have walked in the kingdom. If they can, anybody can, because I think they once hated God."

What a strange, wonderful way to put it, Jason thought. He dipped his head and smiled. Several cameras swept his way again. Jason expected Caleb to turn back to the mike and continue.

But he didn't.

He just stared at them. "That is all I have to say," he said. The smile slowly faded from his face. The crowd stood rooted in silence.

A wave of heat crashed over Jason's head and rushed down his back. The air felt awkwardly heavy. He and Caleb froze like that, staring at each other, somehow trapped in time, oddly expectant.

When Caleb's head moved, it seemed to do so in slow motion. It went backward, still staring at him. The boy's arms still hung loosely at his sides, but his head was now bent back at a right angle. A red mist sprayed through the air behind him. His eyes closed and Jason wondered why. Silence swept through the stadium.

For an endless moment Caleb stood like that, with his head bent back impossibly and his eyes closed to the world. And then his legs suddenly buckled. His body crumpled backward and landed on the plywood with a loud thump.

A great white ball of heat exploded in Jason's mind. That was a bullet that smashed through his little head! Caleb had been shot!

Then he thought, *I've been shot too.*

∽

Banks would have pulled the trigger a second time if it hadn't been for the kid's weird performance at the end. He'd just stood there, and Banks couldn't help thinking that the kid wanted him to shoot.

He leaned against the railing above the press boxes and kept the cross hairs on the boy's temple for five seconds before squeezing his right forefinger. It had been perfect. No report, no flash, just a spit, and the kid was dead on his feet. Banks kept the scope on the boy for three full seconds before it crumpled. The body didn't move. He was dead for sure this time.

And what if they don't pay, huh? Huh, huh, huh?

He hesitated one more second knowing he should've taken out the other two by now. Jason stood stage left, gawking.

Suddenly Banks was running out of time. The sound of a chopper's blades beat through the air high above. That would be the police, and they would know by now. Banks spun the rifle toward the woman, but she was running for the boy already. His time was running out; the stadium was in an uproar.

Banks stood abruptly, shoved the rifle under his trench coat, strapped it in, and ran for the back wall. If Crandal didn't pay, he would pop him, that was for sure. It had taken him twenty minutes to climb up here. It would take him no more than two to descend.

He was unstoppable. Good enough. When he said he would make someone dead, they were dead. At least the boy was—he'd never really agreed to take out the two adults anyway. One point two was nothing. And if it really was nothing—if they changed the rules on him—he had himself a new hunt.

Pop, pop. Good enough.

∽

It took a full three seconds for Jason to realize that he wasn't dead. His head felt as though it had imploded, from shock maybe, but not from a bullet. Caleb—that was a different story.

Cries of shock and unbelief began to build into a sea of confusion. Leiah had already rushed out and fallen to her knees by the boy's body. He thought she might be wailing in horror, but he couldn't be sure because the whole stadium sounded like a warbly siren gone berserk.

The full realization of what had really happened hit Jason then, and he suddenly sucked at the air as if gut-punched.

A groan worked its way past his dropped jaw. "Uhhh . . ."

Adrenaline flushed through his body, and he staggered forward, on unfeeling feet of lead. "Oh, God! Oh, God!"

Leiah was weeping, bent over Caleb, brushing his matted hair away from a gaping hole in the side of his head.

Jason made it halfway to them before he tripped and sprawled to the floor. He clambered to his feet, suddenly desperate to get to the boy. This couldn't be real, of course. Caleb hadn't really been shot in the head. Not now, not ever, not as long as Jason was alive.

His vision blurred and he went down again, but this time on his knees at the boy's side. It was there, close up, that the serene look of Caleb's bloodied face stamped the truth clean through Jason's mind.

Caleb was dead.

Nothing with that kind of damage could possibly be alive.

The breath left Jason completely. His throat ached and his chest screamed with a pain so deep he wondered if things were coming apart in there. This little boy had become his life, and now that life had been ripped from him. First Stephen, now Caleb.

A vague thought stomped through his mind. The thought that this much pain was more than he could bear. It was maybe greater than he should be feeling. Panic ripped up his spine.

"Oh, God!"

The crowd's screaming behind him and Leiah's weeping at his right knee began to fade into a distant world. A dull thumping filled his own. His heart. As though it were slugging up and down through blistering molten steel.

Jason clamped his eyes tight, threw back his head, and screamed at the sky. "Noooooo!"

His voice wailed above the din, strained with agony, frightening in its pitch. And still his heart was exploding. Every nerve in his body seemed to be swimming in the pain. The last reserves of panic raged to the surface, and

Jason knew without a doubt that he was dying. He was kneeling on the stage with his face to the sky, dying of sorrow.

He ran out of breath and inhaled deeply. The sucking echoed hollow, as if he were in a huge drum, and his eyes fell open to the black sky.

But it wasn't black.

It was blue. The same blue air they had swum through in the hills. Now around him a vacuum of silence.

His eyes had been opened again! The pain eased.

Or maybe he was dead and in heaven.

Jason spun his head about. No, he was in the stadium, and the wisps of red and green and yellow floated through the air, as they had in the hills, but now they made slow circles around the stadium instead of skipping over the meadow.

It was the same, and yet it was not the same at all.

Jason pivoted to the bleachers. What he saw stopped him cold.

The people were all out there, all 102,000 of them. But only some of them were standing, staring forward in shock, some of them crying, although he could not hear them. The rest . . .

The rest were dead.

Jason slowly climbed to his feet and walked forward a few steps. They weren't really physically dead, of course, but he was being shown them as if they were. They sat slumped in their seats or lay crumpled on the ground, gray and lifeless, not unlike the boy behind him.

Like a comet from the sky a small shaft of red light suddenly shot in from his left and ripped through his chest.

The pain was immediate—the same searing agony he'd felt a moment ago by Caleb's side. He gasped and collapsed hard to his knees, trembling. It felt as though Jason's skull had been opened and boiling water poured down his spine. And in that moment the source of the pain swallowed his mind.

He was feeling the very heart of God. Not for Caleb, but for these dead souls in the stadium. Because in reality it was these, not Caleb, who were dead.

He gripped his temples with both hands, and an involuntary wail broke from his lips. He wanted to curl into a ball and beg for relief.

In the same way Jason's heart had broken with Caleb's death, God's heart was torn apart by the death littering this stadium.

It was suddenly so plain, so utterly terrible. A sentiment similar to rage coursed through Jason's bones, and he sobbed in long desperate gasps. How could these fools do this to their Creator? To their Father? To Christ?

But the sentiment was immediately replaced by simple profound sorrow. And deep love.

Tears streamed down his face. Jason felt like he might be melting into the floorboards. Begging for them, he reached feeble hands out toward the crowd.

With a blinding flash the skies ignited and then blinked to black.

Suddenly everything was back to normal. At least the stadium was—the sky still swam in colored light. Donna and several of the cameramen broke free of their shock and were racing for the stage. Exclamations of horror rippled through the stadium, and people were leaving their seats and running to the field. It looked like an ant farm gone nuts out there. They were going to swarm the stage.

Jason lowered his arms. He knelt dumbly on the stage, panting, and it occurred to him that his whole vision had lasted mere moments. But he knew now what he had to do.

He stood to his feet, steadied himself, and made for the stand. He snatched up one of the mikes and threw up his hand. "Stop!"

His voice reverberated through the stadium.

They didn't stop. Donna had nearly reached the stage.

He hollered it this time. "Stop it! Everyone stop where you are!"

This time they stopped. But he yelled it again anyway. "Stop!"

Motion seemed to cease—except for the colored lights, which circled, maybe a little faster now. A few whimpers carried on, but otherwise it was only his heavy breathing over the PA that sounded.

He suddenly felt oddly jubilant. He wasn't sure he'd ever used that word before, but it was the kind of moment that required such a word. *Jubilant.* As if he wanted to leap from his feet and join all those wisps floating around. God was going to do something. Something greater than any of them had seen. Not necessarily to him or to Leiah or to Caleb, but to the dead people out there, unaware they were even dead. He smiled.

It occurred to him that while he was standing here breathing hard into the mike, contemplating words like *jubilant,* they were all out there staring at him as if he'd dropped out of the clouds. And not just these faces, but a couple hundred million others through the cameras.

Jason looked back at Caleb and Leiah. The boy was definitely dead. Leiah was definitely weeping. He faced the cameras.

"My name is Jason." The announcement echoed, but it sounded distant to him. "My name is Jason and God has opened my eyes. I told you to stop because something is happening, and I don't think you're supposed to move yet."

He turned back toward Leiah, who was now staring at him too. They were all staring at him. Caleb's blood was making a pool around his head.

The crowd is waiting, Jason.

He put the mike to his lips. "This isn't what it looks like." He felt as if he were standing in one world and calling into another—the one in the football stadium. Maybe he really was dead.

"I mean, I know Caleb's been shot through the head. He really has . . ." He swallowed, thinking about that. "But he's alive. And he was right. I was dead, but now I'm alive too. Alive in his Spirit, I mean. But you"—he pointed to the crowd—"most of you are dead."

He lowered the mike. It occurred to him that he wasn't coming off in the most brilliant of terms.

Donna stood five feet from the stage, white as a ghost. The bare-chested man who'd become a ringleader of sorts stood ten feet behind her, bug-eyed and silent. The cameras whirred there beside him, and the colored lights whipped quietly around the bleachers, riding warm waters of blue. The sky crackled with some static overhead, and Jason thought that was new.

He tried speaking again. "What I'm saying is that God's heart is breaking more for you than for Caleb. You have to turn to him. To Jesus, I mean. Please, you have to let him touch your hearts."

Jason paced to his right. "I mean maybe God does some dramatic things now and then. He heals a boy; he makes skin smooth; he opens blind eyes. But believe me, it's the eyes of the heart that need opening. That's the real miracle—to understand his love for you. To love him."

Above, the sky began a steady crackling—fingers of that static suddenly reaching across the sky. Yes, indeed, something was up.

"God could heal Caleb's dead body if he wanted to," Jason said. "Sometimes when people are so blind, he will do things like that, just to get their attention. He turns rivers to blood, and he turns water to wine, and he knocks down stone walls. But it's your hearts that he wants to heal. Whoever said that a straightened hand was more dramatic than a healed heart?"

Jason glanced at Caleb, and heat spiked up his spine. Leiah had backed away from Caleb's body. The boy lay on his back with one leg folded under his body and a giant hole in one side of his head. The cameras could see that. They could see that he was dead. What they couldn't see was that he was also alive. They couldn't see the blue light swirling all around the body. They couldn't see the red hue surrounding his chest. They couldn't see the static crackling high above.

Jason faced the sky. The fingers of static had gathered into long streams and were circling as if they were on the edge of a whirlpool now. Jason stepped back instinctively, stunned. He was going to do something! God was going to do something to the people!

A warm wind blew through Jason's hair. He scanned the stadium. The wind whipped papers through the air, and people were beginning to look around, surprised by the sudden change. It was a real wind, and to Jason it felt like the breath of God.

He dropped the mike. A loud thump followed by a muffled, rolling sound filled the speakers. He looked to the sky and lifted both hands. "I love you, Father," he said softly. Light rushed from his mouth and streaked to the sky.

Hot wind suddenly slammed into his body, and he caught his breath. He took a step backward on wobbly knees. "Oh, God! Oh, dear God!" Something was up. He felt as though he had been swallowed by the static.

A boom suddenly crashed overhead. White light blasted down from the vortex of that whirlpool and swallowed the stage and everything on it.

Jason's body was picked up and thrown back a good ten feet. He saw it all in the split second that he was airborne: the shaft at the light's core, as round as a pillar swallowing Caleb; the bucking of Caleb's little body; the collapse of the boy's frame back to the artificial turf.

The crowd gasped as one behind him.

Then Jason landed on his seat.

He stood slowly to his feet. The boy's body lay unmoving. Jason glanced at the crowd. Donna stood with her mouth open. The blue light still swirled around the stadium.

Jason walked to the body.

He was still three paces from that dormant form when Caleb suddenly sat up to a sitting position, as if his upper torso were on a spring. Jason stopped. A hundred thousand sets of lungs gulped air in the same instant.

The blue light suddenly vanished from the stadium, as if someone had pulled the plug. *Pop,* it was gone.

Caleb blinked once, wiped some blood from his eye, and then stood to his feet.

Leiah was the first to scream. She rushed Caleb, threw her arms around him, and began to hop up and down with him. Jason already had his arms wrapped around both of them when the full meaning of what they had just witnessed hit the crowd. To say they erupted would be to compare it to a physical detonation. It was more than that. It was the explosion of throats and hearts and minds all in one fell swoop.

Caleb broke free and began to hop. He thrust his fists above his head and skipped across the stage.

Then he began again, hopping vertically now. He lifted his face and cried to the sky. "Jeeesuuusss!"

Like a swelling wave, the cry swept through the stadium.

"Jeeesuuusss!"

Caleb stopped and faced them, as if only now aware of their presence. He ran up to the microphones. "Look to your hearts!" he cried. "He will give you new life as well. That is his greatest power."

The weeping began almost immediately—wholesale, like a flood across the stadium. They had seen. They had heard. Now they understood, Jason thought.

God was bringing them back to life.

Caleb suddenly jumped off the stage and sprinted to the front line where a man knelt with his face in the grass. Beside the man a woman lay facedown in full repentance. A small boy sat in a blue wheelchair between them. His legs were wrapped in metal braces.

Caleb pulled up in front of the boy and then Jason recognized him. It was the small boy from Caleb's first failure. It was the blond child who'd been placed on the Old Theater's stage by a desperate father. And as far as Jason could see, his was the only wheelchair in sight.

Caleb snatched up the boy's hand and pulled him. The blond boy stared wide-eyed as his torso came out of the chair. Then he was standing; it was really that simple.

And then he was stumbling behind Caleb, pulled to the stage. He was running and Jason began to laugh.

The child was staring at his own feet when they reached the stage—a natural enough reaction, considering what had just happened. Consequently he ran straight into the uprights with enough force to break any boy's legs.

But today a break was not in the plan. He stumbled onto the stage and sprang to his feet with a cry of surprise. He spun back to his parents and cried out again—a high-pitched squeal of delight.

The father looked up and saw only now that his son was missing. The mother rose. They stared toward the stage, aghast. And then their faces wrinkled with emotion. They fell into each other's arms and began to weep loudly.

Caleb grabbed the child's hand and together they began to hop, delighted and laughing. It was like ring-around-the-rosies, and it could just as easily have been, but either way, it was because of the Holy Spirit's power.

Jason sighed and sank to his knees. The blue sky was gone, but then it wasn't gone. Not really. The kingdom was right here, beyond the thin skin of this world. His heart was there in that kingdom, and that was all that really mattered. That was the point of it all.

Still, his body was here, wasted with exhaustion.

Caleb and his new friend were jumping back and forth on the stage. People were prone all over the field, crying out to God. They were kneeling between the seats and in the aisles. They were jumping and hopping, and their cries shook the stage. It was Coastview Fellowship Church all over again—only this time with 102,000 people who had never known until this day that God was so real. So very, very, very real.

A balloon rose through Jason's chest and he began to sob. He knelt on the trembling platform, lowered his head, and began to weep.

He was in rapture. He was in heaven.

The kingdom of heaven.

40

Three Months Later

JASON SAT ON THE KNOLL overlooking the small village and watched Caleb picking through the rubble that was left of the monastery he'd grown up in. Leiah sat beside Jason, her hand in his. A light, cool breeze off the Simien Mountains to the south lifted her hair. The small stone house fifty yards behind the construction sight would be their new home for a few years at least. A poetic conclusion, he thought. They'd met divided during the monastery's destruction; now they would live united during its rebuilding.

Only one road led into the Debra Damarro—the same one he'd navigated the Jeep over just four months ago. The authorities had agreed to restricting access on the road during the monastery's rebuilding—two years at least. They'd put a manned gate where the dirt road met the main road leading to Axum. One day they would open the monastery to the public, but the reconstruction would allow a buffer, so to speak: a few years to take a collective breath. Countless thousands would make straight for the boy, given the opportunity. But the time for multitudes had passed. Caleb was a child, and it was time for him to live like one. Perhaps one day he would emerge again.

Jason's mind drifted back to the weeks following the event at the Rose Bowl. It had taken a month to sort out the details, but in the end they were quite plain: God had reached out to the world in a unique way that had even the most ardent skeptics tossing and turning at night.

The Rose Bowl meeting had continued until daybreak. Nothing more was said from the platform; no more spectacular healings or earthquakes or winds followed; no light shows or fireworks. Just the wonderful, heartbreaking, overpowering sound of wailing and laughing and abandoned worship that took on a life of its own. It could easily have been a crusade under the power of the Holy Spirit.

Jason had walked around in a sort of stupor, alternating between tears and wide smiles. When he asked Leiah if he'd said the right things, she just hugged him around the neck and whispered in his ear, "I'm not sure you said anything. God was speaking."

Of course he knew that, but hearing her say it made him laugh, and he hugged her until she gasped for breath.

Caleb was most definitely alive. There was dried blood in his hair and on his cheek, but a doctor examined him and pronounced to the cameras that he couldn't find a scratch. And yes, the blood on the platform was real blood. Caleb's blood. When they found the bullet lodged in plywood at the back of the stage, they found the boy's blood on it as well. And practically the whole world had seen the impact of the bullet itself, replayed a hundred times in slow motion. A week of forensics put the last doubt to rest. The bullet was real; the footage was real; Caleb had been shot through the head with a .308 round and killed.

And no, the boy walking around now was not—*could* not be—an impostor. Caleb was most definitely alive. End of story.

The facts couldn't be dismissed easily. Even Dr. Caldwell, though sticking with her original statements that attributed Caleb's power to psychokinesis, spent most of her time sputtering and stammering on the talk shows. Her explanation of how a dead mind could muster up the power to bring itself back to life had played to polite smirks. The rest of the scientific community offered very sparse comment. Mostly none at all.

Theologians, on the other hand, were speaking freely. In a unique way the event had unified even those of traditionally opposing stripes. It seemed trivial to argue petty doctrine in the face of such an obvious display of truth. No one could argue that God was not glorified. Caleb was clearly not the Antichrist or any such thing. If anything, he was a foretaste of things to come; at least, some pointed to the book of Revelation and said so. Maybe he was somewhere in the book of Revelation.

Either way, Christians from all walks were dispensing with their differences and crossing party lines to boldly proclaim the simple truth of the matter. And the truth was clear enough: God was indeed real; God was indeed sovereign. The revival that swept through the land had a unique way of overshadowing the few spectacular meetings with Caleb. Hearts were being healed, and nobody seemed particularly upset with the fact that hands were no longer being straightened, at least not a thousand at a time.

Some research groups estimated that upward of five hundred million people worldwide had changed their beliefs concerning God in the aftermath of that night at the Rose Bowl. They weren't coming right out to say it, but most people understood that "beliefs concerning God" was too mild an expression for the phenomenon. Accepting Jesus Christ as God was more like it. The world had never seen such an incredible awakening to spiritual truth.

Caleb had performed no more miracles. The small boy in braces had been the last. At least no miracles that Jason knew of. When Donna finally did get him in front of the camera four days after the event, he simply told her that neither he nor Caleb were really so unique from any other follower of Christ. They all had the same power, and it had much more to do with the healing of hearts than the healing of bones. God had made a statement; Jason would let that statement stand on its own.

The fact that Caleb still carried the bullet wound on his belly was not lost on them.

Charles Crandal was out of business. Permanently. Pure and simple. The footage of Roberts pulling the gun with Crandal frowning at Caleb dropped the candidate's poll numbers by a full thirty points in the days that followed. He'd withdrawn from the race on November 5, two days before the election. A week later his body had been found next to Roberts in an old Nationwide Motel outside of Washington, D.C. They both had bullet holes through the head.

The sniper who'd shot Caleb was still at large. Whether or not he was a part of the antichrist gang, tied to the circumstantial sighting of the black-hooded member near that first gun found, no one knew yet. But Jason guessed that either way, the shooting led back to Crandal and that in the end it had come back to bite him.

Jason turned to Leiah and saw that she was looking at him. "We're back to where we started," he said. "So how does it feel to be slipping back into obscurity?"

"Wonderful."

"We're coming back very different people than when we left."

She looked down and he followed her eyes. They were on her forearm. Her skin was a light brown and perfectly smooth. "In more ways than one," she said.

He reached his left hand to her cheek and her lifted face. "You're beautiful," he said.

Her eyes flashed bright blue. She leaned toward him and he kissed her lips tenderly. He pulled back and smiled. "Mrs. Jason Marker. It still sounds remarkable, don't you think?"

"And to think, if I hadn't come along when I did, you'd be a bleached skeleton in a Jeep."

"So you saved me. I'm glad we got that straight."

They chuckled and looked down at Caleb, who was climbing from the ruins and heading their way.

"You know, I still wonder who it was all for," Jason said. "From God's perspective, I mean. Was this whole thing orchestrated for the sake of tearing down Crandal, or was it for all the people who got healed?"

"Or was it for the sake of the world, a reawakening of the church?" Leiah added.

"For that matter, was it for Caleb's sake or our sake?"

"Why not all?" Leiah asked.

"But why did God do this? He must have had a primary purpose."

"Maybe they were all primary." She grinned at him. "*We* certainly were."

"You have a point." Jason watched the boy walking toward them. "And he was primary. It's hard to imagine that within three months he'll be our boy."

"He's already our boy," she said. "The rest is just paperwork."

"I feel like we're adopting John the Baptist or something," Jason said.

She laughed. "He's just a boy. A dirty boy, by the looks of it," she added, looking at his dust-streaked face. He carried a handful of rock and approached with a smile. "The monastery is his life now."

The state had ordered Nikolous to deposit any "profits" from the meetings into a trust in Caleb's name. The Greek had manufactured close to five hundred thousand dollars' worth of expenses, but even so he'd been forced to fork over nearly nine million dollars. The man never did yield to the truth that surrounded him. He'd staked his reputation on a position that was evidently too painful to reverse, that Caleb's power was psychic.

At any rate, the money had been paid, and according to Ethiopian law, Caleb's status gave him full control of those funds—something to do with his position in the church. He'd decided to rebuild the monastery. The construction was slated to begin in three days.

"Selam," Caleb said, using the native tongue.

"Selam," they both replied.

The boy dropped to his haunches beside Jason and let the rock fragments spill to the earth. His dark hair lay in tangles on his shoulders.

"Caleb, I have a question for you," Jason said. "For whose sake do you think all that has happened in these last four months was allowed?"

Caleb lifted his aqua eyes. "You think there is only one reason?"

"No. But if it were mostly one, what would it be?"

"Well, if there is one reason, then it was to show the world the power of Christ. The power of the Holy Spirit. How many worship him who once did not?" The boy thought awhile; then a grin spread across his face and he smiled at them. "But then the reason would also be you two."

"Us? Why?"

"Because, I saw this before." He motioned to them sitting together. "This marriage."

"You did?" Leiah asked, surprised. "When? When did you see . . . this?"

"In the Jeep," he said. "I saw it in the Jeep leaving the monastery."

Jason blinked. So it *had* been designed from the beginning. A lump suddenly rose to his throat and his eyes misted over. The sensitivity was a condition that seemed to have settled on him back in the meadow before the Rose Bowl. Now it was telling him that his Father loved him very much. His Father in heaven.

Leiah kissed his cheek. "I love you," she whispered.

He put an arm around her. And then the other around Caleb. "Well, it was good of you to tell us, Caleb," he said, looking down the hill with a smile. "We could have avoided the whole trip to the States and married in Addis Ababa."

"But then the other things wouldn't have happened," Caleb said. "And without them, you would not have found marriage. I think."

They sat still, facing the Ethiopian breeze under a warm sun.

"I agree," Leiah said.

"Me too," Jason agreed.

And that was the end of it.

Jason lay back on the grass and faced the sun, feeling as content as he could remember.

Leiah lay back beside him, smiling.

Then Caleb dropped to his back beside them and giggled. Jason wasn't sure which felt warmer just now—the sun on their faces or the love in their hearts.

A Word from Bill Bright

THERE IS AN OLD ADAGE which states that our stories do not simply reflect society, they shape it.

Although I have authored more than sixty books over the years, I have come to the conclusion that a good novel on biblical themes can reach many more people than most theological works. God Himself, upon coming to earth in the form of Jesus of Nazareth, chose stories as His primary mode of communication. He used fiction. We call them parables, but they are stories either way—the story of the Prodigal Son, the story of the Sower, the story of the Unjust Judge, and many other similar stories.

Fiction works in a unique way, of course. It's more like a megaphone, trumpeting the truth in grand terms to bring inspiration, than like expository teaching. Fiction uses major themes in a story to speak boldly, and I believe the truth woven throughout this novel is one for which the church is desperate.

It is the truth that God is indeed alive and still moves in supernatural ways today, whenever He so desires and for His purposes, through the lives of those who love, trust, and obey Him. It's the truth that the source of God's power is found in His Son, Jesus Christ, and in the Holy Spirit, not in man's devices. It's the truth that what we see with our own eyes on a day-to-day basis isn't the half of it. There is indeed a supernatural reality all around us that is just as real as the world we see.

And most importantly, it's the truth that, when seen through spiritual eyes, a healed heart and transformed life are far more spectacular than a straightened hand or restored sight. These were the themes of the New Testament church, and they must be the themes that guide our lives today. As dedicated believers, we are on a grand adventure that bristles with power and excitement. But I have been saddened again and again at the lack of enthusiasm and zeal among many who claim to be His followers. A lack of first love among His body—the Church.

The Bible explains that in the last days people will hold to a form of godliness while denying its power (2 Timothy 3:5). Sadly, many believers do not know the reality of living a supernatural life through the enabling power of the Holy Spirit.

The story you have read is spectacular in parts, but in reality the events in this story are no more spectacular than events which occur repeatedly throughout the Old and New Testaments. If they seem more dramatic, it is because we have used a contemporary story to bring them into your world. But if you think about each occurrence of the miraculous, they are no more than what we see in Scripture. The power of the Holy Spirit characterized the New Testament church no less than it did the lives of the prophets of old. The Lord enabled them to do many miraculous signs and wonders (Acts 14:3), many were healed (Acts 5:16), others were raised from the dead (Acts 9:41), and most importantly the good news of Christ began to spread throughout the world.

Jesus said, except you become as a little child, you cannot enter the kingdom of God. Children are generally trusting and dependable and believe what they are told. At Campus Crusade for Christ we have noticed that the response in many parts of the world to the *Jesus Film* is phenomenal. Audiences who see the film say that if Jesus can heal the blind, He can heal them too. And so He does. In fact, we have reported situations where people have actually been raised from the dead, and their communities revolutionized by the message that resulted.

But in the Western world, we are more prone to rationalize and analyze until the true meaning of the gospel is dissipated and often rendered powerless. We become like the churches in Ephesus and Laodicea: we have left our first love and are neither hot nor cold. We find it difficult to believe that Jesus would do today what He did centuries ago, while many of our fellow believers across the seas do believe, and they rejoice in the fruits of their belief.

Without the Holy Spirit, our own strivings are fruitless. It is "Not by might nor by power, but by my Spirit," says the Lord (Zechariah 4:6). The last instruction Jesus gave to His disciples on the Mount of Olives was to wait in Jerusalem until they were renewed with power from on high. "You will receive power when the Holy Spirit comes on you; and you will be my witnesses in Jerusalem, and in all Judea and Samaria, and to the ends of the earth" (Acts 1:8).

Everything in the Christian life involves the Holy Spirit. The Holy Spirit came to glorify Christ, to lead us into all truth, to convict us of sin, and to draw us to the Savior (John 16). We must be born of the Spirit (John 3). Only through the enabling of the Spirit can a person understand the Word of God and live under its power. "But the fruit of the Spirit is love, joy, peace, patience, kindness, goodness, faithfulness, gentleness and self-control" (Galatians 5:22–23).

No book written by man can begin to capture every aspect of the remarkable truths about the Holy Spirit, but I trust this novel has challenged you to reconsider your understanding of God's power. I pray that unity and harmony and love will flow from the discussions inspired by these pages. May we come together as the bride of Christ and worship at His feet together. No matter what your view on how God works in the affairs of men and nations, we certainly can agree that He is awesome and worthy of the grandest telling of His power.

But most of all I pray that every individual who reads this story will be so gripped with the reality of the Holy Spirit's presence that they will personally experience His supernatural love and power.

Lord, may Your light shine brightly on this world of darkness.

BILL BRIGHT

We invite you to visit our Web site at *www.blessedchild.org* for more information and resources about how you can live supernaturally empowered by the Holy Spirit.

ABOUT THE AUTHORS

TED DEKKER is known for novels which combine adrenaline-laced stories packed with unexpected plot twists, unforgettable characters, and incredible confrontations between good and evil. He is the #1 best-selling author of *Blink* as well as *Three, Heaven's Wager, When Heaven Weeps, Thunder of Heaven,* and the co-author of *Blessed Child* and *A Man Called Blessed.* Raised in the jungles of Indonesia, Ted now lives with his family in the mountains of Colorado.

BILL BRIGHT is founder and president of Campus Crusade. Out of his vision came the most widely seen film ever produced, the *Jesus* film, now seen by 3.3 billion people in more than 580 languages. He has written over 50 books and pamphlets, including *Come Help Change the World, The Coming Revival,* and *The Secret.* He hosts a daily radio program, *The Lighthouse Report,* and a television program, *Supernatural Living with Dr. Bill Bright.* He and his wife, Vonette, reside in Orlando.

Also Available from Ted Dekker

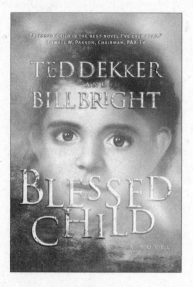

BLESSED CHILD
By Ted Dekker and Bill Bright

The young orphan boy was abandoned and raised in an Ethiopian monastery. Now he must flee those walls or die. But the world is hardly ready for a boy like Caleb. When relief expert Jason Marker agrees to take Caleb from the monastery, he opens humanity's doors to an incredible journey filled with intrigue and peril. Together with Leiah, the nurse who escapes to America with them, Jason discovers Caleb's stunning power. But so do the boy's enemies, who will stop at nothing to destroy him. Jason and Leiah fight for the boy's survival while the world erupts into debate over the source of the boy's power. In the end nothing can prepare any of them for what they will find.

A MAN CALLED BLESSED
By Ted Dekker and Bill Bright

In this explosive sequel, Rebecca Soloman leads a team of Israeli commandos deep into the Ethiopian desert to hunt the one man who may know the final resting place of the Ark of the Covenant. But Islamic fundamentalists fear that the Ark's discovery will compel Israel to rebuild Solomon's temple on the very site of their own holy Mosque in Jerusalem. They immediately dispatch Ismael, their most accomplished assassin, to pursue the same man. But the man in their sights is no ordinary man. His name is Caleb, and he too is on a quest-to find again the love he once embraced as a child. Tensions skyrocket as the world awakens to the drama in the desert. The fate of millions rests in the hand of these three.

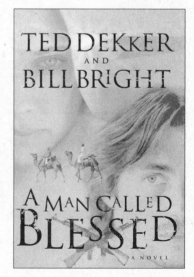

Best-selling Novels from Ted Dekker

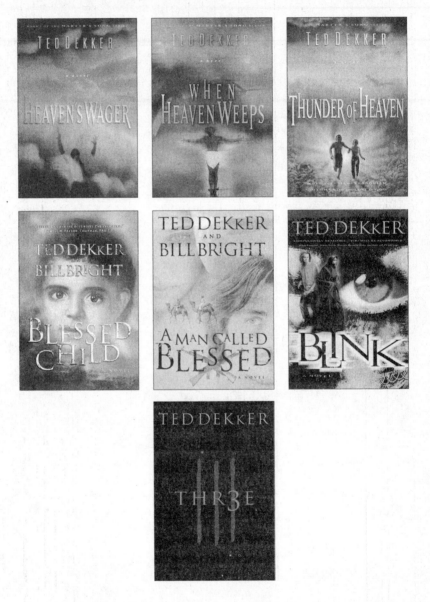

Ted Dekker is the most exciting writer I've read in a very long time . . . wonderful reading . . . powerful insights. Bravo!

—Ted Baehr, President MOVIEGUIDE® Magazine

2004
The Year of the Trilogy

May
2004

September
2004

February 2004

Fleeing assailants through an alleyway in Denver late one night, Thomas Hunter narrowly escapes to the roof of an industrial building. Then a silent bullet from the night clips his head and his world goes black. When he awakes, he finds himself in an entirely different reality . . . a green forest that seems more real than where he was. Every time he tries to sleep, he wakes up in the other world, and soon he truly no longer knows which reality is real.

Never before has an entire trilogy—all in hardcover format—been released in less than a year. On the heels of *The Matrix* and *The Lord of the Rings* comes a new trilogy where dreams and reality collide. Where the fate of two worlds depends on one man: Thomas Hunter

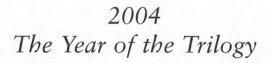

W Publishing Group™
www.wpublishinggroup.com
www.TedDekker.com